Appointment
with
IL DUCE

Appointment with IL DUCE

Hozy Rossi

WELCOME RAIN PUBLISHERS
New York

**In memory of
Neil J. Rossi, Sr.**

Appointment with Il Duce

Copyright © 2001 by Joseph D. Rossi.

Library of Congress Cataloging-in-Publication Data

Rossi, Hozy.

    Appointment with Il Duce / Hozy Rossi.

       p. cm.

    ISBN 1-56649-201-7

       1. Italy—History—1914–1945—Fiction. 2. Eccentrics and eccentricities—Fiction.
3. Dental students—Fiction. 4. Naples (Italy)—Fiction. 5. Young men—Fiction.

    PQ3618.O85 A85 2001

    813'.6—dc21

                        2001017702

Direct any inquiries to

Welcome Rain Publishers LLC, 225 West 35th Street, Suite 1100, New York, NY 10001.

Design by Cindy LaBreacht

Printed in the United States of America by BLAZE I.P. I.

First Edition: June 2001

1 3 5 7 9 10 8 6 4 2

SOME PEOPLE had wanted him to choose music over dentistry.
It was selfishness on their part—better to lose a few teeth
than the local cellist—but also, thanks to what happened later,
advice that could have saved him. A musician never would
have noticed the delicate crack developing in one of Angelina
Perelli's bicuspids, and without that small discovery, invisible
to all but the specialist in the room, it is doubtful that they ever
would have fallen in love, for she was as charmed by his expert
attention as he was seduced by her otherwise flawless mouth.
And without love there would have been no courtship,
no proposal, no heartbreak, no crazy attempt at reconciliation,
and it was the last of these, in conjunction with the use
of amateur explosives, that claimed his life. But how could
he have known that such an end awaited him when, years earlier,
he disappointed the people back home and decided to become,
of all things, a dentist?

ONE

Cortenza is a small town that sits atop a hill two hundred kilometers south of Naples. It looks today very much the way it did almost a century ago when Beppe Arpino was born there. The streets are still narrow and confusing, still paved with broad, uneven stones. The buildings are still the color of fresh pasta, their roofs still finished in clay. A person can still find old men there who stroll the piazza in linen suits and children who play hide-and-seek behind the statues of revolutionaries. And not far from the center of town there still stands the surefooted Catholic church with its two bells and gray windows, its crude likeness of the Crucifixion, its pews that creak at even the slightest touch.

As a boy Beppe spent his afternoons in the shuttered home next door to the church. Father Vincenzo had suffered a terrible fall in his vineyard one day and thereafter walked with the aid of a cane. The tasks that Beppe performed on the priest's behalf were, for the most part, simple ones—some pruning with the garden shears, a quick errand across town—and with a little effort Father Vincenzo could have accomplished them himself—the effort might have helped his condition—but the parish had a few extra lire and, as all knew, the Arpino family refused handouts.

In addition to Beppe, there was Luisa Arpino, his mother; Margherita, his younger sister; and Paolo, the baby of the family. They lived together on the ground floor of an otherwise abandoned building that in ten years' time would collapse on itself. Perhaps Beppe hastened that collapse. At night, as he lay on a mattress unable to sleep—insomnia would curse him the rest of his life—and listened to the demonic snore of Paolo, the asthmatic, beside him, he would extend a hand and slowly pick at the dry plaster wall, first with one blunt fingernail, then another. In the course of the two or three hours normally required for Beppe to fall asleep he would accumulate a small pile of these pickings, which he would then carefully dispose of the next morning for fear that his mother, always within reach of an olive switch, would discover the damage and take action.

Beppe's father, Giuseppe Arpino, did not live with the family. In fact, he did not live in Italy at all. Word from America was that he had been murdered in the corridor of a resident hotel. According to the cousin of a man who had shared a bunk with Giuseppe on the voyage to New York and subsequently worked alongside him in an Italian-owned butcher shop, Beppe's father had been stabbed on his way to the lavatory sometime after midnight by what authorities suspected to be an itinerant bandit. The proprietor of the hotel, however, claimed that the death had been suicide—the clouds of Giuseppe's homesickness still had not lifted after months in America—but the location of the wounds and their abundance made this theory doubtful to both the police and the man in New York who sent word of the incident to the cousin in Cortenza. He had heard Giuseppe mention the town in their cramped, seagoing bunk and in the back room of Bertolucci's Butcher Shop.

Like his father, Beppe—just nine at the time of the knife attack—had a reputation for overcast emotions. The dark circles that surrounded his eyes, for example, were attributed by most people in Cortenza to the extended grief that he no doubt experienced as a result of his father's death. What these people failed to take into account was the fact that Beppe slept just five or six hours a night and therefore spent a great deal of time each day rubbing his eyes with his small, still-dimpled fists in an effort to stay awake, thereby bruising the delicate tissue around the sockets and leaving two purplish, goggle-like rings.

Beppe's posture also encouraged people to think him sad. From the front his shoulders appeared square and, in the manner of most prepubescent boys, delicate, almost feminine, but when viewed from the side or from behind those same shoulders seemed weighted and curiously curved. It was not quite a slouch, though, thanks to the oversized blades that sprang from his back like two dorsal fins. Had Cortenza been a coastal town and Beppe a swimmer, his presence off-shore might have alarmed those unfortunate enough to mistake his partially submerged form for a pair of flesh-colored sharks.

And he was quiet—another reason people assumed that Beppe inherited his father's melancholy. Never much of a talker at home, he had even less to say in unfamiliar company. When any of the wash-erwomen who crowded the banks of the Crati grabbed hold of his cheeks and asked a playful question—"Yes, and what mischief have you been up to lately?"—he usually slipped away without a word, just a shrug and a look of bewilderment. If the grocer whom he some-times visited on behalf of his mother told him to "Speak up, young man!" Beppe simply pointed more emphatically at the cake of soap or wooden matches he desired. Even at school he managed to avoid the teacher's abuse through a shrewd combination of eye contact and solemn nods. For others not as clever as Beppe a career in music would have been unthinkable: Miss Donati alone shattered the hands of a hundred male students, a generation that forever after flinched at the sight of a raised baton.

But contrary to what most people thought, Beppe enjoyed rela-tive happiness as a child. He never cried himself to sleep at night, never wished he had been born elsewhere to other parents—even after his father's death or one of his mother's fits—and never once contemplated suicide. No, for all the hardships that the first decade of life presented Beppe Arpino, his outlook remained bright. One might even say that he considered himself lucky to have only poverty, a dead parent, insomnia, the occasional whipping, and poor posture to contend with. After all, he had the attention of Father Vincenzo. And if he were quieter than most boys, more reserved in conversa-tion, he soon found another way to express himself.

●●●●●●●

Thin and surprisingly pale for a man who drank only dark wines, Father Vincenzo first noticed Beppe at the funeral he conducted soon after word of Giuseppe Arpino's death made its way across the Atlantic and up the twisted road that led to Cortenza. It marked the first time in a thirty-year career that the priest had presided over a funeral with no corpse, no casket, no picture nor mention of the deceased. Shepherds had fallen from cliffs straight into darkness, and at the very least there had been a pine box with an empty cloak inside to sprinkle water upon. Similarly, the family of an elderly woman who had been carried off by wolves one night while she knit on a moonlit porch had followed the yarn off the property and down the road to a prickly shrub on the outskirts of town where they found the needles and unfinished sweater that later accompanied her head-stone. And there had been the arsonist who caught fire in his sleep and, on the insistence of local authorities, was buried in a cast-iron coffin for fear that the graveyard might ignite.

In each case there had been something for Father Vincenzo to work with: a cloak, a pair of needles, the charred remains. But Luisa Arpino, a regular presence at Sunday mass—the left side, always three rows back—seemed convinced that the sudden and somewhat peculiar death of her husband had resulted from a spell cast by gypsies and that any official service held in remembrance of him must be conducted with no reference to Giuseppe by name. There could be no headstone, either. And as for artifacts that might be blessed and buried in place of his body, the widow had already disposed of them according to some ancient pagan rite that most likely involved the blood of a chicken or the hooves of a goat. Her aim was to lose the gypsy curse the way the hunted try to lose their scent—yet another example of the many super-stitions that persisted in rural Italy well into the twentieth century despite the best efforts of the church and advances in modern science that included electricity, indoor plumbing, the telegraph, and, most sig-nificant of all for Father Vincenzo, the work of Louis Pasteur, which forever solved the mystery of fermentation—yes, life without air!

In a place like Cortenza, none of that mattered. People still carried charms in their pockets to clutch as they passed old women on the street. It was still common to see a pail of hot water placed beneath a patient's bed and, if the fever persisted, a potato perched on his or her forehead. A half-dozen drops of breast milk were still recommended for earaches. And it remained socially acceptable for people—even the mayor—to rest their aching feet on a mound of fresh manure.

As noted, the Arpino funeral represented a first for Father Vincenzo. But after more than a quarter century of service and upwards of two hundred funerals—not to mention all the baptisms, first communions, confirmations, weddings, and whatnot the job entailed—he had learned to take such things in stride. That is, he did what he always did, no matter what the occasion: he drank a glass of wine and improvised. On the day in question, with the sun hot upon him, Father Vincenzo opened the service with a talk about paternal devotion and the inexplicable ways of the Lord—peppered with a few personal anecdotes to bring the words to life—then began a quick jog through the Latin since few understood it and the opportunities for embellishment were limited.

Over the murmur of his voice Father Vincenzo could hear the occasional sniffle or choked sob—signs that all was going well—and when he looked up from the page he noticed tears in their eyes—the mother, the younger boy, the daughter, a handful of townspeople. The exception was the older boy, the nine-year-old with what appeared to be a knapsack strapped to his back. After a second glance, the priest hesitated: It was not a knapsack at all but some strange appendage. Wings perhaps? In any event, the boy's eyes were neither wet nor reddened, merely framed by dark circles that made their clarity even more apparent. For the rest of the funeral those eyes remained fixed on Father Vincenzo, and as if eye contact alone were not sufficient, the boy soon began to nod solemnly as though he understood every word, even the hurried Latin. The effect at first unnerved the priest, who had long ago grown accustomed to an audience of blank stares and stifled yawns, bowed heads and tears. But as the service drew to a close that discomfort gave way to mild appreciation and then, oddly, hope.

The grave—rather, the patch of grass and small cross that all had gathered around—dutifully splashed, the group said its final amens and Father Vincenzo hobbled into the shade of a conveniently placed fig tree where, setting aside his cane for the moment, he wiped his brow with a clean handkerchief and lamented the Catholic preference for black. Despite the loose robes and wide hat, he longed for a light-colored suit open at the collar and a matching fedora.

The widow approached, and Father Vincenzo returned the damp cloth to his pocket. "My sympathies," he said and took her hand, which held a warm coin.

"Thank you, Father."

He folded the coin back into her palm and produced a small but heavy pouch. "Please, on behalf of the church."

The gesture was customary when a husband left behind a young family, but Luisa Arpino would not accept the money. The priest tried again only to be rebuffed again. Then he put a hand on her steaming shoulder, the black cloth hot to the touch even under the tree.

"Your son," he said and looked toward the boy with raccoon eyes and unusual posture. "I need someone to help in the afternoons. Perhaps he would be interested."

A third time he offered the pouch, and finally it was accepted.

●━●●●●●●

The instructions were explicit: three sharp raps, no more, no less.

"That's how rich people knock. You understand?"

Yes, Beppe understood, but to hammer the point home his mother demonstrated yet again on the dinner table: rap, rap, rap. A spoon leapt out of a bowl; the water pitcher splashed itself. Beppe noted the disturbances, though he remarked on neither. He just nodded to reassure his mother that he would in no way discredit the Arpino name. If three knocks were what custom required, then three knocks it would be. And if under no circumstances were he to open his mouth or disturb the priest—even so much as sneeze—then all the better.

Still, the question remained: what exactly would he do for the church? No doubt one chore involved a brush and a bucket: at mass the previous December, Beppe had noticed cobwebs slung beneath the altar and a layer of dust on top of Jesus's feet. But work in a church required diligence, and despite nine Easters and an equal number of Christmases—the children attended on select occasions—Beppe could not for the life of him remember the pattern he was supposed to trace when he sampled holy water: head, chest, left-right-left, or chest, head, right-left-right? Also, would he be expected to kneel as he moved from pew to pew or would a single, especially long genuflection suffice?

It was all a mystery to him, and it would continue to be a mystery, because during the entire time that Beppe spent in the employ of Father Vincenzo—a total of four years and eleven months—the church itself never figured prominently. A peculiar woman, however, did.

After Beppe knocked on the rectory door—after he wiped his palms on his trousers, rubbed his eyes, cleared his throat, wiped his palms again for good measure, then knocked—he leaned his head close to the door and listened for the uneven sound of Father Vincenzo's approach, but he heard only the pulse of blood through his ears before the door swung open and a towering woman appeared in an ankle-length apron over a charcoal-gray dress that almost touched the floor. She looked at Beppe as one might a bruised tomato, then leaned out the doorway and surveyed the street.

Had the knock Maria Teresa heard, that insistent rap, rap, rap— an attack almost—truly come from the creature that stood before her: dark eyes like a rabid dog, trousers worn through and patched and worn through again, shoes that looked as though they had been stolen from a buried corpse? Or was the boy but a decoy? Last year a woman carrying an infant had stood in the same spot, and while Maria Teresa warmed some milk in the pantry, the candlesticks disappeared. The year before that two aged veterans had knocked, and while Maria Teresa buttered two slices of bread for them—again, in the pantry— the men unbuttoned their tunics so that upon her return to the door she bore witness not only to their impressive battle scars but to their slack and lopsided genitalia as well—the image forever seared in her memory. And how could she forget the parcel that she discovered smoldering on the step one day and foolishly stamped out, thereby ruining a favorite pair of shoes—the smell never did go away—and suffering the jeers and catcalls of the neighborhood delinquents?

Her mother had warned her long ago: "The church attracts eccentrics," she said, "the way a mutt attracts fleas." The priests were of particular concern. According to Maria Teresa's mother, most had servants not merely to cook and clean. "Men are all alike, my dear." But Maria Teresa was chaste, and Father Vincenzo apparently uninterested, and the occasional theft or practical joke not enough to prevent her from earning a wage. As for the boy who now stood before her, he appeared to be alone.

"What do you want?" Maria Teresa asked.

Beppe had not anticipated such a question and had no ready reply. His mind at that moment was as blank as it had ever been, as blank as the white apron that stood before him like an impenetrable wall: nothing. Beppe stared at the apron, and the apron stared back. If the woman behind it spoke, he never heard her; there was a silence in his head comparable to the emptiness. But then, as if by magic, Beppe noticed a spot on the apron, then another spot. They were bumps, tiny beige bumps: batter that had splashed from a mixing bowl. The baker, Mr. DeBono, had given the children sweets after the funeral, and he, too, had bumps. Beppe wanted to reach out and pick at the bumps on the woman's apron—first with one fingernail, then another—and he was about to do so when the bumps all of a sudden jumped.

The woman grabbed hold of both his arms and began to speak in an exaggerated manner, as though Beppe were deaf and visiting from a foreign country. "I said," she all but yelled, "what . . . do . . . you . . . want?"

"Beppe!" he managed to squeak, then added, "Arpino." And no sooner had he uttered those words than he realized the mistake: two words, just two words, and already he had soiled the family name.

"Beppe Arpino?" The woman released his arms and shook her head. "Never heard of him." She pointed across the street. "You might try . . . "

"No!" Beppe interrupted, as sweat began to pool in his socks. "That's me. I am Beppe. The Father said he wanted . . . "

"Oh, the Father." The woman made room in the doorway. "Remember to wipe your feet."

●○●○●○●○

Although the rectory may have been small and plainly furnished by Vatican standards, to Beppe it seemed opulent. There were carpets, for one thing, and electric lights. In the room where the woman told him to wait, two hundred—no, more like three hundred books lined a wall of wooden shelves. A leather chair of a design Beppe had never seen before sat in one corner, graced by a brass lamp with a thin brass chain that ended in a scarlet tassel. In another corner: a globe on a pedestal. Even if Beppe had stretched out his arms as wide as he could and tried to encircle the globe like a long-lost brother, his fingertips would have failed to meet on the other side. By comparison, the globe at school seemed ridiculous.

Beppe leaned over a polished table and examined his reflection in the surface. His face appeared dim and rather distant, as though age had intervened. Beppe wrinkled his nose. He scowled at himself; he grimaced and frowned. He made a face like the face he imagined would be his in, say, fifty years. It looked nothing like his father's, though his father died at half that age. Beppe had accompanied him the morning he left Cortenza. Together they walked to the edge of town, where a stranger and two mules waited. His mother had stayed home, hysterical, with the younger children. A nine-year-old could find his way back alone.

Beppe had carried a tin box wrapped in a checkered handkerchief. The box held the last home-cooked meal his father would ever eat: green beans in tomato sauce, a little beef. It made the tin warm in places, especially the bottom. Beppe's father carried a small valise in one hand, a rope tied around a rolled blanket in the other. On his feet were the only shoes that Beppe had ever seen him wear—black except at the cracks where the brown showed through. Old shoes, comfortable shoes. And now, carpet: softer than the mattress Beppe shared with his brother, like standing barefoot in damp grass, or perhaps what the mayor felt when his soles kissed manure.

"Excuse me." Father Vincenzo touched the startled shoulder. "Here, sit down for a moment and catch your breath."

The boy complied . . . into Father Vincenzo's prized chair. But no matter; he would have Maria Teresa wipe it down later.

"And how about some milk?"

Father Vincenzo lifted a pewter bell from a low table and shook it. He then pulled a straight-backed chair to a spot opposite Beppe, though in the process his cane slipped to the floor and nearly tripped him.

"How I hate that thing," he said after he finally settled. "And where is Maria Teresa?" He picked up the bell again. "If that cane doesn't kill me, that woman will."

But a moment later Maria Teresa appeared, and within minutes Beppe and the priest were sharing a plate of warm biscotti. The cookies were shaped like half moons and fragile as china, their taste reminiscent of licorice. Beppe ate several and washed each down with a mouthful of warm milk flavored with what must have been coffee, while Father Vincenzo worked his way through a bottle of wine.

Thus far, Beppe could not complain: cookies and milk and no questions that required a verbal response. The priest rattled on, and Beppe nodded and stared, no brush or bucket in sight. What could be easier? The woman who answered the door had not even asked to inspect his hands when the snack arrived, a routine Beppe's mother performed before each meal. He would unclench his fists for her one at a time, and no matter how clean the palms, she would tell him to wash. She feared disease and infection, as any mother would, but more than that she feared gypsies. Touch something a gypsy just touched—a doorknob, a counter—then touch your lips, and you developed a stutter. Wipe your eyes, and you would need glasses.

Run a hand through your hair, and a gray streak appeared overnight. Worst of all, using the outhouse—so bad, in fact, that Beppe's mother refused to provide details, though he had seen old men urinate in the recesses of the public gardens and from the look of their organs— dark and reptilian, not spongy and pink—he had an idea what the damage might be.

"But enough about me." The priest paused for the first time in ten minutes and set aside his empty glass. "How are your studies, young man?"

Beppe nodded, then smiled, rubbed his eyes out of habit, but the priest persisted.

"You go to school, yes? What do they teach you at school?"

Beppe felt the last traces of moisture abandon his mouth. All of that milk, and suddenly nothing.

"You speak, do you not?"

Beppe braced himself. "Yes, Father."

"Good, very good. You had me worried there for a moment." The priest poured himself another glass and settled back in the chair. "It reminds me of the time—oh, this happened years ago, long before you were born—the time Pope Leo XIII forgot the words—ha, ha, ha—to the 'Hail Mary.' You see, I was a novitiate then, visiting Rome for only the second or third time. Perhaps it was the third time, because it was on my second trip that I met those two nuns from Australia. What were their names? Margaret and Joan? Now, *there's* a story. But you're too young for that. Suffice it to say that I was in Rome—we'll call it my third trip, shall we?—and I had just lunched at a lovely trattoria but a stone's throw from St. Peter's. Now, contrary to what the Neapolitans say, Rome does have the better restaurants. The food may be comparable—I will concede as much—but the Romans truly know how to match their wines. If you order veal, for example—a breaded cutlet is always nice—you can rest assured that . . . "

And the story went on a few minutes more until when the priest promptly fell asleep.

∞∞∞∞∞∞∞

Father Vincenzo's fondness for long, digressive monologues perhaps explained his continued presence in a remote and somewhat primitive outpost like Cortenza. Granted, the town had its charms—an unhurried pace and unspoiled vistas—but the night air carried venomous fevers— one reason the streets emptied at dusk—and the only physician, the druggist contended, still wrote prescriptions for leeches. There were no intellectuals to speak of and seldom outsiders: the nearest train station was a squalid affair that spooked all but the hardiest travelers, though a frail English poet did spend one night at the local inn—a visit he later commemorated in an otherwise forgettable sonnet.

But if a mere tendency to digress were enough to warrant exile to an isolated southern town, then Cortenza and its neighbors would have been crowded with clerics. The fact was that only the youngest or most abusive priests were banished to the far reaches of country- side: the enthusiastic beginners, the polygamists and blasphemers. What, then, had been Father Vincenzo's crime? In a word, wine. As Beppe soon discovered, the history, production, and consumption of that beverage were foremost among the priest's obsessions. Or as the bishop rather bluntly stated in response to Father Vincenzo's appeal for a new appointment, "I think it's safe to say that you're a drunk."

Beppe, however, had no conception of such matters—nor of the appeal that the world beyond Cortenza might have held in the mind of another—and found it in no way peculiar that in the first hour of his first visit the priest consumed an entire bottle of wine and passed out. No doubt Father Vincenzo had been thirsty and tired, Beppe rea- soned. He felt the same way himself on occasion, and if it had not been for the dreaded insomnia, he would have enjoyed a nap, too. But alas, Beppe remained alert in the chair twenty or thirty minutes longer—it rivaled the carpet for comfort—until the apron reappeared and escorted him to the door.

Why Father Vincenzo invited the boy had not been explained to Maria Teresa. If not to scrub poor, dusty Jesus and those neglected pews, then what? Merely to nod, to clean a plate? But as she closed the door behind the odd little figure with his exaggerated stoop, she recalled what her late mother once told her about priests and their desires: "Young boys," she said, "the younger, the better." Her mother had also offered some practical advice: "No matter what, my dear, never turn your back at a baptism."

Yes, of course. And that explained the absence of innuendo between Maria Teresa and the priest—two years together in the same apartment and never once had he proffered so much as a suggestive good night. The realization comforted Maria Teresa in a manner that even she recognized as unbalanced. Certainly she had no desire to sleep with the crippled priest—she paled at the thought of such a transaction—but vanity had begun to get the better of her. At twenty-five she wondered whether her attractiveness had already fled. Her hair of late seemed thinner and weak. In recent months her face had taken on a wrinkle or two. And in her bedroom mirror at night the candlelight revealed the shadow of a mustache. Alone these flaws might not have been a problem—her bosom had lost none of its bounce—but Maria Teresa also had height to contend with. To put it simply, she dwarfed most Italian men.

But whatever solace she found in the sudden connection between her mother's words and that peculiar child was short-lived. No sooner had her ego been restored—yes, a glimmer of hope—than she remembered the innocent victim and, at that moment, understood her duty: she would protect him from the evil sinner asleep in the next room. Their meeting that day in the study, she now understood, had been but a prelude to wickedness—her cookies, bait. Maria Teresa shuddered to think what acts the priest might have in store for the hunchbacked boy. A piece of graffiti scrawled on the confessional wall immediately came to mind.

Never again would her diligence lag. Never again, at least when the boy came around, would she tune out Father Vincenzo's voice—a skill learned during her first weeks of employment and improved upon after the accident to include the sound of that infuriating bell. Ah, the accident: A man his age—a man of the cloth, no less—out there in the yard behind the church like a peasant girl, his robes hitched up to his knees as if he were about to prance through daisies. And just as she expected, one day he fell.

Although Maria Teresa had been within earshot when it happened—inside, but with the shutters open—a neighbor down the street first heard the calls and alerted her.

"The Father," the neighbor said after Maria Teresa unlatched the door, "I think he wants you."

Indeed, that appeared to be the case: sprawled on the ground between two row of vines lay Father Vincenzo, his black robes brown with dirt, his broad hat flat beneath him.

"Where have you been?" he whispered in a hoarse yet angry voice when Maria Teresa finally approached. "I've been here for almost an hour. You didn't hear my calls?"

She felt a twitch of guilt and helped the priest inside. She sat him at the pantry table, forfeited her last bottle of sherry, and sent for the town physician. Father Vincenzo still blamed her for that final decision, and with good reason: even Maria Teresa was not surprised when a year later the fracture had not healed.

•◦•◦•◦•◦•

Life in Cortenza, as in other places, had its unexpected twists and turns, and what at first seemed a terrible burden could later become a welcome endowment. Consider Father Vincenzo's fall in the vineyard. When Luisa Arpino first heard the gossips along the riverbank describe the spill—the doctor had been alerted just moments before—she knew instantly that tragedy would strike close to home. A priest, a symbol of the church she attended, had been brought down on holy ground: it must have been gypsies. Luisa dropped to her knees right there at the water's edge and covered her face with both hands. The previous week her husband had left to find work in America; the ship must have capsized.

The ship had not capsized—the mayor telegraphed Naples later that day and learned that it had not even departed—but for the next nine months Luisa waited for what she knew in her heart to be inevitable, and when word of her husband's death arrived, she felt a cool wave of relief wash over her before the feverish grief settled in. At once she resolved never again to take chances where gypsies were concerned. On the advice of a local expert whose identity she swore never to reveal, Luisa burned all her husband's clothes and petitioned the priest—still not recovered from his accident—to keep the services anonymous. She also began a secret ritual designed to protect her children. On Sunday nights she would gather their fingernail clippings and bury them in the graveyard not far from Giuseppe's nameless plot. She did this week in and week out, rain or shine, though Beppe's contribution usually consisted of the merest sliver. His nails were always blunt and flush with the skin, as if he filed them every morning. No wonder he, of all the children, seemed possessed by a dark spirit: those eyes, that stoop, the silent nods. It was disconcerting, especially for a mother.

Fate soon took a slight turn, however, and the priest's ominous fall became Luisa's blessing. The pouch Father Vincenzo presented at the funeral alone doubled the family savings, and as long as Beppe worked at the church, the compensation would likely continue. With that thought in mind, Luisa greeted her son affectionately when he arrived home after his first few hours at work. She ushered him to their table—cluttered as usual with bundled clothes and chipped dishes—and produced his favorite snack: a crust of bread. Her mood bordered on happiness, and the questions poured from her mouth: Had he scrubbed floors as she suspected? Or had the priest sent him up a ladder to scour the windows? And what about those grimy pews, the dirty Savior?

To each question, Beppe shook his head—no, no . . . no—while Luisa's expression went from curiosity to frustration to anger. The first time in weeks that she wanted to him to speak, he refused. She slapped the bread from his hands and pointed at the bedroom. "Tonight, you go to bed early!"

If Luisa suffered from a shortness of temper, she had good reason. A young widow, just twenty-eight—still young enough to remarry, yes, though that would never happen—she had three children to support and meager resources. The money she earned as a washerwoman barely paid for their pathetic groceries: picked-over tomatoes, trod-upon string beans, indecipherable cuts of meat, and palsied butter.

To compound matters, handouts were not an option: to accept one might deny a gypsy.

But how could Beppe ever have explained that first afternoon with Father Vincenzo? "Mama, I sat in an elaborate chair in an elegant room and ate delicate cookies while the priest napped before me." He would suffer more than a slap on the wrist with that response. Fortunately, he understood that his mother's outbursts had little to do with him directly. Her moods, though never altogether predictable, had become downright erratic after his father left. When her arm swung around and the crust went flying, the element of surprise was all but negligible, and Beppe left the room as impassive as he had entered it.

The bedroom: three cheap mattresses on a bare stone floor, one rickety chest of drawers. Beppe parked himself on the mattress he shared with his brother. It sank less than an inch beneath him. He stood up, then stepped on the mattress, walked around a bit. Without a doubt, the carpet had been softer. He sat down again and began to untie his shoes. His brother and sister, huddled in a corner over Old Icardi, glanced up and smiled. The doll appeared even more tattered than when Beppe first found it waist deep in a pile of rubbish on the walk home from school. He had cleaned it up and given it to his sister, who named it after the man next door: Old Icardi, an ancient widower whose efforts every morning to dislodge phlegm unnerved the neighborhood.

As Beppe watched, Paolo held the doll in place while Margherita subjected it to various treatments. First she tried to force a stick down its throat, and when that failed she began to beat Old Icardi across the back. The children's giggles brightened the room, though not Beppe. He watched but did not smile. Had Margherita and Paolo glanced again, perhaps they would have noticed the furrow that creased their brother's brow and how the intricacies of shoelaces now escaped him. And with a dose of intuition, the children might have guessed the cause of his anxiety: Father Vincenzo. The priest had fallen asleep with no mention of any chores. Did that mean Beppe had no job? If so, he could well anticipate his mother's reaction. He had no choice but to return in twenty-odd hours prepared to scrub, scour, polish, and wipe.

●●●●●●●●

The vines had been planted years ago by priests now dead and buried. The church needed wine for sacramental purposes, and local supplies at that time were unreliable. Although the half acre behind the church lacked the gentle slope recommended and broad shadows settled in at midafternoon, the vines nonetheless took hold and the priests never once had to dilute their precious beverage. But now that a railroad connected Cortenza to wineries all over Europe, the church plants, at least in the mayor's opinion, had outlived their usefulness.

"A vineyard in the center of town?" he complained to Father Vincenzo after mass one Sunday. "Why not a playground for the kiddies or a garden path—you know, birdbaths and marble busts?"

The priest resisted. "A clerical legacy is at stake here," he said, "a part of church history. And you, a Catholic, want me to root that up?"

The mayor let the proposal drop for the moment, despite the fact that in the past it had been no secret that the priest preferred statues and grass.

When Father Vincenzo first arrived in Cortenza direct from a Florentine seminary, he had fancied himself a refined young man— a musician, a scholar—who had never dirtied his hands in peasant soil and had no desire to make it a habit in the future. As a result, he tended the vines behind the church as one might roses—gloves and all—and pruned according to aesthetic, not horticultural, principles. The plants, though attractive, yielded little—a few grapes for the crows to nibble or the sun to dry into raisins. With wine production soon out of the question, Father Vincenzo devoted his time to the numerous books he had brought with him and the music that since childhood had been a passion. But, in the manner of slow diseases, the boredom of rural life began to gnaw at him—he had no one to discuss the books with, no concerts to attend—and the once-eager priest became more and more despondent. A moderate drinker until that point, he started to raid the church reserves.

The cellar where Father Vincenzo sought relief provided an unexpected prize as well: a mildewed diary that had been kept by another priest who, though he dated each page, neglected to sign his name. The penmanship resembled that of a cloistered monk—patient and impeccable—and some pages contained drawings and graphs, yet none of the contents pertained to their author. Instead, the book described the day-to-day ritual of a small parish vineyard—the pruning, the harvesting, the processing, the aging. No mere instruction manual, though, the diarist had rendered it all an emotional landscape: *I awoke this morning before sunrise and ventured out at first light to inspect the grapes. Their color reminded me of the blush that had been brushed on my sister's cheek the day of her funeral: a powdery red with a blue undertone. The grapes will be perfect tomorrow, though I may not be if poor Gabriella appears tonight in a dream.*

Father Vincenzo, who until then had viewed the cultivation of grapes with, at best, indifference—a task on the order of, say, raising chickens—found that the book in his hands held the power of revelation. The thoughtful accounts of the unnamed writer turned an otherwise grim enterprise into a noble one—an art, so to speak, with the same opportunities for insight as classical literature, the same demand for attention as baroque music. By the time he reached the journal's abrupt end, Father Vincenzo understood the implications, and within a year's time the vines behind the church had blossomed once again.

When obliged to defend his new obsession—as happened in conversation with the mayor or in correspondence with the bishop—Father Vincenzo pointed to historical precedent and, as priests are inclined to do, quoted biblical verse to reinforce his point. A favorite passage from the book of Genesis described Noah's actions after docking the ark upon Mount Ararat: *And Noah began to be a husbandman, and he planted a vineyard. And he drank of the wine and was drunken.* Even Beppe, who never once questioned the vineyard's presence or the priest's sobriety, heard the quotation numerous times over the course of his tenure with Father Vincenzo.

The second visit Beppe paid to the rectory, as well as the third and the fourth, proceeded much like the first—no mention of chores, no scrub brush or bucket—and soon a routine developed: Beppe would sit quietly—though never again in the comfortable chair—and stuff himself with cookies while the priest talked and talked and then fell asleep. Maria Teresa, almost always just around the corner, would at that point enter and, with a sigh of what seemed relief, usher Beppe to the door. On those occasions when she did not appear the moment the priest became silent, Beppe would occupy himself with the crumbs that remained on the vacant plate—picked up with a licked fingertip—and the spectacle of a priest asleep: his cheeks shuddered with each breath, an eerie wheeze escaped his windpipe. If Father Vincenzo happened to wake when Maria Teresa entered— her size precluded a dancer's grace—he would offer the boy a weak, hungover smile, reach into a hidden pocket, and produce a single coin, which he would then deposit into the small hand—softly, as one might a wafer.

The afternoons, though, were not without responsibilities. During the second week alone the priest asked Beppe to run a note to the town vintner—a tubby man with fat purple fingers who rolled his eyes after reading the message—and to help with an inspection of the vineyard.

As Father Vincenzo showed Beppe the shortcut through the pantry where Maria Teresa puttered, he explained that plants needed a great deal of attention. "A bit like children," he said, "and stubborn as well." He hobbled a step ahead of Beppe along a stretch of tile floor, the cane in one hand, apprehension in the other. At the end of the room he leaned against a thick wooden door that, as Beppe soon discovered, opened onto the vineyard.

"Hello! Hello!" the priest called out. "And how are my babies?" He moved toward a knotted vine and, with the support of his cane, cupped a handful of berries. He held it for a moment, perhaps to gauge its weight. "The size and shape of a human heart."

Beppe followed the example, then let his fingers bump along the plump clusters.

At first he had not noticed the cello, almost hidden behind the massive globe, but after several afternoons of watching the priest sleep, the novelty wore off and Beppe's eyes began to wander. He started to count the books that lined the wooden shelves—one, two, three . . . ten—but lost track somewhere near thirty. He picked up the crumbless plate and, turning it over, discovered that it came from China. He looked at the globe across the room and searched for a place with that name—impossible at that distance. Then he caught sight of the instrument.

Beppe thought it large for a violin and could not imagine how a person might play it: Seated? Standing? At the shoulder? The elbow? In a room full of neglected objects—books that he had never seen opened, a globe that never spun—it alone seemed most forgotten. The awkward child: a thin stump of a leg, a pear-shaped body, a stretched-out neck, and a slender head topped with effeminate curls. It all but cowered in the corner—until the rain one day dripped a thought into Father Vincenzo's consciousness.

The summer had been wet—the first time in recent memory—and though the Arpino family owned a decent umbrella, Luisa needed it most days to protect the laundry. Beppe, therefore, traveled between cloudbursts whenever possible. But the forecasts he made were by no means scientific, and on occasion he found himself a distance from home and unprotected. Not that rain bothered him—it felt rather nice, in fact—but adults disapproved. His mother, for example, feared the worst—malarial fevers and assorted plagues, not to mention electrocution—and kept him at home when a large storm threatened—a fact that, thanks to Beppe's silence at school, went undetected by the vigilant Miss Donati. Even Maria Teresa acted peculiar the time he arrived wet with rain.

"Are you crazy?" she asked as he dripped outside the just-opened door.

Again, a question he felt unprepared to answer. Two months had passed since that first encounter, and Beppe had grown accustomed to their exchange: he knocked—the same rap, rap, rap as always—and she reminded him to wipe his feet. Why should today be any different?

Of course, the rain explained the change in Maria Teresa's behavior. The boy was drenched, as though he had just stepped from the river, and even a dozen towels would not keep the odd drop from staining the carpet. Under normal circumstances, she would have asked him to take off his clothes so that they could be wrung out and ironed. But that would send the boy into the study naked except for a towel, and all her efforts to protect him from the degenerate priest might come undone, might slip away with a quick twist of a wrist. She settled on a compromise instead: remove the shirt, throw a towel over the bare shoulders—which did, as the gossips had informed her, resemble fins when fully exposed—and hover in the hall as usual.

Thus far Maria Teresa's efforts had, from what she could tell, deterred the priest. Yes, there were those days when an errand forced her to leave the house or the oven demanded frequent attention, but even then she felt assured that no evil transpired in her absence. When she ushered the boy into the study, she always made careful note of the priest's position relative to the youngster and the condition of the latter's clothes. If a chair had moved or a button been undone, she would have noticed—the carpet had its indentations, the grip of a grown man's hand made wrinkles. Also, the talk that Maria Teresa heard bore no suggestive overtones—merely new versions of the same monologue the priest always delivered, though now he had a captive audience, one that never interrupted or feigned another engagement as the adults of Cortenza often did when cornered by their priest. What the boy lacked in physical appeal he made up for in diligence.

Or perhaps he was slow, as his reaction at the door the first day suggested—a blank look when she questioned him, an abnormal fascination with her apron. Another explanation might be rickets, which affects the bones, yes, but maybe the mind as well. The curve of that back—in a word, amphibious—lent credence to this theory. The emotions, though, might also be to blame. One heard rumors around town about a suicide in the family, and that mixture of grief, shame, and confusion would have numbed anyone to the priest's monotonous blather.

Whatever the cause of the boy's unnatural patience, he deserved Maria Teresa's protection. As her mother had often said, "A big girl like you must look out for the little ones." Her mother had been tiny herself. Maria Teresa inherited her size from her father, a man she knew only from stories. "Just how big was he?" she once asked, and her mother replied with typical candor: "Let me put it this way, my dear: childbirth was the least of my worries."

●●●●●●●●

No matter how genuine and well intentioned Maria Teresa's concern, it was entirely misplaced. Father Vincenzo had other thoughts on his mind the afternoon Beppe appeared before him with a towel draped over his shoulders.

"All is lost," the priest muttered with a sigh, "all is lost."

As usual, Beppe took his seat in the straight-backed chair, which poked the points of both shoulder blades and forced him to lean forward as if he hung on the priest's every word.

Father Vincenzo appreciated the attention. "What has it been?" he asked. "Four days? Five?"

As always, Beppe replied with silence.

"It may as well be forty," the priest continued, "as far as I'm concerned. Once the roots are soaked . . . " But he did not finish. Or if he did, Beppe never heard him. With each day of rain, the priest had appeared to sink deeper and deeper into the chair, and now he seemed to call out from a dark and distant place. It made no difference, though, since Beppe had heard the complaint before: waterlogged soil would ruin the crop.

"Forty days." The priest mumbled another few words, then added, "It reminds me of Noah."

Noah? Again? Beppe braced himself for the inevitable recitation, but to his surprise it never occurred. Instead, the priest described a theory he had developed that concerned the Old Testament figure, a theory he had once presented in confidence to a fellow priest who, rumor suggested, later used it to advance his career. Father Vincenzo, however, remained philosophical: "Such are the risks one takes with all friendships."

According to the priest's theory, Noah had used music to entice the animals aboard the ark and, once captive, to keep them subdued. "Imagine, if you will, lions and llamas side by side on an old wooden vessel—the animals were arranged in alphabetical order, of course—for forty days and forty nights. The rough, choppy seas, the violent thunderstorms . . . Noah must have been an accomplished musician, perhaps Noah's wife as well. Yes, matrimonial duets."

Beppe knew lions from school, and though in stories they sometimes ate children, he nevertheless liked them. Besides, there were more than enough children to go around—fifteen in his class alone. And some, like Dino DeBono, the baker's son, could have been counted twice. A lion would have liked Dino, who no doubt tasted sweeter than most since he ate more sweets than most. Beppe thought about that for a moment, then thought about the spots on Mr. DeBono's apron. And occupied with that thought, he almost missed Father Vincenzo's confession: he, too, had been a musician.

"For many years," the priest said, "like an addiction." He emerged from the chair's depths and pointed in the direction of the globe in the corner. "Fetch that for me, will you?"

Beppe hesitated—the globe?—but so seldom did the priest make a request that he felt obliged to comply. "Lift with the knees, not with the back," his mother had warned him whenever she needed help with the baskets of laundry; she claimed that his posture resulted from improper technique. Beppe prepared to do as his mother instructed—he adjusted the towel and squatted into position—when the priest called out.

"No, no, young man, I meant the cello!"

By process of elimination, Beppe determined what the priest wanted, and his heart made a little jump. At last, the time had come to rescue the orphan. Again, he squatted to pick up the object—how could he have known that cellos were hollow?—and when he lifted almost fell over backward. He recovered, though the towel slipped from his shoulders—Maria Teresa gasped in the doorway—and presented the instrument to the priest, who did not lift it to his chin, as Beppe feared he might, but made a V of his legs, pulled back the robes, and positioned it between his knees. Beppe stood there in anticipation, just inches from the instrument and moments from hearing the sound that would change his life.

The priest tugged one of the strings with the fleshy part of a finger. A dull, flaccid tone emerged, a burp. The priest tugged other strings and turned the flat knobs at the top, which made the pitch waver. He seemed revived by the process, as though the rain no longer mattered, the grapes no longer mattered, and the wine that remained at his elbow could evaporate without consequence.

Finally, when all was adjusted, Father Vincenzo sent Beppe back for a stick he called the bow. The priest turned a small screw at one of its ends and bounced the bow on his knee. A puff of dust sprang up. He then scraped the bow across the strings to produce a sound not unlike that of a man clearing his throat—a civilized man, that is, not Old Icardi. What happened next would remain clear in Beppe's mind for the rest of his life, until those final tragic moments when the explosives detonated. He would remember it with the clarity of an afterimage, the effect that occurs when you stare at something—a tooth, for example—then close your eyes and still see the object in darkness: a tooth, perhaps even the crack.

The music went straight to Beppe's knees, which wobbled and weakened and forced him back into the uncomfortable chair. His shoulder blades, however, did not protest. The music had a sedative effect, as though he had fallen under the spell of a kind hearted gypsy. Whether the priest was accomplished or not, Beppe could not say. The only music he had heard until that moment came from the local accordionist and a teacher at school who tortured violins. What the priest played sounded different. It rose and fell much like laughter, yet at times had a melancholy edge. Some notes were long as the walk home that day Beppe's father left, others quick as blinks. The tone itself was warm, like a blanket, and reminded Beppe of the bells on top of the church that he would never clean and of his mother years back when she would wash young Paolo and hum to herself and fill their home with the sounds of a woman, a baby, and water. Beppe sat there, stunned, and watched the priest work the instrument, watched the bow glide over the strings like a gondola, the left hand contort itself like an old spider, the face twist in a painful grimace.

When the priest finished—it may have been the whole piece or just the beginning, Beppe had no idea—he propped the bow against the cello and the cello against the chair and complained of his shoulder, the fall in the vineyard, his need for refreshment. He reached for the glass, and Beppe reached for the bow.

●●●●●●●

A week after the vineyard spill Father Vincenzo had brought out the cello and tuned it up with the hope that a dose of music might bring some comfort. Instead the act proved to be a terrible mistake. His technique, once impressive, had withered over time to the point of embarrassment. But he understood the demands of performance and had expected a deterioration. What he had not expected was the ache that burned in his right shoulder after a few dozen strokes with the bow. He must have landed on that side when he tripped or else developed acute bursitis. Whatever the cause, the pain soon forced him to stop and perhaps never start again. The cello fell away from him and died on the carpet; he tossed the bow after it like a branch onto a pyre.

Who would have thought that the end, when it came, would feel like a funeral? After all, Father Vincenzo had not played the instrument in years. The desire that possessed him as a young man began to dissipate once he settled in Cortenza. It happened, like most things there, in slow increments: The practice sessions became shorter and less frequent, the trips to the cellar more predictable. And the cello, propped in a corner alongside the globe, soon took on the look of furniture—an attractive piece of wood with curved surfaces ideal for the collection of dust.

It had been a gift from his teacher, a disciple of Merighi who, with equal parts envy and admiration, would on occasion describe the time the master had purchased a Stradivari cello on the streets of Milan from a man who carried it unprotected in a wheelbarrow. Antonio Stradivari had built just thirty of the instruments during his lifetime, and to discover one under such peculiar circumstances was indeed remarkable. As the teacher put it, "Like finding the Pope's ring on a prostitute."

Needless to say, Father Vincenzo did not receive one of the precious Stradivari for his eighteenth birthday. Rather, it was thought to be a Guadagnini—small and somewhat abused but with a warm and sonorous voice. The young man cherished the instrument and with renewed fervor vowed to surpass the achievements of even the acclaimed Merighi. Unfortunately, his technique, though formidable, lacked the grace and finesse of a professional, and his playing, emotional depth. The generous gift had been an attempt on the teacher's part to compensate for a flawed curriculum. But even a fine instrument could not disguise the student's deficiencies, and at age twenty he was encouraged by a visiting soloist to pursue another line of work. He turned to the priesthood for solace.

Despite the frustrations associated with an aborted career, Father Vincenzo continued to believe that music in one way or another would always be part of his life, and even years later when the cello went neglected while he became obsessed with the cultivation of grapes, the instrument's presence across the room never failed to comfort him—a familiar face in a favorite pew. But the pain in his shoulder, just a week after the fractured ankle, put an end to those thoughts. Father Vincenzo realized that he had become an old man, and that awareness pressed upon him with the weight of a hundred cassocks. He looked at the cello facedown on the floor before him and wondered how long it would be until he, too, was lifeless and prone.

The boy reached for the bow. He wore no shirt, and the outstretched arm showed itself to be no thicker than what it sought and in all likelihood as fragile. The boy as a whole seemed fragile: the sunken chest and battered eyes, the girlish neck and shoulders. Yet he acted now with a boldness that belied fragility. He grabbed the bow without hesitation or permission when at other times one had to frighten him for an audible reply. The music surely accounted for the difference. The boy had become transfixed at the cello's first notes. And although Father Vincenzo focused most attention on the slippery intonation and the stab in his right shoulder, he had been trained both as a priest and as a musician to make periodic eye contact with audience members; therefore Beppe's expression did not escape him—as though the youngster had discerned the face of Jesus in the instrument's patterned grain or heard his departed father speak through one of the sound holes. Let him play with the bow, Father Vincenzo decided. It's useless to me now.

●●●●●●●

Beppe ran a hand along the hairs that just moments before had made music. They were coarse, almost abrasive, and slowed the progress of his fingers. What sort of creature had they come from? he wondered. A mule? A llama? A wrinkled old witch? He bounced the bow on his knee as the priest had done—it hopped like a rabbit—then fit the end into his hand and sawed off thick slices of air to the accompaniment of the music that still echoed in his ears.

"Watch yourself," Father Vincenzo said. "Your grip is too tight. It should be loose and flexible." He set down the glass to demonstrate. "Imagine that you're painting a wall. See how my wrist moves?"

Beppe studied the motion—back and forth and back and forth—and though he had never painted a wall, merely picked at one, he found the comparison helpful.

"Yes, much better," the priest said. "But it's best to practice on an instrument." He motioned for Beppe to stand beside him. "Here, I'll hold it while you play."

Beppe, eager to hear more music, took a position next to the cello, lowered the bow into place, and mouthed the words *loose* and *flexible,* but the bow skittered across the strings as though it were afraid of them.

"You have to press harder," the priest advised. "Don't be shy."

Beppe tried again, now with a firmer grip, and an actual tone emerged. He could feel it tingle in his wrist and travel to his shoulder.

"That was an open C, and a good one, I might add."

Beppe smiled at the compliment, and the priest smiled, too. But their smiles were broken by a crash across the room.

"Whoops!" Maria Teresa assumed a look of what she hoped would communicate surprise—she opened her eyes wide and threw a hand over her mouth as if to stifle a yawn—paused for a moment to let the performance register, then bent over and attended to the shattered cup. She had dropped it twice on the carpet, but the carpet refused to cooperate. In desperation she rammed a heel down and crushed it like a bug. The remnants were small and plentiful: assorted bits of porcelain, a spoonful of white dust. She brushed them into a palm with her fingers and watched in vain as the priest continued.

"As I said, an open C." He put a hand to the boy's elbow. "And the secret? A firm yet supple grip."

Maria Teresa almost toppled. Although she had never slept with a man—and had begun to doubt that it would ever happen—she recognized seduction no matter what its guise. In other words, attempts had been made. The first came from Giovanni Ciano, twenty-eight when she turned fifteen but gentle, artistic, and clean. He introduced her to the Renaissance masters through his own distorted reproductions and called her Venus in a sweet, familiar way. It may have been love, as he claimed, but she refused to pose nude on the scalloped platform he constructed in her honor. Next was Borghi Verbano, an older and stouter man who suffered chest pains the night their stroll through the gardens turned into a chase as soon as he suggested a detour. Even the mayor had tried—at the vegetable market, no less, where he parted her lettuce with a thrust zucchini. And last but not least were the two aged veterans whose crude exhibition still haunted her like a scene from Giovanni's *Homage to Hieronymous Bosch*.

Maria Teresa poured the cup into an apron pocket and proceeded toward the towel. "You'll catch cold," she told the boy as she covered his bare shoulders and, with her knees, nudged him into a seat.

"Believe it or not, young man, Maria Teresa has a point." The priest set aside the cello. "Disease lurks in these hills like an assassin." He sunk back in the chair and took up the wine. "And thanks to the talents of our dear physician, even a minor ailment will have grim repercussions."

A comment clearly directed at Maria Teresa, who responded not with scorn but with a sigh of relief. The crisis averted, she could return to her chores and the preparation of dinner. Tonight it would be pork chops and boiled peas with a plate of buttered pasta. Not that it mattered, of course, since the priest just nibbled on breadsticks.

●●●●●●●

The rain ended within hours of the cello's appearance, but the lessons continued for years. Beppe had a natural feel for the instrument and gave it, people later remarked—people who heard him from the street or prior to having their teeth examined, even those who never met him but read the obituaries in dental publications—a magical charm. Likewise, Father Vincenzo proved himself a patient and insightful teacher despite the fact that he had no interest in the rigors of musical instruction. The program he had followed as a youth seemed in hindsight more like persecution: the merciless finger exercises, the metronome's iron fist. As a result, he would offer Beppe just brief demonstrations—though padded with the usual digressions—and few drills or exercises. He adopted an informal approach to the process and, unlike their work in the vineyard, did not insist on a rigid schedule.

The vineyard: With meticulous care the grapes had to be picked each fall—the most laborious task Beppe performed for the priest, but the one that, for obvious reasons, he liked best. After that, the vintner would be summoned to cart away the fruit and begin the procedure that ends with wine. Then, when the leaves fell a month or so later, the plants had to be pruned, a step that required great insight and care: if too many buds remained, the next year's crop would, in the absence of summer rains, be ample but the wine inferior; too few and the quality would be high but the yield modest.

"A balancing act," the priest once remarked as he guided Beppe snip to snip from atop the stool he had appropriated from Maria Teresa's pantry. "Consider yourself a circus performer. You've been to the circus, right?"

Beppe, tangled in a vine at the moment, still managed to shake his head.

"Well, that's a shame, because all children love the circus. When you're ten years old there's nothing quite like a woman with a dozen chins or a pair of Siamese twins dressed as sailors. And then there are the acrobats—you know, the people who jump around in tight-fitting clothes? You have midgets as well and men who will swallow almost anything. And would you believe that I once saw an elephant catch fire at the circus? Yes, I was your age or just about. No, come to think of it, I must have been older. Let's see, I had my first communion at . . . "

If with the shears, as the priest suggested, Beppe were a tight-rope walker, then with the bow he became an illusionist: From the time he first performed in public, when all he could manage were the quiet little tunes that Father Vincenzo had taught to him, listeners claimed that the cello seemed to whisper just inches from their ears; a few even said it tickled them. Similarly, the manner in which Beppe held the instrument—embraced it, really—made some people wonder whether it were, in fact, polished wood and not disguised human flesh.

But no sleight of hand took place. It was simply music performed with an open heart—not meant to impress, not meant to reward, not meant to fulfill an obligation. Beppe played because it gave him a pleasant sensation. He could close his eyes and relax that relentless stare or attempt to repair the damage inflicted by a night's worth of asthmatic snores. Meanwhile the thoughts that he kept to himself throughout the day could flow from the cello like rainwater down a sloped cobblestone street.

For Father Vincenzo, the future seemed less bleak when he could lean back and listen to Beppe replicate the sounds he had grown up with. Major scale, minor scale, Mixolydian, whatever—it all had the power to lull him into the most pleasant dreams he had experienced since the night before he entered the priesthood. For Maria Teresa, Beppe's performances provided comfort of another sort. They assured her that, at least while the music continued, the boy was out of harm's way. After all, the cello required a seated position when played in the conventional manner and introduced a large, impenetrable object between the legs.

∞∞∞∞∞∞

When the priest remarked on her son's musical abilities at the close of mass a week after the first anniversary of Giuseppe's death, Luisa thought that he must have been mistaken. "Beppe?" she asked with all due respect.

"Yes, a natural musician."

The liquor, she assumed; once again the gossips had been correct. "Beppe Arpino? Dark eyes, sloped shoulders, quiet as ricotta cheese?"

"Yes, Beppe. And believe me, he'll make all of us proud one day."

Luisa thanked the priest for the kind words and hurried home to applaud her son. He still worked at the church most afternoons—the coins she received proved it—and had mentioned music once or twice, but the details remained vague in Luisa's mind. With Margherita and Paolo to keep her occupied, not to mention that stubborn grief and the neighborhood laundry—just the handkerchiefs alone from Bruno Icardi took a full hour to clean—she had neither the time nor the patience to coax information from her eldest, though he did tell her about the grapes when she demanded an explanation for the stains on his fingers. But the sad truth was that mother and son had drifted apart since Giuseppe's departure.

Although Beppe bore little resemblance to his father—a broad man with a bricklayer's shoulders who, contrary to appearances, had worked as a butcher—they shared the same wide-eyed stare, the same quiet reserve, and the same fondness for scraps from the dinner table. On those occasions when the budget permitted a roast chicken —stuffed with onions and a sprig of rosemary—father and son would remain together after the meal and dismantle the bird in silence. The sight of Beppe seated alone with that familiar determination focused on a few overcooked string beans stirred in Luisa both sorrow and exasperation. On the one hand, he looked pitiful hunched over their all-but-empty plates; on the other, somehow defiant.

Stubborn, Luisa thought as she wound her way through the maze-like streets, stubborn, stubborn, stubborn, yet oh so indifferent. She could yell at him, send him to bed at six, hit him in the head with stale bread or across the bottom with an olive switch, and his expression would remain the same. He never even cried at the funeral. It seemed impossible to Luisa, a woman with little control over her own emotions, that a child like Beppe could have sprung from her womb. If she had not been present when it happened, she would have had serious doubts.

And now Father Vincenzo proclaimed him a natural musician. Luisa stepped aside to let a clattering cart pass and to gather her thoughts. Yes, she had hummed before Giuseppe left—most recently to soothe the baby—and her husband had whistled, she recalled, at the moment of each child's conception—a gap in the teeth the blame—but no other music—if hum-dee-dum and *sheew!* could be considered music—had entered their home. The fact was that no one, as far as she knew, on either side of the family had ever owned an instrument—well, except for Uncle Antonio, who brought a bugle to their wedding and sprayed spittle all over the cake and the maid of honor.

But what about the rhythms she produced while she pounded wet clothes upon the riverbank? Or the strange melodies that her spoons composed inside her pots? And how could she forget Edoardo, the local accordionist, who squeezed out a tune whenever he picked up his laundry—a special thanks for the efforts Luisa made to remove those inevitable strap marks? Nor could she rule out the influence of gypsies, who, rumor had it, played their guitars late at night in the vacant piazza and waited in anticipation for the wolves to appear as required for their more elaborate rituals. Once, as she tiptoed to the graveyard with a week's worth of fingernail chips, Luisa had heard—or thought she heard—the strum of a gypsy thumb over catgut and the not-too-distant howl of a predator.

She resumed her walk—the cart had been loaded with wine bottles—and followed the final curve home. As usual, Margherita and Paolo would be huddled in a corner over that frightful doll. And

Beppe . . . Luisa searched her dress for a handkerchief and found one tucked under a sleeve. Her Beppe: a natural musician. If only Giuseppe were alive to share in her pride. If only he had remained in Cortenza or selected a different hotel or waited until daybreak to relieve himself. If only the priest had exercised more caution when he stepped over that injurious vine. The unfairness of life wearied Luisa; no tears were left. She returned the handkerchief to her elbow and fished out a coin from somewhere among her dress's many folds. For Beppe, she thought as she opened the door.

∞∞∞∞∞∞

A single comment at the riverbank, a mother's little boast—no harm intended—but within hours Beppe's world had changed. The washerwomen now competed for his cheeks. The grocer's bellow softened overnight into a polite meow. People on the street—adults, complete strangers—now smiled and winked; even the mayor wiggled his toes. And Miss Donati, with all her militaristic charm, requested a classroom recital.

"How about tomorrow?" she asked as the tip of her pointer came to rest on his nose. "Will tomorrow be okay?"

The heads in the room all turned to face Beppe for what might have been the very first time: Giulia, the pubescent eleven-year-old who, even seated, clutched a book to her chest; Carlo, just eight but already able to roll cigarettes like an infantryman; Dino, the baker's son, the class clown, the plump comedian; Francesca, whose handstands behind the school inspired restless fantasies; and Filippo, the boy with the indigo tongue. In all, fourteen students stared at Beppe while, at the thick end of the pointer, their teacher waited . . .

The room began to swim.

. . . and waited . . .

Beppe's chest threatened to explode.

. . . and waited . . .

Always these questions, never the answers.

. . . until the silence was broken. "I know," Miss Donati said, her pointer still poised, "I will invite our own violinist, and you two . . . "

"No!" The word leapt from Beppe's mouth before he could restrain it, but then the clarification: "I mean, I have no instrument."

The heads all turned to Miss Donati.

"A minor detail," she said. "I'll take care of it." And then, with the precision of a fencer, she swung the pointer from its perch on Beppe's nose and cracked it across Filippo's index finger, the tip of which had just emerged from an inkwell and appeared headed for his mouth.

"Aaaaah!" Filippo collapsed to the floor.

Beppe would have screamed as well if he had not suffered from shock. The unwelcome attention had taken its toll. The stares, the cheeks, Miss Donati, the mayor. What, he wondered, made people think he had become an expert musician? Had Maria Teresa blabbered it all over the vegetable market? Had Father Vincenzo mentioned their sessions in yesterday's sermon? Hmmm, Father Vincenzo. And that would explain the coin Beppe received when his mother returned home from church and cried, "Treat yourself, my boy! I'm proud of you already!" She offered no explanation for the kindness, though Beppe had grown accustomed to her erratic behavior and, with a thank-you and a smile, pocketed the coin—just enough for a fresh cannoli.

Father Vincenzo, however, would never have boasted. Beppe knew a few tunes, the scales and modes, the hand positions, and simple notation, but he still had much to learn. He still, for example, had a tendency to grip the cello too tight with his knees. "It's not a wild horse," Father Vincenzo would remind him. "It's not going to throw you." The priest also told him again and again to sit up straight. "A cellist is supposed to lean forward and meet the instrument, yes, but you look as though you're about to defile it."

If Beppe were ever to perform in public—an act that, until Miss Donati's request, he had never considered—it would happen in ten or fifteen years and not twenty-four hours. The thought made him nauseous. He pictured Giulia, Dino, Carlo, and the rest, their eyes glued upon him. The cannoli would have to wait, at least until Miss Donati abandoned her search. And the odds were not in her favor. Cortenza had no orchestra or music store, no instrument makers, and Father

Vincenzo, as far as Beppe knew, possessed the only cello between Palermo and Rome—a misconception that was soon corrected.

The decrepit approximation that Miss Donati unveiled at school the next day looked to Beppe, accustomed to the beloved Guadagnini, as though it had been fashioned from the remnants of an unearthed coffin. Indeed, he would not have recognized it as a musical instrument if the teacher had not identified it as such. Beppe approached with skeptical caution and, as he drew closer, detected a familiar odor, one that he identified with infants and forgetful children. He took a deep breath—held it, as he did in the public latrine—and tried to remain focused on the task at hand.

He sat down and positioned the instrument between his knees. There were cracks in its surface, jagged lines, as though at some point it had been smashed and reassembled—the handiwork of an apprentice carpenter. Beppe dusted off the limp strings with a sleeve—aware that whatever afflicted them might be contagious—and made an attempt, at least, to tune up. Then, without so much as a word of introduction, he launched into the first piece Father Vincenzo taught him: a diminutive waltz that brought to mind the voices one heard at a puppet show. Although the warped bow threatened to slip from his fingers and the instrument's tone ranged from shallow to weak, Beppe soon found relief in the music and a pleasant calm settled over him.

Had the acclaimed Merighi stumbled upon the scene just then— impossible given that he had died more than fifty years earlier—he would have recognized in the slight tilt of Beppe's head and the almost imperceptible bounce in his thighs the expressive quirks of a born musician, quirks that Father Vincenzo, despite years of practice, never developed. Even the students in the room, as ignorant of music as Beppe once had been, knew that the otherwise quiet classmate who now sat before them generated sounds altogether different from their resident violinist. Whereas her performances became painful endurance tests, the children, with one notable exception, found Beppe's as enjoyable as an unsupervised recess. They applauded when he finished the piece and asked him for another.

∘∘∘∘∘∘∘

"Teacher's pet! Music lover!" Dino DeBono jabbed a fat finger into Beppe's chest, turned, and waddled back into the bakery.

Beppe rubbed the sore spot—as if a rib had been dented—then bent over and picked up the soiled cannoli. Dino's outburst surprised him. He had until then considered the baker's son to be a jovial sort. Was the person who just threatened him the same person who a week before had stuffed an olive up his nose and shot it clear across the classroom so that it plunked right into the rubbish can? The same person who joked about men's meatballs and had a hundred names for you-know-what? The same person who once spilled a pocketful of confectioner's sugar on a desk and traced Giulia's bookless profile into it with a wet finger? The same person who cleaned his ears with a fork?

Beppe brushed off the pastry as best he could—a mixture of dirt and odd-shaped hairs—then took an eager, blissful bite: the crunch outside, the smooth inside. No matter how delicious Maria Teresa's cookies—and they were quite delicious—he preferred even a scuffed cannoli. But on the second or third chew, Beppe heard, as well as felt, an ominous crack and, after a quick shift of the contents in his mouth, realized that a tooth had been chipped—on the right, at the back, on the top, a sharp edge. He tongued out a small white fragment—the partial tooth—and a smaller, darker one—what appeared to be a stone. He dropped both to the ground without further inspection and finished the cannoli in the careful manner of an octogenarian.

Years later Beppe would ponder the broken tooth at the back of his mouth—a sixth-year molar, he would then know—and attempt to recall the circumstances of its damage. That memory, however, would prove elusive, no doubt overshadowed by what at the time seemed to be more important matters: the school performance that he had just completed, the threat of violence from an overweight classmate, the rapture of a favorite dessert.

If Beppe had been born into one of Cortenza's wealthier families—the Bergamos, who helped settle the town, or the Carbonis, who all but owned it—he might have traveled north to see a trained specialist, a person with knowledge of the latest techniques to repair a broken tooth. Instead, he proceeded straight to Father Vincenzo's apartment and spent the afternoon as usual. The fact that there were people in Naples who filled teeth and replaced them would have come as a surprise. Beppe knew that a tooth could be pulled—the barber charged two lire, three with a shave and trim—but that marked the extent of his dental wisdom. It would be another four years before he learned more about the subject or had the desire to learn more.

He was fourteen when that happened and still insulated from the outside world. In general, the events that made headlines in metropolitan newspapers had little impact on rural southern towns. Although the war that had occupied Europe claimed a few of Cortenza's men—as noted on a plaque in the central piazza—and the Fascists had installed themselves with a flourish in Rome, both events seemed remote and failed to spark much conversation. Instead, the townspeople gossiped, as usual, about the indiscretions and ineptitudes of their neighbors. They attended mass and washed clothes and procreated and died. The grapes ripened in the summer; the vintner crushed them in the fall. And most afternoons, Beppe cradled the cello and serenaded the priest.

•••••••••

The letters stood tall and demanded attention: *S. Russo, Painless Tooth Extractions.* Above them a cartoon showed a fat man with an imperfect but nonetheless radiant smile. Below them a paragraph described the wonders of a new medication that made the removal of teeth, in the words of an unnamed patient, a thrill and a pleasure. Beppe folded the handbill in quarters, slid it into a pocket, and continued on toward the market. His mother needed soap and had sent him on an urgent mission. Still, Beppe paused once more before he left the piazza and watched the man—presumably S. Russo—set down a small leather case similar to what the town physician carried, open it, and reach inside. He wore a dark flannel suit—again, similar to the physician—and when he bent over its seams revealed their imperfections.

When Beppe returned with the soap ten minutes later—as always, he had detoured to avoid the bakery—he did not see the man with the handbills in the piazza. But when he went to visit Father Vincenzo that afternoon, he passed him on the street—the leather case in one hand, what appeared to be a cookie in the other. Beppe stopped once again and watched the man, until he disappeared around a corner, then proceeded on toward the cello. As he had done hundreds of times before, he knocked on the door—rap, rap, rap— and waited for what had become as inevitable as Old Icardi's coughs or Father Vincenzo's digressions, the white apron and the repetitive hello: "Come in, Beppe. And remember to wipe your feet."

Maria Teresa offered that same reminder to all the priest's visitors, even the church officials who appeared at odd intervals. The words now came out as a reflex whenever she welcomed someone inside. Without them, the carpets would be ruined in a matter of months or she would be forced to spend hours down on her hands and knees—"A vulnerable position," her mother once remarked, "and dangerous near a priest." Yet how peculiar Maria Teresa's reaction when, as she ushered Beppe down the hall, she noticed footprints on the carpet: a flush came to her cheeks, and the humidity beneath her skirts started to rise.

The footprints were large—a man's feet, almost as large as her own. Maria Teresa touched the handbill hidden in her apron pocket. At long last, the man of her dreams—attired like a professional, the hint of some exotic cologne. He had traveled great distances and arrived at her door unannounced, but she knew the moment their eyes met that he would be the one to loosen her stays. How shameless, she thought, and with the child at her heels. But ah, that merciless gaze. It had so overwhelmed her that even her reflexes had failed. She left Beppe with the priest and returned to the footprints. On the one hand, the carpet might be ruined; on the other, it was as if he had never left. She knelt down and touched one of the marks: more dirt than mud. A stiff brush would do the trick, though that could wait until later.

Maria Teresa ducked into the pantry and unfolded the handbill: *S. Russo, Painless Tooth Extractions.* The words alone sent shivers up her thighs. What did the *S* stand for? she wondered. Siro? Silvio? Sante? Salvatore? She had always liked the name Salvatore. Salvatore Russo—that had a nice ring to it. Dr. Salvatore Russo—he must have studied female anatomy in school. Maria Teresa Russo—yes, that would do fine.

She returned the handbill to her apron—though not without a quick press of her lips—and loaded another plate with cookies. The visitor had eaten them all within minutes. It had been a message to her, she understood, and she returned it as he departed: "Excuse me, sir, would you like another?" Naturally, he accepted—a masculine handful. It saddened her that the priest had monopolized their time, but how could a lecherous old man with a limp be expected to recognize true love? He had talked and talked about aches and pains and, for some reason, the Middle Ages, oblivious to the glances that connected the face opposite him with the face in the hall, oblivious to the charged atmosphere, the boisterous hearts. But through it all, Salvatore—yes, he looked like a Salvatore—had endured with grace and vigor. The man had stamina.

With the replenished plate in hand and a cup of warm milk, Maria Teresa returned to what she now called the music room and, careful not to spill, let her feet retrace Salvatore's steps. He would be back tomorrow, she had heard him tell the priest in a voice loud enough for her ears. She handed the milk to Beppe and stooped to set the plate on the table next to the wine and another, smaller bottle. When she straightened up, she felt, with neither surprise nor alarm, the intimation of a toothache.

●●●●●●●●

The ankle had gone from bad to worse, and the shoulder now complained regardless of its position. As for the wine, which had numbed these and other pains with moderate success over the years, it no longer made a difference. The afternoon recitals helped, though, and the diarist's entries—both instilled in him peace—but the pain itself remained: simple and straightforward, relentless, unperturbed. At times it seemed more than he could bear. Had the dentist arrived the next week or the week after, it might have been too late.

Well, nowhere on the handbill did the man use the word *dentist*. Instead, he described himself as a tooth extractor, which prompted a chuckle from the priest. "Perhaps I should change my title as well," he said. "How about Father Vincenzo, Eucharist Dispenser?" He could not resist a degree of familiarity with the visitor. After all, their respective professions had been aligned for centuries, ever since the Middle Ages, when the practice of dentistry was limited to monks. The church later outlawed that monastic service, but an interest in the subject continued despite the prohibition, and a brotherhood of sorts developed between those devoted to the soul and those devoted to the teeth and gums. Even in Father Vincenzo's time books written for dental practitioners passed between seminary bunks and furtive discussions spiced with words like *caries* and *halitosis* took place in the alcoves of darkened cathedrals.

"There's a young man who comes to mass," the priest explained as the visitor consumed a cookie, "rather fat, the baker's son, and from the way he winces after communion I suspect it's a second molar. You must pull a lot of those, I imagine. Just climb right in there and yank—the faster, the better. At least that's the idea, right? The element of surprise? Yes, not unlike a baptism."

Father Vincenzo, both hands on the awkward bottle, refilled their glasses with red sloshes. "Perhaps I should have become a dentist myself." He set down the bottle: a clunk, a sigh of relief. "You never know, I might have made an excellent dentist. And I could have worn white, all white, though I see you prefer—is it brown or black? Either way, the blood doesn't show—a wise decision. But flannel? I would have selected linen or a lightweight cotton, and in the summer months, short sleeves."

The visitor finished the last cookie and began to lick the crumbs from each finger. "I notice your hands are a bit scarred," Father Vincenzo continued, "but I suppose that's unavoidable. Yours is a dangerous profession; it's a wonder you still have ten fingers. But the priesthood also has its dangers. Need I mention the vise-like embrace of new widows or the indigestible pies and cakes that are served at peasant receptions? I've heard confessions that would make most sinners faint—bizarre acts, barbaric, beyond the scope of even a lunatic's imagination. And then there is the confessional itself: a sauna in July and August."

Father Vincenzo nodded toward the cane propped beside him and told the visitor about another burden: the fall in the vineyard and its wicked legacy. "Just the short walk to the church now exhausts me," he explained. "Even to lift this glass—but I'm sure you hear people talk about their pain all the time. Which reminds me, what do the dentists use nowadays? Is it still ether?"

No, as Father Vincenzo discovered, S. Russo favored another painkiller. He used the leaves of a coca plant to create a powder that, when dissolved and injected into the gums via syringe, made the entire mouth numb and inspired mild elation. The powder, the visitor added, could also be sniffed.

"Really?" Father Vincenzo said. "From the leaves of a coca plant? I've never heard of that concoction before. I would be curious to test its effects. But alas, I have remarkable teeth. Ironic, isn't it? While the rest of me collapses, the teeth remain strong as ever. Of course, I give them a good workout at supper—the breadsticks the housekeeper bakes are ideal—and scrub them most nights with a badger's-hair brush. And once or twice a week I give the tongue a good scraping. If only my ankles were as resilient as my incisors. The pain, as I said, it's . . . "

The visitor reached down and opened the small leather case that he had set on the floor when he arrived. Father Vincenzo noted the manner in which the sleeves of the man's coat seemed to separate from the shoulders—ventilation perhaps—then inventoried the contents of the case: a dozen or so miniature bottles, a metal syringe, a pair of antique pliers, and other assorted implements. The man removed one of the bottles and pulled out its stopper. He then handed the bottle to Father Vincenzo, who cupped it in a hand—as fragile and light, he noted, as a dried flower. The priest sniffed the bottle as one might perfume but detected no odor. The visitor encouraged him to pour out a pinch of the white powder and inhale it like snuff. Father Vincenzo did as suggested, and a bumblebee zoomed up his nose, whereupon it transformed itself into a swarm. The two men soon agreed upon a price.

∞∞∞∞∞∞

An extra wineglass on the table and a medicine bottle. The familiar handbill under the corkscrew and what had appeared to be a cookie in the pedestrian's hand. Beppe assembled the evidence and reached a conclusion: the man in the tattered suit, S. Russo, had been a recent visitor. And as advertised, the patient exhibited no discomfort. In fact, Father Vincenzo seemed euphoric. Beppe had never seen the priest like that before, and the unusual behavior befuddled him. He neither drank the milk when it arrived, just set it aside, nor touched the cookies, and when Father Vincenzo asked him to pull a book from one of the shelves, Beppe hesitated.

"That's all right," the priest said with uncharacteristic haste, "I'll get it myself." And to Beppe's surprise, he did just that. He leapt from the chair, bounded over to the bookshelves, pulled out the desired text, and returned to the chair—no cane, no complaints. A miracle, Beppe thought, I have witnessed a miracle.

Father Vincenzo opened the book: a thin volume bound in red leather with the word *Teeth* stamped into its cover. "One of the classics," he said. "I must have read it a dozen times." He browsed a few pages and laughed—a schoolgirl's giggle. "Yes, the periodontal membrane, I remember it well."

Beppe no longer recognized the priest. What had happened to the exhausted posture and the half-shut eyes, the frequent mutters and sighs? Had a toothache, not the vineyard spill, been the real affliction? Or had the visit from S. Russo reawakened a dormant passion? Beppe inched the chair forward and tried to peer at the book's contents.

Father Vincenzo raised an eyebrow. "Curious?" he said. "Well, take a look at this." He handed Beppe the book and pointed to a picture. Beppe examined it: a detailed illustration that showed three teeth.

The first appeared flawless, while the second had minor imperfections —a dark spot and grooves; the third resembled a puckered vegetable —broccoli when he squinted.

"It's a shame I never became a dentist," Father Vincenzo said as he leaned back in the chair. "I would have liked the independence: just me and my satchel." He leaned forward and smiled. "And plenty of tools." He reached over and picked up the corkscrew, tested its point with a finger. "There's one—a turnkey, I believe it's called—that with a twist will loosen even the most stubborn tooth." He made the appropriate gesture, then tossed the corkscrew aside. It ricocheted off the globe.

The priest stood up and walked once around the chair where Beppe sat with the mysterious book—a tooth that appeared infested, three teeth without gums. He then rested a hand on Beppe's shoulder. "Let me have a look in your mouth."

Beppe regarded the hand—the excited tremor in particular— then craned his neck and searched Father Vincenzo's eyes for reassurance.

"Just a peek, now. Open up."

Beppe found no consolation in the dilated pupils, but he could not refuse the man who first introduced him to the cello and who still, five years later, presented him with the coin each week that bought half the family groceries. He leaned his head straight back and opened wide—cheeks taut and strained, lungs stilled—while the room—the world—grew quiet except for the shush of air that rushed through Father Vincenzo's nose and rustled Beppe's lashes. The flared nostrils hovered above him: two fathomless holes lined with a head's worth of hairs and dusted with a fine white powder.

"A catastrophe!" Father Vincenzo exclaimed and returned to the leather chair. "Fourteen years old and the teeth of a derelict's cadaver."

Beppe lowered his head in shame. The family had one toothbrush at home, and all four members were supposed to share it. Beppe, however, had not used the brush in more than a year. It drew blood, he remembered, and smelled as he imagined the mayor's feet must.

Father Vincenzo slapped a hand down on the armrest. "No cello until that mouth is in order."

A punishment severe even by Miss Donati's standards. "But Father . . . "

Another slap. "I repeat: no cello." The priest stood up again and again circled the chair. "You see that picture?" Beppe had forgotten that a book sat open on his lap. "Let that be a lesson." Father Vincenzo then snatched up the medicine bottle from the table and stomped from the room. The milk quivered in its cup; the cookies trembled on their plate.

Beppe looked over at the cello in the corner. He could feel the taper of its neck in his empty hand, the places where the varnish had worn off but the wood remained smooth. He could feel the pressure of the strings beneath his fingers, the pleasant indentations. He could feel the drag of the bow when he played a whole note, the scamper of sixteenths. And he could feel the chair that he sat on vibrate as a thud like thunder sounded overhead.

••••••••

The candied fruits for the panettone—the red-red cherries and the emerald jellies—were stored in a metal canister on a shelf beside the nuts and spices, which meant that Dino could reach in and sample them whenever he measured out a half kilo of blanched almonds or a quarter cup of cinnamon. The fruits, moist and sweet, stuck to one another as though glued and, when eaten on their own, left red and green stars in the crevices of Dino's molars—a phenomenon that he noted in the mirror but otherwise ignored. With time, though, one of the stars lost its points and became round: the shape of a planet or an unburst pimple. Dino then began to experience a peculiar sensation when he drank certain liquids or sucked air through his teeth, a sensation that later became constant and severe. When Dino climbed the stairs at home a throb accompanied each step, and when he went to bed at night an ache settled into his jaw just as his head settled into the pillow.

The discomfort began to dampen Dino's spirits. No more olives shot across the classroom, no more meatball humor; even the sight of

Francesca's bloomers failed to inspire him. The only relief came on Fridays when Beppe Arpino, the teacher's pet, the goggle-eyed hunchback Dino had taunted since third grade, took a seat next to Miss Donati's desk and played the school's dilapidated cello. What pain Dino felt went wherever the music did once it sounded in the air. It vanished, evaporated, died, and a smile spread across Dino's face while his foot tapped out a cheerful rhythm. He began to look forward to Beppe's performances as once he had feared them—a fear, he now understood, unwarranted and unfair. Beppe showed no desire to steal Dino's place front and center. To the contrary, it seemed that Beppe disliked the attention Miss Donati forced on him at the end of each week.

But the cello performances never lasted more than fifteen minutes, and as soon as the applause subsided the unwelcome pain returned. Still, Dino kept it a secret. He had seen the barber's bloodstained apron and heard the screams from the barber's patrons; he would rather die than submit to that inhuman torture. Yes, he would starve himself to death first, then the whole town would mourn him. A plaque would appear in the central piazza, perhaps a statue as well—Dino astride a general's stallion—and his father, who had wanted him to take over the family business, would name a dessert in Dino's honor: a mixture of candied fruits and milk chocolate dollopped on an anisette-soaked cookie. In short, Cortenza would never be the same.

The tooth, not surprisingly, worsened, and Dino's appetite, as a result, did suffer—he began to eat normal portions at dinner and snacked less and less—but death still stood far in the distance when his mother, who believed that the best insurance against diseases—the plagues and fevers that claimed poor people—was an aristocrat's diet, detected a decline in Dino's otherwise prodigious intake and went to fetch the town physician.

"He looks gaunt," she explained to the woman who answered the door. "He's lost that DeBono shape. I've seen carcasses with more flesh on their bones."

The physician, however, could not be disturbed at the moment. As the woman informed Mrs. DeBono, the experiments he conducted—

experiments, the gossips reported, that crippled helpless animals—
had reached a critical juncture. Dino's mother had no choice but to
leave her name with the woman and comfort her son until the experiments ended. Dino rejoiced at the news when she told him and, thankful for the reprieve, pretended to be cured. He waited on customers as
though it were Christmas Eve and swallowed unchewed handfuls of
sweets. The charade continued for an hour until, like a phantom, Dino's
savior arrived.

It was midafternoon when the man in the dark suit who carried a
small leather case walked into the bakery and ordered a hard roll.
After Dino handed him the roll, the man tapped it on the counter as
if to test its toughness. He then took a loud bite, which provoked in
Dino a visible shudder. The man smiled and asked about the condition of Dino's teeth. When he received no answer, just a stunned
expression, he presented the baker's son with a piece of paper: *S.
Russo, Painless Tooth Extractions.* Within minutes the molar had
been removed, much to Dino's delight: Despite the fact that his
mouth now dribbled blood, he felt happier than he had in months and
carefree. He danced around the shop while his mother settled the
bill, and when he twirled in front of the window and saw Beppe run
past, Dino smiled at the blur and waved.

●●●●●●●

Maria Teresa, needle and thread in hand, had mended most of her
nightgown when a boom sounded somewhere in the house and the
stool that she sat upon seemed to shiver and shake. She realized then
that the music had never started and that perhaps Beppe might be in
danger. She set down the garment—a sheer cotton shift, immodest but
appropriate for the occasion—the needle and thread, and stepped into
the hall where Beppe then bumped into her. He looked concerned.

"Upstairs," he said. "Father Vincenzo, I think he's fallen."

Impossible, she thought. Another fall? Well, it would be the next
housekeeper's concern. In a week, if all went as planned, Maria Teresa
expected to be far from Cortenza and the priest's ailments. It might
be Naples, the birthplace of her dead father; or Venice, the perfect

destination for two mature lovers; or Rome, where, if she dropped her handkerchief on St. Peter's steps, the pontiff himself might pick it up for her.

A hand touched her sleeve.

"Oh yes," Maria Teresa said, "the priest." She led Beppe up the stairs—"Father Vincenzo?" she called. "Father Vincenzo, where are you?"—and down the narrow corridor that connected their bedrooms. Some nights, unable to sleep, Maria Teresa would listen for the creak in the corridor floorboards that would give her permission to clobber the priest with the ladle she kept under the covers for protection and, she blushed to recall, amusement.

She leaned into Father Vincenzo's room. The bed remained unwrinkled, just as she had made it; the night tables were still in order, the walnut dresser. Beppe dashed past her to the figure unconscious on the floor. Maria Teresa gasped, clutched her breast, then fainted.

Beppe heard the housekeeper fall, but the sounds she made—the thump of her shoulder on the doorjamb and the clump of her head on the carpet—seemed distant and indistinct, as though a woman at the market across town had fumbled an onion or let a pear slip through her fingers. He focused instead on the priest. He spoke to him in whispers—"Father Vincenzo, wake up"—patted a flaccid cheek, lifted a shut eyelid, slapped the same cheek, all to no avail. He then went to Maria Teresa and repeated the procedure, with better results. She sputtered and spat and sent him to find the town physician.

Beppe ran as fast as he could and as fast as he ever would in the years that followed. At fourteen he had already passed the midpoint of his life. Of course, he did not know that as he sprinted through the streets that afternoon. A young man propelled by fear and concern does not pause to ponder fate or visit a fortune-teller. No, he runs as though chased and follows the most direct route possible, which meant that Beppe passed right in front of the bakery where Dino DeBono worked. But when Dino waved at him through the window in midtwirl and smiled, Beppe missed the gesture. His attention was focused on the uneven pavement underfoot and the rhythmic slap that his unhinged soles made when he lifted them off the ground. He rounded a corner and caused a cart loaded with figs to swerve and tip—close but not quite. The man who pushed the cart cursed loud— "The scrotum of Jesus, you worthless kid!"—but Beppe neither stopped nor apologized. He did, however, slow when he saw the mayor barefoot in the wake of a horse-drawn carriage.

"The priest!" Beppe yelled. "The doctor!" He pointed in the direction of the church—"The priest and the doctor!"—then continued until at last he reached the section of town where the Bergamos, the Carbonis, and the other affluent people Beppe's mother had instructed him to respect lived. He ran up the steps to the physician's residence—an inconspicuous placard marked it—and pounded on the front door—no polite raps—until someone opened it: a woman cut from the same cloth as Maria Teresa. Winded, Beppe tried to explain the situation. The woman, though, just shook her head and said that the physician could not be disturbed at the moment.

She had almost shut the door when Beppe stopped it with a shoulder. Although he had spent enough time in the company of Father Vincenzo to be familiar with the physician's reputation—"The man couldn't diagnose a mosquito bite, much less set an ankle"—the priest required attention, and Maria Teresa had requested the physician.

Beppe pleaded with the woman. "Please," he said, "please, please, please." When that failed, he resorted to violence. He pushed against the door, kicked the woman in the shin, and slipped past her. The doctor, seated in the next room at a table covered with strange equipment, held a kitten in one hand and a clamp in the other. Beppe blurted out the news, then crawled under the table to avoid the housekeeper's attack, but in the process he jostled the table and something on top fell over. The doctor then dropped the kitten, which ran to Beppe, and proclaimed the experiment a disaster.

"I hope you're satisfied," he said as he shoved back the chair and stood up. "And for your sake, it better be more than a twisted ankle."

●●●●●●●

Luisa arrived on the scene just moments after the mayor and minutes before the physician and Beppe. The news had reached the riverbank with its usual haste—that is, at about the same time Beppe abused the housekeeper's shin—and Luisa, mindful of the evil that had resulted from Father Vincenzo's previous fall, rushed to protect her son. She stepped through the open front door, closed it behind her, and followed the footprints down the hall into an elegant room furnished with a plush chair, several bookshelves, the notorious cello, and the largest globe that she had ever seen. The room, however, lacked people. Luisa wandered the house until she found a small group gathered upstairs in a bedroom.

Father Vincenzo appeared to have fallen asleep on the floor. He looked calm and relaxed there, very different from the way he had seemed in church the past few years—a pained expression when he offered communion, as though each wafer weighed ten kilos. Next to the priest kneeled a woman Luisa knew to be the housekeeper— Maria Teresa, the gossips called her. Luisa recognized her from the market, the church, and elsewhere around town: a tall woman with a flirtatious manner who bruised vegetables and prayed too loud. She had never married, Luisa knew, nor entered the convent, which led to much speculation on the riverbank. A tease, some guessed, or a tramp, while others believed the inevitable: Maria Teresa and Father Vincenzo shared more than their meals.

Over the years Luisa had questioned Beppe about the afternoons he spent with the priest, and while she knew that her son would never be one prone to effusion, the silence that characterized him at nine and ten had matured by fourteen into a reticence that permitted occasional replies. From the little he told her about Maria Teresa, Luisa had expected to find an immaculate home. But the condition of the carpets and the thick dust that covered the priest's dresser—like a handful of flour—suggested that Beppe might have exaggerated a point or two. If so, then perhaps the baker's son did not harass Beppe after school as he claimed and the teacher, Miss Donati, did not threaten students or strike them across the knuckles. Still, Luisa preferred embellishment to wordless nods and stares.

Behind the housekeeper stood the mayor, who had removed his hat and now clutched it beneath his chin as one might a blanket on a winter's night. For years Luisa had heard him deride Father Vincenzo's vineyard as an eyesore and an old man's indulgence, which led her to believe that the two men were rivals. But the look of despair that distorted the mayor's face as he watched the fallen priest suggested otherwise. The hat soon dropped to the floor, and the mayor rested a hand on the housekeeper's tall shoulder—either to steady himself or to comfort her.

Luisa, in an attempt to stave off the panic that she feared would soon consume her, attended to the hat. As she bent over to pick it up, a small bottle on the carpet beside the dresser caught her eye; she retrieved it as well. The bottle, Luisa observed, once had been filled with a white powder that now coated its insides like breath on a chilled window. She set it on the dresser next to the hat, blind to the resemblance between the dust she had observed earlier and the bottle's former contents. The front door then banged open, and all heads turned toward the hall.

For an instant, Maria Teresa thought it might be her mother, who had died almost a decade earlier. And why not? The afternoon had thus far been more eventful for Maria Teresa than the sum of all the afternoons that had preceded it. First the man of her dreams had appeared on the doorstep, then Father Vincenzo suffered a sudden and perhaps fatal attack, then the blackout—like a damsel in distress—and finally the mayor, a man who traipsed through manure and had attempted a not-so-subtle seduction, offered the gentle comfort that Maria Teresa needed. It seemed natural that a ghost should appear next. And when it turned out to be Beppe, the dolphin-shaped musician, Maria Teresa breathed with relief. Just one breath, though, because as soon as Beppe entered, the woman beside the dresser—where had she come from?— grabbed hold of him and bolted from the room. Maria Teresa almost gave chase, but then the town physician appeared, and the presence of a dark suit and a small leather case—ah, Salvatore—held her like a leash.

The physician joined Maria Teresa beside Father Vincenzo. He prodded the priest with a finger. He lifted a wrist off the floor and let it fall. He twisted the tender ankles and squeezed the blood-filled nose. The blood-filled nose? Yes, it startled Maria Teresa as well: thick blood, slow and gelatinous, that oozed from inside. She watched as the physician opened the leather case and produced a swab. He dabbed at a nostril, then reached into the case again and retrieved a lens attached to a handle. He examined the swab's stained tip through the lens. "Just as I suspected," he said, "human blood."

And with that, the examination ended. The physician handed the swab to Maria Teresa and snapped shut the leather case. He stood up, brushed off the carpet lint, and addressed the mayor. "A hemorrhage," he explained. "I'd wanted to amputate after that fall in the vineyard, but . . . "

The two men talked into the hall, words that never reached Maria Teresa, who, still on her knees with the swab in her hands like a taper, offered a prayer for the priest.

● ● ● ● ● ● ● ●

Beppe could not leave home. He could not attend school or Father Vincenzo's funeral. He could not even answer the door when someone knocked. Again, the instructions were explicit: remain in the bedroom until told otherwise. A week elapsed, another; the confinement continued. Not that Beppe complained. No, whatever interest the world once held for him ended the instant he realized that Father Vincenzo had expired. The streets no longer beckoned; the classroom lost all appeal. Solitude suited him fine. He had four walls to pick and a kitten to pet. And he had much to consider.

When Beppe first returned home—after the sprint for the town physician and the ambush that followed—he sat down on the same stiff mattress that he had walked on five years earlier and convinced himself that the priest, still asleep on the carpet, would soon wake and that their afternoons together would resume without further interruption. He vowed to scrub his teeth as ferociously as his mother scrubbed clothes and promised himself that he would never again doubt Father Vincenzo, no matter how bizarre the request or invigorated the behavior. And at first the trick worked. He unlaced both shoes and relaxed

both feet. He unbuttoned the shirt he wore and removed the frightened
kitten, which he then introduced to a delighted Margherita and a ten-
tative Paolo—the former stroked it, the latter sneezed.

But as the sun settled behind Old Icardi's house and the stone
floors in the bedroom cooled, Beppe grew anxious: a mild suspicion
that prickled a recess somewhere developed into a lump in the stomach and a brick in the throat. The church bells chimed at an unfamiliar hour, and worried voices echoed in the street. When their
mother appeared at the bedroom door a few minutes later, the look on
her face, accentuated by the late-afternoon shadows, told Beppe all
he needed to know. He curled on the mattress and pulled the kitten
close: a clump of rust-colored fuzz with a pink nose and no teeth. He
had asked Margherita for a name when he first produced it, and she,
without a moment's hesitation, had answered, "Papa!"

Two weeks later, the resemblance still escaped him. Their father
had been dark-haired and solid and not prone to meows. If he spoke
at all, the words were low and rumbled together: mittened fingers on
a poorly tuned cello. Beppe picked up the kitten—almost twice the
size it had been when he rescued it—and set it in on what used to be
a pillow but now functioned as its bed. He scratched around the tender ears and watched the kitten fall asleep. He then went back to his
own mattress, reclined, and stared up at the unpicked ceiling. A ladder, he thought, or a long pole.

Knock, knock, knock.

The accordionist, Beppe reckoned, which meant that a tune
would soon follow. It would be the same tune he played whenever he
paid a visit. In fact, all the tunes the accordionist performed sounded
more or less alike: waltzes that Father Vincenzo once claimed
inspired people to drink, not dance. Beppe had smiled at the mild
insult—Father Vincenzo could be humorous when he wanted—even
though he happened to enjoy the accordionist's music. He liked its
cheerful aspect, the lift it provided. And he liked the comfort he
derived from the familiar and the predictable.

But no music ensued, and the manner in which Margherita had
summoned their mother suggested that it must be a stranger—perhaps

S. Russo, the painless tooth extractor whose handbill was tucked under the mattress. Beppe rose from the bed and approached the bedroom door. The kitten he refused to call Papa—the name belonged to their father—stumbled out, too; the knock must have awakened it. Beppe scooped up the kitten and peered out toward the front door. Whoever knocked had not yet entered. Instead, he or she remained on the step and listened to their mother, who had Paolo affixed to her skirt, chatter in a voice that Beppe could not decipher from where he stood on the room's perimeter. He willed the visitor to come inside and hoped that it would be S. Russo. Beppe wanted to ask the man with the small leather case and imperfect seams what he had discussed with Father Vincenzo that afternoon or removed from him. In other words, he wanted an explanation for the priest's odd behavior and unexpected death.

Beppe ventured into the main room, off-limits to him except as a route to the outhouse, and at once the conversation became more distinct. He heard their mother, as if she were right beside him, pronounce the word *dangerous* twice and watched as she shooed Paolo from the door. Yes, Beppe thought, a tooth extractor, even a painless one, would unnerve her. He allowed himself another few steps. And then, as distinct as an olive switch upon contact with tender flesh, he heard a voice that in the two weeks since Father Vincenzo's departure he had almost forgotten. It belonged to Maria Teresa.

"You must," she said. "For heaven's sake, please."

∞∞∞∞∞∞∞∞

The instrument looked out of place in their home—a silk kerchief in the underwear drawer—but the housekeeper, Maria Teresa, had insisted. "No," she said, "it's not a handout but an inheritance from the priest." And when Beppe joined the discussion—he hugged the woman as though it were she who had borne him—Luisa realized that further protests would be futile. She relented, though with a condition attached: the instrument could not be touched until she first consulted her expert on ancient spells and charms. The fingernail ritual prescribed four years earlier continued to do its job, and the most recent antidote—a lamb shank suspended over the front door—had kept Beppe safe since the priest's death. But when Luisa went for the consultation after Maria Teresa left, the advice she received surprised her: administer four generous spoonfuls of castor oil to her eldest son, wait twenty-four hours, then untie the shank and dispose of it. After that, Beppe could do as he pleased—handle the cello, attend school, even wander the streets at night and light matches—with no more risk of harm than a normal boy.

Luisa had her doubts—castor oil seemed too simple a solution— but she trusted the expert—had no choice but to trust—and knew that she could ill afford to keep Beppe prisoner in that room much longer. Her budget had suffered a tremendous blow when the coins he brought home from the priest disappeared. The lamb shank had almost depleted their savings; what if another were required? Meanwhile, their meals had become little more than variations on tomato soup. The income that a washerwoman earned would never support four people. Beppe therefore needed to work. And now it would have to be a full-time position. Yes, Luisa reasoned, he had grown too old for school. Her own education had stopped at ten, while her late husband's continued until eleven. Their son knew more at fourteen than most teachers.

Luisa spooned the castor oil into a glass. She remembered the foul taste from years back—her mother had claimed it even cured colds—and decided to sweeten it with a pinch of sugar. Beppe liked sweets; she would call it syrup. Perhaps some color would help convince him. She searched the kitchen for brightness, but the shelves were for the most part barren and lifeless. The red-wine vinegar would be too fragrant, the tomato soup too familiar. On a high shelf, though, she noticed Giuseppe's liquor. A dash of that and the mixture would look like honey. Luisa pulled over a chair and brought down the forgotten bottle—her knees trembled as thoughts of her husband raced—then stirred a splash into the oil and carried the so-called drink into the bedroom, where she found Beppe on the mattress transfixed: the instrument gleamed before him.

"A sweet medicinal syrup," she said and handed him the glass. "Now drink it quick, and tomorrow night you can entertain us with some music."

Beppe, who had abandoned all hope that he would ever see the beloved Guadagnini again, took the glass and drained it: a swig from a spittoon. Yet despite the fact that he almost retched, he would have downed another such drink in an instant if required. He would have licked the mayor's feet as well or gnawed the rotten shank above the front door. Whatever illness he might suffer would be worth it. Since Maria Teresa's appearance a few hours earlier, the cello had tempted him like a three-foot cannoli after weeks of tomato soup. And although she had not remembered the all-important bow, just to hold the instrument as he used to would be sufficient. Tomorrow, he thought, tomorrow night.

A moment later—at least what seemed a moment to Beppe—Margherita entered with the kitten. "Papa, Papa," she cooed, "your poor little paws." She set it down on the pillow and came to Beppe's side. He sensed her presence but chose to ignore it. When he first recognized Maria Teresa's voice, he had dropped the kitten on the floor and run to the front door. Since then Margherita had behaved as though he were as cruel and unkind as the town physician, a man who abused frail animals on a regular basis.

"So that's it?" she asked with obvious disdain. "An old piece of wood?" Her hand moved to touch the instrument.

"No!" Beppe said. "I mean, please." He looked at her resentful face and, aware that he might have been too harsh, reconsidered. "Well, all right," he said. "But be careful."

Margherita smiled and nodded her assent. She patted the cello's hollow torso as though it were a hound and peered at length into the sound holes. "What if you dropped something in there?" she asked at last. "Like a string bean or a carrot? What then?"

The longer Beppe pondered the question the more suspicious he became.

●●━●●━●●

The handbill, split and tattered, still burned like paper. Whatever human qualities Maria Teresa had ascribed to it did not hinder the flame. A pass of the match: the smoke rose, the ashes fell. She pushed open a shutter to clear the air, then rinsed the remnants down the drain. He had never returned. Rather, he had vanished completely. No one even knew the man's full name. Salvatore Russo? It would remain a puzzle in Maria Teresa's mind. But the time had come to minimize her losses. She had spent the better part of two weeks brandishing the handbill—at the funeral, in the shops, the public garden—and in the process no doubt become the subject of lurid speculation. With the new priest's arrival imminent—direct from Rome, no less—Maria Teresa decided to put the sad episode behind her. "A fresh start," she told herself, as surprised at her sudden resolve as she had been at the sorrow she experienced when Father Vincenzo died. A part of her, she realized now, must have loved the irritable old priest. "Remarkable," she said. "Who would have thought?"

Maria Teresa closed the faucet and shutter, and the house returned to silence. In the past she would have heard the cello about now; even if she were upstairs its sound would have found and relaxed her. Well, perhaps all priests appreciated music, and Father Vincenzo's replacement would invite Beppe over for the occasional recital. If not, then Maria Teresa would just have to visit the Arpino household herself whenever the need arose. And if Beppe's mother objected—she had all but slammed the door the last time—Maria Teresa would call on Old Icardi, a man who still spoke of her father as though he were alive and well, and take a seat near an open window and listen for the sweet recuperative sound that Beppe somehow pulled from the meager instrument.

A child when he first arrived—unable to speak when she questioned him, slouched, the clothes of an underpaid gravedigger—and now a renowned musician. Maria Teresa felt the pride that a mother might, or a sister. Of course, the slouch had not improved in five years and the clothes were no better and the deferential manner still a source of frustration, but in other respects Beppe had become a man—the closest she would ever have to a younger brother or, she feared, a son. And regardless of the new priest's taste in music, Beppe would be welcome the same as before: all the cookies he could eat, all the milk he could swallow.

Maria Teresa straightened her apron and made a final inspection of the house. The carpets had been scrubbed—no more evocative footprints—the furniture polished until it shone like silver, the windows washed inside and out. She had convinced the priest who performed the funeral—a man who happened to be the same height as Father Vincenzo—to take the spare vestments with him when he returned home to Catanzaro. The cello had been delivered to Beppe and the globe donated to the local school. All that remained were the books—hundreds of them, enough to last an avid reader a lifetime— with titles such as *The Iliad* and—her heart sank—*Teeth*. Maria Teresa had thumbed through some and, since the contents either upset or confused her, deemed the collection worthless and inappropriate for schoolchildren. Despite the clutter the books introduced into an otherwise unspoiled room, she decided in the end to let the new priest determine their fate.

The floorboards in the upstairs corridor creaked as usual. Maria Teresa took a step back and balanced herself on a sensitive spot. She shifted her weight from heel to toe and toe to heel, and the pitch responded in kind: high to low, low to high.

"A bit like the accordionist," she said and laughed for the first time since the nervous titter that was her response to S. Russo's provocative farewell: "Good night," he had told her in broad daylight. But once the laughter passed and the floorboards hushed, the house seemed even quieter than before. The silence had a sound all its own, a hum or drone that reached deep into the inner ear.

"Good night," Maria Teresa said out loud to relieve the pressure, then moved on to the master bedroom.

She never used to talk to herself—not until Father Vincenzo died—but never before had she lived alone, either. How much did it have to do with solitude, she wondered, and how much with grief? Or perhaps she had reached the age when that particular trait developed. All the older people she knew or had known, without exception, muttered to themselves or just plain yelled. Her mother had offered advice whether or not Maria Teresa was in the same room. Sometimes she would walk in and catch her mother's words: ". . . a jar of olive oil next to the bed. I tell you, it works like a charm." Even Father Vincenzo, unaccompanied in the music room or at the dinner table, had lamented the weather and reminisced.

Yes, he had jabbered too much and exhausted Maria Teresa's patience, but now, thanks to the tattered journal that dropped from his cassock pocket when she lifted him onto the bed, she understood: he had lost a sister he loved to fever and joined the priesthood soon afterward. The fact that he had never mentioned the sister in conversation—Gabriella was her name—proved to Maria Teresa that the sorrow had burrowed deep. No matter where he looked, even at grapes, he saw her innocent face. When Maria Teresa first read the journal, the night her own disaster struck, she soaked an entire bedsheet with tears. The journal she kept as a personal memento, as well as the cane—it made an excellent weapon—and the small pewter bell, which had lost its clapper when Father Vincenzo hurled it at her once in disgust but worked fine now as a candle snuff.

Maria Teresa marveled at the bedroom's transformation. Who would have suspected that two weeks earlier a priest had died right there on the carpet? At one point a dozen people crowded the room: the undertaker, the mayor—he kept vigil, to universal surprise—the pastor summoned from Catanzaro, an assortment of unkempt parishioners—more curious than devout—and the token Bergamo or Carboni. Beppe, however, had never come back to bid Father Vincenzo farewell, nor did he attend the funeral. The woman who abducted him—Mrs. Arpino, Maria Teresa inferred—had, for mysterious reasons, put him under house arrest.

"Overprotective," the grocer claimed when Maria Teresa mentioned it after she had dropped off the cello. "You know," the grocer continued, "her husband had to leave the country in order to kill himself."

"Very peculiar," Maria Teresa had replied, the fearful refusals and the stench of rancid meat—was that a lamb shank mounted above their front door?—still fresh in her mind at the grocer's stall. She repeated the words to herself now as she fluffed the pillows one last time before the new arrival, then added as an afterthought, "No wonder some men never wed."

●●●●●●●●

A lie: He heard it and knew it to be untrue. And he knew that she knew it, too. "I'm afraid not," she had told the tall woman with the handbill. "But you might try the butcher." Dino's mother had lied, and when he asked her about it later, she said that he would understand in due time. In other words, the tall woman and the tooth extractor she wanted to find were sinners. Dino savored the information like a chocolate truffle. Now that he had recovered from the operation and the gymnastic Francesca become more and more self-conscious, he craved titillation no matter what form it took. An inference based on a lie would do just as well as a peek beneath a classmate's skirts. The imagination of an adolescent could fill in whatever gaps remained.

For Dino, the contents of the small leather case—in particular, the pliers—and the woman's unusual size provided the most inspiration. In the week that followed the visit, he found himself lost in thought numerous times. Miss Donati struck him twice, and he burned an entire batch of biscotti. Then, as if the dreams had come to life with all their absurd possibilities intact, he saw the tall woman march down the street in front of the bakery with an object in her arms that resembled—could it be?—a cello. Dino reeled. Had the tall woman, unable to locate her out-of-town lover, taken up with the much younger, not to mention slouched, Beppe? Was that why he had abandoned school?

Dino ran into the street to follow, but he had never been fast or possessed a keen sense of direction and soon lost her. He did, however, find the stick that went with the cello a few doors down. The tall woman must have dropped it and, anxious to reach her destination and perhaps blind with lust, not noticed the loss. Well, he would return it to her when she next passed, and the thanks she showed, Dino supposed, would be both effusive and risqué.

But a week later he still had not seen her. And the bow, hidden in a back corner beside the nuts and spices, began to weigh on Dino's conscience. Granted, he was not the most pious adolescent in Cortenza or the best behaved or, for that matter, even amiable. No, he harassed classmates with obscene humor—"Why did the nun eat two meatballs?"—and demanded at all times to be the center of attention—witness the nasal projectiles—and lied more often than the town's worst gossips—a trait, he discovered, that ran in the family— but Beppe had helped Dino through a difficult stretch, and the bow— up close, just wood and white hairs—had played an integral role. Even if Beppe used music to seduce the tall woman and bend her to his will—a will that, based on Beppe's posture, Dino assumed must indeed be bent—he deserved the bow and whatever pleasures it might procure. Such are the rewards that befall an artist. Dino had witnessed the same phenomenon with Giovanni Ciano, the middle-aged painter beautiful Giulia now posed for—portraits never displayed in public—and Edoardo, the accordionist who, though a drunken bachelor, had fathered at last count three children. And neither of these men, from what Dino could tell, was half as talented as Beppe.

What a shame, then, that Dino's parents had refused to purchase the bugle he wanted last Christmas. Even when he promised not to blow it—he would just hold the instrument and let the women wonder —the request had been denied. "A bugle? Are you kidding? The way you shoot those olives, you're liable to kill someone." As for the bow, it looked too much like a cane to attract much interest from the opposite sex. Women would mistake him for a cripple, which had its advantages—their sympathy might take on a physical dimension—but seemed rather extreme, perhaps a last resort. Humor, therefore, would have to be Dino's weapon. Thus he could return the bow to Beppe and the favor: the recitals at school that had eased that awful pain.

He went after work, with the bow and a cannoli in hand. And though he did not know the exact location of Beppe's house, he soon heard and followed what sounded like cello music. He followed it right to Old Icardi's door, upon which he knocked the instant he realized a mistake had been made. Without a doubt, the music issued from the next house. Dino pondered the options before him—hide and risk discovery or remain and suffer embarrassment—and chose the former. He squeezed into the narrow walk that separated the two structures and crouched low.

The old man who opened the door called out a few times, hacked and spit, but never saw Dino, who in the meantime had become acquainted with the kitten he almost stepped on. It appeared to be abandoned—no mother in sight—yet quite tame for a stray. Dino picked it up and, when the old man disappeared, emerged from the walk. He had never felt much affection for cats—pests that scattered rubbish at night and clawed—but girls liked them, fawned over them, and a cute little kitten might achieve the same results as a bugle. Dino retrieved the bow, which had slipped to the pavement, with the same hand that held the cannoli, then drummed the appropriate door with a plump knuckle.

••••••••

The predicament distilled to its essentials—gratitude versus fear— Beppe chose the former. He invited the baker's son inside and, when Dino asked, even agreed to perform a few tunes as a thank-you.

"I'd like that," Dino said. "Fridays just haven't been the same."

No longer confined to the bedroom, Beppe seated himself in the middle of the main room, where the sound that the cello produced could climb the ruined stairs unimpeded and echo throughout the condemned upper floors as it might through balconies. All the while he tried as best he could to maintain an appreciative expression. For he was, indeed, appreciative, since the bow that he had used prior to Dino's appearance—from a violin that the accordionist never played—was too short and threatened to snap. In addition, Maria Teresa, though at a loss to account for the original bow's disappearance, had nonetheless welcomed Beppe with cookies when he came in search of it and allowed him to borrow—insisted that he keep—the red-leather volume entitled *Teeth* that Father Vincenzo had produced just moments before he died. And last but not least, Beppe had survived the night of a dozen outhouse visits, an ordeal that began an hour or two after he drank that so-called medicinal syrup.

Beppe had reason, then, to be appreciative, several reasons, but he could not quite overcome the fear that Dino's presence evoked in him. The class clown, harmless to others at school, had bullied Beppe for years without apparent justification. And as if that were not enough, Dino carried with him the dreaded kitten that Beppe had thrown out after it scratched the backside of the cello bare. Margherita had protested the eviction, but Paolo, whose asthmatic condition had worsened since the kitten's arrival—the strange remedies their mother administered offered no relief—sided with Beppe. Did Dino intend to return the kitten as well as the bow? The question occupied Beppe's thoughts as he finished the second tune.

"I remember that one," Dino said. "You used to play it at school." He set a small cylindrical package on the table but kept the kitten with him. "It sounds better now. I mean, the cello's different, right?"

Beppe eyed the package. Because of Dino's threats, it had been a long time since he last tasted cannoli. "Yes, it belonged to Father Vincenzo. The housekeeper, Maria Teresa, she gave it to me."

"Maria Teresa? Is she the tall one, the one with the large . . . you know." Dino raised both eyebrows and nodded.

"Apron?" Beppe ventured.

Dino laughed. "Funny," he said. "I like your sense of humor." The kitten seemed quite comfortable on the well-padded lap. "But seriously now, you're a musician; you know what I mean. That Maria Teresa, is she . . . " More nods and such.

Beppe, though not sure where the musicianship fit in, began to understand what Dino meant—it followed an established pattern—but he had no desire to speak ill of Maria Teresa and tried to change the subject. "So, how's Miss Donati and Carlo and the rest?"

"Aahhh, Miss Donati." Dino closed both eyes and smiled, then opened them and leaned toward Beppe. "You ever notice how," he whispered, "when she hits someone with that stick, her tongue slides out of her mouth and curls and sometimes, when it's warm and she takes off her coat, you can see her bra and even, if the light's just right, what's underneath?"

○○○○○○○○

The fact that Beppe had a visitor—with the exception of the woman who delivered the cello, the first ever—did not go unnoticed by Margherita even though she had hidden herself in a dark corner on the second and forbidden floor in an effort to the escape her conspiratorial brothers. She had heard the knock before Beppe but refused to answer. If he wanted to play music from dawn until dinner and avoid school and read that little red book and disown poor Papa and more, he could also open the door. And if their mother found out that he had not responded to the knock of an important client because the music entranced him and made all other sounds unhearable, she would punish him—the olive switch unleashed—and, Margherita hoped, demolish that repulsive cello.

A few scratches? It was scratched from the start. And what difference did a pebble or two dropped inside an object that size make? He had overreacted in both cases and turned Paolo against her. Margherita seethed, but she listened as well, could not help it. And when her vigilance lapsed, the music that resonated the floor beneath her cooled that scalded temper and made her, for the moment at least, a cheerful person. It happened again when he performed for the unknown guest, and by the end of the second tune Margherita wanted to thank him. She reached the top of the stairs just as the conversation started and stopped there to listen.

"I remember that one. You used to play it at school."

The voice, clearer now that Margherita had moved closer, was still unfamiliar. She began the slow descent, careful to avoid the broken boards and rope-like spiderwebs.

"Maria Teresa? Is she the tall one . . . "

Very tall. When Margherita had opened the door to her last week and expected to see the accordionist, her gaze had to rise an extra meter.

"Aahhh, Miss Donati."

The teacher most feared. Margherita had been spared and studied under the lesser of two evils—the tone-deaf violinist—but Paolo would not be as fortunate.

Now, as Margherita reached the bottom step, the visitor's voice lowered to a whisper. Perhaps he had seen her and spoken softer because what he said concerned her. She turned to look and . . . Papa!

The girl, arms outstretched and mouth open, ran toward Dino as countless others had in dreams, but she was much younger than the ones he had imagined, not to mention clothed, and the name she called out sounded more like Papa than Dino or sweetheart. In the instant before she arrived, Dino, as happened on the neighbor's step a half hour earlier, faced a split-second decision: stand up and meet her or pitch the cannoli at her head. If she were a little older or more developed, the answer would have been obvious. Alas, Dino wavered. Beppe, however, did not. He shielded Dino and caught the girl, then pulled her across the room. In the process, a chair fell over, and the cello. The commotion woke the kitten, which attempted to jump from Dino's lap before he restrained it.

"Papa!" the girl cried. "It's me, Margherita!"

Dino knew that Beppe's father had died overseas—Miss Donati announced it to the class—but had never heard about the lunatic sister. Did their mother keep her locked upstairs? Yet the girl's face looked familiar—perhaps from the public gardens, where invalids roamed—and normal in comparison to Beppe's. Still, it seemed clear to Dino that she mistook him for her father.

"Papa!" she called out again and again and motioned for him to join her. But her brother had a firm hold.

"No," Beppe explained in an apparent attempt to calm her, "it just looks like Papa."

The scene unsettled Dino—had he stumbled upon an asylum?—and he headed for the door. "You know, I was supposed to stop at the grocer's," he lied. "See you two later, okay?" He tucked the kitten under an arm and reached for the tarnished knob.

When the door clicked shut, Beppe released Margherita. Aside from the fear that the kitten might escape and the cello fall face first—it landed on its back—her performance had pleased him. Dino's conversation held little interest, and the cannoli, well, it beckoned like the red book that Beppe had spotted in Father Vincenzo's collection and asked Maria Teresa to borrow. He peeled off the paper wrapper with care and lifted the dessert to his lips. But he stopped there and, a reconciliation in mind, offered the first taste to Margherita, who shook her head and declined.

●●●●●●●●

The children had been at it once more. Luisa could not leave them alone for ten minutes without a quarrel to settle when she came home. What had happened to the pleasant threesome that shared its dolls? Yet another reason, she thought, to mourn the past.

"That's it!" Luisa announced with a slam of the kettle. "No dinner for anyone tonight!"

Just as well, too, because there was little to eat. The rent was a week overdue when she paid it that morning, and now three customers were delinquent on their bills. And it seemed that no one in town, not even the new priest—a nice man, if somewhat obese—needed a fourteen-year-old assistant. Luisa asked all her acquaintances on the riverbank and at most shops in town; not one person had expressed an interest in Beppe's services. Which left Rosselli. But Luisa refused to speak to the butcher. Thanks to him, Giuseppe had traveled to America and never returned.

New York, New York, New York—Rosselli talked about New York as though it were Naples. What a stupid, ill-informed man. If New York were as magnificent as Rosselli claimed and its wealth as plentiful as olives, why did he remain in poor Cortenza? Luisa had asked the same question of Giuseppe a hundred times, but he believed whatever Rosselli told him and was as stubborn as an arthritic mule. No, if Beppe were to ask the butcher for a position—and it had come to that—he would have to do it himself. Luisa had not set foot in the shop since her husband's departure—the lamb shank and occasional treats were purchased through surrogates— and refused to do so now. She would coach Beppe instead—what to say, how to say it—but first, a little relaxation.

"Beppe!" she called. "Please, some music for your mother."

Luisa watched her son walk across the room, set a red book on the table, pick up the instrument, and pull over a chair. His posture, she noted, had never improved. If only he had lifted those baskets with the knees and not the back.

"Fast or slow?" Beppe asked.

"Slow, but not too slow. I don't want sad."

Beppe nodded, paused for a moment with the bow in hand—it seemed different, Luisa thought, more substantial—then commenced with a low breath-like tone. The effect on her was immediate: a thumb at each temple. Although she appreciated the accordionist's recitals for their enthusiasm and charm—like Maria Teresa, he had a reputation as a flirt—it was not until Beppe first performed for Luisa a few nights earlier that she considered music a tactile experience. And it disturbed her, that invisible touch. It suggested the influence of gypsies—witchcraft and the like. But then she remembered that a priest had taught Beppe to play, a priest who then died, and no doubt the priest now watched over the instrument, perhaps even guided the bow. Her heart calmed; her head lolled to one side. Luisa would miss such moments once Beppe left home—as happened four years later—miss them even more after the fatal explosion, but no allusions to far-off doom clouded her mind the night she listened to her son stroke the cello as a favor and then, in concert with Paolo's reverberant snores, mumble what sounded like numbers—". . . ten, eleven, twelve . . . "—while he slept.

Beppe made a slow circle of the top row—eleven, twelve . . . — then the bottom, with a tongue that touched each tooth as a clock ticks off seconds. There were twenty-eight in all; the other four would not appear for at least two years. He had learned their names—central incisor, lateral incisor, cuspid, et cetera—and their function—some cut food, others tore, and molars, of course, were grinders—from the thin red book he studied when not at the cello. A revelation, that book. It had turned Beppe's mouth into a world crowded with information. No longer did he pick at the walls to pass the time before he dozed but instead explored the nooks and crannies between adjacent teeth and compared their various contours with pictures remembered from the book.

The three teeth that the priest had pointed out comprised just one of its illustrations. Another showed the two half moons, upper and lower, of an immaculate mouth. A third contained several oversized cross sections of individual teeth with arrows that identified the enamel, cementum, and dentine, the nerve and the nerve's root. And, as expected, one illustration revealed how the professionals brushed: a circular motion on the outside surfaces, back and forth for the rest. Beppe attempted the procedure himself, first dousing the communal brush with their father's leftover liquor and then, as the book suggested, sterilizing it with salt. And he noticed a marked improvement; in fact, he felt as if he dropped a few kilos in the process.

The book became a constant companion, as cherished as the Guadagnini, and Beppe read it from cover to cover innumerable times. Still, he never found the passage he most wanted to discover, the one that would explain Father Vincenzo's death. He had hoped that the book would provide some insight, a revelation or clue, but neither caries nor the worst halitosis seemed sufficient to kill a person outright. The search would continue.

●●●●●●●

The bell on the door jingled; a customer had entered the shop. Rosselli, clad in a blood-spattered apron as usual, looked up from the meat grinder and at once recognized the figure silhouetted against the front window. But perhaps he had just imagined the bells. He blinked several times to make the apparition disappear, but it did not. Instead, it blinked back, then rubbed its eyes and smiled. Rosselli moved toward the cleaver. Giuseppe Arpino, as he recalled, had been much thicker and unslouched, but those eyes . . . unmistakable. And besides, five years in the ground would weaken even the strongest man.

A vendetta, the butcher suspected, as a shiver traveled the length of his spine. Why did he ever encourage an employee like Giuseppe to leave Cortenza and pursue fortune in America? The advice seemed pure recklessness now. After all, the man had a wife and three children, and New York, murderous thieves.

"Giuseppe?" he called out, a hand around the cleaver. "Giuseppe? Is that you?"

"No, sir," the figure replied. "My name is Beppe Arpino, and I would like a job."

Beppe? A nickname picked up in the afterlife? Impossible, Rosselli thought, yet he also wears short sleeves; such are the mysteries of heaven. "It's been quite a while, Giuseppe." Rosselli readied the cleaver.

"Excuse me, sir?"

A stall tactic, the butcher assumed. Giuseppe had always been a quick thinker. "I said, 'Long time, no see, old friend.'"

The figure shuffled. "My name is Beppe Arpino, Giuseppe Arpino's eldest son, and I would like . . . "

The cleaver dropped to the floor with a clank. "Of course," Rosselli said with breathless relief, "how stupid of me, of course." He rushed from behind the counter and extended a red hand. "Welcome to the business, son. Your father was one of the best."

Beppe took the hand and squeezed it just as his mother had taught him the previous night. The touch of blood did not disturb him, nor the fact that his shoes stuck to the floor once he stepped behind the counter or that a black cloud of flies buzzed over the rubbish heap visible through the back door. No, from the start, when Beppe first tied an apron around himself and became Rosselli's apprentice, he mopped up blood without hesitation and sorted entrails as though they were socks. He had a tolerance for what might otherwise offend—inherited from Giuseppe—a tolerance that would prove useful later in life when the time came for him to open up pus-filled gums or leverage stubborn molars. And as he had done at harvesttime under Father Vincenzo, Beppe proved himself a tireless worker: from seven until six at the butcher shop, then several hours with the cello, then a chapter or two of *Teeth*.

Soon the whole town knew Beppe's schedule, and a procession of sorts developed outside the Arpino house in the warmer months each year. People who otherwise would have headed straight to the central piazza for an evening stroll now detoured through unfamiliar streets in order to hear a tune, perhaps two, from the butcher's assistant, who remained behind closed doors but, because of the temperature, kept a window open. A few who passed and expected to see the performer seated on the front steps like an unwashed chamber pot were disappointed and claimed that the music came from a hidden Victrola, but these skeptics were soon disabused of such notions by the baker's son, who waddled up and down the street whenever the cello sounded—a cat named Cuddles in hand, a pocketful of candies, and a leer that unsettled even sightless women.

"It's Beppe," Dino would assure people, "not some contraption." And if the listener were female and neither too young nor too old, he would add, "Come back later and I'll introduce you."

Luisa herself, mellowed now that their finances had improved and the threat of immediate disaster waned, could have put an end to the speculation with a propped-open door, but in the back of her mind she recalled that music attracted wolves, and the fear that a carnivorous animal might traipse into her home and devour all the children meant that a Victrola's presence would remain plausible to some. Margherita did not help matters when she told her friends at school, who in turn told their parents, that the instrument her brother owned was just a wooden box filled with rocks and rotten vegetables. Nor did Old Icardi: The widower resented the dust that the strollers kicked up—he said it thickened phlegm—and insisted that the performances were a sham. "You buncha suckers!" he barked from a window one night until someone hit him in the head with what appeared to be an olive.

If Miss Donati had heard Old Icardi's taunts, she also might have struck him down. The schoolteacher considered Beppe, who no longer attended classes but still, now and then, could be coerced into an afternoon recital, her greatest achievement. In other words, Miss Donati took full credit for Beppe's musical prowess. On the street she boasted that she had taught him all he knew, and in the classroom, in an effort to replicate a past success, students for decades to come, even Paolo, were required to take turns at the school's decrepit cello and assume what their instructor called the Arpino slouch.

Although the mayor, who loved music but suffered from tender feet and therefore missed the summer performances, made no attempt to trace Beppe's abilities back to himself, he did share with Miss Donati a fondness for private recitals. On more than one occasion Beppe was summoned to the mayor's office to entertain a visitor—a Fascist from the capital, a wanderer from Trieste—or to the mayor's home if a special reception were scheduled. But when the new park behind the church opened and a request came for another performance, Beppe felt compelled to decline. The reason he provided— "The park has no fence, sir, and my mother, you see, fears a wolf might nab me"—bordered on untruth. The main impediment was that the park stood on the spot once occupied by Father Vincenzo's vineyard.

Rosselli, unaware of Beppe's musical skills when he hired him, did not anticipate the interruptions the recitals would cause or the abuse he would suffer when customers saw their favorite cellist covered with blood from head to toe or, as happened once, almost strangled while he wrestled with a cow's intestine.

"He's an artist, Rosselli. Have some respect."

Another employer might have objected to such remarks and, when coupled with the time lost for performances, even fired the worker in question, but not Rosselli. He considered it a favor to Giuseppe, compensation for the bad advice, and would have kept Beppe on the payroll even if the boy professed an aversion to knives.

The fact, though, was that Beppe's presence seemed to help business. Maria Teresa, for example, now purchased three or four times as much meat as before, an increase that Rosselli attributed to the affection the housekeeper showered upon Beppe the moment she walked through the door and not to the new priest's circumference.

But Rosselli could not be faulted for having reached that conclusion. Maria Teresa did sometimes let her emotions overflow in the shop and occasionally ask for six chops instead of four. It was clear that she adored Rosselli's assistant and, like the butcher himself and the mayor, the mother, brother, and sister, and others in Cortenza, would miss Beppe once he left to pursue a new career.

TWO

N aples: Home to thousands, perhaps millions, perhaps more. A true metropolis, with two castles and a volcano in the distance. It has cathedrals and convents, a renowned opera house, and apartments so tall and close together that sunlight never reaches the lower windows. And wherever one looks there are people: men gathered around newspapers, women bent over babies, children who prowl the streets in packs and crowd the air with their voices, a fruit vendor at each turn—watermelon for sale, apricots and cherries; just to count the flower sellers would take at least a week. And the smells: blossoms sweet enough to make the eyes water, basil like a stiff breeze, the ammoniac hit of fresh lemons, of urine in corners, of drunks in their undershirts, of suds spilled from front steps.

Beppe walked in a daze the first few hours—a bandaged valise in one hand, the cello harnessed like a backpack. The directions he had requested at the train station were forgotten as soon as he stepped outside and entered Neapolitan life. He followed a darkened street for what seemed like forever—a tunnel connected at intervals with other tunnels. At times horses jostled him, soldiers, nuns. A cow pushed him into an open door when it passed; the tenants pushed back. A mutt snarled as he continued down the street, a rooster barked, but the people who came and went took no notice of the newcomer in their midst. Another recent arrival, as Beppe imagined their thoughts, another unsophisticate.

He had been warned to expect a cool reception. Rosselli, who had apprenticed in Naples, and the mayor, once a frequent visitor, both told Beppe that the people there would be at best indifferent to him. The urban atmosphere, he was informed, made them rude and mistrustful. Rosselli went as far as to call the Neapolitans thieves. "And clever, too," he added. "They'll steal the coins from your pocket while you're sitting down, the strings from your cello while you're playing it, the dirt from under your fingernails while you pray."

Rosselli embroidered some, though with honorable intent: He simply wanted Beppe to avoid Giuseppe's mistake. If he had encouraged the father to leave, he would dissuade the son. But Beppe, despite the nods of assent he offered the butcher's comments, never wavered. He let Rosselli and others like him speak their minds—let them put forth unsolicited advice, protest, moan, gesticulate—out of politeness and respect. So when the mayor remarked, "A butcher, I could understand. A musician, too. But a dentist? In Naples? What a disappointment!" Beppe thanked him for the concern and promised to think it over.

Even those who supported the decision to move did so with an important qualification: music must come first. Miss Donati was perhaps most insistent. "No," she told Beppe, "it's as simple as that. I've invested far too much time in your musical career to have you fussing around in some Neapolitan's mouth." Others quoted Father Vincenzo's appraisal—"a natural musician"—until it began to sound like a kind of chant. But again, Beppe did not succumb. These people, he realized, would never understand the motivation.

Unlike the cello, it had been a private obsession. Only Paolo, Margherita, and their mother knew about the little red book. Maria Teresa, it seemed, had even forgotten its existence. When Beppe explained to her, in the course of a bittersweet visit to the house where he first discovered music and a mentor had died, the house now occupied by a different priest, that he would soon depart for Naples in order to become a dentist, her face turned pale and her mouth opened wide. It was as if she had seen Father Vincenzo float past in a transparent casket. But she then recovered and wished him well, offered a tearful embrace, a faint but effective smile. "I will miss you, little one."

As for the Arpinos, reactions varied. Margherita expressed enthusiasm from the start and, though she had never absolved him for the kitten affair, defended Beppe's ambitions from maternal assaults. "He's eighteen, Mama. Let him do as he pleases." If that approach failed, as it often did, she appealed to their mother's financial sense. "Think of the money he'll send, Mama, when he's Dentist Arpino."

Beppe appreciated her support and, as usual, avoided interruption, but he did offer a clarification now and then. "You know, it's not like I'll be away forever." Yes, Beppe planned to return as soon as possible. The future he had in mind was modest, straightforward: however much time dental school required—reports varied, from six months to years—then a little office in Cortenza near the central piazza, with discounts for children, sterilized tools, a bookshelf in back, and several comfortable chairs. He described it to their mother a half-dozen times, but still she had reservations, once called him insane—that is, doubted her son. Understandable, of course, since her husband had made similar claims, but unfortunate for Beppe, who meant what he said and, later, felt remorse when it proved to be untrue.

The farewell, to no one's surprise, had been strained. After coffee shared in silence, their mother stuffed a valise with elixirs to protect Beppe from various ills—bad water, rats, and, heaven forbid, knife attacks—and presented him with a tin filled with pasta. In return, Beppe offered to perform a final tune before he left—her favorite Boccherini—but she declined, kissed him quickly, and resumed folding handkerchiefs. Margherita kissed Beppe as well but did not follow him past the front door. It was Paolo, in a scene reminiscent of their father's departure, who accompanied Beppe across town to the mule that would take him to the train headed for Naples.

●●●●●●●●

Another recent arrival, another unsophisticate.

At last, thanks to the assistance of a concerned fruit vendor who had seen Beppe turn the same corner ten times—hard to miss, Beppe supposed, with that cello strapped to him and that tattered valise— the destination came into view. It was four o'clock then, four-fifteen when Beppe mounted the final step inside, opened the door with the stenciled letters on it that spelled LINATI PUBLISHERS, sniffled once to alert the receptionist, and asked for Dr. Leonardo Puzo.

"Leonardo who?" The woman behind the desk—her nails, Beppe noticed, were painted red—appeared puzzled.

"Puzo," Beppe said, "P-U-Z-O."

The woman shook her head, and the bow in her hair—also red—wobbled. "No, never heard of him. You sure you have the right place?"

Beppe, surprised but not discouraged, bent down—no small feat given the size of a cello and its fragility—opened the valise, and, careful to keep the elixirs upright, removed the well-worn and revered *Teeth:* first shown to him by Father Vincenzo four years earlier, published by Linati twenty years before that, and written by Dr. Leonardo Puzo even farther back in time. It was slick, Beppe discovered, with an oily substance; a bottle must have leaked. He wiped the cover with a sleeve, then presented the book to the receptionist as one might a newborn to its mother.

"For me?" the woman asked in a hands-off manner that told Beppe he should keep it. "Really, I . . . "

He took the book back and opened it to the place where the names Linati and Puzo appeared together. "Here," he said and pointed, "P-U-Z-O. I came to meet him."

The woman copied the name on a slip of paper. "I'll see what I can do," she told him, then vanished down a corridor, her heels soon a hammer in the distance.

Alone now, Beppe studied the room: polished wooden floors as dark as espresso, claw-foot furniture—the desk and the chairs that matched it—walls that were almost white but not quite, and, in a place of prominence on one, the framed photograph of a square-headed man—stern, no hope of a smile—surrounded by soldiers with their arms raised as if they all had questions. Beppe stood on tiptoe to look for a caption.

"You're in luck," the woman announced. He had not even heard her staccato return. "I found an address—an old address, but it's worth a try."

She spread out a form on the desktop blotter—a contract for a book entitled *Thorough Mastication*—scribbled down an address, and handed the information to Beppe, who thanked her but made no move to leave.

"Ah," the receptionist said after a moment, "you need directions. Well, it's not far; I'll draw a map."

As the woman sketched out a route to Via Cavallina and Beppe watched her hands, the nails attached to those hands, Dr. Leonardo Puzo sat in a house on that street—in the den, to be specific—and put the final touches on another book, one that surpassed all his previous efforts in terms of breadth and ambition. He called it *Personal Hygiene of the Future*. Yet even with that cunning title Dr. Puzo would in all likelihood be forced to publish the book himself. "Too radical," the Linatis of the world would claim. "You'll frighten people."

True, the material would be unpleasant to some. One illustration showed the misshapen feet of a retired fashion model who had adored heels, while another revealed the unclothed profile of a woman with posture so poor her only suitors were circus performers. Autopsies were quoted throughout: bones described as rotten slats, skulls filled with what smelled like manure, tumors the size of full-grown chickens . . . Dr. Puzo included it all. And with good reason: People, he believed, even educated people, even doctors, medical professionals, needed to be scared, shaken, choked if necessary, in order to be broken of their suicidal habits. Otherwise the Italians of tomorrow would be freakish and diseased and, with few exceptions, all perish in their teens.

•••••••••

The plaster statuette outside the residence, on a waist-high pedestal shaped like an ancient column, differed from others on the street in that it featured neither angels nor souls in hell nor multicolored flowers. Instead, a muscular figure held aloft a tablet in one hand and what looked like a tomato in the other. Beppe checked the information once more—yes, the numbers matched—then followed the narrow walk past the statuette—no, a plaster apple—and up the two steps that ended at a double door. An impressive entrance, Beppe noted, an impressive home. He set the valise on the top step beside him and wiped both palms on his trousers.

The moment had finally arrived. Once Beppe lifted that heart-shaped knocker and let it fall, life as he knew it would be no more. A similar realization had come over him earlier in the day when he boarded the northbound train, and in both cases he felt the need to look back, as though the transformation he was about to experience would also reorder the world. At the station he had resisted the impulse—the train never even came to a complete stop—but now he complied and turned to view, for one last time, the planet before its mutation. An old woman, stooped and shawled, pushed an unoccupied stroller. A breeze headed in the same direction battered the hull of a newspaper. Across the street a hand on the second floor pulled two shutters closed.

"Whatever your business, I'm not interested."

Beppe almost let out a scream. As happened with the receptionist when she returned from her errand, a person had startled him from behind. Rosselli, if he had known, would have been furious at Beppe. The first and most important lesson for a butcher's apprentice concerned distractions. In their profession, attentiveness was as essential as a sharp knife and fresh meat. "Without it," Rosselli had repeated at least once a week, "you'd be safer jumping out of trees." Even a brief lapse—to admire a severed blood vessel or recall a childhood scene—could terminate a career and a butcher's life as well. "I've seen it happen," Rosselli claimed. "We tried to plug the wound with bone marrow."

But Beppe's former employer would have had another reason to be upset, because it was more than a workplace directive that had been twice overlooked. A traveler, the butcher had cautioned since the trip was first announced, must be alert at all times, but never more so than in urban places. "And Naples," he insisted, "it's the worst." To Rosselli's credit, he supported that assertion with a provocative notion: "The monuments, the cathedrals, the mosaics—all built to capture a tourist's attention while the Neapolitans strip him clean."

Again, Beppe was instructed to behave as though stalked, even in bed at night behind locked doors. "You'll have to sleep like a cat, I'm afraid. No, make that an insomniac." But what if someone did enter and attempt to steal all his clothes? Rosselli had thought of that, too. And on the eve of Beppe's departure, as the two men said farewell, the butcher produced a slender stiletto that at first Beppe mistook for a pen. But then the blade appeared, followed by the somber admonition: "Remember, son, what happened to your father."

Beppe now reached for the knife and would have pulled it out had he not, as he soon remembered, earlier stowed it in the valise. Inexcusable, he thought, and dumb.

"Are you deaf? I said I'm not interested, which means leave."

A shock shot through Beppe, as though the knife had somehow entered him. The words he heard had come from Dr. Leonardo Puzo's mouth; he felt sure of that. It was the same voice that read to him whenever he opened *Teeth*—authoritative, almost harsh, and pitched at low tenor. Beppe pivoted slowly, anxious to see at last the master's face but flustered because of the reprimand.

"A cello, is it? Well, minstrel, peddler, it makes no difference, I . . . "

A head with hairs like pinfeathers, spectacles that made the pupils plums, a nose that flared then thinned then flared, and hands that clasped the instrument, unharnessed it, then took hold of Beppe's shoulders.

"For heaven's sake, even a tramp should stand up straight."

Beppe offered no resistance to the forced realignment. He let himself be squared, flattened, arched, and tucked until Dr. Puzo appeared satisfied. "Now, isn't that an improvement?"

"Yes," Beppe said, "it does feel better," though that was as far from the truth as possible. He ached in most places and thought he might pass out. Walk in that position? Never. Breathe? Not quite. But if someone ever asked him what it felt like to be skewered, then he would have the answer.

"A textbook case," Dr. Puzo remarked with both admiration and, Beppe suspected, disdain. Thanks to comments at home about an improper basket technique and whispers overheard in the butcher shop about a hunchbacked cellist, Beppe knew that he did not possess a cadet's posture. But the matter had seemed inconsequential until then. A stoop, he used to think, suited him best. It was comfortable, like carpet, familiar, and relaxed; he could do it for hours without complaint. But now, with Dr. Puzo's approval at stake, Beppe wanted no more than to be as stiff-backed and barrel-chested as the man in the off-white outfit and oversized shoes who studied him in a manner reminiscent of how Rosselli inspected cows.

Stiff-backed? Barrel-chested? At the point in life when most people succumbed to heart attacks and cancer, strokes and pneumonia, Dr. Puzo remained in excellent shape: somewhat shriveled in places perhaps, almost bald all over, but still capable of graceful calisthenics. In addition to regular exercise and a clean diet, one reason Dr. Puzo thrived was that he would not swallow a mouthful of food until he had chewed it exactly thirty-two times—a number not arrived at by chance. Another reason was that he considered the modern handshake a source of disease—in fact, he had lectured on the topic as far north as Milan—and held an even lower opinion of the Italian preference for a kiss on both cheeks between acquaintances.

"Why not put a gun to your head?" he liked to ask students when he saw them embrace one another in the halls of the school he had established and still provided with advanced instruction. But did that deter them? Of course not. Without exception the students showed no more respect for what he said outside the classroom than might be expected from a corridor filled with apes or Sicilians. Their interest in health did not extend beyond the teeth and the connective tissue that held them in place. The sad fact, as Dr. Puzo knew too well, was that few people shared the passion that flamed inside him.

～～～～～

The mental confusion and apparent fatigue—dark circles around the sockets like an assault victim—no doubt resulted from an accumulation of blood in the liver and intestines—common in habitual slouchers. In all likelihood the young man also suffered from headaches and constipation and experienced a coldness in the hands and feet. The splanchnic circulation, in short, had been impaired. It was a diagnosis that, due to the abundant visual clues, provided Dr. Puzo with little satisfaction. A veterinarian, he believed, would have been able to reach the same conclusion. And the treatment was just as obvious: a few weeks in a corrective brace, with exercises to tone atrophied muscles, and an hour each night facedown in bed with a pillow placed under the abdomen.

No surprises, therefore, at least from a medical standpoint—no need to invent new techniques or prescribe untested remedies, no need even to puncture the flesh—but notable nonetheless: Dr. Puzo had before him a specimen both pristine and anxious to please. Whatever adjustments he made to undo the poor posture had been completed without protest and still held a full minute later. By contrast, most of the patients he had treated in the past for similar conditions needed to be trussed up like fowl or threatened with invasive procedures, and even then the progress was slow. But here the transformation, immediate and profound, rivaled the shift that a woman's torso underwent after giving birth to twins. Dr. Puzo would have to re-create the procedure before a photographer's lens.

"I have a proposition to make," he told the visitor, who now appeared slightly blue in the face. "Please, take a breath, relax." Dr. Puzo patted him on the back and watched as the shoulders drooped but not too much. When a blush returned to both cheeks, he continued: "You see, I'm a doctor, a writer as well, and I . . . "

"Dr. Leonardo Puzo?" The name came as a surprise. "P-U-Z-O?" To thwart spiteful students, no placard identified the house.

"Yes, but who . . . "

"Unless food debris and other filth are removed from the teeth, an ideal home is furnished for undesirable germs that can cause disease in the mouth and elsewhere in . . . "

Although Dr. Puzo, an author, researcher, educator, and tireless public-health advocate for several decades—a Renaissance man if ever there was one—had started out as a simple dentist and composed those words for a textbook published in what seemed another lifetime, he still recognized them as his own. And despite the fact that he had administered countless student exams over the years and listened to more recitations than he cared to remember, never before had he heard the material delivered with the reverence it deserved.

" . . . because there are certain places in the mouth that are difficult to clean and because the overall health of the individual may have been undermined by improper diet or disease."

Beppe would have continued, but once Dr. Puzo began to mutter the words in unison with him, like a supplicant at mass, self-consciousness set in. For a minute, though, an uncommon but not forgotten boldness had powered him. He still recalled how he had persuaded the town physician—commanded him almost—to visit Father Vincenzo on the afternoon the priest died. And there was the time Beppe first sat in front of the class and, nervous as he had been, drawn music from that crippled cello. Then, as now, he startled himself—the determination he possessed no matter how perilous the act. But what made the present situation different from those others was that Beppe had wanted it to happen, had traveled two hundred kilometers so that it would happen. The crisis he faced now, in other words, had been planned. And the plan—travel to Naples, meet Dr. Puzo, enroll in dental school—had thus far proceeded without serious impediments. If Dr. Puzo bore no resemblance to the writer who had appeared in Beppe's head—less hair in real life, more wrinkles —and their conversation still left much to be desired, then at least he had not moved into another home since the publication of *Thorough Mastication* or, as Beppe had sometimes feared, a mausoleum.

He blotted a hand, then held it out and spoke the introduction just as he had rehearsed it. "Beppe Arpino, sir. I've read your book a thousand times."

The dazed expression soon faded as what appeared to be a smile curled the corners of Dr. Puzo's mouth. Still, he refused the outstretched hand. "Arpino, is it? I knew an Arpino once, an expert on venereal disease."

"Oh," Beppe said, "I see." He decided that Neapolitans did not shake hands and withdrew the one he had proffered.

"From Salerno or thereabouts. A relative perhaps?"

Beppe had passed through Salerno on the trip north and, because it looked more prosperous than home and possessed a wondrous coast and because Rosselli had told him to mistrust even the conductor's words, at first confused it with Naples. If not for a fellow traveler, a bullish old woman who knocked him to the floor in her push to reach the train's door, he would have disembarked there and been stranded for hours. "No, sir, I'm from Cortenza, which is farther south."

Dr. Puzo nodded as if he had just returned from a visit to Cortenza and could still feel the stones that paved the piazza there beneath his feet. "Farther south," he repeated, "which explains the posture and the clothes, the suitcase, even the—well, the cello is a bit queer. But tell me, please, the book you just quoted from, where does that fit in?"

●●●●●●●

The den rivaled Father Vincenzo's for splendor, with more books, a desk, and a human skeleton. And to think that Beppe, who now sat across the desk from its owner and next to the suspended skeleton, soon would live there—not in the den, of course, but in the house that surrounded the den. He would live upstairs, to be precise, in a bedroom all his own. It would be the first time he had ever slept alone. Surely now he would sleep better.

"I don't know what to say, Dr. Puzo." Beppe searched for an adequate phrase to express his appreciation. He had come to Via Cavallina for advice—could Dr. Puzo recommend a good dental school in Naples? a reputable butcher?—not an apartment, but as a conversation developed between him and Dr. Puzo, first on the porch, then in the den—more an interview than a chat—room, board, and even tuition were mentioned. All Beppe had to do in return for these was eat what Dr. Puzo ate, join in Dr. Puzo's exercise sessions, and obey Dr. Puzo's rules.

"No siestas, no drunken sprees, no cards or mindless distractions." Dr. Puzo stood and motioned for Beppe to rise, too. "A person should never sit when he can stand, never stand when he can walk, and never walk when he can run."

Beppe then followed Dr. Puzo down a long hall that led to what would prove to be the exercise room. Curiously, though, their pace never exceeded that of a saunter.

"It will be difficult at times, Mr. Arpino, make no mistake." Dr. Puzo paused at the door to the exercise room, turned, and rested a hand on Beppe's shoulder. "But indolence, as I wrote in *A Battle Plan for Health*—I don't suppose you've read that one as well—is a hostile foe whose armies surrender to discipline."

Better, Dr. Puzo believed, for him to be honest from the start and avoid later disappointment. There had been others in the past, just as hopeful, just as anxious to commit themselves, and all deserters within the first month. Youthful enthusiasm, he had learned as a result, would not alone suffice. A cold-blooded determination was required, a warrior's spirit: kill or be killed. The few who had joined him before underestimated the opposition and suffered almost immediate defeat. Dr. Puzo blamed himself in part. Perhaps he had expected too much too soon and not provided an honest assessment of the difficulties involved.

Certainly the life held enormous allure from afar: the bleached smock, the weight lifter's chest, the formal address—"Dr. Puzo, I presume?"—the scientist's demeanor. And it paid well, too: he owned a spacious home and in the past maintained an office that window shoppers often mistook for a jeweler's. As such, it was inevitable that some people, dazzled and bewitched, would misinterpret their attraction and insist that more than financial reward or the desire for distinction motivated them. These confused souls, with a boost from Dr. Puzo, would adopt their landlord's habits with what looked like enthusiasm, but as soon as the first obstacle appeared, in the form of a muscle ache or cerebral exhaustion, a profound indifference would be exposed and the project abandoned. Was it wise, then, to expect more from a vagabond named Beppe?

So obvious was the answer that Dr. Puzo chose to dismiss all questions for the moment and concentrate instead on the peculiar sensation that now visited him, rare in a man who studied Italians and their health: hope.

Had Beppe Arpino, a butcher's son from a small rural town, achieved the sort of fame reserved for statesmen, explorers, poets, and prima donnas, the letters he wrote home when he first arrived in Naples would have become collector's items after he died. And had the person who acquired them—the biographer, historian, or well-to-do fanatic—sifted through that correspondence—faded with time and filled with misspelled words and abhorrent punctuation—to find its start—a note addressed to Luisa Arpino and dated a week after her son's departure—he or she would have learned that Beppe's first impressions of Naples were, on the whole, positive—though he did lament the overcast streets—and that, if all went well, he would start dental school in the near future. While Dr. Puzo received a brief mention—it looked on the paper more like Dr. Pozo, which forever confused Luisa—no details of the pact that Beppe formed with him were offered. Instead, Beppe promised to write more when time permitted and, as in all the correspondence that followed, closed with an affectionate farewell.

What the document lacked in elaboration it made up for in enthusiasm. It was Beppe's first attempt at a formal letter, and despite its dashed-off appearance, he labored over the task for an hour in an effort to achieve the appropriate tone. On the one hand, he wanted to put to rest all unwarranted fears. He had not been robbed, bitten, or abducted, stabbed or seduced, and did not sleep on the streets or wander the dark halls of resident hotels. On the other hand, Beppe had no desire to foster unreal expectations at home. Yes, he had been provided with a room in Dr. Puzo's house and admittance into the dental school that Dr. Puzo established, but neither beneficence was without conditions that must be met if Beppe hoped to continue as both tenant and student. In the end, he decided that a cheerful letter slim on specifics would be best, and once it was drafted and sealed in an envelope, he consulted Dr. Puzo on the matter of its transport.

"A post office?" Dr. Puzo turned from the stove, spectacles steamed over. "We'll pass one later on our stroll. Remind me, and I'll point it out." He hoisted an enormous spoon. "Now, wash up and help me set the table. It's almost time for dinner."

The stroll Dr. Puzo referred to, as Beppe knew from recent experience, took place after dinner and followed a crowded route to the waterfront and back. Its purpose, though, was neither scenic nor social but practical—to promote normal digestion—and at no point did Dr. Puzo pause to admire the view or trade pleasantries with other pedestrians. Even the violinist who serenaded the pier failed to slow Dr. Puzo's pace. And while Beppe would have liked to stop and listen to a piece—the musician sounded accomplished—he dared not, because Dr. Puzo maintained a strict schedule that permitted no lapses. "A minute wasted," Dr. Puzo had told him, "is lost forever."

Beppe washed up and set the table. Because of the effort that went into the letter, as well as the calisthenics beforehand and the strain to keep his shoulders square, he was now quite hungry and would have consumed an entire salami—a food that no sane butcher ate—had one been offered to him. But there was little chance of that, because Dr. Puzo, as Beppe had discovered in the week since he left Cortenza, banned cured meats and most spices from the diet. Rank cheeses, fresh bread, and pies were also forbidden, as were butter and cream, liver and pheasant. The meals that Dr. Puzo prepared— he had no Maria Teresa to do it for him—consisted instead of steamed vegetables and bland chicken, stale loaves, sliced fruit. Whereas Beppe's mother tended to cook beans until their color disappeared and boil potatoes to pieces, Dr. Puzo favored the almost raw: asparagus spears that still snapped and peas that rolled around the plate like pellets.

How Dr. Puzo ate these foods also surprised Beppe, who had never counted chews. But as Dr. Puzo explained, the evils of insufficient mastication numbered in the hundreds: inadequate use of the teeth and jaw led to dental disease and worse; too little saliva mixed with food and poor subdivision of that food meant slow and imperfect digestion; the failure of taste nerves to alert the stomach to the kind and amount of chemical output required caused nausea and heartburn; the list went on.

"You ready out there?" Dr. Puzo called from inside the kitchen. The clock had just chimed seven, the hour when dinner was served.

"Yes," Beppe answered as he made a minor adjustment to reposition a fork. Though most southerners, Beppe included, would have considered nine or ten a more appropriate time for dinner, Dr. Puzo claimed that the later the meal, the less healthful. It inclined one to rush, he said, to swallow the food not chew it, and allowed little time for an adequate stroll.

Dr. Puzo set a full platter on the table and sat down. "Please, hand me your plate." Beppe did so and watched as Dr. Puzo served him—from a platter laden with broccoli and cauliflower, zucchini and carrots, bread, black olives, beans—the wafer-thin fillet of a fish that appeared to have suffered from starvation. He centered it on the plate with the precision of a watchmaker, then nodded once to indicate that Beppe should take the plate back. "Remember," Dr. Puzo said as he helped himself to an identical portion, "those first four mouthfuls make all the difference in the world; set the pace, so to speak."

Beppe, known to devour an entire cannoli in two bites and a dozen cookies in six minutes, considered the fish set before him. It resembled a skinned sardine and would have required three mouthfuls at most, even with the miniature fork that he was now expected to use. "Meant for children," Dr. Puzo had remarked when he first showed where the utensils were kept, "but ideal for adults." Beppe now understood the rationale at work—to keep the mouthfuls small—just as he knew that proteins such as fish should be eaten first and in modest amounts. Dr. Puzo had explained it all to him over the course of that lecture-filled week, but the desire to revert to unhealthy behavior still threatened at times, in particular when Beppe accompanied Dr. Puzo to the photographer's studio. It was across the street from what purported to be the best bakery in the hemisphere, and regardless of whether or not that boast were true, the butter aroma alone weakened Beppe's knees and caused him to ponder a ruinous act. But he resisted the temptation when it had come, as he did now at the dinner table where a platter beckoned and an appetite burned. He would nibble the fillet as Dr. Puzo had shown him, then crunch carrots and such until deaf—the harsh bread the loudest, like a percussionist in the next chair—then came the fruit, the cleanup, the stroll, and last, before bed, the beloved Guadagnini.

The fish dissolved like whipped cream once it touched the tongue and carried with it no discernible taste, but Beppe nevertheless performed the requisite chews and commented on a delicious flavor. "And tender, too," he added.

"Well, that's to be expected." Dr. Puzo dabbed himself on the lips with a napkin's corner, then made a notation in the pocket-sized pad that he produced at each meal and exercise session. "No cellulose, I'm afraid, and cellulose, as I've explained, is an intestinal must. But fear not, because the food we have here"— he tapped the platter with his pen—"will scrub our colons clean."

∙∙◆◆◆◆∙∙

An upscale trade school, a haven for timid men. Indeed, most students at the Naples Institute for Dental Arts enrolled not out of love for pristine teeth or science but in order to secure stable careers. No matter who assumed power in Rome or how the lira fared in comparison to the pound, Neapolitans would continue to need the services of well-trained dental practitioners: Incisors would weaken and molars rot and sooner or later pain would announce its unwelcome presence. Fascists and Socialists alike, in times of both peace and war, would find the school's alumni indispensable, and that fact helped fill the classrooms.

It saddened Dr. Puzo, of course, to see the ideals that had prompted him to establish the institute some three decades earlier become replaced now in the students' minds with mere economic concerns, but dentists, he consoled himself, were not unlike carpenters or stonemasons in terms of their respective skills; even the tools overlapped, as Dr. Puzo, who had used an awl for some extractions, knew quite well. A chimpanzee, he had come to believe, could be trained to pull a tooth or fashion a crown, and if its hands were clean and the rates competitive, patients would line up outside the door.

What Dr. Puzo once considered the noblest of professions, a notch above the priesthood because it administered to heathens as well as to the baptized, now seemed too narrow and specialized. The mouth was but one orifice that demanded attention. After all, people who brushed their teeth and flossed immediately after each meal still succumbed to fatal ailments. The entire person, therefore, from scalp to soles, nostrils to buttocks, needed treatment, but not just what medical doctors provided. Whereas those impetuous men used scalpels and hacksaws to eradicate disease, Dr. Puzo looked toward prevention: exercise, diet, posture, even the cut of a patient's clothes.

It had amounted to a midcareer leap for Dr. Puzo. One moment he was a dentist and headmaster, the next a recluse. He canceled all appointments, entrusted the school's administration to others, and devoted himself to research and frenzied experiments. A year later he resurfaced, an expert on all topics related to health. And while he continued to present lectures to advanced dental students and proctor the school's annual exams, he spent most time elsewhere: at home, where he exercised and wrote books; in the converted dental office, where he treated hunchbacks and insomniacs, obese priests and emaciated nuns; and before conferences and assemblies, wherever he found people who would listen to what he had to say.

An upscale trade school, a haven for timid men. The risk was that Beppe would become infected with the materialism and narrow ideas that now pervaded the institution. He had potential, in Dr. Puzo's opinion, was serious and unspoiled, but peer pressure could ruin him for life. Dr. Puzo waited a week to enroll him, waited another few weeks until the term had started and further delays would be counterproductive. With the core beliefs that Dr. Puzo held spelled out and a modest exercise routine established, the time had come to put the newcomer to the test. Either he would sink to the level of his classmates, in which case Dr. Puzo severed all ties, or he would rise, as Dr. Puzo had risen, to search out obstacles more difficult to overcome than cavities and receding gums.

●●●●●●●●

The students, loud and informal with each other—one conversation across the aisle concerned the weekend, a review of indecent exploits —silenced the moment an older man walked into the room and approached the podium. He carried no notes with him, nor a paddle, just a tin box that he placed on a table at the front. The presence of this container, almost identical to the one that had held Beppe's final home-cooked meal, comforted the new student and put to rest whatever worries that had occupied him since Dr. Puzo announced that the time had come to start dental school.

It happened in the exercise room, while they took turns with the wooden clubs. First Dr. Puzo would demonstrate a movement with the heavier pair—a lateral sweep, for example, which started with the clubs held out in front like two inverted wine bottles and ended with them pointed at opposite walls—then Beppe would attempt to copy the exercise with the hollowed pair, but the effects that Dr. Puzo achieved, the fluid arcs and precision stops, proved elusive to the novice. Dexterous at the cello, Beppe was still inept in these silent pursuits after weeks of practice. He suspected that adding music would help, even if it were just seeds that rattled inside the stout clubs.

"You'll start tomorrow," Dr. Puzo said as he executed a two-handed crisscross. "I've discussed it with the headmaster, and all the particulars have been taken care of." He stopped and, with a deep exhalation, set the clubs down on the canvas mat. "You'll join the foundation course—a must for all students—and attend a few hands-on labs."

Beppe smiled at the news, but the smile masked concern. Until then dental school had remained an abstraction for him, idealized and indistinct. But so had education itself. Beppe was fourteen when he last attended a class, and since then he had somehow convinced himself that the methods Miss Donati used were in no respect representative of the profession. Dr. Puzo, however, had much in common with the disciplinarian back home, and there was no reason to think that the teachers he hired would not follow the stern example he set. Also, Beppe supposed that the students in Naples would differ from their rural counterparts—more competent, which would not be hard, and much better behaved. But what if he were expected to battle their wits in classroom debates? And the lab: it brought to mind Cortenza's sinister physician. Did that mean Beppe would have to torture cats?

Dr. Puzo waved a hand in front of Beppe's face. "Is something wrong, Mr. Arpino?"

"No, sir," Beppe answered, then lifted the trainer clubs and attempted to trace Dr. Puzo's last pattern. And he almost had it until one of the clubs sailed across the room and shattered a framed chart that identified the skeletal muscles.

The professor clasped the podium and cleared his throat—a shovel scraped over stone—then commenced with the lecture: "We continue our discussion of historical perspectives." He paused for a moment, as if he expected applause, which Beppe, had the professor waited another second, would have gladly provided: the fulfillment of a dream. "As I mentioned in the previous session, cavities were rare in primitive man. Recent archaeological studies tell us this. And remember what we learned from the Eskimos, who tear leather with their teeth."

Beppe, thankful for the review—it pained him to have missed the first classes—recorded the information in a hurried scrawl that even the speaker, had he asked to look over what he had said, would have assumed was written in code. But speed was only part of what made the mess indecipherable. Some words the professor used had never been uttered in Beppe's presence before, and to render them he invented a makeshift alphabet that relied on pictures as much as consonants and vowels. Nevertheless, Beppe kept pace and in the next hour filled a good portion of the tablet Dr. Puzo had given him. But even without the notes he would have remembered each detail. The lecture fascinated him, most of all the tales about tooth transplantation and how Napoleon's men had raided the mouths of opponents wounded on the battlefield so that upper-class Parisians could eat crust.

A bell sounded, at which point the professor picked up the unopened box and exited the room—perhaps, Beppe thought, to have lunch. The talk between students then resumed, mixed with the slap of book covers and the shuffle of chairs. As Beppe stood to leave— he had a lab to attend next—someone bumped him from behind.

"Excuse me," a voice said, more sarcastic than sincere. Beppe sat back down and let two students pass. The first, who carried a cane but had no limp, looked over his shoulder at Beppe. "That outfit," he remarked to the other, whose coat was draped like a cape, "perfect for a clown."

The words made Beppe wince. He had hoped to slip into the school unnoticed, just another face in the crowd, but it was foolishness, he now realized, to have entertained such an idea. Dr. Puzo's old clothes, which were much too loose for Beppe and not the common black or dark brown, made him stand out in the classroom like a sour note in a scale, and the orthopedic shoes that Dr. Puzo purchased for him—"I shape them to fit the feet," their maker boasted, "rather than force the feet to fit them"—were no less conspicuous.

Whether he appreciated the clown comment or not, Beppe knew that it contained at least a kernel of truth, because when he first tried on the suit at home, even he could not help but chuckle. The trousers became a sail when he walked the hall, while the jacket covered him like a shawl or, to be more precise, an elephant's blanket. But Dr. Puzo insisted that the fit was perfect.

"The question of dress," he told Beppe, "is related to the question of ventilation, and as I've said before, fresh air is as important to health as exercise and a fibrous diet." A loose outfit, he went on to explain, one made from porous and light-colored fabric, was undoubtedly best. "There should be no restriction of the airflow and no pressure on the torso. You've heard of a corset, right? Well, if I were a woman, I'd rather be buried alive."

In other words, Beppe should have known better than to have questioned the suit's fit, just as he should have expected, no matter what he wore, a measure of unwanted attention when he first arrived at the school. He was an outsider, for starters, and late to the term, but also someone who, since childhood, had never meshed well. Even in Miss Donati's classroom, where one student snacked on ink and another shot olives from his nose, Beppe had attracted special notice. But at least then he had the cello to hide behind and the music to climb inside, whereas now there was no shelter other than what could be fashioned from the excess material of his oversized clothes.

●●●●●●●●

Alone at his desk in the den, Dr. Puzo removed from a shirt pocket the small pad in which he tabulated calories burned and consumed. He flipped the pad open, picked up a fine-tipped pen, and started the slow transfer of information into the master journal. It was a tedious chore, even for a man who counted chews, but Dr. Puzo believed that the answers to tomorrow's medical questions would be found in records like these. To that end, he had made plans to have all his personal papers housed at the Naples Institute for Dental Arts after he died. The Puzo Archives, as he liked to call them, would also contain a report on his postmortem examination, as well as blood samples, teeth, what little hair remained, and detailed pictures. Yes, the same photographer who documented Beppe's posture, before and after the fix, would shoot Dr. Puzo's corpse in its full state of undress; he would even hand color the prints to account for blemishes and such.

Dr. Puzo stopped for a moment to admire the work before him: the neat columns, the careful addition. All meals were accounted for, all exercise sessions, the strolls, the errands, the unfortunate fevers. He stepped on the scale at dawn and recorded that number, too: never more than two kilos in either direction. "A precision machine," he often remarked after his 7:15 evacuation. If flaws existed in Dr. Puzo's metabolism, he failed to admit them, just as he overlooked potential problems with the planned archive. Suppose he outlived the photographer, who had been paid in advance for both labor and supplies? It happened. And what if Dr. Puzo, like Beppe, met a violent end, one that did not lend itself to blood samples or autopsies, not to mention colored pictures?

He resumed the meticulous entries—*deep knee bends: 20 repetitions*—but soon paused again and lifted the pen. For the first time in weeks Dr. Puzo had the house to himself—Beppe was off at school—

and the solitude, as never before, seemed palpable to him: no foot-steps in the hall, no flush from upstairs, no silverware clatter, no questions. He sat back in the chair, even allowed himself a curved spine, and listened. Except for a chirp-chirp from outside and the drum-like rumble of a distant motorcar—obscene, those inventions; catered to laziness and polluted the air—no sounds could be heard from where Dr. Puzo sat, and that put a smile on his wrinkled face.

Perhaps more than most people, Dr. Puzo understood the impor-tance of quiet. It induced a meditative state, as he knew from numer-ous studies, which lowered the blood pressure and calmed one's nerves. Music, it was rumored, produced similar effects, though Dr. Puzo had reservations about that claim. As a matter of fact, recently he had come to believe that the opposite was true. For proof he point-ed to the cello that Beppe played at night after their postprandial strolls. Granted, the lithe melodies lulled Dr. Puzo to sleep, but the dreams he then experienced disturbed more than soothed.

A bachelor for life, Dr. Puzo had nonetheless taken part in sev-eral romantic affairs. Not that he had fallen in love with the partici-pants—either patients or professional assistants—or expressed a desire to wed. No, he rejected the notion of courtship and viewed the liaisons, even those that continued for months, in Darwinian terms. Humans, Dr. Puzo believed, differed little from other mammals when it came to their sexual needs. "Visit the zoo," he once advised a woman who had called him insensitive. "Five minutes in front of the primate cage should do the trick."

It was quite a surprise, then, when Dr. Puzo, under the spell of the newly arrived cello, started to dream of moonlit walks and inti-mate whispers, even tearful farewells—the stuff of melodrama in a scientific mind. Faces from the past appeared as if frozen in time: he kissed a beautiful Cecilia, whom he had last seen reclined in a cof-fin, and proposed to a ripe Caterina, now under the care of a live-in nurse. At the climax of these fantasies—outlandish but vivid and real—he would awake with a start, as if kicked in the groin, short of breath and stunned to be alone.

A knock.

What? Someone at the door? Dr. Puzo, who still had sums to enter, columns to finish, waited for another knock but heard none. With luck, it was that talkative bird, smack into the door, and not a peddler or, as still happened, someone in need of treatment. Despite the fact that he had retired from full-time practice and never mounted a placard outside the house, Dr. Puzo occasionally received visits from people with backaches and stubborn addictions, skin disorders and abdominal pains. How these would-be patients found him, he never knew, but because the services he provided were unique in Naples and, as he too often heard, considered radical, he found it difficult to refuse the periodic requests.

Another knock.

Well, so much for solitude. Dr. Puzo capped the pen and, with a mixture of disappointment and anticipation—his last unannounced visitor had rekindled hopes of a successor—went to the front door, where he encountered neither a peddler nor a patient but his former publisher, Giacomo Linati, carrying a newspaper under one arm.

"I was in the neighborhood," said the squat man Dr. Puzo had not talked to in five years, "and saw the statue from the road. I never forget a face."

Although Dr. Puzo had conceived the work himself—an apple for health, the tablet for education—and served as its model, the artist had been a primitivist, which meant that the likeness Linati referred to did not exist except in a cartoon sense. Dr. Puzo offered the caller a suspicious stare.

"Have I come at a bad time?"

Their last encounter almost ended in blows. First Linati had refused to print Dr. Puzo's treatise on the handshake, then he confessed that all unsold copies of *A Battle Plan for Health* had been burned to save warehouse space. "Criminal!" Dr. Puzo had screamed as he climbed over the publisher's desk, but when he took hold of the plump arm and squeezed that pliable flesh—no resistance between sleeve and bone—he felt sick inside and stormed from the room. But now there was a new book to consider—*Personal Hygiene of the Future*—and a desire to reach the most readers possible. Perhaps a cease-fire could be established, a truce struck.

"I have a few minutes." Dr. Puzo opened both doors wide and stepped aside to clear a path for the overfed visitor. "Please, Giacomo, I'll fix a special tea."

* * *

The recipe: combine a half kilo precipitated chalk, two hundred grams light carbonate of magnesia, one hundred grams bicarbonate of soda, and twenty-five drops flavored antiseptic—either oil of cloves, oil of wintergreen, or oil of sassafras; mix well and store in a sealed container.

Satisfied that he had copied the information from the board correctly, Beppe closed his notebook and, now that all the other students had left the lab, stood up himself. The tooth powder he concocted—with clove because it reminded him of a cookie Maria Teresa used to bake—sat in a jar at the front of the room. There were ten jars total, one for each student, and soon all ten would be donated to the state, which then, as the instructor explained, passed them on free of charge to orphans, prisoners, and members of the armed forces. Tomorrow a convict somewhere—a murderer, a purse snatcher—could coat his toothbrush with that same powder and save himself from future pain. Such twists of fate astonished Beppe, left him dizzied and drained. No wonder he then stumbled in the corridor outside the lab and slipped as he descended the staircase.

"Bravo! A pratfall from our clown!" Applause, applause.

"No, dear sir, I think we've witnessed an attempted suicide!"

Beppe, embarrassed but unhurt, pretended not to hear. He picked up his notebook, the scattered pen, then dusted off the suit and hurried toward the nearest exit.

"Oh, Mr. Circus-Tent Pants! You dropped a . . . "

Another few steps and—thank heaven—Beppe was out the door. But the hecklers, he was surprised to find, pursued him.

"Wait! Wait! We have your . . . "

Beppe broke into a sprint, enormous shoes and all. He passed a flower seller, a newspaper stall, almost clobbered a drunk, then slowed when he saw himself reflected in a pharmacist's window. How foolish he looked, in a suit inflated to monster size, on the run from a man with a cane and his caped counterpart. Even when Dino had threatened real violence, Beppe did not show such cowardice. He stopped and let the two students catch him, prepared to take whatever abuse, verbal or otherwise, they offered.

The first to arrive leaned on his cane, winded but not the least bit violent. "Impressive run!" he exclaimed between breaths. "And in those clothes, those shoes!"

The other, a step behind and equally spent, unshouldered the coat and agreed. "Yes," he wheezed, "I expected to see our friend here—whew!—lift off like a kite."

If not flush from the exertion, Beppe would have blushed at the praise. Burdened with a notebook and the inherited outfit, he had not run nearly as fast as he did the afternoon Father Vincenzo died, but still he bested the Neapolitans, and he had done so on their own streets.

"Aw," he waved off the comments, "please."

The one with the cane extended a hand. "I'm Stefano, and that's Marcello."

A dilemma—violate Dr. Puzo's laws or jeopardize friendship—but no time to think. Beppe took a quick look around, as if his mentor hired spies, and decided to compromise with a brief squeeze. "Beppe," he said and made an unspoken promise to wash at the nearest fountain.

"Beppe? A child's name, not one for a doctor." Stefano tapped the cane on the pavement and wondered out loud. "Beppe . . . Beppe . . . I know!" He flourished the cane like a sword. "Bonaparte! A dentist we can all admire."

"Yes," Marcello chimed in, "and we'll find you some tight britches and one of those Napoleonic hats."

Beppe began to doubt the earnestness of his new friends. Was it all a tease? Was he just the butt of jokes? He made ready to leave. "Well, it's time for me to . . . "

"Wait, Bonaparte." Stefano reached into a pocket. "Your pen, it's here somewhere. I picked it up off the steps."

What did the Neapolitan take him for, an amnesiac? Beppe had retrieved the pen himself when he first dropped it; no doubt Stefano now planned some kind of hoax: a stink bomb perhaps, an obscene photo. But no, Beppe was mistaken. He owned the object Stefano produced, and it did, when sheathed, resemble a pen: the stiletto, Rosselli's farewell, which Beppe, as directed, now carried with him in case of attack.

"You know, I never even noticed." He tried to sound nonchalant, but when Marcello snatched the so-called pen from his partner, Beppe's voice climbed an octave. "Careful," he told them, "it's a . . . an heirloom."

"Solid for a pen." Marcello reached for the cap. "What it is, silver?"

The flourish came to mind: Bonaparte! Beppe pictured a duel, bloodshed, scenes from the butcher shop. He considered another run.

"Marcello, I think I see heaven." Stefano pointed across the street with the outstretched cane, where Beppe discerned, once the strollers passed, a little café with two unoccupied tables in front and a waiter slumped at the third.

Marcello, a smile spreading across his face, seconded the comment. "Yes, heaven indeed." He returned the still-capped knife to its owner, reshouldered the coat. "Shall we?"

"At once, before we lose the scent." Stefano turned to Beppe and bowed. "Adieu, Bonaparte."

Marcello tipped an invisible hat. "A pleasure, dear sir."

Beppe then watched as the men—fellow students, friends—crossed the street and headed toward the café—the waiter stirred—but at the last moment their path took a sharp turn to the left and put them on the heels of two women, unnoticed until then, whose dresses,

Beppe could tell, were unhealthful and whose shoes, in accordance
with Dr. Puzo's laws, should have been banned.

∞∞∞∞∞

It was late, a quarter to four, and the workout was scheduled for half
past three. Beppe set his notebook on the table, his jacket on a
hook, and rushed upstairs to don the short pants and sleeveless
shirt that Dr. Puzo said was more appropriate for exercise than the
traditional leotard: ventilation, ventilation, ventilation. Without a
second to spare, Beppe unbuttoned his pants while he hurried along
the hall and kicked off both shoes as soon as he entered the bedroom—behavior characteristic of an adulterer pressed for time,
which Beppe, needless to say, was not nor had ever, even for an
instant, wished to be.

Call him a late bloomer with regard to sexual matters; call him
naive. Whereas a former classmate like Dino DeBono had been a
pawn to his hormones since he turned thirteen, Beppe would not
experience full-blown lust for another year. For him Francesca's
handstands behind the school had been a show of coordination, not
fuel for salacious dreams, and the two women who had attracted
Stefano's attention and distracted Marcello from the knife were ini-
tially mere obstacles to Beppe's view of the café. A flash of under-
clothes or a well-buttressed bosom would not suffice; he needed an
emotional spark to kindle his libidinous coals.

Dressed now in the workout clothes, Beppe checked himself
quickly in a tall mirror before dashing back downstairs. With just a
glance he could see the difference between the troll he had been in
Cortenza and the Neapolitan man. The shoulders that he worked so
hard to keep square—never once had he worn the brace—were
padded now with flesh, and the muscles that had carried him faster
than Stefano and the almost-as-swift Marcello—the quadriceps, that
shattered chart had said—could be seen when he lifted a knee to run.
Even the circles that had darkened his sockets since childhood
seemed to have faded some.

Diet and exercise, Beppe knew, accounted for these improvements, but when it came to sleep—another important factor—he fared no better now than when he lived at home. The posture Dr. Puzo prescribed for slumber—flat on the back with as low a pillow as possible; a cracker would have provided more cushion—made the blood rush to Beppe's head, while the window over the bed let in a draft that, because he had a mother who sealed the house at night to keep out wolves and fevers, Beppe found unpleasant at first. He wanted to close the window, to roll over on his side and, in a return to old form, pick at the wall with a blunt fingernail. But doing so would restrict lung expansion and bend the spine.

"The den, Mr. Arpino! I'm in the den!" Dr. Puzo must have sensed Beppe's surprise to find, after all that effort, the exercise room vacant. "Good news!" he continued. "There's reason for hope!"

He was sitting at the desk when Beppe entered, dressed as he had been at breakfast, with a newspaper folded before him—the first Beppe had seen in the house—and the pocket-sized pad on top of an open journal. "I seem to have lost track of time," Dr. Puzo confessed. "But for once our workout can wait."

Beppe was speechless, dumbfounded, numb. What about the schedule? A minute wasted, as the expression went, was lost forever.

"Come here, Mr. Arpino. Pull up a chair."

It could be a test, Beppe reasoned, so he called Dr. Puzo's bluff with an appropriate quote. "A person should never sit when he can stand, never stand when he can walk, never . . . "

"Sit down, Mr. Arpino." Dr. Puzo rolled the newspaper until it resembled a club. "Now's not the time for performances."

Beppe thought it best to follow orders and save the rest of the quote for later. He would also wait to ask Dr. Puzo about the Eskimos, a people who, based on what had been said in class, Beppe pictured with teeth like the shoemaker's tools.

Dr. Puzo returned the newspaper to the desk and smoothed it flat with both hands. "A question." He looked at Beppe, pupils as plum-like as ever behind those spectacles. "Are you familiar with what's called radio?"

Radio? Beppe had heard a description once—on the train to Naples, when the man opposite him tried explaining the invention to a friend who insisted that a disembodied voice must be witchcraft: "This radio business, the telephone—it's all hocus-pocus." Yet Beppe had since seen telephones in action—people with canisters pressed to their ears, mouths close to metal flowers—and none of the users, at least as far as he could tell, seemed possessed of evil spirits.

"Yes, sir," Beppe answered. "I believe it's a telephone without wires."

Dr. Puzo appeared pleased. "A telephone without wires . . . I'll have to remember that." He pushed the newspaper toward Beppe and pointed to a block of text. "Here, take a look at this."

Beppe leaned forward and started reading. The article described a radio program for children soon to be broadcast on the new Naples station, but since Dr. Puzo did not own a radio and had never expressed an interest in children, Beppe was somewhat confused. He scanned adjacent articles—the wheat harvest, an attempt on the prime minister's life—just to be sure, then continued with the radio piece until he came to the sentence that explained Dr. Puzo's excitement: *The program will feature stories about Italian heroes, educational rhymes, and fables and lectures about hygiene.*

Beppe looked up from the newspaper at Dr. Puzo, who smiled in return and winked.

●●●●●●●●

"The forest was quiet and still. The birds were asleep in their nests. The squirrels were curled into balls. Even the owls did not hoot. All was calm in the forest, all was peaceful. It was a wonderful night. Then from deep in a cave came a terrible sound: 'Hack! Hack! Hack! Hack!' The birds flapped their wings. The squirrels shivered with fright. The owls called out from the trees. 'It's Mr. Dragon,' they said, 'and he's smoking again.' Soon the whole forest knew there would be no more quiet that night."

The voice—perhaps a woman's, perhaps not; it was impossible to tell—rasped on, buffeted at times with static, scuffed and scratched, as if the announcer stood in a sandstorm and spoke through a tin megaphone. Still, the words could be discerned, and there were pauses where pauses should have been placed, stress on the appropriate syllables. Dr. Puzo almost wept. Satisfaction? Too weak a word to describe how he felt. Elation? That would be closer to the truth. Triumph? Even better. But no matter what the choice, he was more hopeful at that moment than he could ever remember. First Beppe Arpino, a potential heir; now radio, access to the masses. And Dr. Puzo had, for the latter, an old nemesis to thank.

"I'm speechless, Giacomo. It's all happened so fast."

Indeed, just a week after the reunion, when Linati knocked on the front door, Dr. Puzo found himself in the publisher's office seated before an electrified console. And while the fable issuing from inside was familiar to Dr. Puzo—he had written *The Problem with Mr. Dragon* a decade earlier to protect children from the tobacconist's charms—it still held him rapt, still unnerved him when, in the final scene, a lost squirrel discovers the protagonist shriveled and dead.

"What a waste of life," Dr. Puzo remarked to his host after the unnamed announcer reached the end.

"Tragic," Linati agreed, "a damn shame." He lifted the lid off a box of cigars. "Care for one?"

"Uh . . . " Dr. Puzo, in his present state of mind—triumph, hope, grief, disbelief—did not rant as he would have otherwise. "Not at the moment, thanks." And just as well, because he owed Linati now, and the least he could do was show some restraint. *Personal Hygiene of the Future* would be published the following month, with a hundred copies shipped to Rome alone. In addition, Dr. Puzo had been commissioned to write a series of fables for publication in book form and broadcast on *Neapolitan Youth*. It was an all-out attack on the populace, in print and via the airwaves, one that Dr. Puzo would not have conceived, much less accomplished, without Linati's help. But what did the squat man now sniffing a cigar receive in return? Even Dr. Puzo, overcome with emotions, did not for a minute think that Linati Publishers had suffered losses as a result of his absence from its rolls. In fact, the firm seemed to have prospered in the interim: new

offices, handsome furniture, framed pictures on the walls, a mani-
cured receptionist with a bow that matched her nails. What reason,
then, for the sudden interest in an author whose books the publisher
once burned?

The answer stared Dr. Puzo in the face. Had he read more closely
the newspaper article that Linati left behind—not fixated on the references to health—and taken more of an interest in political affairs
—the little he knew came from rallies that diverted his strolls—he
would have realized that the man who authorized the radio broadcasts
also looked down on him from Linati's walls: in a black shirt, black
slacks, and spats; in a frock coat with wide white cuffs exposed; in a
top hat and upturned collar; a different outfit in each photo but the
same stern expression, the same square head. That is, what had started
decades earlier as a small press devoted to the works of unknown
writers—a project destined for failure—and later turned its focus to
academic and medical titles, as well as the occasional manifesto,
flourished at last when the Fascists took power.

Linati struck a match, then puffed a cloud across the room. That
should do it, he thought, that should hasten Dr. Puzo's exit. There was
no need to waste more time with that lunatic man. The risks, after all,
were serious. One never knew when he would snap—jump atop a
desk and make insane threats. Linati had put his life on the line when
he visited Dr. Puzo at home—that special tea, its laxative effects still
haunting him a week later—but now that he had him under contract
and convinced, thanks to the broadcast, that the fables would indeed
reach masses, further contact seemed unwise. Linati launched another
cloud and watched it float toward his visitor.

The truth be told, he had liked the dragon best. No matter what
those know-it-all owls said about tobacco and exercise, the dragon
refused to bend. Stubbornness: the squirrels of the world be damned.
Linati would have done the same himself. A person—or, for that matter, an animal that smokes—sometimes needs to stand alone. Where
would Linati be now if, as his brothers wanted, he had not sold his
share of the olive farm and relocated to Naples? And suppose he had
remained, like a hundred publishers now out of business, a slave to

aesthetic concerns and championed gifted authors? And what would have happened, to cite one final example, if he had told the Fascists, as did many in his profession prior to the March on Rome, to take their manuscripts elsewhere? What favors would that earn him now? A fire at the presses? A broken nose?

"Perhaps I should be off." Dr. Puzo stood to leave, a stricken look upon his face. "I have a book to write, remember?"

"Of course." Linati waved the offensive wand. "You're the doctor. You know best."

"Farewell, Giacomo." Dr. Puzo hurried out the door, then stopped in the waiting area and breathed deep—ah, sweet relief—in the manner of a weight lifter: inhalation, exhalation . . .

"Shall I call a doctor, sir?" It was the receptionist, who had left her post behind the front desk. She grabbed hold of Dr. Puzo's elbow and ushered him to a chair. And he let himself be led—the touch of such well-tended hands, hair that smelled of fresh flowers—and almost accepted the chair, but as he studied her face, so close as to fill his field of vision, the makeup she wore became apparent: the obstructed pores, the artificial luster, the eyelashes like spiders.

"But I *am* a doctor!" He broke free. "Please, leave me alone." The stairs, Dr. Puzo discovered, could be taken three at a time.

◦◦◦◦◦◦◦◦

Finally, a letter from home. Beppe picked it up off the table where Dr. Puzo had propped it next to a handwritten note—*a business appointment . . . start the workout without me*—and went directly to his room. First he sat on the bed, careful to keep the letter away from the window where a draft could catch it, then moved to the small desk where he studied each night. It was covered with books, several of which had L. PUZO printed on their spines. He removed the books and placed the letter in the vacant space before him like a make-believe dinner plate. He positioned a hand on either side, where the utensils should have been, and examined the meal.

In one corner, a stamp, no bigger than a thumbnail; in another, a brownish smudge, the postman's trace, perhaps a remnant of his lunch. The address was in Margherita's script; Beppe recognized it at once: more ornate than his own, with curls at the end of words that resembled added vowels. But what about their mother? She, too, could write—the account she kept of her customers, the slips that identified their bundled clothes—and all three of the letters that Beppe had sent thus far were addressed to her. Had she been in an accident and sustained injuries that made it impossible for her to pick up a pen? Beppe pulled out the stiletto and sliced open the envelope expertly, as though he were Rosselli in the presence of a fattened sow.

Dear Beppe . . . The first words provided no clues; he hoped that what followed would calm him. *We miss you. We hope you are well.* Whom, Beppe wondered, did his sister include with herself? *People ask, "How is Beppe? Have you heard from him?"* Her command of punctuation made it read like a book. *Mama tells them that soon you will be home.* An untruth, a lie, but at least their mother could speak and, even if confined to bed, accept visitors. *She tells them that then you will fix everyone's teeth.* Yes, that was the plan: an office off the piazza with comfortable chairs. *She is proud of you. I think the anger is gone. I think in another week she will write.*

The outbursts that had preceded Beppe's departure—the verbal assaults, the doubts about his mental health—seemed so ancient to him now—like those prehistoric teeth mentioned in school—that it was a minute before he understood what his sister meant, and while he had no desire to recall the displeasure that their mother expressed about his leaving, it did comfort him to know that she was not incapacitated or worse. But the comfort soon passed, because other townspeople, as Beppe learned in the next lines, had not fared as well since he moved. Mr. DeBono, who provided the Arpino children with sweets after their father's funeral, had dropped dead while icing a cake—Dino now ran the shop—and the mayor, in office since before Beppe's birth, had been dismissed on orders from Rome and replaced by a Fascist.

With affection, Margherita . . . Never had the distance between Naples and home seemed so immense. An earthquake could strike

Cortenza and level the town, and Beppe would not feel even a tremor under his toes. There could be a firestorm there, and the temperature in Naples would not rise a single degree. Disease, a pack of wolves—the possibilities were too numerous to consider. Beppe returned the letter to its envelope, tucked the envelope inside a book, and collapsed on the bed facedown, clothed, the orthopedic shoes off the end like two broad, awkward, useless oars.

That was how Dr. Puzo found him: passed out in a hazardous position, the pillow stained with drool. It was half past three, the appointed hour for their workout—he had jogged the last stretch from Linati's to make it back on time—but Beppe was sound asleep. Except for the outfit, he could have been a sailor returned to his bunk after an unsupervised night ashore.

Dr. Puzo went to the desk and picked up the book that sat atop it. The excitement of the broadcast diminished now thanks to the smoke and the makeup, he would not hesitate to wake Beppe as he did students who dozed at school. But as he lifted the book above the desk upon which it would land—loud as a pistol shot—he noticed an envelope's corner, which reminded him of the letter that had arrived earlier. Bad news from home? He set the book down next to the pen. No, it was a scalpel. Dr. Puzo felt his collar turn to ice. Perhaps that was not drool on the pillow after all. Hopes of a succession quickly faded.

He rushed to the patient's side and examined both wrists: no sign of cuts or contusions, but one could not rule out poison. "Mr. Arpino?" He jostled a shoulder. "Mr. Arpino, please."

A voice roused Beppe, distant but familiar: a man, an older man, more formal in address than most. He rolled onto his back to see who it could be, but when he opened his eyes the room appeared to waver, expand and contract, shine brilliant then dim.

The voice again, close and concerned: "Can you hear me?"

Beppe could not remember a more restful sleep, nor one as unshakable, but at last, after numerous blinks, the speaker came into focus: clad in white, ethereal. Beppe saw a mouth, an ear, spectacles, two dark nostrils, and was at that moment transported in time to an

afternoon he had revisited on countless other occasions, the afternoon Father Vincenzo died, but one detail that had been misplaced
in the past presented itself now: while the soon-to-be-deceased priest
pretended to be a dentist, Beppe had noticed a fine white powder
inside the cavernous nose.

A hand slapped Beppe on the cheek and catapulted him forward
in time. "Mr. Arpino!" The voice he identified—Dr. Leonardo
Puzo—the room as well, and the nap he remembered, too.

"I must have fallen asleep," Beppe said, up now on an elbow.
"Sorry if I worried you, Dr. Puzo."

⚬⚬⚬⚬⚬⚬⚬⚬

The workout—deep knee bends, the medicine ball—went forward as
planned once Dr. Puzo determined that his boarder was not suicidal,
but for the benefit of those concerned it should have been canceled,
because Beppe's performance showed none of the improvement he
had made in the previous week. He lost balance at the midpoint of
most bends, and the one time he caught the medicine ball, he failed
to send it back. "Mr. Arpino, either toss the ball or roll it, but don't
nurse it like an infant."

Beppe stumbled at dinner as well. He either executed half the
required number of chews or stared off into space, and when Dr. Puzo
enthused about the broadcast, Beppe displayed no apparent interest.
He failed even to smile when Dr. Puzo joked that the smoke-filled air
inside Linati's office had smelled—ha, ha—like a mortician's hands.
As before, Dr. Puzo blamed the letter. And since mental perturbation
was as much a poison to humans as hemlock or fashionable clothes,
he decided to venture a question or two and use the occasion to teach
an important lesson.

"Mr. Arpino, the letter that arrived, did it contain unwelcome
news?" He set his fork aside and awaited the outflow.

An astonished look but no tears. "As a matter of fact, sir, it did."

Dr. Puzo asked for details and was surprised to learn that the
problems concerned a baker and a politician and not, as he had supposed, a relative or best friend. Still, one man's nick was another's

laceration. Pain varied from person to person, in particular emotional pain, and Dr. Puzo knew from experience that appeals to reason or common sense were in most cases futile. If a patient wanted to believe that a prescribed treatment—an enema, for example, or a corrective brace—bordered on torture, all the denials and statistical support in the world would not convince him otherwise. And if a sexual partner claimed that she had been made to feel like an object—it would happen sooner or later—the best solution was to feign sleep.

But Beppe had insisted from the start that he wanted to lead a healthful life—not the first words out of his mouth, nor unprompted, but Dr. Puzo saw no reason to belabor the finer points—and in order to reach that goal he would need to master his emotions. As in all else, moderation was essential. A tantrum now and then provided a release for accumulated frustration, while a burst of song or a chipper hello did the same for bliss and enchantment. Repression, though, was to be avoided, as were morbid obsessions and depressive broods. The mind was like an opium fiend in its appetite for self-abuse, and those prone to sulks were no different from the addicts a traveler might see on a visit to a Chinese bazaar.

"Feel free to scream," Dr. Puzo said after explaining the risks of pent-up melancholia to his reserved tablemate. "If nothing else, it stimulates the salivary glands, and that, as you know, helps digestion."

Beppe thanked his mentor for permission to vent but deferred to a later date and, anxious to redirect the conversation, praised Dr. Puzo's skills in the kitchen. "Great peas," he remarked, "just the right amount of crunch."

The maneuver worked, and soon steam was the topic under discussion. Not that Beppe discounted what Dr. Puzo had told him about emotions. No, with a mother prone to tantrums and a former schoolteacher possessed of a similar temperament, he had witnessed firsthand the cathartic effects of an occasional howl and would have offered one up, if just to please Dr. Puzo, had the stimulus been there. But it was not homesickness or sadness that accounted for Beppe's preoccupation at the dinner table and, earlier, in the exercise room. The vision of Father Vincenzo's nose had supplanted remorse for the baker—cannoli would never taste the same—and concern for a man who had befriended Beppe but also uprooted the church vines. A fine white powder like confectioner's . . .

"I have a book on emotions." Somehow Dr. Puzo had circled back to the original subject. "I planned to save it for later, once we finished with the flesh, but an adjustment at this point shouldn't disrupt us too much." He helped himself to a crust of bread and made a notation. "It's called *The Habit of Happiness*. I think it will help."

Another book? Beppe had more in his room upstairs—eleven at last count—than most people touched in their lives. How would he ever finish them? The schedule he had kept in Cortenza—butcher shop, cello, little red book—was an invalid's vacation compared to life in Naples. Between the calisthenics and the meals and the strolls and the book-book-books and the classes, as well as the impromptu lectures and the odd newspaper article, Beppe found little time for music—fifteen minutes at most—or correspondence—just a few notes home since he started school—or friends: Stefano and Marcello had twice invited him to join them at the café, but an excursion of that nature, even for a quick tea, would have been unthinkable.

No wonder he had fallen asleep earlier: exhaustion, plain and simple. Yet Beppe knew, in the place reserved for such awareness, that a hundred books could collect on the desk upstairs, two hundred, enough to bow its legs, enough to lower the first-floor ceiling, and he would not abandon the project, would never lose hope, would under no circumstances settle for less. Since the fateful day of the tooth extractor's appearance—S. Russo, Beppe still remembered his name—and the enthusiastic response of Father Vincenzo—like a new man, like a schoolgirl—the belief that within the dentist's realm one could discover happiness had not diminished. Granted, music had its charms, its exceptional appeal—nothing soothed Beppe like the cello—but the mention of teeth was what finally woke the dormant priest. His last hours on earth were giddy and carefree—remember how he tossed the corkscrew?—and Beppe—call it fate, call it luck—had been a witness: the miracle fixed itself in his mind like a tumor.

●●●●●●●●

The title did not inspire hope in Giacomo Linati, who had published hundreds of books in his lifetime and rejected hundreds more, some simply based on their titles. He skimmed the manuscript: Puzo to the core, with its emphasis on health and insistence on self-discipline. A rabbit, all smiles before the race, triumphs over a somber turtle—a nice twist. But the title? Well, what difference did it make? Aside from the copies that would be distributed in Rome and the ones that private schools purchased, the remainder would likely be burned at a later date to save warehouse space. Such was the case with books lacking a specialized readership. Oh, Dante sold well, and families still liked to put a Manzoni on the shelves next to their Verdi librettos, but most Italians, even those who posed as scholars, never bothered with more than the newspaper headlines, which meant that to survive in Linati's profession one had to maintain a certain dispassion about the fate of individual books. Some observers would have added that in the south, where illiterates outnumbered the insects, a bit of dementia was also required, since being a publisher there made about as much sense as selling winter coats in Palermo or bicycles in the Alps.

Linati set down the manuscript and initialed the attached memorandum with all the zeal of an overworked bureaucrat. How unlike the idealist who had arrived in Naples filled with false notions about literature and its place in people's lives: older now and wiser, powerful, rich. But not as powerful as he wished. Shrewdness had kept Linati afloat while his competitors sank like untethered anchors—medical students, he had observed, purchased books, as did political extremists—and the lucrative state contracts of late, for manuals and educational pamphlets, had moved the business into new suites, and put Cuban tobacco inside the office cigars. But with an ex-newspaperman now in command of the nation, Linati's success as a book publisher seemed no more than a prelude.

He looked at a picture on the opposite wall and in the stern face staring back at him saw several men: the editor who shared with

Linati a dependence on the printed word and an interest in the price
of paper; the adroit orator whose speeches incited violence—even
Linati once raised a fist; the rebel who broke ranks with the Socialists
and, despite setbacks, came to dominate them; the appreciative vic-
tor whose minions ensured that businesses helpful to the cause now
shared in the rewards; the prime minister who, if all went as Linati
planned, would appoint the publisher to an important post.

Turtles Never Win was part of that plan. As Linati learned from
newspaper reports—his breakfast consisted of coffee and two dailies
—a concern for public health had taken hold in Rome. There was
mention of low birthrates and preventable disease, even a piece on
how peasants in rural areas seldom washed their feet, but not until
the announcement of radio broadcasts for children—in particular, the
placement of *fables* and *hygiene* in the same sentence—did Linati
think of Dr. Puzo or his books. And despite the time that had elapsed
since their last encounter, the crazed expression that the doctor wore
when he climbed atop the desk remained as vivid as if it had just
occurred. So, too, did the words that had prompted that behavior, and
Linati, who had not flinched then, shuddered at their recollection.
Yes, he had turned Dr. Puzo down and, worse, revealed a trade
secret: all unsold books became ashes. A special effort would be
required on Linati's part to reclaim lost trust, perhaps a show of
penance, but the humiliation would be worth it if a few well-placed
people in Rome—cabinet ministers and other officials—noticed the
books left on their doorsteps and mentioned Linati's name—it would
be printed above Dr. Puzo's—in the presence of their leader. As for
the radio broadcasts, which credited Linati Publishers whenever its
fables aired, he had less hope for those. Outside Naples no one
would hear them, and the local listeners all would be children. Still,
it was the broadcasts that had most interested Dr. Puzo and, as a
result, preserved Linati's pride.

He reached across his desk for the cigar box. In less than five
minutes the second installment of *Neapolitan Youth* would commence,
and Linati wanted to have a nice haze in place in the event that Dr.
Puzo appeared unannounced. To refuse him a seat at the console,

where he had been welcome the week before, could prompt an altercation; better if he left of his own accord.

But the likelihood that Dr. Puzo would disturb the publisher's peace was almost nil. He had not recovered from the last visit to Linati's office: painted women still entrapped him while he slept, and it seemed as if tobacco strands had been sewn into his clothes. In addition, Dr. Puzo now had a radio of his own at home so he could monitor the broadcasts.

●●○●○●○●

A bell sounded, and the professor, as he had after the first class and the handful since, picked up the tin filled with who knew what—it could have been pasta or gunpowder—and exited the room without comment, another lecture finished, another part of the foundation in place. For the session just ended, he had discussed the nerves inside teeth and how these were but branches of a more substantial nerve that spread throughout the head. "Thus," he explained, "a problem tooth will sometimes cause discomfort elsewhere—an earache, a sore throat, nasal distress. We call this reflected pain." He released hold of the podium and stepped over to the blackboard, where he drew a crude face—the face of a swollen ape—then shaded a beard on its chin. "Irritation in the lower incisors will be felt here." He erased the beard and added sideburns. "Pain in this area can be traced to the upper second molars." Next he darkened the cheeks, then the nose, the temples, the forehead, and in each case identified the teeth responsible.

It was valuable information for a dental student to possess, and Beppe, who tended to be somewhat maniacal in dictation, took special care now that the class was over to touch up the miniature faces that populated his notebook: fill in their misplaced mustaches, their peculiar tattoos, their painful bruises and awful birthmarks. He sketched, lost in the world where artists live, while the classroom emptied, and soon it seemed as if he were alone. But, as Beppe discovered when a crumpled-up piece of paper hit him on the head, two other students also remained.

"Bonaparte, the lecture's ended." It was Stefano, a few rows back.

"Yes, I'm afraid the professor, he left." Marcello, of course.

Beppe closed the notebook and pocketed the pen. "Hello, Stefano." Work on the faces would have to wait. "Hello, Marcello." Besides, their lab was about to start. He stood up to leave.

"What's the rush, Bonaparte?" Stefano, still seated, held the cane like a scepter. "Take a break, relax."

While Beppe would have liked to visit with the Neapolitans, the clock did not permit such luxuries. "We have a lab now, remember?"

Stefano chuckled. "Oh, can't be late for that. There would be riots if the prisoners were denied their tooth powder."

"Indeed," Marcello added, "a national crisis."

Nevertheless, the two men, despite the derisive nature of their comments, followed Beppe's lead and headed for the door. The coercion, though, continued. "How about after the lab, Bonaparte? Join us for a drink?"

As much as Beppe hated to disappoint people, once more he would have to refuse a request. "No, I just . . . I just don't have time."

"Well, what's so important?" Stefano wanted to know. "We all have our studies. What is it? A job? Chores?"

"Not quite," Beppe answered as he steered them toward the stairs.

"I know!" Marcello dashed ahead, the cape a stubborn shadow. "There's a woman somewhere, isn't there?" He blocked Beppe's ascent. "You've a rendezvous planned, correct?"

"No," Beppe protested. "A rendezvous? Never."

"And I'll bet she's older, married, a woman experienced in the . . . "

"An illicit affair!" Stefano cheered. "Good work, Bonaparte."

Beppe, whose father some people in Cortenza still insisted had killed himself, knew firsthand the power of unchecked rumors. "There's no woman, no affair." He stepped past Marcello. "I have to be home at three, that's all." And with the lab around the corner and the bell ready to announce a new hour, the questions ceased and the students turned their attention to the lab and producing an alkaline wash that would, when forced between the teeth, remove particles of food and neutralize harmful acids. But when the session ended—the ten jars of lime water in a line at the front, the instructor now departed —Beppe found himself subject to further abuse.

"So, Bonaparte, tell us what she's like?"

"Yes, details, details."

More queries in the corridor and down the stairs and, to Beppe's surprise, out the main exit and across the street. In fact, Stefano and Marcello accompanied him the whole way home, and no matter what Beppe said to confuse them—the denials, the evasion—it all seemed to support their belief that he maintained a secret life. Yet Beppe avoided the truth. He feared what would happen if students at the Naples Institute for Dental Arts learned that their classmate lived in the same house as the school's founder: jealousies, reprisals; the next object to hit him on the head would not be a piece of paper.

Beppe wanted to run, but he knew that such behavior would just make the next encounter with Stefano and Marcello more difficult. Instead, he decided to bid them farewell on the doorstep, with no invitation to enter—a course of action that would have worked if not for the statuette perched on the pedestal out front.

"I've seen that face before." Stefano pointed with the cane.

Marcello nodded. "I seem to remember it from church. The Stations of the Cross?"

Stefano stepped closer. "No, it's from school, if I'm not mistaken. You know the portrait behind the headmaster's desk?"

Yes, the same artist who fashioned the statuette also dabbled in oils and had sold Dr. Puzo both two- and three-dimensional renditions, a fact that Beppe, because of the unusual nature of his admittance into the school, did not know since he had never met with the headmaster to discuss tuition, attendance, and related matters and as a result never looked around the headmaster's office out of boredom and inspected the cartoonish portrait and its brass nameplate: DR. LEONARDO PUZO, FOUNDER. In other words, soon Beppe's secret would be made public. He braced himself for the worst.

"So, Bonaparte, what's with the statue here? A relative or . . . "

But, as happens in the theater as often as it does in sacred texts, a voice then called out from somewhere hidden and interrupted the action: "Aaaahhhh!"

Stefano and Marcello both retreated, while Beppe, accustomed to Dr. Puzo's exclamations, stayed put. He was trapped there, snared, defenseless, as lame as an etherized kitten. Without a doubt there would now be introductions to make, explanations, forced smiles and pleasantries.

The door then opened, and out flew a small paperback book that fluttered like a conjurer's dove before coming to rest with a slap in the middle of Marcello's chest, where it remained clutched as he tumbled to the ground. Well, not quite the ground, since the jacket that he wore draped in the manner of a cape spread itself out like a blanket the instant before he landed and helped cushion the fall.

Meanwhile, Stefano, who had taken an ill-aimed swipe at the book with his cane as the object approached Marcello, made as if to rush the door in defense of his friend, but Beppe, jolted into action, put him in a wrestler's hold. The time spent with the clubs and the medicine ball had not been wasted, for he was just about able to stifle Stefano's taunt for whoever threw the book to step outside. Another week of exercise and the words would have remained trapped inside Stefano's chest, but as it so happened Beppe could not quite contain them, and Dr. Puzo did appear in response to the squeezed-out invitation.

●●●●●●●

"Just turn the knob and wait a minute; it's as simple as that."

At the radio shop the trick had worked. There had been music when the console warmed—music of a distant and distorted sort, but music nonetheless. Now, however, all Dr. Puzo could hear was static, a sound not unlike that of a faucet at full throttle. He consulted the instruction manual, but it was useless. The illustrations, arrows and concentric circles, were as incomprehensible to a man trained in medicine as a map of the cerebral cortex would have been to an electrician, while the text that accompanied the pictures read as if it were the work of illiterates. Dr. Puzo could make no sense of the manual and, as the time for the program that he had waited all week to hear approached, tossed it out the front door: catharsis.

The relief lasted but a moment, though, because the book struck someone—inevitable, Dr. Puzo supposed, as the population of Naples increased—which prompted an altercation that did not resolve itself until Beppe, even slower to speak than usual, identified the victim and the rabble-rouser as acquaintances from school—evidence of how low the institute's standards had sunk in recent years—whom Dr. Puzo then attempted to scare off with a brusque hello and mention of the annual exams. What kept the visitors—and what later put them in Dr. Puzo's favor—was the fact that the fallen one, when he handed back the now-tattered booklet, professed to own a radio of the same design and offered to adjust Dr. Puzo's set if poor reception was what prompted the earlier outburst.

"All I hear is noise," Dr. Puzo replied and started for the front door. "Please, follow me." He was skeptical, to be sure—was that a cape the would-be repairman picked up off the ground?—but desperate, too. The radio had not come cheap, and he hated to miss even one broadcast of *Neapolitan Youth*. Dr. Puzo's concern for the health of others aside, he was as vain as the next man. No wonder each room inside the house sported at least one mirror, and volumes with L. PUZO stamped on their spines appeared on most bookshelves, and the statuette out front was supposed to resemble its owner. A radio broadcast that featured a Puzo fable was but another occasion for self-appreciation.

The student—Marcello was his name—did, to Dr. Puzo's surprise, have a touch of the technician in him, and after a few twists and tweaks at the console the voice of that unnamed announcer—male or female, Neapolitans would forever take sides—filled the den. The tale had just started—the rabbit was teasing the turtle—and Dr. Puzo invited Marcello and the one with the cane, Stefano, to sit down and listen and, if desired, join him and Beppe afterward for their calisthenics routine. The last request was, as Dr. Puzo had anticipated when he made it, refused—capes and canes do not hint at athletic prowess—but the spirit of celebration could not be dampened: access to the masses! Beppe alone seemed preoccupied, tense and ill at ease. Could it be, Dr. Puzo wondered, that Beppe's sadness over the death of that acquaintance back home somehow had been rekindled? A baker, believe it or not, a peddler of disease, an active participant in the ruin of mankind. The world would be a better place if all practitioners of that vile profession toppled over into their cakes—a sentiment that Dr. Puzo, for obvious reasons, could not communicate to Beppe, at least not for another few weeks. Instead, he decided to open the discussion to a different topic now that the announcer had finished and a musical performance was set to begin.

"So, Marcello and Stefano, tell me about school. How are your classes so far?"

A squirm or two, a nervous twitter, much like patients before their rectal exams.

"School, sir?" Stefano examined the cane for a moment, then gave a salesman's smile. "Splendid," he answered, which was similar to what all the students said in the presence of their school's founder. "I couldn't be happier."

Marcello, hands held up to better emphasize the point, was no less immodest. "Teeth, teeth, love those teeth!"

Dr. Puzo, accustomed to overdone enthusiasm from dental students, pressed on if for no other reason than to lure Beppe into the conversation. "And Mr. Arpino, how is he as a classmate?"

The visitors looked at one another, traded puzzled expressions, looked back to Dr. Puzo, then finally attempted an answer. "You mean Bonaparte?" Stefano asked. "He fills notebooks faster than da Vinci ever did!"

Chuckles from all except Beppe, who remained quite removed from the discussion. And the reasons? Well, one, as Dr. Puzo suspected, was the fear that he would be embarrassed in front of new friends. A second reason, of which Dr. Puzo had no awareness despite the fact that it now controlled Beppe, was what came from the console: a cello concerto, to be specific, one that soared from a tower somewhere near Naples and settled into Beppe's head. It mesmerized him—beautiful music—but also left him perturbed. Could it be, Beppe asked himself, that no one else heard the bowed instrument, its occasional cries? Were their ears filled with butter, their hearts solid bone?

As much as he liked Stefano and Marcello and appreciated Dr. Puzo, perhaps even loved him now like a father—the void was there to fill—it saddened Beppe to think that he alone felt the music. Was he so different from them? Were all dentists tone deaf? Yet Beppe's classmates had made reference to concerts attended; the sadness must have another source. Beppe listened for a moment while the cellist roamed free. Yes, he missed music, the place it once occupied in him. He practiced now a mere fifteen minutes before bed, rather than for several hours, and had not learned a new composition in months. Such was the price to be paid for a free education, free room and board, but someday, perhaps after graduation, when Beppe moved back to Cortenza and opened his own dental shop—with comfortable chairs, remember—he would spend more time playing the cello, both after work and between appointments, whenever he had a few minutes to spare.

••••••••

Ventilation, ventilation, ventilation: as noted before, Beppe was required to sleep with a window open, a situation that he at first found unpleasant but now, after a year under Dr. Puzo's roof, rather liked. In fact, apart from those times in the winter when a draft had chilled him, and the two or three occasions before and since when he succumbed to childhood fears that a wolf might nab him—irrational, Beppe knew, since Naples had no wolves and the bedroom was on the second floor—he had adjusted to all Dr. Puzo's prescriptions: the exercises, the diet, the oversized clothes, even the open window. And while it was not always easy—a drill sergeant would have found the regimentation excessive—and homesickness sometimes made matters worse—no one from Cortenza had yet visited, and letters were infrequent—Beppe knew even during these difficult stretches that, deep inside, Dr. Puzo meant well.

The window overlooked a narrow lane, and despite the calls of lustful cats and the shouts that accompanied domestic quarrels, Beppe never once found the outside sounds to be a nuisance. For more than a decade he had slept—or attempted to sleep—within earshot of Paolo's asthmatic rasps and for even longer had awakened to Old Icardi's sunrise retches; the sounds that entered now and then from the lane alongside Dr. Puzo's house were whispers in comparison. And since these varied little from week to week—shouts or howls, howls or shouts—a sound needed to be new and unusual to capture Beppe's attention. Once, as he read an article about the latest dental fixtures, he heard a man down below express affection for another man by changing the words to a popular song. On another occasion, while Beppe battled the never-to-be-defeated insomnia, he heard the unmistakable bleat of an accordion outside—could it be that Edoardo had followed him north?—then the ricochet of thrown objects—aimed not at the musician, as Beppe had supposed before he looked, but at the instrument itself, which sat in a heap, tattered and bashed, as a well-dressed woman tossed stones at it, pieces of refuse, and took the Lord's name in vain. But as odd as these and other performances were—and odder still the circumstances that must have produced them—none compared to what Beppe witnessed late on an autumn night one year after his arrival in Naples when he heard, over the cello's pianissimo voice, what sounded like an ambush outside: sudden footsteps in the lane, muttered threats, the thud of fists sunk into flesh.

He jumped to the window and peered out, just in time to see a man fall to the pavement and a few others crowd around. The tallest of these men then produced what Beppe took to be a knife. At least it looked like a knife from the bedroom window, flashed as a knife would flash in the presence of a street lamp, and this in the opinion of someone who had apprenticed in a butcher shop and over time developed a close relationship with knives of all shapes and sizes. Yes, Beppe decided, a crime was imminent, and in spite of Rosselli's cautions—"Trust me," the butcher once remarked in reference to

Naples at night, "its jail is the safest place"—he bolted for the stairs
and did not, as a true Neapolitan would have done, remain a specta-
tor or pull the shutters closed.

And what reason for the fearlessness? Was it Beppe's kinship with
sharp objects that emboldened him just then or mere innocence?
Granted, in an earlier era Dino DeBono had shoved Beppe a half-
dozen times with too much force, and Luisa Arpino never missed a
chance to plant an olive switch on the backsides of her children, but
otherwise Beppe had little firsthand experience with violence. At most
he had heard tales of wolf attacks—an old woman was rumored to
have vanished from her porch—and of people stabbed to death—in
New York, however, a far-off place—and had rescued a kitten from a
would-be torturer and witnessed the demise of countless calves—
"Sweet dreams," Rosselli said before he clubbed them down. In short,
Beppe came from a place where criminals, polite as nuns, would surrender their knives rather than draw blood from an unarmed witness,
and as a result he expected the men outside Dr. Puzo's house to run
when he appeared; if not, the mention of police would surely scatter
them. People feared the police, Beppe knew, even back in Cortenza,
where the two officers who made up the local force were neither mean
nor armed. But in the end no threats were needed and, counter to what
Rosselli would have predicted, no backlash happened. Instead, the
men all sprinted when Beppe burst upon the scene—that is, all except
the intended victim, who remained sprawled on the pavement ten
meters from where his savior stood. Had a photographer been present
to capture the scene, the film, when developed, would have revealed
an inhuman form: the loose white pants and shirt that Dr. Puzo prescribed still filled with air after the leap downstairs so as to make their
occupant appear twice his normal size. No wonder the men had run,
and no wonder the fallen one, immobile until then, soon started a
crab-like retreat that made it appear as if he feared himself in the
presence of a phantom from Pompeii.

"Wait!" Beppe called and hurried to the man's side, where he
noticed that the pavement underfoot was soaked—he almost
slipped—as was the front of the man's torn dinner jacket.

"I'll fetch a doctor," Beppe told him and, careful not to slide on the slick pavement, turned to leave, but then he recalled that the last time he had carried out such a mission—in the wake of Father Vincenzo's collapse—he failed to make it back in time—the patient had expired—so despite the nearness of the present destination—up a few stairs rather than across a small town—Beppe lifted the man— lifted with the knees, not the back—and carried him inside, laid him on the kitchen table, and roused Dr. Puzo from a naked slumber: ventilation, ventilation, ventilation.

∞∞∞∞∞∞

Tomassino Perelli, still in his twenties, still unblemished and slender, his head still encased in pomade, had been out on the town with friends—dinner at a favorite restaurant, coffee next door—when an unpleasant sensation visited him, a sensation in the midsection not unlike the cramps he experienced when his father asked if ever he planned to wed. Perhaps, as one friend ventured, it was the shellfish he had eaten that caused the discomfort or, in the opinion of another, the undiluted vermouth taken beforehand. Whatever the reason, Tomassino felt the need for fresh air, for movement, and excused himself from the table in order to stroll home. Such walks never failed to please him because at that late hour Naples was different, more subdued, quaint almost: the vendors became less abrasive, the filth less apparent, and the air seemed as fresh as if it had just blown in off an Alpine lake and not a putrid port.

Once outside, Tomassino's condition improved to the extent that he decided to follow a detour home and loop around to Via Cavallina, known for its statuettes and street lamps, its expensive charm. The idea seemed at first a wise one, then a foolish mistake, and in the end, in retrospect, destined, fate. Suppose Tomassino had remained at the café with friends: unthinkable now. Yes, it was meant to happen. Tomassino had no choice but to leave when he did and take that circuitous route home, pause when he did to inspect a statue, freeze when the ruffians passed, offer a nervous chuckle when one called him a name. And when it seemed that an attack would happen, what else could he have done but run down that lane and hope to lose them?

The punches hurt, of course, the few kicks. As for the derisive name—delivered with a lisp—he had heard ones like it back in school. Most distressing was the castor oil treatment. He had seen victims of these attacks—incredible doses, obscene—left to wake in a piazza, soiled and subject to embarrassed stares. Thus when the man kneeling beside him pulled out the spoon and bottle, Tomassino lost all hope. He pictured himself smeared and foul, passed out in a well-traveled place and, when the blows wore off, unwelcome in a car for hire, and went limp with dread. First one spoonful slid down, a second and a third, then the visitation from above.

It took Tomassino a moment to realize that he had, in fact, been saved. Although the ruffians ran off—their oil spilled, their spoon tossed—he now faced someone just as sick and twisted: white robes sized for a sail, a Samaritan's ecstatic smile. Tomassino clawed the pavement in an effort to escape: all he needed now was to be indebted to a freakish priest. But even when it appeared that the man was not a cleric—the robes turned out to be pajamas of some sort— Tomassino hesitated. It was only a matter of time before the castor oil took effect, and he wanted to be close to home when that happened, close to a bathroom and clean clothes.

The man promised to find a doctor, a task that should have given Tomassino plenty of time to leave. But then, in a movement both swift and gentle, the man—he looked nineteen at most—picked Tomassino up off the pavement, as if he were a doll, and carried him into an austere home that seemed, at least from Tomassino's held perspective, part bookshop, part morgue. In one room he glimpsed a skeleton, in another the picture of a skinless man, and upon shelf after shelf there was book after book.

Tomassino ended up on a table fitted with two chairs. Above him an incandescent bulb came to life, and above that the sound of footsteps could soon be heard—perhaps the man went to find a coat— then a brief exclamation from someone else—"Caterina!" the voice cried out, "I do! I do!"—then murmurs, more footsteps, then trampled stairs. Tomassino had planned to wait until the pajama man left the house so that he could do the same, but that proved impossible because the doctor, Tomassino learned, lived on the premises. And if the one who rescued him appeared odd and imbalanced, the so-called healer looked even worse: stripped to the waist and barefoot, spectacles askew, a head topped with dust or pollen—or fuzz—and a line of dried saliva from the corner of his mouth that resembled scar tissue.

"What's the problem?" Dr. Puzo asked, not quite awake but relieved to have left Caterina at the altar. It was the cello that had prompted the dream: erotic at first but soon traumatic.

"A stab wound," Beppe answered. "To the chest, I think." He pointed. "The jacket, it's all wet and torn."

"Yes, I can see that, Mr. Arpino." Dr. Puzo undid the buttons— not the outfit of a healthful man, not loose and too dark; just as well it had been ruined. "But the blood, where's the blood?" He raised both hands to show an absence of stains. "This is oil of some kind." Dr. Puzo then addressed the patient, scratched and bruised but otherwise intact: not a hair out of place. "Where's the incision, son?"

The patient replied in a faint voice, one that hinted at a private education. "No incision," he whispered. "It was a spoon, not a knife, and that's castor oil."

Dr. Puzo's awareness of current events, while it would never be much to boast about, had improved somewhat since the radio entered the house. Not that he ever listened to the news broadcasts or political speeches. No, he confined his hours at the console to *Neapolitan Youth* and let Beppe tune in a musical program occasionally. Still, examples of what passed for news in Naples did slip in here and there. Sometimes his favorite show was interrupted on account of a bulletin—the prime minister this, the prime minister that—to which Dr. Puzo responded with a letter to the station. In addition, there were portions of *Neapolitan Youth* devoted to news written for children, and Dr. Puzo did listen to these with interest ever since he heard the one about recent discoveries in the field of nutrition—a report that pleased him despite a few inaccuracies: the announcer praised pasta, for example, as an Italian wonder food but made no effort to promote dried fruit.

As a result of this exposure, albeit haphazard, to news, Dr. Puzo did not frown at the patient's castor oil comment as he would have a year earlier. He knew that in Rome and elsewhere measures had been taken to reduce the incidence of Blackshirt attacks now that their man had assumed power. And while Dr. Puzo saw little harm in an occasional forced evacuation—believed that for most people it was long overdue—he understood that those who administered the doses did so without full cooperation from their patients and under conditions that were less than ideal. He therefore felt inclined to offer some care to the lean beat-up man with the painted-on hair who was spread out on the table before him and, once it became clear that no serious harm had been suffered, tried to make him comfortable.

"Mr. Arpino, show our friend here to the bathroom, where he can wash himself and, well, relax."

⊗⊗⊗⊗⊗⊗

A week passed, then an unexpected envelope in the mail slot: an invitation, written on paper of such fine quality that at first Dr. Puzo mistook it for silk, to dine at the home of a Mr. Alfredo Perelli. The occasion? A banquet in honor of the two men who rescued Perelli's son.

Dr. Puzo threw the invitation in the trash. The idea seemed preposterous to him, more like punishment than a reward: all the protein that rich people ate, all the tobacco and alcohol. And a banquet would be even more decadent than usual. He imagined mountains of undercooked meat, its fat like glistening larvae, and cream-filled desserts with enough calories in each piece to fuel a decathlete for weeks, and obese people stuffed into clothes cut to fit famine victims, and smoke in the air, smoke, smoke, smoke, as if the carpets were on fire and the windows sealed shut. What on earth would make him want to endure a meal in an aristocrat's home? He winced at the thought.

But then, upon further consideration, Dr. Puzo realized that Beppe might benefit from the gruesome spectacle. He had lived a sheltered life thus far—he still thought patients would follow their dentist's advice—and had never, to Dr. Puzo's knowledge, been exposed to excess. An evening with the Perelli crowd could do him good, show him how far one can stray from the healthful path. And to make it easier for Beppe, to make him feel less out of place, Dr. Puzo decided that he would loan him a formal set of clothes, perhaps the linen suit purchased in Milan and worn for the reception that followed his handshake lecture. Yes, contrary to what the hostess had claimed in the course of her toast, it was a lecture, not a diatribe.

Little wonder, then, that when Beppe returned home from school he found, perched on the table where letters from home awaited him on other occasions, an opened envelope with, when he felt for its contents, a swatch inside, a swatch so soft that for several pleasurable seconds Beppe let his fingers linger between the envelope's leaves. It was an invitation, he discovered—it was paper!—from the man who had been accosted and the man's father. And it was scented—not with perfume, though; more like old potatoes.

Beppe, excited but doubtful that Dr. Puzo would share the excitement, returned the plush paper to its sleeve and went upstairs to dress for their afternoon exercise session. It would be another hour before he learned how wrong he had been about Dr. Puzo's reaction.

"Just because I have no interest in attending this affair doesn't mean it's of no value." Dr. Puzo offered Beppe a towel, their workout finished, their armpits soaked. "Frankly, there's a lesson for you in seeing how the Linatis of the world live."

Beppe could appreciate the wisdom in Dr. Puzo's words. The banquet seemed a natural addition to their pact. Still, he had no desire to be the center of attention at the Perelli home—the event was half in Beppe's honor—not without a cello to hide behind or an escort, someone like his mentor, someone more adept at public speaking and more familiar with etiquette.

"Now, I should warn you," Dr. Puzo continued, his hand now on Beppe's shoulder, "a banquet is not a pretty sight—on par with an autopsy or a train wreck—but don't flee; observe, take it all in, even sample the food if you like."

That last comment, the one about food, did not seem to Beppe to have exceptional importance. He listened and nodded and accepted as inevitable the fact that he would embarrass himself in front of the Perellis and their friends. Even Dr. Puzo gave the comment no special treatment—the same professorial tone, the pause afterward the same as what followed others: a second at most before he headed for the shower. Yet the comment was significant, perhaps the boldest expression to date of the trust that had developed between teacher and student.

Needless to say, Beppe had trusted from the start, when he first stood on the doorstep and permitted Dr. Puzo to grab hold of him in order to correct his deformed posture. The Neapolitan could just as easily have bound Beppe's hands behind his back and, as if to prove Rosselli's point, emptied Beppe's pockets. But Luisa Arpino's son was, for the most part, a credulous young man. Whereas his mother grew more suspicious over time—she now asked customers to surrender their fees in advance—he remained trustful. It was Dr. Puzo, not Beppe, who shared Luisa's caution. He, too, was reluctant to place confidence in his fellow man, above all a new disciple. He had been disappointed in the past, and Beppe's struggles the first few months—the loosed clubs and sudden depressions—did little to encourage blind faith. The idea of sending him unchaperoned to a banquet at that time would have been ridiculous, like pushing an altar boy into a brothel: whatever resolve he possessed would evaporate in the presence of such abundant temptation. And then, as before, Dr. Puzo would be alone with no prospects for a successor. But he was willing to take that risk now, to trust that Beppe would not abandon their project even if, as the comment about food proposed, he tasted the tender veal and nibbled the indecent pastries.

●●●●●●●

Stefano and Marcello, the best-dressed students in dental school, had much to offer Beppe in terms of advice when he approached them after a lecture on molar removal: what to do with his coat after arriving at the banquet, how to introduce himself to others in attendance, where to sit when the meal was served, which hand to use for his fork. The three students were headed home—Dr. Puzo's home, that is—to join their school's founder for another installment of *Neapolitan Youth*. It was an ordeal at times for Stefano and Marcello—once a week with a fanatic, an hour of juvenile nonsense—but if the results from their annual exams were any indication, the effort had paid off. The visits also gave them a chance to peek beneath their classmate's puzzling exterior. Almost a year after that first encounter with Beppe, when he tripped on the stairs and received a French nickname, he continued to be a source of fascination. Who would have guessed that he owned a cello? Or that he followed a fitness regimen developed by a dentist? And now, the latest surprise: Beppe had rescued the son of none other than Alfredo Perelli. It was too much to fathom. Indeed, neither friend believed Beppe when, a block from their destination, he named the site of the soon-to-be-held banquet.

"Where?" Stefano stopped and let his cane—now topped with a small lion—drop to the pavement. "At Alfredo Perelli's? Please, Bonaparte, have another drink."

Marcello's cape, still without decoration, also threatened to fall. "Yes, sorry to say, but Alfredo Perelli wouldn't even invite me to one of his parties."

Unlike remarks made in the past, these did not affect Beppe. He understood now that Stefano and Marcello meant no harm. It was their way, he knew, their personalities. Whereas some people—Miss Donati, for example—screamed and hit children, others teased or carried capes. Beppe had grown accustomed to the harassment—expected it now—and preferred a little cleverness to violence or mute snubs. Nevertheless, he had no explanation for the disbelief shown him in this case. For reasons unclear to him an invitation from Alfredo Perelli seemed as improbable to Stefano and Marcello as an appointment to lunch with the Pope.

Beppe, who seldom held a newspaper and even then never made it past the front page, could be excused for his ignorance. And Dr.

Puzo, who had read the invitation as well but experienced no revelation when he saw the host's name, also could plead innocent. A person can accomplish only so much in a lifetime. Priorities must be set, decisions made: will it be the intricacies of teeth that receive the most attention today or the names of socialites? To attempt both could lead to confusion, which, of course, explained why Stefano and Marcello would never be among the nation's best dentists. An inordinate amount of their time was spent bent over the society pages: who attended which ball, what dress the diva wore. It was no surprise, then, that the name Alfredo Perelli stopped Stefano like a bullet to the head.

"Yes, there it is, in black and white." He held the invitation that Beppe had pulled from a pocket as if it were a relic. "Alfredo Perelli," Stefano repeated, "Alfredo Perelli."

Marcello looked over his partner's shoulder. "And it's spelled the same as in the newspapers."

A slow sigh escaped Stefano's mouth. "Oh, some people have all the luck." He returned the invitation to Beppe, stunned and defeated, as if it were he who had been beaten in that darkened lane.

"So true," Marcello added, the familiar cape now a leaden mass. "It's not fair. It's just not fair."

More expressions of injustice followed, more oppressed poses, before the two men, now behind Dr. Puzo's door, finally rallied in support of their friend. "It will be an event to remember," Stefano promised, "a once-in-a-lifetime chance." He propped the cane in a corner. "Just the artworks alone—splendid, I'm told, a private museum."

"You've heard of Medici, no?" Marcello placed his cloak on a hook. "Well, Perelli makes him look like a pauper."

An overstatement, to be sure—the Neapolitan businessman had nowhere near the collection of that Renaissance patron—but indicative nonetheless of Alfredo Perelli's wealth. It all started with paper—a small investment in a mill that had been idle—and grew to include vast stretches of land, hotels and restaurants in Naples and Rome, an electronics plant near Pisa, a furniture store. Paper, though, still accounted for the bulk of Perelli's income. It was the foundation upon which the rest stood and consequently received most of his attention: hours and hours on the telephone or in conference, at the mill itself or in the forest. He followed the process from start to finish, from lumberjack to reader, and could speak for weeks about watermarks. In fact, he knew so much about paper that sometimes he felt part tree. And he did seem, from a distance at least, a bit arboreal: tall and expressionless, with pale skin like birch bark and hair that, when the wind blew it, resembled autumn leaves.

●●●●●●●●

At the appointed hour—seven o'clock—on the appointed date—the fifteenth, the ninth month—Beppe approached a mustachioed man in a police uniform who sat atop a horse.

"Excuse me, officer," he said, hand cupped to his mouth in order to make himself heard over animal's breathing, "I seem to be lost."

It was true: so preoccupied was Beppe as he walked to the banquet, so filled with dread and excitement, apprehension and delight, that he turned a street too soon and within a block became confused. He had never ventured into that area before—the houses more like palaces, their facades decorated like cakes—and could not reorient himself relative to his destination. The horse and rider appeared just as Beppe had begun to panic: suppose he missed the banquet . . . oh, a once-in-a-lifetime chance.

The relief he experienced, however, did not last, because when asked for directions to Alfredo Perelli's house, the officer refused. "What?" he replied, the mustache thick and immobile. "Do you take me for a fool?"

Stunned, Beppe offered the invitation as proof. "Look at this, officer"—he held the swatch aloft—"please."

Yet even with this evidence, the officer seemed unconvinced. "Well, how do I know for sure? You could have fished this out of— let's see here—Mr. Arpino's trash."

Perhaps it was the mothballed clothes, Beppe reasoned, the linen suit Dr. Puzo loaned him, that made the officer skeptical. It did emit a peculiar odor—but no worse, he believed, than what came off the horse—and retained its wrinkles like a handkerchief left unlaundered. But aside from the faded pants and jacket, Beppe found his appearance quite respectable. Stefano and Marcello had insisted on a striped cravat instead of a necktie, and on his head the two had perched a handsome bowler. Also, Beppe's nails had been trimmed and buffed at the end of class that afternoon—the first time another person had tended his hands since childhood, when Luisa Arpino would collect her children's clippings once a week and tiptoe off at dusk in the direction of the graveyard.

"But that's me! I'm the Mr. Arpino mentioned on that invitation." Beppe, desperate now, all but clutched a stirruped boot. "Take me to the Perellis, officer, and I'll prove it."

And that was how Beppe arrived at the banquet: with a police escort, a commotion at the door. Tomassino, summoned from down the hall, vouched for Beppe, welcomed him inside, then addressed the officer. "There are wild mobs out there," he said, "madmen armed with spoons and laxatives. Put that horse to use, sir, and leave people like Mr. Arpino alone."

Tomassino paused for a moment. It was an uncharacteristic outburst, to be sure—and dangerous, too—but while this policeman had been harassing an innocent man, a pedestrian somewhere—on the next block even—was in all likelihood being medicated against his will. The unfairness of it made Tomassino want to scream, but then he looked again at Mr. Arpino and decided to thank the officer instead. Perhaps it had been best to exercise some caution. Mr. Arpino, after all, must have appeared out of place in their neighborhood—thank heaven for the cravat and bowler—and if he flew at the officer excited and inflated, as he had Tomassino in the lane when he disrupted the attack, well, then it was a miracle that the officer had not aimed and fired or the horse reared and trampled their honored guest.

Tomassino took Beppe's hat and led him to the ballroom, a place that would soon be filled with people he detested: the tedious men who talked business, the shrill unpartnered women, the overzealous suitors. If not for the few close friends situated in a corner, the event would be intolerable for Tomassino. Most banquets taxed his patience, but this one promised to be even more strenuous. As usual he would have to smile at obnoxious people and stand for innumerable speeches and answer personal questions: forever the same questions—about women and children, about the future—and never the desired answers. But on top of all that, on top of these inconveniences, Tomassino would be forced to relive a most unpleasant experience—the assault off Via Cavallina—in front of a hundred people. What next? he wondered. A reception to celebrate the removal of a cyst? Yet he understood that this banquet was the worthiest to date. In spite of appearances, Mr. Arpino was a hero and deserved to be treated as such. Since the newspapers would never report his brave deed out of respect for their paper supplier, a banquet would have to suffice: a toast to his fearlessness, a loud round of applause, slaps on the back and handshakes, the presentation of a pocket watch. When the time came for Mr. Arpino to leave—ten or eleven in all likelihood—he would know that the Perellis appreciated him.

Tomassino asked a servant to interrupt his father, who stood, stiff as timber, with two other men and explained how the amount of bleach added to sulfite pulp was crucial: too much weakened the fibers, whereas too little resulted in paper the color of newsprint.

"Whoever measures the chlorine must be a master." Tomassino's father let the servant know that he would be with him in a moment, then took a swallow of wine. "I have a man at the mill," he continued, "and that's all he does—handles the stuff as though it were nitro."

●●●●●●●●

First there was the Arpino home: the unstable furniture and unfinished floors, the flattened mattresses, the pickable plaster walls. Then came Father Vincenzo's residence next to the church: carpets and bookshelves, a leather chair, a brass lamp. And after that was Dr. Puzo's house: the statuette outside on the pedestal, the double doors, the skeleton in the den, the upstairs toilet. But none compared, even in a superficial sense, with the place Beppe now found himself in. Was it a mansion, he wanted to know, or a castle? And was that wallpaper over there or, as Stefano predicted, an enormous fresco? "You'll see chandeliers the size of battleships," he promised Beppe, "and rooms that could fit an entire fleet."

Yes, the space that Tomassino led Beppe into was quite impressive: as expansive as the ocean, as brilliant as the sun reflected off the sea. But when Beppe entered the ballroom and waited while Tomassino made a request to a man in black tails, he experienced a sudden and unexpected sadness. The maritime descriptions that Stefano had used prompted an unfortunate association: Beppe now pictured his father crammed into a narrow bunk on a boat bound for New York. How the air must have smelled in that crowded cell and the swells been unbearable at times. How the men must have traded names, traded hopeful speculation, and clutched their few possessions as if it were these—the cheap valises and dented tins—that kept them all afloat. How distant home must have seemed as the hours passed, more remote with each minute but never as indistinct as what awaited them. And how imperiled the men now seemed to the son who stood, cravat at his throat, on the threshold of a ballroom.

"Mr. Arpino, I'd like to introduce my father, Alfredo Perelli."

The brood abandoned as quickly as he had adopted it, Beppe turned his attention to a tall, impassive man with a glass in one hand and, to Beppe's dismay, nothing in the other. He had discussed the question of handshakes with Dr. Puzo that afternoon and hoped to reach a compromise, if just for the banquet, but on this matter his mentor would not bend. "You have to be careful around these aristocrats," he explained. "You can't let appearances deceive you. Believe me, a rich man's hands can still be slathered with tubercular mucus."

The solution Dr. Puzo recommended was a polite bow of the head, an example of which Beppe executed after Alfredo Perelli's introduction. "A pleasure, dear sir. I was honored to receive your gracious invitation."

While the action Beppe performed was of Dr. Puzo's contrivance, the words came from Stefano and Marcello. Both had coached their friend for hours in anticipation of the splendid event, as though he were an untrained actor in a starring role. And it was not just individual lines that were rehearsed but entire speeches. Beppe knew how to respond if asked for his opinion of the latest fashion trends, and despite never having seen the artist's works in person, Beppe could describe in detail what he liked best about Titian. He had even studied pictures of political leaders in the event that he found himself seated beside one. In short, Stefano and Marcello were relentless in their efforts to prepare Beppe: before school, after school, as if their own reputations were on the line.

"No, it is I, Mr. Arpino, who should express honor." Beppe had expected a more decorated man: diamonds, he supposed, sewn into a silk cape, perhaps a cane topped with a fat opal. "You see, I've only one son"—Alfredo Perelli gestured toward the pomaded and fair Tomassino at his side—"and who knows what would have happened to him if you hadn't intervened." He turned to a man in black tails— a different man, Beppe noticed, from the one Tomassino had spoken to earlier. "Please, get Mr. Arpino some wine."

As the man crossed the room, Beppe suppressed a desire to call out after him: a request for carrot juice or warm milk. He had not consumed so much as a drop of wine since moving in with Dr. Puzo, and now he would be expected to down an entire glass. Too bad Father Vincenzo was not on hand to assist in the effort; the priest, Beppe remembered, could finish two and three bottles at a time without apparent effect.

"So, Mr. Arpino, Tomassino here tells me that you have a home on Via Cavallina—a beautiful street, those statues, beautiful." The servant, or one just like him, returned with the wine.

"Well, sir"—Beppe was surprised to find the taste still familiar —"I have a room there, yes, but the house belongs to Dr. Puzo."

"Dr. Puzo? I . . . " Perelli paused while Tomassino whispered something in his ear, then nodded as if in agreement. "Of course, Dr. Puzo. I'm sorry that he couldn't make it. You'll have to give him my regards."

Beppe promised to do so, then, in order to fill the silence that followed, decided to launch into one of his prepared monologues: a lament about the unfortunate disappearance of spats. The paper baron, however, saved Beppe from needless embarrassment.

"Dr. Puzo, is it? That name"—Perelli tapped himself on the temple—"I'd swear I came across it just today if I'm not mis—oh, excuse me." He bowed as Beppe had bowed earlier. "I see a publisher I need to speak with."

That left Tomassino and Beppe alone, as alone as two people could be at a banquet in a ballroom. The space had filled since Beppe entered, but the bodies and the noise were not unpleasant. No, provided he did not have to stand on a platform and answer difficult questions or resuscitate a dead conversation, Beppe enjoyed the spectacle. The costumes people wore: No wonder Dr. Puzo lambasted the rich. It was hard to believe that some of them could breathe squeezed into such ludicrous outfits. The women in particular seemed confused about the purpose of clothing. Their shoulders were exposed, their calves and ankles, while at the same time their heads sported fur hats. And the posture of both sexes reminded Beppe of those pictures taken of him soon after his arrival in Naples and included in Dr. Puzo's latest book: curved backs and twisted hips, extended necks and contorted spines. The notable exceptions were Alfredo Perelli—a back flat as a planed board—and the men in black tuxedos: six or eight of them at work around the room, their platters filled with breakables, their chins tucked in like soldiers.

●●●●●●●●

The air: a mixture of smoke and familiar phrases, conversations and what passed for conversations. At least that was how it seemed to Tomassino as he led Beppe to the corner where his friends had positioned themselves. Until the announcement for dinner, this would be their home: near where the quartet would soon be sitting down and its music would be least disturbed. The friends had come more in support of Tomassino than for the free drinks and food, and he rewarded them with an ensemble made up of the finest musicians in Naples—

so fine that singers at the opera house were sure to be displeased when informed that their favorite string players had been hired away for evening.

"These are my friends, Mr. Arpino." Tomassino introduced each of the five men to Beppe and explained that all had attended the same university. "We studied literature together," he added, "and Latin, with the exception of Alonzo here, who, as you probably can tell, studied math." The comment received the laughter Tomassino had expected from his friends but not so much as a smile from his rescuer, who seemed preoccupied at the moment, his attention focused on the quartet now taking its place.

"Are you fond of music, Mr. Arpino?" Tomassino waited for a response, waited several seconds, then looked to the others for assistance. His friends, though, merely shrugged, so Tomassino tried again. "Mr. Arpino?" he asked, louder this time but still to no effect. Was the man awestruck, Tomassino wondered, to find himself in the presence of semifamous musicians, or—heaven forbid—had he slipped into a coma? Tomassino reached for an elbow. "Excuse me, Mr. Arpino, but perhaps you should sit down."

Beppe allowed himself to be lowered even though he had no desire to take a seat just then—not unless it was the seat behind the cello: a beautiful instrument, polished like an antique clock. Indeed, it appeared to be in pristine condition, better preserved than the beloved Guadagnini, which had more than a few bumps and bruises thanks to Margherita and her misnamed cat as well as the abuse it suffered while strapped to Beppe's back: the bullish old woman who flattened him when their train stopped at Salerno, the faceless pedestrians who later jostled him in the street. Yet despite that mistreatment, the cello's voice remained the same: sonorous and warm, a shelter from the storm. If ever Beppe felt weak—so far from home and such an inflexible schedule—a few minutes with the instrument would make him feel better.

"You don't look well, Mr. Arpino. Please, have some more to drink."

The musicians, Beppe noticed as he sipped and swallowed the wine—just fruit, he reminded himself, picked from vines and stored in barrels—were dressed the same as the servants—crisp bow ties and pointed tails—and their posture was equally impeccable. No doubt Dr. Puzo would have been impressed; Father Vincenzo, too, who had never been satisfied with what Miss Donati dubbed the Arpino slouch.

"Perhaps some fresh air would help." Tomassino persisted when it became apparent that the alcohol had failed. "I know it often works for me." Another torturous pause—the seconds seemed to stall—then at last an answer.

"If it's not an inconvenience, I'd prefer to stay right here."

"Certainly," Tomassino said, "that's fine with me." And the corner was, without question, where he wished to remain as well. In addition to its nearness to the musicians and the five former classmates, the spot afforded Tomassino a haven within the ballroom: a cove of sorts, an inlet. Yes, the sharks had begun to circle. These were the suitors who infested the waters that surrounded Tomassino's sister. Who invited them, he had never determined—denials came from all sides—but without fail the men—sometimes two, sometimes ten—now appeared at each banquet and competed with one another for Angelina's attention: a pursed smile, a pleasant hello, but never more than that, never a hand to squeeze or cheek to kiss or even a glimpse of her white, white teeth. As a matter of fact, Tomassino's sister expressed about as much affection for the suitors as she did for the people who now ran the country. And while her aloofness clearly worried their father—almost nineteen and still no announcement—Tomassino understood that the men who pursued his sister were too coarse for her, too immodest, the sort of men who, after the banquet—a polite affair—would abuse someone out for a stroll, call that person names and chase him down a lane. It was plain to see, Tomassino believed; just look at their bared teeth.

And now, not a moment too soon, the much-anticipated music.

●●●●●●●●

A curious sound, Alfredo Perelli noted as he searched for the publisher, the product of friction—animal hairs on steel—but pleasing nonetheless. Tomassino in particular liked music and had taken it upon himself to hire the performers. Finally, some initiative from Perelli's son. Perhaps the attack two weeks earlier had shaken it loose. Still, Tomassino would need more of that, much more, if he hoped to excel as an executive. One could not be a follower, no matter how well schooled or sensitive, and hope to succeed in the position. Decisiveness was essential, but until the attack it had seemed a trait Tomassino lacked. Even in personal matters, he tended to wait: a handsome man in his midtwenties, the heir to an empire, Perelli's son remained unattached and, worse from a parental point of view, unconcerned about the situation.

"When I meet her, I'll know," Tomassino would answer when asked for an update. And if pressed for specifics—Perelli sometimes could not restrain himself—the words would become hurtful: "I'm not sure, Father. Perhaps I'm destined to lead a bachelor's life."

A stake to the heart.

A shove into the chlorine vats.

A tumble in the pulp refiner.

To a man who, wealthier than most monarchs, would surrender untold assets in order to see his children wed, the statement caused unbearable pain. But it was not just a desire to see them paired off that continued to be denied. No, what Alfredo Perelli, a widower for almost two decades, wanted most of all at this point in life was to be a grandparent. He wanted little ones around the house, a troupe of novice Perellis, to spoil with candies and send down the banister and spin overhead like pizza and, best of all, thrill with exotic stories, tales about Chinese papers and India inks.

He scanned the room once more for the publisher: still no trace of the rotund businessman who, in a blink, had disappeared before Perelli could reach him. Either he was still in the room and Perelli failed to see him—possible, since the space was almost filled—or he had stepped outside for some fresh air, as Perelli would have liked to do himself. Banquets had become a form of torture for him ever since Tomassino reached adulthood. A hundred beautiful women, all ripe and desirable, all as poised as ballerinas, had been ushered into the ballroom for past functions—not a coincidence, to be sure—but none of them, not one, had met with Tomassino's favor. It was a lack of interest—as if Tomassino did not see them—that baffled the elder Perelli and led him, at last, to abandon the project unfinished and put as much, if not more, effort into his daughter's future. With a female, he had assumed then, the task would be easier, since no initiative was required on her part. A woman could just stand there and, as the saying went, be swept off her feet. But alas, the disaster threatened to repeat itself now: in the same way that Tomassino was oblivious to the beauties who once packed the ballroom, Angelina rewarded her suitors with chilled indifference. Perelli, however, would not be frustrated a second time. If she did not choose a mate on her own, he would find one for her—a venture that, he felt certain, would not be too difficult. Angelina possessed a luminous smile—teeth so white, so perfect, that her dentist refused all fees—and stood to inherit a fortune; the trick was to find a candidate whom she would endorse. And here the skills that Perelli used to locate new properties—the hotel just acquired in Rome—and influence textbook publishers—a stubborn lot if ever there was one—would prove invaluable.

He took a final look around the room, then headed toward the music. Not that Perelli wanted to dance or even find that fat publisher now; he would see him at dinner. Rather, his intention was to locate Tomassino, the music lover, and send him in search of Angelina. Perelli wanted her to meet the hero, Mr. Arpino, even if just to express her thanks. And that, he feared, was all she would have for him, because Mr. Arpino did not quite measure up: a boarder, as Tomassino described him, a student of some sort, and a peculiar dresser. Yes, Mr. Arpino would look like a tramp next to the usual suitors and make no impression on Angelina. Perelli had tried, though, and even now it seemed a sensible plan: the man who had risked life and limb to save Tomassino would benefit from a sister's love for her brother and—who knows?—succeed where the suitors had failed. What other reason could Perelli have had for hosting the banquet? If it was just thanks he wished to express, a cash reward would have sufficed.

Now, past another clutch of people—smiles all around, hello, hello—he could see the musicians in their half circle—arms in motion, bodies not—and, off to one side, Tomassino with a few other men, one of whom—it appeared to be the rumpled Mr. Arpino—sat in a chair. Perelli considered the name the hero had mentioned, Dr. Puzo, which did sound familiar, as if Perelli had come across it just hours earlier. Was it printed on a sample he reviewed when he visited the mill? Stenciled on a door he passed as he walked alone after lunch? The answer eluded him; the stress of not one but two unmarried children must have blunted the point on his rapier-like mind.

⬤⬤⬤⬤⬤⬤⬤⬤

"Some water, sir? A martini?"

No, Giacomo Linati refused all refreshment, so the receptionist, who had looked in on him at noon to comment on a rescheduled appointment, returned to her desk at the main entrance and inspected her hands: the nails now painted pink instead of red but still coordinated with the bow affixed to her hair.

"As pale as a plucked chicken," she later explained when a coworker asked about the publisher's health after the cancellation of an afternoon meeting. "I believe he went home."

But Linati had not returned home. And neither was he sick, as the receptionist suspected, at least not sick in the medical sense. Despite appearances, he had not ingested poison or experienced heart failure nor contracted a virus or suffered a hernia. Aside from a cancer still to be detected and the more obvious case of obesity, an indulgent lifestyle had thus far left the publisher unscathed. The wan complexion and premature exit from work were rooted elsewhere.

As Linati had looked over the newspapers in his office that morning and sipped from a cup of coffee—the routine never varied—he noticed, next to a letter that supported the loyalty oath now required of schoolteachers, an editorial on the state of Italian radio. But because he had lost interest in the new medium since its premiere in Naples—he seldom touched the console—and had a full schedule ahead of him, Linati skimmed the text as he would an article on exercise or the profile of a noted poet. It came as a surprise, then, when the words *Neapolitan Youth* jumped out at him from the newspaper and, after those words, the name—shock of all shocks—of someone he knew: Dr. Leonardo Puzo.

Months had passed, months and months, since their last encounter—when Dr. Puzo retreated from the smoke—enough time for the publisher to have abandoned all hope that a mere book would help win him a political appointment. In fact, Linati now wondered how he ever could have been so foolish. None of the cabinet ministers or other officials had responded to the free copies left on their doorsteps, and to make matters worse, the one piece of correspondence he did receive that mentioned the book had been mailed from a mental institution. Thus when it became clear that the effort had failed, Linati distanced himself, as he had once before, from Dr. Puzo—an assistant now handled the fables—and banished the episode from his head. But it came back to him when those fourteen letters leapt off the newsprint: *Dr. Leonardo Puzo.*

Linati read the editorial from start to finish, much as it hurt him toward the end, while the coffee turned cold beside him. The writer—a public servant, believe it or not—praised Dr. Puzo's fables as a perfect example of what Italian radio could do for the masses and called their author both a talented artist and a true Fascist.

It was, Linati had to admit, a powerful statement—pure falsehood, of course, but powerful nonetheless—and if he had not known the individual described better, or that individual's works, the editorial would have convinced him that Dr. Puzo was a good person. But what about Linati himself? After all, he had been the one to approach Dr. Puzo about the fables, the one to print those initial manifestos, the one to stand for hours in the sun, shoulder to shoulder with the so-called masses, in order to hear the prime minister speak. Dr. Puzo, on the other hand, wrote stories about weak hearted squirrels and brewed poisonous teas and climbed over office furniture in order to issue threats. The editorial felt like a slap in the face for Linati, and he reacted in kind. He fumed for some minutes—half-uttered curses, a fist to the desk—then ranted and raved—the newspaper torn into confetti, a cigar snapped in half—before he finally calmed down and let the cloud he knew to be depression envelop him. Tomorrow's newspapers, Linati suspected, would profile Dr. Puzo, and after that there would be personal appearances and, sooner or later, an invitation from Rome.

He stared at the walls around him, at the pictures on those walls, at the man in the pictures, and at the man's quarried face. Appointments were canceled, an afternoon meeting, and at one o'clock the publisher left his office without explanation. He went to a restaurant where he ate nothing but unbuttered bread, then to a bar where he ordered plain soda water, then to a brothel where he never undressed, and then to a banquet where he avoided the host.

●●●●●●●●

"The founder of an institute? I don't think so. It must be another Dr. Puzo I have in mind."

Beppe stared at the man whose posture deserved admiration and whose house resembled a castle. He stared, nodded and smiled, well aware that Stefano and Marcello had coached him for such moments but unable now to recall their speeches. The music, close and deliberate, distracted him. It spoke to Beppe, called out his name, while the man opposite him chatted and sipped wine.

The violinist had just started a solo when Alfredo Perelli approached and, in whispers, sent Tomassino from the ballroom. Beppe remembered the violinist's tone—warmth seemed to radiate from the instrument—as well as the tune, the solo, from the strolls he and Dr. Puzo took after dinner, the hour when this same violinist serenaded the waterfront, head tilted and oblivious, Beppe understood, to all but the music, a series of notes: hand positions and strokes. And now, in the midst of the banquet, Beppe stood—for he had risen when Alfredo Perelli addressed him—not more than four meters from the violinist but still could not listen to the full composition, prelude to coda, without a detour or a discussion.

"So, Mr. Arpino, if it's not too much trouble, describe for me, please, Tomassino's rescue."

Beppe knew that such a request would occur at some point, but the response Stefano and Marcello helped him prepare seemed too theatrical now. With music behind him, their parries and thrusts would look more like dance movements. Besides, Beppe had never been one to boast, and what he had done to help Tomassino was unremarkable compared to what the violinist accomplished in each measure: feats that, except for a small audience of six—Beppe and Tomassino's classmates—went unnoticed in the ballroom and uncelebrated.

"Well, sir, there's not much to describe." Beppe focused on Perelli's features: the autumnal hair and pale skin, the lips wet with saliva and fermented fruit. "I heard noises outside—not the usual sounds, cats and the like—and looked out and saw, in the lane down below . . . "

"Ah, here she is at last."

Beppe, concentrated as he was on Perelli's face in an effort to block out the music, was surprised to see that Tomassino had returned to their corner with a woman beside him, perhaps a wife or fiancée. She planted a kiss on Alfredo Perelli's cheek, and he then turned her toward Beppe.

"Mr. Arpino, I'd like you to meet my daughter, Angelina."

She resembled her father, Beppe noted, more than her brother, stood taller than Tomassino and appeared sturdier, and her hair showed no trace of pomade; instead it consisted of curls that fell to her shoulders, the kind of hair, Beppe knew, that often rendered the scalp inaccessible. "Difficult to cleanse," Dr. Puzo had once told him, "a paradise for lice."

"It is a pleasure, Miss Perelli, a sincere pleasure." Beppe nodded as he had at others, then added a few more rehearsed words. "Miss Perelli, never before have I seen such a beautiful dress." The truth, though, was that the dress was less stylish than others at the banquet: a cloak as opposed to a sheath.

"You're too kind, Mr. Arpino." She produced a fan and fluttered it, as if to compensate for the dress's poor ventilation. "And we're all so thankful that our Tomassino was rescued."

Beppe, never comfortable with praise or other forms of attention, even when he expected them, and anxious to hear more of the music, hoped that Alfredo Perelli or Tomassino would take charge of the conversation, but neither appeared inclined. The father just sniffed his wine, while the son moved to rejoin his former classmates. Thus Beppe, for the first time ever, was forced to entertain an aristocratic female. He reminded himself of what Stefano had said in preparation for the banquet: "You must flatter the women, Bonaparte. The more compliments, the better."

"Miss Perelli, that dress, it's . . . it's . . . exquisite."

Yes, Beppe almost repeated himself, but at the last moment he found an appropriate substitute for the word *beautiful*. The effect, however, was no different than if he had offered the same remark twice: an awkwardness that was as apparent to others as were the wrinkles in Beppe's suit. Even Angelina sensed the discomfort in him and tried to ease it with more thanks. "You're too kind, Mr. Arpino, much too kind." And while that effort seemed to work—he then commented on her fan—she could not ignore her own disappointment. Angelina had hoped, based on how her father talked about heroes, that Mr. Arpino would be an exception to the suitors, and from a distance, as she watched him from a secret perch earlier, he did appear different. He lacked the strut that others had perfected, their burnished suits, and was more interested in the musicians than in the whereabouts of women around the room. But as soon as Angelina heard him speak, she realized her mistake. His words were similar to those of all suitors: hollow compliments, in this case for a dress that was old and needed alteration. But she could not turn her back on Mr. Arpino as she did the others, not after all he did to rescue her brother. The question, then, was how much more would have to be endured before she could excuse herself and sit with Tomassino's friends, the few men in attendance whose comments were sure to be spontaneous and whose motives could be trusted. Wealth was not the object of their affection.

"As a matter of fact, Mr. Arpino, I do admire Titian." Angelina looked to her father for support, aware that he expected more of her and would be disappointed with her impatience. Still, he had never denied Angelina in the past, and this time was no exception.

"Mr. Arpino"—he stepped forward and spoke as if to a friend—"let's hear some more about that rescue, shall we?"

The interruption was a relief for Beppe, too. He had exhausted his repertoire of compliments and questioned the wisdom of discussing art with a patron's daughter. For all he knew, the ballroom itself could have been painted by Titian. The rescue of Tomassino, on the other hand, was familiar terrain.

"Well, sir, as I said before, there were noises in the lane down below, and when I looked out, I saw several . . . "

Another interruption: a delicate chime, like a bell mated with flutes, that blended with the string instruments, that shared its pitch with them and captured Beppe's attention. The sound lasted for several seconds, an interval that gave Beppe time to conclude that it was too refined to report a fire and too sedate to delineate the hour. It was, he decided after Alfredo Perelli made a reference to food, the announcement for dinner.

●●●●●●●

Salad, pasta, veal, beans: Beppe had sampled each dish set before him—all overcooked and overseasoned—drank more wine than was wise, recounted the rescue in full—though minus any mention of Tomassino's time in the bathroom—and listened for an hour to Alfredo Perelli discuss paper—manufactured in the Far East, Beppe learned, five centuries before its appearance in Europe—but the real test was still to come. Kind to Beppe until then—he had seated him in a place of honor at the main table and toasted him at the start of dinner—Perelli now wanted to hear about Beppe's plans for the future. It was the one speech that Stefano and Marcello had not helped him prepare.

"Well, sir"—Beppe watched as a servant removed their plates—"when I'm finished with dental school, I intend to . . . "

"What?" Perelli spoke as if startled. "You're in dental school?"

Beppe nodded. "Yes, the Naples Institute for Dental Arts." It helped that others at the table were deep in their own conversations. "That's the one I mentioned earlier, sir, the school Dr. Puzo founded."

"The infamous Dr. Puzo."

"Yes, and he wrote a book called *Teeth*." Beppe warmed to the subject. "It's a classic in the field."

New plates were set before them . . . for the fourth time.

"*Teeth*?"

Dessert plates: cannoli: the dead baker.

"Huh?"

A fine white powder like confectioner's . . .

"The book, it's about teeth?"

Beppe returned to the banquet. "Yes, teeth." No more bakers, no more priests. "I memorized it from cover to cover."

"What a coincidence," Perelli said, "an expert on teeth." He prodded the cannoli with a fork: massive, the size of an expensive salami. "Then I suppose you've noticed my daughter's teeth." He broke off a small piece and lifted it to his mouth. "Her dentist says they're the finest he's ever seen."

Beppe copied the proud father, nervous with anticipation—it had been more than a year since he tasted cannoli—but, after the first bite, disappointed: sweet, much too sweet. Was it the death of Mr. DeBono, he wondered, that made a once-favored dessert now distasteful? Was it the Neapolitan recipe? Was it Dr. Puzo's dietary influence? He could not decide; all three seemed reasonable, unlike Perelli's last comment. If a woman had such beautiful teeth, she would smile, show them off, and not be so quick to flee. But Beppe did not want to disappoint. "I'm sure that she has excellent teeth, sir."

"Very diplomatic." Perelli set the fork on his plate. "I admire that, Mr. Arpino." He clapped Beppe on the back. "You'd make a fine businessman. In business, as in life, it's better to avoid decisions based on secondhand information." He removed the napkin from his lap and placed it crumpled on the table. "I often visit the forests where we harvest just to feel the bark, and no matter what, I insist on spending at least one night in a hotel before I'll purchase it. So I understand your hesitation, Mr. Arpino, and admire it, but at the same time I can't help feeling like you don't trust me. And there's nothing I hate worse than that."

Perelli then called over a servant and whispered instructions—Beppe heard the words *chair* and *lamp*—stood up, tapped a glass with his fork—Stefano and Marcello had explained that this meant a speech would soon follow—and addressed the dining room: ten tables, each with ten people.

"Attention!" he called out. "Attention, please!" Perelli reached down and took hold of Beppe's lapel, then pulled on the loose fabric until the two men were side by side. "Mr. Arpino here, our hero, is, I've come to find out, also a dentist."

Beppe, with the hundred heads turned toward him and a heart about to detonate, wanted to offer a correction—he would not be a professional for some time still—but suspected that it would make no difference.

"And who better than a dentist," Perelli continued, "to appraise the worth of a woman's teeth?"

Angelina almost choked on her cannoli. What had been a pleasant meal until then, protected as she was from harassment in a seat between two of Tomassino's friends, now promised to become painful. What her father proposed was akin to an auction, and while her teeth, Angelina knew, were exceptional, a feature that she had never wanted to trade—her frame, by contrast, could have been smaller and her hair finer—she had no interest in their public appraisal or in an examination at the hands of a disheveled impostor. Yes, Tomassino had said that Mr. Arpino was a student when she asked for details before the banquet; now he claimed to be a dentist. What other lies had he told their father?

She scrutinized him, this Mr. Arpino—if that was his real name—who stood at the end of the table: somewhat different in appearance from the other suitors but just as opportunistic. For all she knew he could have helped plan the attack on Tomassino. With the Fascists, even an act like that was possible. She read the leaflets, heard the rumors. The prime minister himself was said to have had opponents killed. Yet some of Angelina's female friends found the man attractive—a few even clipped pictures of him from the newspapers—and tried to convince her that a square head was a sign of intelligence, a broad chest indicative of vigor, and an interest in music—he played the violin—revealed a sensitive nature. But Angelina had her own ideas. The sort of man she hoped to marry would not be so vain as to pose bare-chested on a pair of skis, and he would never associate with hoodlums. He would be articulate but not loud, clean but not polished, and honest, modest, and handsome.

Her father motioned for her to come forward—a chair had been placed beneath a lamp—and told those who wanted to observe the inspection to form a circle. Angelina then felt herself rise from her place at the table and approach the chair—illuminated there and expectant—as if she were suspended from strings: a puppet en route to its execution.

●●●●●●●●

Beppe appealed to Tomassino, seated beside him—a quick look intended to communicate need—but the man he had saved in the lane responded with silence. Likewise, the would-be patient, seated across the table between two of her brother's friends, raised no protest. Expressionless when Beppe first met her in the ballroom—he held the dress responsible—she now headed toward the chair, calm and passive, as if such requests were part of all their banquets, like the musicians who had followed them from the ballroom—to distract Beppe and taunt him—or the salt that polluted their overcooked food.

"Come, Mr. Arpino, and prepare to be impressed." Alfredo Perelli—a tall man, a tree—walked Beppe to the soon-to-be-occupied chair while people at the other tables followed suit, their collective racket, their voices and footsteps, so much like the sounds of penned cattle that for a moment Beppe expected Rosselli to appear armed with a cleaver.

"But sir, perhaps I should wash first." He could never put his hands into someone's mouth without at least a rinse; that would be akin to murder.

Perelli snapped his fingers—"Some water and a napkin!"—and within seconds Beppe's hands were cleansed.

He then drew nearer to the woman, dark-haired and cloaked and still closemouthed, but stopped when he noticed what looked like sparkles on her forehead and on her upper lip. He blinked, rested a palm on the back of her chair, blinked twice more. It was the lamp, Beppe realized, its heat—her perspiration—so he adjusted the device as his instructors did before their demonstrations. If Perelli wanted to call him a dentist, then Beppe would act like one. The question was what sort of examination should be conducted. Beppe's first impulse was to keep it as brief as possible, just a peek to please Perelli. But with the people now around him—an audience, a mob—a performance seemed in order. Well, he would let the teeth determine what happened next. As the instructors at school so often said, "Each mouth has its own agenda."

Beppe leaned forward, lower and lower until his face was on the same plane as hers and the distance between their heads was such that lice in search of new pastures could have leapt from one to the other with ease. He paused, bent there, and waited, waited as one would await the appearance of dawn, but the mouth before him did not open. It remained closed, sealed, impervious, shut. She could have had a mouse hidden in there, a little chick.

"Please, Miss Perelli, I'll make this quick."

The comment, which sprang spontaneously from Beppe and surprised him as well as her, was bold, but once spoken it seemed appropriate—the kind of thing a dentist would say—and that, in turn, provided Beppe with a sense of relief. Yes, despite the lamp and the sparkling perspiration, he now felt a coolness about him, a coolness not unlike the breeze from an open bedroom window. And perhaps there was a breeze, an open window, because Beppe then heard, at the instant that her lips began to part, what sounded like a door slam somewhere in the house.

A door did close—the front door—but air was not the reason for its movement. The publisher pulled it, and while he would later fear that he had used too much force in the effort, no one other than

Beppe, not even the tuxedoed servants, noticed the sudden exit, which led Alfredo Perelli to wonder afterward whether the stout man ever attended the banquet. But Linati had been there, as those who sat beside him could confirm, and he did eventually attempt to socialize. At first it was difficult for him to pretend that all was well— as stubborn a depression as he had ever known—but as the dinner continued, a smile started to form on the spherical face. The answer, Linati saw, was twofold: burn all of Dr. Puzo's books, all the manuscripts and proofs, and spend more time in Rome. The first act would help stall the dentist's ascension, while the second would make it easier for the publisher to befriend those in power. He would host dinner parties, not unlike Perelli's banquet, and invite all the top officials, even the prime minister himself.

The plan cheered Linati, and his appetite returned in time for the cannoli. Now he would be able to thank the host, a most important paper supplier, with all the enthusiasm that protocol required. But just as he was ready to approach the main table, the announcement came that sent another cloud his way. "Attention . . . our hero . . . a dentist." And while Linati knew that it was impolite to storm from the house— not to mention reckless since contracts hung in the balance—he had no choice but to leave as soon as possible. He could not endure what promised to be a celebration of Dr. Puzo's profession. It was as if the lunatic had taken a seat at Linati's table, so palpable was his presence in the room. Even the hero's clothes, fashioned from what appeared to be wrinkled curtains, reminded Linati of his foe.

From warm to cool to cooler, from fall to winter.

Alfredo Perelli had spoken the truth. Her teeth could not have been whiter or more uniform nor the flesh around them more pink and vibrant, while her breath, even after their overseasoned dinner, smelled as if she had just rinsed with flavored antiseptic. Compared with the illustrations found in textbooks—even those in color—and the mouths he had viewed at school—people off the street and fellow students—what Beppe saw before him now was somehow different, not natural at all but the product of an artist. Each tooth looked as if it had been taken out and polished, buffed to a luster, then reset so that the fit between teeth was seamless, flush as boards in a bleached dance floor or hairs in a taut bow. The result was almost too perfect to be real: a mouth as it would appear in a dentist's dream or, if the place existed, in dental heaven.

As Beppe studied the teeth, oblivious to the promise he had made to be brief and the rise and fall of the cloaked bosom below him, he returned once more to the afternoon when he sat for Father Vincenzo as she now sat for him. How different it would have been if Beppe's teeth had looked like hers. "A catastrophe!" the priest exclaimed minutes before he left the room and collapsed upstairs; the words still echoed in Beppe's head.

Since then Beppe had tried to make amends, with brush and powder, mouthwash and floss, and improvements did occur—Dr. Puzo went so far as to compliment him once—but never would Beppe's teeth be likened to pearls nor would their order be better than haphazard. Unlike poor posture, which could be corrected with exercise, and internal ailments that responded to an improved diet, Beppe would have to live with teeth that were nowhere near as perfect as the ones now before him, just as he would live forever with the pain that he inflicted upon Father Vincenzo, a pain that no doubt helped kill the priest.

Still the breeze, the coolness—a splendid view, as from atop a steeple—but then, like smoke trails from a distant fire, the flaw revealed itself: a shadow on the lower left side, a crease in the second bicuspid.

Beppe doubted himself at first. He was new to examinations and must be confused. Plus, the mere suspicion that what he saw was a hairline fracture filled him with despair. How nice to believe that one mouth in the world was free of imperfections, even nicer to think that he stood in its presence. A second later, though, the realist in him took over. "Miss Perelli," he said, "open wider, please, and, if at all possible, tilt your head back a little more."

A murmur went up behind Beppe, who would have seen, had he turned around at that moment, a hundred people on tiptoe. And had he continued to watch those people he would have noted the disbelief on their faces when, with a matter-of-factness that left no room for denials, he lifted a hand, palm open as if for alms, and requested a butter knife.

Astonished? Yes, and dumbfounded, too. Alfredo Perelli was all that and more before it occurred to him that the comment was a joke. Of course, he reasoned, a butter knife, of course, at which point he laughed. "You've a keen sense of humor, Mr. Arpino!" He pointed at the prankster's expectant hand. "You almost had me there for a second."

It was a rare show of excitement for Perelli—the tree transformed into a child—and all the more exceptional because it occurred at a banquet. Finally someone had cheered him, had enlivened the frustrated matchmaker, and for that Perelli wanted to embrace the man, the hero and student, but he quelled the desire when it became clear that Beppe's expression would not turn into a smile. It seemed that the request for a knife—as droll as it was preposterous—had been, Perelli now understood, serious.

The realization delivered a thud to Perelli's midsection, and another thud arrived soon afterward—two blows from a blunt ax— when a servant returned with the knife. Perelli had no choice then, thanks to the audience, but to stand there and watch as the knife was proffered and accepted and, as in some carnival routine, inserted into his daughter's mouth. Never before had a piece of flatware assumed such a horrific aspect. But worse than the fear that it would harm her—the tip was rounded, the blade was dull—was the suspense. Perelli, otherwise patient as a monk, felt as if he would explode. A butter knife? What business did that have in a woman's mouth? Well, whatever the dentist intended to prove, the outcome had better be favorable. The last thing Perelli needed—if he hoped ever to have grandchildren—was for Angelina's most salient feature to be maligned in public.

There was a buzz when he struck the tooth—miniature, like an invisible tear in her fan—that she could still hear an hour later and still
feel as a small vibration in her jaw as she touched her face to her pillow. She could also feel the hand on her chin and the breath on her
cheek—an intermittent brush—just as she could still smell moth-
balls and soap, ricotta cheese mixed with saliva. It was as if the
examination continued or that it had never ended. Either would have
pleased Angelina. In fact, she wished that he had tested all her teeth:
the knife a mallet and her mouth a marimba. But had he done that,
her interest would have waned. Because what she liked about him, at
least what she liked first, was the professionalism with which he carried out the chore. From the manner in which he washed his hands—
as a painter would clean prized brushes—to the soft tones that he
used for directions—"Miss Perelli . . . please"—to the reassurances
with which he consoled her father—"It's a simple procedure, sir, and
the discomfort will be minimal"—he had won her trust and confidence. Not once did he attempt to flirt with her or to lean on her
bosom. A flatterer no more—another suitor would have abused the
situation—he made her feel at ease. It was a feat that Dr. Luccetti,
her dentist since childhood, could never have accomplished.
Whereas Mr. Arpino was serious and focused, the other favored dra-
matics: applause when she opened her mouth at the start of an examination, tears when she stood up to leave, and threats if her father
attempted to settle the bill. He would be hurt to learn that she had an
appointment with a competitor, but the fact that the appointment was
with a man referred to as the finest dentist in Naples—Mr. Arpino
promised to coax him out of retirement just for the operation—should
provide some consolation. The news comforted Angelina, as did Mr.
Arpino's offer to assist with the procedure. She knew that she would
feel safe with him there, would feel protected. In contrast to her
father, who acted as if the paper mill were threatened with demolition, she saw no cause for alarm. Rather, she looked forward to the
date—uh, the appointment—with much anticipation.

As happened before, Angelina felt her cheeks heat. The pillow was cool, but her face was on fire. How unusual for her to blush alone in the dark or, for that matter, under a lamp at a banquet. The reason was Mr. Arpino, who had somehow moved her, but attempts to picture him now proved fruitless. He was a voice, a collection of smells, wet hands hidden in a napkin, and a temperament that was neither slow nor rushed but deliberate. What Angelina wanted, though, were visuals—a nose, an ear, an outfit—and their absence hampered her swoon: a reminder of just how brief the encounter had been and how dangerous it was to suppose too much. For all she knew he now resented her—an imposition, a burden—and deemed her unattractive: weak teeth and thick hair, a dress that fit her like a raincoat— almost nineteen but still no interest in fashion—and cheeks red as a peeled tomato.

"I hope that didn't hurt," he had said after removing the knife from her mouth.

No, he had not hurt her—just the opposite—and now, in bed and anxious to know what the future held—the answer was love, a proposal, and heartache—she found it difficult to believe that such a calm and considerate man would ever hurt her. But he would hurt her, later, as happens in all relationships. And after the final hurt occurred—a desperate act meant to impress her—she would think back to the moment two years earlier when, alone following their first contact, she had not been able even to picture him in her head. And she would ask herself then, at that later date, whether, despite the time that had passed since the banquet, he had ever come into focus.

●●●●●●●●

The musicians paid and departed, the invited back in their own homes, the servants excused until next time, the father upstairs and dressed for bed, the sister as well, and Tomassino alone below in the ballroom, where the darkened chandeliers were now slow ships, their undersides covered with shells, and he a man thrown overboard whose pockets were filled with stones. Even the quiet, so odd after a hundred loud farewells, was like water in his ears.

He had come there, to the ballroom, to the spot where he sat beneath the center chandelier, because experience told him that upstairs he would curse the smallness of his room—not small at all but seeming to be so at times like this when his thoughts wished to wander. If he could have walked outside then without fear of attack, he would have done that instead. But the ballroom sufficed, with its papered walls in shadow now—an effect that lent them extra depth— and its several chandeliers: sometimes ships viewed from below and sometimes clustered stars.

It was not the first time that Tomassino had used the ballroom for contemplation, though he had never before needed it after a banquet. Under normal circumstances, the events left him too tired to do more than mount the stairs and put himself to bed—all those hands to shake, all those fake smiles. But sleep was inconceivable to him now as he pondered the last few hours. Was it love? he asked himself. Was that what he had witnessed?

Whereas most men in their midtwenties were married or in the midst of one or more courtships, Tomassino had no experience with romance apart from what he read in books and saw at the theater. He had never even loved from afar or nursed a broken heart. In other words, it remained an abstraction for him, much like advanced mathematics. And as such, he did not at first trust his own conclusions. Perhaps it was another emotion that had caused his sister to blush. It could have been embarrassment: there were a hundred people anxious to look inside her mouth. Or fear: when Mr. Arpino asked for the knife, even Tomassino, just an observer, felt his temperature rise. Embarrassment, fear—either would explain the reddened complexion, but Tomassino also had to account for the smile that followed the examination and her uncharacteristic titter. Indeed, though the news from Mr. Arpino was not uplifting—it almost felled their father— Angelina behaved as if she had been awarded a prize.

Tomassino studied the chandelier overhead—its circle now a barnacled ship's bottom, now a telescope filled with stars—and remembered how, when he and his sister were both children and home a modest apartment, their father would suspend himself from a similar but smaller fixture and impersonate an ape: upside down and ill mannered, the silliness in him infectious. Sometimes he pretend-ed to be an acrobat, the World Famous Mr. Papa, and would perform impressive stunts for them: somersaults across the carpet, pirouettes off the wall. How different that man from the one upstairs—not just older now but beaten, drowned; the barker—"Attention, please!"—transformed in seconds into a melancholic mute. And all because of a small human flaw, invisible even to its possessor.

What peculiar circumstances, Tomassino noted from that spot beneath the water's surface, beneath the artificial stars, for love, if it was love, to awaken. The poets spoke of colorful fields and the moon's influence on the heart; none had ever mentioned, at least that Tomassino could recall, encounters at crowded banquets or the use of butter knives. He wanted to ask Angelina for clarification, an expla-nation, but she, too, slipped off to bed as soon as the house emptied. Thus Tomassino found himself alone and left to wonder about the secrets hidden in people's mouths and the appeal of wrinkled clothes.

∞∞∞∞∞

"Mr. Arpino, I was about to summon the police."

Except for the times when their bladders disrupted their sleep at the same instant and demanded to be emptied, this was the latest—well past eleven—that Beppe had ever seen his mentor out of bed. But unlike those bathroom encounters, Dr. Puzo was now dressed—no pendulous privates to watch out for—and alert, so alert that he had opened the door before Beppe could reach the handle.

"What a relief, Mr. Arpino. I feared those aristocrats had won a new convert."

Beppe, by contrast, was exhausted and had no interest in the tea Dr. Puzo offered once the door closed behind them nor in another conversation. His voice, worn thin, now needed rest, as did his mind, which could hold no more information, could decipher not one more word. How he made it home from the Perelli's house would remain a mystery—the route had confused him earlier—as would the exact manner in which he informed Dr. Puzo that an account of the banquet would have to wait until later. In a trance Beppe climbed the stairs, brushed and flossed, then washed and went to bed, where he soon fell asleep as if clubbed unconscious, the insomnia pummeled into submission, overpowered, floored, thanks to a woman, to a look into her mouth, thanks to love.

Dr. Puzo suspected otherwise. Based on articles that he had read about soldiers returned from the battlefield, it seemed clear that Beppe suffered from a kind of shell shock. A sensitive person, a musician, he had visited the trenches and been exposed to scenes barbaric and cruel; thus traumatized, he would need time to recuperate. So Dr. Puzo let him sleep, despite his own desire to hear about Beppe's reaction to the banquet and to tell him about the miracle that occurred soon after he left: a request for a newspaper interview. At last Dr. Puzo would have a forum, an adult one that reached thousands, to expound on matters related to health. The reporter who had made the call also left behind a newspaper that mentioned Dr. Puzo and the fables, and while Dr. Puzo had never before considered himself a man of one or another political stripe, the kind words expressed in the piece convinced him that to be a Fascist was perhaps best. The editorialist made it sound as if the welfare of the masses mattered to the people who now held power, whereas in the past Dr. Puzo had felt as if he were alone in his efforts to break backward habits, to educate and clean.

It was a disappointment, therefore, when Beppe declined Dr. Puzo's invitation for tea, but at least he had returned from the banquet. There was that to celebrate, too. For Dr. Puzo had panicked when at ten and then eleven Beppe did not appear. He found the trust he possessed tested as the hours passed, and now, the ordeal behind him, he felt chastened. Beppe had proved himself again: the heir apparent, a worthy successor. No trace of that hunched creature from Cortenza remained save for an occasional blank stare and the fixation with teeth. That was the last hurdle for Dr. Puzo to clear: he must convince Beppe that childhood dreams were meant to be abandoned. It would be a crime if, as still planned, the boy moved back to his hometown after graduation and spent the rest of his life removing plaque.

Dr. Puzo poured himself a cup of tea and settled down to prepare for the interview. For once, sleep would have to wait—unhealthful, Dr. Puzo was quick to admit, but unavoidable given the circumstances. As a doctor, he knew from experience that the opportunities for embarrassment in the course of even a brief interview were plentiful. Too often had patients, in response to serious medical questions, revealed secrets that one hoped their mothers never lived to hear: a past indiscretion, an embezzled sum. One woman, when asked to describe her health as a child, mentioned what she used to do after school—it involved cold cream, Dr. Puzo recalled, and a neighbor's pet—while another woman, acned but refined, confessed her desire for a scandalous tattoo. He had a male patient, a watchman addicted to caffeine, who sometimes alluded to thefts, and a retired naval officer with an ulcer who once referred to himself—a slip, Dr. Puzo assumed—as Isabella, Queen of the Open Seas.

Needless to say, Dr. Puzo harbored no secrets. For all he cared the newspaper could print the names of former sexual partners in boldface and ask them for quotes. Nevertheless, he felt it important to appear as credible and articulate as possible in the interview no matter what the topic. Since the editorial described him as a true Fascist, Dr. Puzo would learn more about what that meant. He would learn much more, in fact. Little did he know it at the time, but the subject soon would become for him an obsession. Weeks he would devote to it, months; even after Beppe finished school, a dentist himself now, Dr. Puzo still would be enthralled.

THREE

Rome, not Venice or Milan, not Palermo, not Florence, and not Verona or Trieste, Parma or Assisi, or even Naples, is the center, the navel, the place where north and south meet, where laws are written, where leaders take residence and keep mistresses, where Julius Caesar was killed—just off Via de Chiavari—and schoolchildren tour ruins and, across the river, the Pope sits for his haircuts. It is famous for its seven hills, all rather small—the Celio the smallest— and its fountains and churches. People in China know what the Colosseum looks like, and Eskimos have visited the Sistine Chapel. Before London and New York, the world had Rome. And now Rome had Beppe.

He arrived on the first train from Naples—it was dark when he climbed aboard—and despite the private compartment and the clean sheets, he did not so much as nap. Unlike most travelers, even fellow insomniacs, even recruits headed to their first battles, Beppe did not find a train's movement restful, reminiscent of the crib. He never felt lulled on trains. To the contrary, the scenes outside the window, sunlit or black, captivated him much like music. But more than the visual stimulation—the farmhouses and beaches, the shepherds and tramps—it was the anticipation that excited him, the wonder of what was ahead: the unfamiliar and unknown or, on a return trip, home.

A man met him at the station, a man who held a placard with DR. ARPINO printed on it in neat script. He picked up Beppe's new valise—

it contained clean socks and undershorts, toiletries and papers—and led him to a car. Beppe had driven in cars before—Alfredo Perelli hired them for weekend excursions—but never before had he been in Rome: the nation's capital and home to the Catholic church; the prime minister lived there, and not far from him slept the Pope. Yes, it seemed that Beppe had known about Rome all his life. He remembered how back in school Miss Donati would hammer its names into their heads—Romulus and Remus, the Tiber, the Pantheon—and how in the afternoons Father Vincenzo would also talk of Rome, a place where novitiates, Beppe learned, went to meet nuns.

The driver remarked on the weather—hotter than usual—and pointed out a few landmarks—palaces, ministries, a theater closed for repairs—as he shuttled Beppe from the station to the hotel, the streets as crowded and chaotic as those in Naples but the insults different. Whereas a Neapolitan would slander one's relatives—in most cases, one's mother—the Romans, at least from what Beppe heard in the car, favored direct attacks and made use of metaphors that, more often than not, included some mention of food. A pedestrian's buttocks, for example, were likened to mounded polenta, while the driver's brain was compared to a prune.

"You see that over there?" Beppe looked to where the man behind the wheel now pointed: a vacant lot. "Last week it was all houses, and soon it will be a parade route."

The comment could have been a boast or a lament; Beppe could not tell. He did not know the driver well, nor the condition of the homes before their removal. But the comment still provoked a reaction in Beppe: Ever since he learned that the home back in Cortenza had collapsed on itself—the picked walls no doubt a factor—rubble or references to rubble or to land once littered with it made him think of his mother and brother and sister—all, thank heaven, outdoors when the floors met—and his promise to return once he finished school. For someone who considered himself decent and truthful and who, even as a dentist, tried to protect others from pain, the demolition served as an awful reminder: a needle pushed into him and twisted, wrenched so that it scratched bone.

The car slowed before a semicircular drive—curses sounded in response—made the awkward turn into it, and rolled to a stop. Beppe's door opened, and a man dressed in a crimson jacket leaned in and smiled. "Dr. Arpino," he said, "welcome to Rome." Beppe returned the man's smile, then stepped out of the car, thanked the driver, and walked into what would prove to be his final home.

●○●○●○●○

The report had taken Dr. Puzo months to finish—not a word left to chance—but a week before he was to leave for Rome, the illness struck him down. No one saw its approach, not even Beppe, who still lived with Dr. Puzo despite the fact that he was now finished with school and had opened his own dental practice. He was with Dr. Puzo just hours before the first seizure, and his mentor had seemed fine: as emphatic as ever—"A person should never sit when he can stand, never stand when he can walk . . . "—and optimistic about the future. "Success," Dr. Puzo had announced over their usual breakfast of fresh fruit and whole-wheat toast, "is near at hand," a prediction that he followed with excerpts from a speech to be delivered later at a luncheon—the luncheon at which he collapsed—that described what he wanted the report to accomplish. His plans for the Italian people were, to be sure, ambitious: collective sports and field calisthenics, classes on health for expectant mothers, a national radio program— *Adventures in Hygiene*—and an essay contest for children: "How Cleanliness Affects Me." And while these initiatives were certain to face resistance in some circles—even the prime minister had to twist arms—Beppe knew that in the end Dr. Puzo would prevail. He was much too determined to settle for less, too stubborn and idealistic, too forceful, too intense. Thus it came as quite a shock to Beppe when, that very afternoon, a nurse from the hospital appeared at the office to tell him that Dr. Puzo was under its care.

"He's conscious," the nurse explained—her outfit even whiter than the one Beppe wore—then added in a somber voice, "but I would come sooner rather than later," so Beppe canceled his next appointment—a routine cleaning—and rushed to where Dr. Puzo had

been taken after he disappeared behind the podium in midspeech—
the audience at first convinced that the fall, like the pauses in other
places and the passionate hand gestures, was for emphasis—and now
rested on pillows of the sort he had deemed unhealthful in books now
out of print: thick as filled flour sacks, wicked on one's spine. But Dr.
Puzo was too weak to protest. And the pillows, it so happened, eased
somewhat the discomfort: not the feverish chills that made him shiver or the blurred vision that dizzied him or the unstable bowels and
bladder, the countless cramps and pinches, the wooziness, the shortness of breath, no, but the backache that the bed induced thanks to
a mattress that offered less vertebral support than even feather pillows. Dr. Puzo was, to state the obvious, in trouble, and he understood
that to be the case. Since the luncheon, when the words before him
started to swim and the listeners' heads faded from view, he had tried
to arrest the affliction, but those attempts had failed, and now he
found himself captive in a hospital staffed with men no more interested in the preservation of life than most morticians. Dr. Puzo knew
their kind, these so-called professionals with their bleached coats
and stethoscopes; it was only a matter of time before the scalpels and
saws appeared, the mops for sopping up blood.

He shifted position and, like a break in the painful haze that
enveloped him, experienced relief, as if he drifted free, but it lasted
only a moment before the ailments returned. Whatever the illness, its
advancement was swift and ceaseless. At first, as people surrounded
him and the podium, he suspected a bacterium, but he had eaten at
home beforehand—never trust prepared food—drank plain water at
the luncheon, and not touched another person's flesh in weeks. Then
he decided, in those lucid bursts that came and went like the hospital's nurses, that he must have contracted a virus. Perhaps it was
influenza—he did hear a sneeze at one point in the speech—or
mononucleosis and, in either case, would soon pass. But the pains
were so acute and varied—like a sampler of medieval tortures—and
his mind so confused that Dr. Puzo, an expert on complaints too elusive for traditional practitioners, could not determine what he had nor
predict its outcome. Even death seemed possible. In fact, death

seemed more and more probable as the minutes passed and the discomforts multiplied, which forced Dr. Puzo, athletic and never drunk, a responsible chewer—in short, a man whose personal habits were faultless—to admit for the first time ever that he, like others less careful, was mortal. Ah, but the time for such a revelation could not have been worse, because the dream had almost been fulfilled. And that awareness, without a doubt, caused the worst soreness: to have come so close—the report had been printed and bound, the train ticket issued—and still be denied.

The coarse hospital sheets now pinned Dr. Puzo into place, while the pillows threatened to suffocate him. He tried to readjust these but could not lift an arm, and the call he made for a nurse's assistance came out as a shallow rasp. Yet someone did appear after a pause: a white shape at the door, blurred and indistinct.

Beppe rechecked the room number—it matched—then blinked several times in quick succession, but the numbers remained identical. Some mistake had been made. After all, was he to believe that the person on the bed before him—a face sunken and mournful—was the same person who had championed calisthenics a few hours earlier? The same person who just the day before had tossed the medicine ball as if it were a brown balloon? No, the patient here looked more like someone transferred from a rest home.

Beppe turned to leave, and the patient rasped what must have been farewell. A wave in response, then Beppe started down the hall. Yet ten paces on he stopped and reversed direction. Ashen skin and cadaverous expression aside, that rasp had sounded familiar. It took a moment for Beppe to recall the specifics, but he soon made the connection. Yes, he had just returned home late from the banquet when Dr. Puzo accosted him at the front door: "What a relief, Mr. Arpino. I feared those aristocrats had won a new convert."

As with the patient's rasp, the voice remembered from the past communicated, also in anxious tones, a desire for Beppe's presence, which hurried him back down the hall. To be wanted again: it warmed Beppe to think that the distance between him and Dr. Puzo was about to close. Indeed, since he first announced that he would establish a dental practice rather than follow Dr. Puzo's lead and become an advocate for public health, Beppe had suffered the strain in their relationship. Sometimes he felt more like a patient late for an appointment than a friend, a student, or even a tenant. Never once since the announcement had Dr. Puzo inquired about personal matters—so eventful for Beppe now—or the just-opened dental practice. Perhaps he had no time for these topics—the report seemed the new focus—and assumed that because his former apprentice was set to wed a Perelli he had adopted her family's aristocratic practices. The truth, though, was the reverse: over time Beppe had introduced numerous improvements to the Perellis' dinner table and convinced them all to take more strolls.

He approached the bed, and the resemblance soon became apparent. It was Dr. Puzo there beneath the sheets, fevered and stressed: a source of heat, Beppe noted, not unlike a fire.

oo oo oo oo

"Yes, I promise. Rest assured, sir, I will."

The first step down the spiral staircase. But how could he have refused the desperate request, even if acceptance meant difficulties both at home and at work? As Beppe saw it, he had no choice but to honor Dr. Puzo's wishes, and it pleased him at the time to comfort the man who had done so much for him in the past. A trip to Rome seemed small in comparison to the shelter and the food and, most important, the education that Beppe had received after he arrived from Cortenza, the cello strapped to him like a backpack, the battered valise filled with slick bottles. The elixirs inside those bottles were supposed to protect him, and though he never drank the strange fluids—the memories of previous treatments still too vivid—little harm befell Beppe while in Naples. He found a mentor when he needed one and two friends—Stefano and Marcello—a woman who loved him and, later, office space at a reasonable rate. Even Dr. Puzo's disappointment in him vanished at the end.

"Do well, son," he rasped between spasms, and the old closeness, much to Beppe's relief, returned with that familial address. And not a moment too soon, because death came quickly to Dr. Puzo. Beppe just had time to send for the cello—at the office to soothe dental patients—and perform a slow E-minor waltz at bedside—a proven painkiller—before the last utterances and the final, failed attempts to breathe.

"Caterina!" Dr. Puzo called out—not the first time Beppe had heard her name, but never a face to join with it. "The forest was quiet and still!"—the opening of an anti-tobacco tale for children, one that the radio station still broadcast occasionally. "A minute wasted is . . . is . . . "

The words then trailed off as consciousness seemed to leave Dr. Puzo, so Beppe, in a voice almost as labored, finished the statement for him: "A minute wasted, sir, is lost forever."

And that, Beppe came to believe, was the moment Dr. Puzo expired, for there were no more outbursts, no new movements save a few twitches, no further respiration, and no response when the nurse, summoned from down the hall, slapped the impassive patient. But Beppe was mistaken, because Dr. Puzo's mind lived on for another minute: He visited Milan once more and lectured the nation's dressmakers, then traveled south to Pisa where a woman with a crooked spine invited him into her boudoir. Next he joined the prime minister to demonstrate deep knee bends before the assembled masses in Rome, then returned to Naples where a fat man tried to sell him books for use as firewood. The scenes flashed and shifted, the plausible and the absurd, a kaleidoscope inside the head of someone more dead than alive and soon not alive at all.

Health Advocate, the headline read, *Dies After Brief Illness*, and in the narrow column that followed Dr. Puzo's career was reviewed for those unfamiliar with it: the start as a simple dentist, the establishment of the dental institute and the authorship of its first textbooks, the switch later to comprehensive health—prevention as well as treatment—the fables written for broadcast, the public presentations, and the planned visit to Rome. The illness that prevented the trip, though, was never specified. Even the doctors Beppe asked could provide no answers. Thus another person close to him had expired in a sudden and inexplicable manner: first a father doubled over in a distant corridor, then a priest collapsed on the carpet, a baker flopped atop an unfinished cake, and now a mentor propped up on pillows. Life seemed a series of these surprises, and one could not avoid or hope to understand them. An itinerant bandit could be poised around the next corner, knife unsheathed, or it could be a woman with spectacular teeth. In the first case death was almost certain to occur soon after the encounter, while in the second it would take a bit more time.

●●●●●●●●

A look at the pocket watch presented to him at the banquet—after the crack had been discovered and Alfredo Perelli's fears somewhat eased—told Beppe that he had more than an hour before he was scheduled to meet with the man who, if all went as planned, would help him deliver Dr. Puzo's report, the report that now sat in Beppe's valise, which in turn now sat unopened on a squat platform that appeared to have been built for no other reason than to support valises. The man in the crimson jacket had placed the case there a moment earlier when he escorted Beppe to the room. He had also opened the shutters and, before he left, pointed to a velvet rope that hung in one corner from the ceiling. "If ever you need assistance, sir, just pull this." The room even had a handsome Victrola.

Beppe should have known that he would receive special treatment. In less than three months he and the hotel's owner would be related; it made sense, then, that the room Beppe occupied at the Perelli Grand would have sophisticated touches: Oriental carpets, for example, and a painted urn. Still, he would have preferred to do without these features. Suppose he tracked in mud or toppled the decorated vase? And that rope: Dr. Puzo would have ripped it from the ceiling. Such modern conveniences, he had stated more than once, simply catered to laziness.

Beppe stepped over to the window and, as learned from the master, took a deep inhalation—ventilation, ventilation, ventilation—then paused before he exhaled to admire the view: a small piazza with its own stone fountain. It was quiet and peaceful, a space protected

from Rome, from what surrounded the hotel. The curses and conges-
tion seemed as distant as home.

Beppe released the air that filled him and pulled the shutters
closed. Just a little past noon, but already he wanted to leave. If not
for Dr. Puzo's deathbed request, he would have departed then, without a moment's hesitation. It made no sense, minus that errand, for
Beppe to be alone in a place he had planned to discover with someone else. No wonder Angelina had tried to dissuade him. But there
were other reasons, too.

Another look at the pocket watch told Beppe that only three minutes had passed since its last inspection, which meant that he still
had more than an hour until the appointment. A nap was out of the
question, while a stroll—suppose he wandered too far? What Beppe
needed was music; that would help pass the time. To be specific, he
would have liked at that moment and for the next half hour to have
the cello close at hand and let the sounds it produced distract and
relax him as those same sounds distracted and relaxed dental patients
before their examinations and made them, Beppe had learned in the
months since he finished school, easier to treat: their mouths opened
wider after a chorus or two, and their inclination to scream lessened
provided the tune was not too somber. Of course, novocaine was still
required for some procedures—extractions and the like—but music
helped those patients as well. And while the interludes added several
minutes to each appointment, which meant that Beppe saw fewer
patients per week than most dentists and therefore could expect a
smaller income, their inclusion provided him with more time at the
cello than had been possible since childhood.

But the instrument was not in Rome. Beppe had left it back at
the office, with the other painkillers. Scars from the last train ride,
when he followed the coast north to Naples, were still visible on its
surface. He would not risk additional trauma, not for such a brief
visit. Fortunately, there was the handsome Victrola.

He lifted the arm—it resembled an inflated dental implement—
and set the point down on the platter. It took hold; it followed the
curve. A scratch next, a scrape, like a comb drawn across the listener's

scalp, and then, as the violins arrived, the eerie surprise: a composition first heard at the first concert Beppe ever attended, which was also the first event to which he ever escorted a woman.

Stefano and Marcello had recommended that he ask her to the concert, even offered up their seats for the occasion—"Our Bonaparte with a hand on a Perelli's knee!"—and Beppe, desperate to make a favorable impression, had followed their advice. If the friends had told him to walk her past the nearest prison and toss her hat over its fence, he probably would have done that as well. For when it came to women and courtship, at that time Beppe still lacked experience.

"You've never had a sweetheart?" Stefano asked, the cane across the desk beside him. It was a week after the banquet, and the three students had just listened to a lecture on dental oddities, those rare but memorable cases that kept practitioners on their toes.

"A sweetheart, Stefano?" Beppe shook his head. "I'm afraid I haven't."

"Not even a sister's friend?" Marcello, for reasons unknown to Beppe, had left his cape at home.

"No, her best friend was our brother." He remembered the tattered doll, Old Icardi, and their attempts at resuscitation. Beppe had found it waist deep in a rubbish heap on the walk back from school; what made him think that an aristocratic woman would want to be seen with someone who used to climb around in rubbish? A reasonable question, to be sure, but not one that Beppe could have answered then with words or pictures. It came down to how she looked at him and how that look made him feel: a boldness similar to what had carried him from Cortenza to Dr. Puzo's door twelve months earlier now pushed him toward her. He would ask Stefano and Marcello to coach him and, when he went to check on the repairs as requested, would repeat their words to her as at the banquet. And he would do it no matter how improbable the union. Otherwise he would be forever haunted: that mouth, those teeth, the ease with which she accepted her flaw.

"Miss Perelli, I have tickets to a concert this weekend, and I wondered if . . . "

Stefano corrected him: "I would be honored if . . . "

"And I would be honored if you would accompany me."

•○•○•○•○

A voice broke the silence—"Bravo!"—then another voice "Bravissimo!"—and then applause such as he had never heard before. It sounded like the arrival of several trains into one station, and it churned like trains, rumbled like them, sent vibrations like enclosed locomotives.

Beppe joined in the applause, but he did so as much from relief that the concert was over as in appreciation for the excellent performance. It had been a mistake, he realized too late, to have scheduled two firsts for the same occasion. He could concentrate on neither the music nor the woman beside him; the minute he focused on one, the other would distract him, and for an hour and a half he went back and forth: from the snare drum to the bare arm at his elbow to a clarinet solo to the ankle exposed when she adjusted her skirt. Thus it surprised Beppe to find that melodies from the concert, entire sections, came back to him later when he picked up the cello. Because at the time, with the orchestra before him and a date to one side, he had felt distracted and dizzied, self-conscious and tense: as if he were about to be called up from the audience and handed the baton.

Yes, Beppe could neither calm himself at the concert nor relax—a common complaint from new suitors—but Angelina had her anxieties, too. A woman who, until the banquet at least, had been able to control her disposition, it disarmed her now to find her palms moistened and her heart aflutter and a smile pasted on her face that made her look, she suspected, like a recent parolee. And that titter! Even as a child she had resisted such emissions. The worst, though, was the fear that he would kiss her. Suppose she fainted when their lips touched? It had never happened before—widows fainted, and anemic children—but she had once found Tomassino passed out in the ballroom; perhaps their blood carried that weakness. Yet at the same time—and this was what most confused her—she hoped that he would kiss her. Not in the concert hall—too public, too soon—but on her doorstep later. And if she fainted there, well, he had carried her brother to safety, so a precedent of sorts existed. But whether or not he kissed her then and no matter what her reaction, at least she had a better idea now, thanks to the invitation, of how he felt.

"Miss Perelli, I have tickets to a concert this weekend, and I would be honored if you would accompany me."

He had just inspected the work done to her mouth—"Dr. Puzo," he reported, "did a masterful job"—and the request somewhat shocked her. Her father was still in the room with them—a matter of life and death one would have assumed based on the rate at which he paced—as was Tomassino. But their presence did not deter Mr. Arpino. No, he seemed above the usual protocols. Whereas other suitors would have waited for a moment alone and then produced boxed chocolates, he spoke what was on his mind without hesitation or expensive props. And the look with which he accompanied the words—a stare that made her feel as if no one else in the world mattered—just added to their impact. It was all she could do not to leap into the air and click her heels.

"Well, I think I can," Angelina replied and looked, out of deference, to her father, but he seemed distracted and did not offer consent or voice objection. Tomassino, on the other hand, who stood behind their father, nodded in what appeared to be approval. "Yes," Angelina said at last, "a concert sounds like a fine idea."

If the response pleased Mr. Arpino, he concealed it well. Perhaps there was a smile that flickered in the pause that followed, but otherwise he just stood there for a moment and stared, then blinked a few times and returned to the subject at hand: "So, Miss Perelli, does it hurt to chew?"

Some women would have taken offense—a suitor, it seemed, was expected to dance in the streets when he received an acceptance— but Angelina understood that this man was different. The frills and flourishes common in others had been traded for a simpler, more modest demeanor. He was serious and at the same time had a tenderness about him. But most important, Angelina believed that she could trust him. Whereas she once doubted his motives—at the banquet before he looked into her mouth—she now wanted to tell him all her secrets. And that would happen in due time. For the moment, though, she contented herself with the fact that he had invited her to a concert. That he failed to toss confetti when she accepted did not disturb her. Rather, she envied his reserve and tried to match it.

"A little," she answered, then put a hand to her jaw near the place that had ached. "It's still sensitive."

•••••••••

He took no tea or coffee, just warm milk, which he sipped between sentences at the café across the street from the concert hall, the café that later became known to them as Our Café but then was just a convenient place to sit and chat after the performance. She had asked him about school, and in response he described for her a recent lecture.

"There was one with roots that formed an arch—a bicuspid that must have been—and a molar with holes in it that whistled when the patient breathed. Our professor said the man sounded like a referee."

She tittered at that—no control—while her date sipped more milk.

"Another molar was soft and smelled like cheese, and there was one cuspid"—he measured an invisible fish—"well, a friend of mine, Marcello, insists it was a tusk." He told her about other oddities: the two teeth fused like twins, the tooth with worms in it, the tooth that resembled a Catholic saint; some were black, he said, and some transparent, but all were kept in the same peculiar place.

"A tin box? And the professor carries it around with him?" Suspicious now, she watched for traces of a smirk or smile. Teeth with animals in them, teeth that whistled.

"Yes, I used to think it held his lunch."

She would have chuckled then—no more titters—had her companion not maintained such a credulous expression. He offered no indication that what he said was untrue. And he would look equally sincere a week later—the same café, a different table—when he told her about Dr. Puzo—wooden clubs and prescriptive clothes, a handshake ban and disdain for all restaurants—and described, the week after that, some of the people back home in Cortenza: the barefoot ex-politician, the vintner-priest, the anti-Neapolitan butcher. Never once in the course of these tales did he show the least disbelief. There was no misdirection that she could see, no attempts to tease, which after the wisecracks of Tomassino's friends and the polite lies of most suitors became another attraction. It refreshed her to be with someone so unaffected and pleasant. But as she learned on that first date—the discussion had moved on to more personal matters—he also knew pain and disappointment.

"Stabbed in an American hotel," he explained when she asked how it had happened. "I was nine at the time."

She waited for him to continue—the sorrows of life without a father—but the pause only expanded: a second, then ten seconds, then a minute, then more. It was not an uncomfortable pause, though, not awkward like some she had endured. It did not make her want to revive the conversation or stand up and leave. Oddly, she felt herself drawn closer to him as the wordlessness persisted. In a crowded post-concert café, a shared silence, she discovered, could be quite intimate, and the louder the sounds around a couple, the more private and insulated its space. Thus when a sudden cheer went up inside the café, it seemed then as if she were alone with him in a secluded cave or on a precipice somewhere distant. The exact location did not matter provided that the place isolated them and, more to the point, inspired affection.

She reached a hand across the table. That is, she made the next move.

●○●○●○●○

Advice had come at him from all sides: from Stefano and Marcello, whom Beppe had asked for help; from Dr. Puzo, whose counsel was unsolicited but nonetheless welcome; from Alfredo Perelli, whose paternal cautions were expected; and from Tomassino, whom it was a nice surprise to hear from. And while the comments of one man sometimes conflicted with those of another, Beppe tried his best to take it all in and form a mental consensus.

"Like a cat, Bonaparte," Stefano explained the afternoon before the first date. "You have to be prepared to pounce at a moment's notice." He made a paw with his free hand for emphasis.

"Yes," Marcello added, "when she least expects it." He copied Stefano's paw and made as if to pounce, but because of the cape—back after its unexplained absence—he looked more like a bat than a feline. Still, Beppe understood: the element of surprise, the hunter and the hunted.

"So, if I'm a cat," he ventured, "then that means she's a mouse?"

"Excellent, Bonaparte!" Stefano presented him with the cane. "The poor girl doesn't stand a chance."

Marcello draped his cape over Beppe's shoulders. "I suspect she'll never know what hit her."

An hour later, Beppe received advice of a different sort from Dr. Puzo. He had been directed into the den—"Please, Mr. Arpino, have a seat"—and thereafter addressed from across Dr. Puzo's desk, which was covered, Beppe noted, with open newspapers and Fascist books.

"The time has come, Mr. Arpino, for us to discuss an important matter." The matter, Beppe soon learned, was venereal disease. "Now, I'm familiar with the misinformation that prevails in backward places like Cortenza, and for that reason I think we should start from scratch." Dr. Puzo then held up a picture of an unclothed woman. She resembled someone who used to shop at Rosselli's, but that woman, Beppe was certain, never left home without at least a shawl. "Attractive, no?"

Beppe studied the picture some more, but before he could form an opinion about the woman's appearance Dr. Puzo answered the question.

"Of course, Mr. Arpino, just as nature intended. And these"—he pointed to her lips, then her breasts, then her pelvis—"are the major enticements." Dr. Puzo set the picture aside and focused on Beppe. "But beware, because a man takes his life in his hands when he approaches a woman." He paused for a moment as if to reflect. "Yes, terrible afflictions: blindness, joint disease, peritonitis . . . rational minds can be turned into mush." Dr. Puzo then described the fate of a renowned mathematician whose demise he had witnessed. "A hopeless case," he said, "and such a waste. Toward the end, as I recall, the man couldn't even drool without assistance."

Beppe was therefore instructed to take certain precautions. "First, assume that all women are infected. Some will offer denials, but don't be fooled; I've treated more nuns for this than prostitutes." Dr. Puzo opened a desk drawer and produced what appeared to be a coin purse. "Second, never leave home without one of these." He opened the purse—well, more like a packet—to reveal what he called a contraceptive sheath. "Don't underestimate its value, Mr. Arpino. Men have been known to kill for these." Beppe, however, found it difficult to feel much enthusiasm for an object that looked for all the world like a scrap that had been picked up off the floor of a butcher shop. Nevertheless, he pocketed the purse and assured Dr. Puzo that it would remain with him at all times.

Alfredo Perelli's turn came next. Another few hours had passed, and Beppe was now seated on an upholstered sofa—the cloth featured raised flowers—in what looked to be the mansion's parlor. The servant who led him there had said that Miss Perelli would be down in a minute. The servant had also offered him a drink—"Wine, sir? A cocktail? Some mineral water perhaps?"—but Beppe declined. He wanted to remain lucid. There was much to remember, much more to come, and even a little carbonation could be trouble.

"Ah, Mr. Arpino!" Alfredo Perelli marched into the room. "I had hoped we would have a moment alone." He picked up the chair closest to the sofa and moved it closer still; the fabrics, Beppe noticed, matched. "A concert," he said as he lowered himself into the chair, "I think that's wise. She likes music; Tomassino, too. But what about after the concert? What then?"

Stefano and Marcello had suggested a waterfront stroll. "Well, sir, if it's not too late, I thought we could walk down to the . . . "

"A café, Mr. Arpino." He clamped a hand on Beppe's knee. "I took my wife to one on our first date. Trust me, a café."

"Without a doubt, then, a café it will be."

"And don't order for her. Angelina hates it when I do that."

Beppe appreciated the warning, though not the pressure being applied to his knee. "I'll remember that, sir. Anything else I should know?"

"She has her idiosyncrasies, Angelina, as all people do, but don't let them discourage you." The hand held like a vise. "What I'm saying is, keep at it, Mr. Arpino. You've come farther than most."

At the sound of footsteps, Alfredo Perelli stood and repositioned the flowered chair. Beppe rose as well and almost faltered: a soreness in his knee. But it was not Angelina who appeared at the door as expected. It was her brother, hair as slick as ever, who soon seated himself at Beppe's side.

"So," Tomassino started, "this is quite an occasion."

Beppe nodded. To call it a milestone, he felt, would be to underestimate its importance.

"And has Father here—oh, I see he's left." Alfredo Perelli had drifted from the room. "Well, did he have any last-minute advice?"

"As a matter of fact," Beppe said, "he did suggest we visit a café."

It was Tomassino's turn to nod. "There are plenty in that area. Just keep to the main streets. Remember what can happen in a deserted lane late at night."

Beppe remembered, though it seemed like months had passed since the assault that introduced them.

"It's also best to avoid that park not far from here"—the same park Stefano and Marcello had recommended for its darkened paths—"which is where Blackshirts are rumored to lurk." Tomassino looked toward the door then back at Beppe. "Which reminds me, Mr. Arpino: steer clear of politics if at all possible. It's a subject that gets my sister—oh, here she is now."

●●●●●●●●

As soft as a velvet cushion. No, softer than that and moist, more like a moss perhaps, but cleaner and sweeter . . . and soft: cannoli without the crust.

He kissed her first on the doorstep. Or she kissed him. Their heads moved toward one another, and whether he led and she followed or vice versa seemed irrelevant since neither resisted. It was a brief kiss, though, as polite as passionate, after which Beppe excused himself and hurried home, where he then climbed into bed and waited: too late for the cello, too restless for sleep. The window, open as usual, let in a breeze that should have cooled him, but it did not cool him. Or it cooled him too much, sent shivers into him. Hot one moment, cold the next: temperatures of late had been subject to wild fluctuations. First he ordered warm milk, then he wanted ice. Amid the cheers that went up when the conductor paraded past the café— no baton but still an arm aloft—she had reached out and touched Beppe's wrist with a hand that could have been frozen or in flames. Yet he did not flinch or recoil. No, he let her hand remain there, where she had put it; he would, with a smile even, suffer the burns or the frostbite, whatever happened as a result of her touch. It was as Dr. Puzo had said: women did inspire a certain recklessness in men. And Beppe was no exception. Soon he would cover her outstretched hand with one of his own—in a café of all places—and later, on the walk back to the Perellis' house, he would crook an arm for her to take— the streets no less crowded than before—and on the doorstep, despite the suspicious shadows visible in two windows, he would lean into her and pucker.

The shadows? Tomassino behind one thin curtain and Alfredo Perelli behind another, both men anxious to find out how the date went and both surprised when the farewell took the form of a kiss.

Well, it was not the kiss itself that surprised Tomassino. He had seen the couple's approach, taken note of the linked arms and the unison steps, and knew that these often foretold more. In a book or at the theater it would have been no different. What made the scene exceptional was its particulars: how restrained the embrace—almost imperceptible—and how awkward and unsure the kiss and abrupt its finish. Even the best actors overlooked these details—the frail hesitations, the meek departure—and instead all but wrestled their partners to the floor. Such coarseness had never appealed to Tomassino, refined and slender, but until then there seemed no real alternative. A lover needed to be confident and dramatic in order to win affection. Yet the episode on the doorstep proved otherwise, and it was this realization that jolted him and awoke in him a sudden desire, one new for Tomassino, to render the scene in verse.

Alfredo Perelli also experienced a shock in response to what happened on the other side of the window, and while it prompted no meditation in him on the nature of romance, no new vocation, neither was he displeased. In contrast to those fathers who would have rushed outside and crippled the would-be defiler—quite a few kept implements at the door just for that purpose—Alfredo Perelli wanted to invite him in and propose a toast. He restrained himself, however, because an interruption at that point would have been foolish. The celebration could wait. All that mattered for the moment was that a suitor had breached the first lines of defense. As for the fact that she had appeared to offer no resistance, where did one surprise end and the next begin? After all, who would have guessed that a rumpled-up dental student, a man too timid even to shake hands, would have succeeded where men far more sophisticated had failed? He was polite, Mr. Arpino, and he was sincere and had a talent for his chosen profession. Were these the attractions? Perhaps. But the truth was that Alfredo Perelli had no idea, and although he could have asked, in the end it made no difference to him what the reasons were provided that the couple married and proceeded to breed. A house filled with rambunctious children: for the first time ever the prospect seemed more feasible than fantastic. And to think that a cracked tooth had started it all. No, an assault had started it, the incident in the lane. Hard to believe, but those Blackshirts deserved some credit, too.

∞∞∞∞∞

Scrape, scrape, scrape, scrape . . .

Beppe finally lifted the arm—a molar pick blown up in size—and returned it to its cradle. Somewhere, maybe on the other side of that platter, the piece continued. He would listen to the rest later. For now, he had to prepare for the appointment. A look at the pocket watch told him that there was only half an hour to spare. The music, as predicted, had worked on him like some narcotic.

Like some narcotic: an apt metaphor in Beppe's opinion, for music did, he believed, have medicinal qualities. And what a shame it was that Dr. Puzo never researched the subject. It could have opened up new frontiers for a man who favored nonintrusive methods. Beppe, at the valise now, both hands on its buckles, could almost see the titles lined up on a shelf: *Pain Relief and the Piano, The Conductor's Smile, What Mendelssohn Cures, Oboes: A New Treatment for Hives*. But alas, those important books were never written. Instead, Dr. Puzo devoted his final years to the report—its cover now visible inside the unbuckled valise—and occasional speeches, the fables for broadcast, and the little new research he conducted was more historical, more political, more personal than scientific. An idol to others—Beppe, to name one—he had at last found someone else to revere.

"I'm impressed, Mr. Arpino. He's different from the others. He's a breath of fresh air."

Beppe could still hear the enthusiasm that was in Dr. Puzo's voice when he made that pronouncement. In what seemed like an instant now—a month or two at most—the man Beppe most admired had become an admirer himself, a follower, an obsessive devotee. He went from someone who lamented the ineptitude of Rome and called its few health initiatives criminal and insane to a supporter of state policies who all but worshiped the man behind them. It was a radical shift, one that at first stunned Beppe, but soon he realized that it also made perfect sense. Like Dr. Puzo, the prime minister, as Beppe learned, wanted Italians to improve themselves: less pasta and wine, less excess, and more self-control. The fact that the man exercised at dawn and drank a special tea before bed and wore oversized shoes no matter what the occasion and favored a salute over a handshake just added to the attraction.

"Did I mention that he refuses to use elevators? Yes, and he's known to climb stairs four at a time."

No detail was too trivial, and Dr. Puzo shared them all. Some surprised Beppe: He had never suspected that such a stern man—the square head, the humorless expression—could possess the sensitive nature of a musician. Yet Dr. Puzo said he owned a violin. And others confused Beppe: "I'm told he changes his uniform five times a day." But whatever their effect, Beppe soon knew more, thanks to Dr. Puzo, than most Fascists about the editor-turned-politician known to all now as Il Duce.

The platter stilled, the valise split open, and the documents in hand—the report and related papers—Beppe headed downstairs to the car that the hotel—Alfredo Perelli—had reserved for him. But unlike the overdone apartment, with its urn and imported carpets, the vehicle seemed appropriate, even crucial, under the circumstances. Rome, the nation's capital, home to the Catholic church, was immense and complex—its train station alone warranted a street map—and Beppe needed a driver who could be trusted to deliver him and the report to their first, and hopefully final, destination: an address, written in Alfredo Perelli's hand, on a slip of expensive paper.

The man in the crimson jacket held open the door for Beppe, closed it once Beppe was settled, then raised an outstretched arm as the car eased itself back onto the road. A wave? A salute?

Beppe read the address to the driver, who nodded once—"I know a shortcut"—then honked twice to spur the cyclist before them. In the distance, past the other cars, Beppe noticed a crumbled structure that appeared to be shrouded in dust. Another parade route? Another collapsed house? He clutched the report, held it close. If all went well, tomorrow he would hold her. And he would kiss her as he had on that first date and all the dates since then. And the kiss, as happened whenever their lips met, would be returned in full. But for such a kiss to occur, first Angelina would have to calm down.

ꝏꝏꝏꝏ

Tomassino had warned him to avoid the subject—in the parlor before the first date—and apart from Alfredo Perelli's café recommendation, it was the best advice that Beppe received. And for their first few dates he had been able to follow it. Instead of politics, the conversations had focused on school—he never missed a class—and Cortenza

—she seemed to find the place peculiar—and Naples—her birth-place—and music—a shared interest. He told her about what happened in New York, and she, in turn, described for him her own mother's fate: a fever when Angelina was still an infant. It was almost a month into their courtship before Beppe learned the reason for Tomassino's caution.

They had just taken their seats in the café when applause started—not uncommon, since the conductor made the rounds after each concert. When Beppe looked out onto the street, though, he did not see the man he expected march past. One arm was held aloft, and if not for a uniform instead of tails he could have been another conductor, but the resemblance ended there. Whereas the maestro smiled and escorted blondes, the officer scowled and surrounded himself with soldiers. In addition, the applause he received sounded different: less exuberant than respectful, without the loud bravos. And perhaps it was that audible difference that caused Angelina to turn her head—otherwise she stared at Beppe—and then, once she had done so, release Beppe's hand, which he assumed meant that she also wanted to clap. But what she wanted, he found out the second he burst into applause himself—the man must have been a hero of some sort or an ace or a renowned commandant—was to remove an irritant from her lashes.

"You'll have to excuse me if I don't join in," she said a moment later as she studied the once-bothersome speck. "I have a problem with Fascists."

The comment silenced Beppe as a stroke would its victim. What sort of problem? he wondered, concerned now that he had somehow offended her. Then he remembered Tomassino's advice: steer clear of politics if at all possible. "So, will it be tea as usual?"

"I mean, what's there to clap about?"

She did, Beppe could tell, seem puzzled, but he persisted: "I think I'll stick with warm milk."

"It amazes me," she continued, undeterred, "when a man like that, someone who deserves about as much applause as a . . . well, a convicted felon, can walk down the street and all these people"—she waved a hand to indicate the café patrons—"will jump to their feet. It just amazes me."

It did not amaze Beppe. He lived with a man who a few weeks earlier had been flattered to find himself described in print as a true Fascist. There were books related to the subject now scattered about the house, and the conversation at each meal was peppered with their contents. Indeed, had Dr. Puzo been in the café, he no doubt would have been the first to stand and the last to be seated. What a relief, then, that Beppe's mentor avoided such places. But the problem still remained: how to move from politics to a new topic. Beppe tried music—"Is it just me or was that soprano a little flat?"—then casual observation—"I hear it's supposed to rain tomorrow"—then an anecdote from school—"The teeth were so rotten, it looked like a mouth filled with licorice"—all to no avail.

"I don't understand," she said after that last remark, "because the more I learn about them, the more obvious it seems."

The choice now was between silence—just the usual nods and smiles—and a response based on what Dr. Puzo had told him about Fascism and the masses. Beppe chose the former, which proved, as he discovered when he did quote Dr. Puzo in subsequent discussions, to be a time-saver: another minute in amazement—"But he's a dictator, for heaven's sake"—then she seemed to shake it, and her stare returned to Beppe, her hand returned to him, and the desire these stirred in him returned as well.

○●○●○●○●○

A spell, a dream-like state, a sustained hallucination: how else to describe those first months, when flawed mates are perfect and their presence soothes like a balm applied to the heart? A charmed condition for the parties involved—enviable, too—but one that sooner or later, as with ointments and anesthesias, wears off and allows for discomfort to enter and discord—impossible to fathom earlier—and sometimes distrust and, in the most extreme cases, even dislike and hate.

She sat opposite him in the café. It was another date, a week or two later, and another ovation had just started, which prompted

Angelina, as on that first date, to extend a hand across their table—
the secluded cave, the precipice somewhere distant—but when her
hand reached Beppe he felt tense, and when she looked at him he
appeared distracted, and from the corner of her swoon Angelina saw
the uniformed reason.

"Authoritarian rule," she remarked as the Fascist marched past
them, "its appeal escapes me."

But unlike what happened the previous time she mentioned politics, Beppe did not attempt to redirect the conversation now with
unrelated comments. Instead, he responded, after a brief pause, as if
asked a direct question.

"Well," he stated as the applause subsided, "some people think
the discipline is overdue."

It made sense that such a compassionate man would take into consideration the other's side no matter how ludicrous its position. Still,
Angelina could not leave the statement uncontested. "Discipline?" she
asked. "As if we're all children? Who in the world wants that?"

Again, Beppe made her feel like an interviewer. "I can name one
person," he said, "as an example. Remember Dr. Puzo?"

Dr. Puzo: the man who had tended her mouth; the best dentist in
Naples. "You mean the Dr. Puzo I met? With the white pajamas and
spectacles?"

Beppe nodded. "He's happier now than I've ever seen him."

The picture became clearer. Angelina recalled the stories Beppe
had told her about Dr. Puzo on previous dates—the wooden clubs,
the handshake ban—and the brusque manner in evidence at her dental appointment did, thanks to this new information, seem to her now
rather imperious.

"So, does that mean Dr. Puzo is a . . . "

But the question did not need to be finished, because in Beppe's
face she could read the answer. Yes, incredible as it sounded, a
Fascist had worked on her teeth. And the man, believe it or not, was
her date's mentor: incredible, simply incredible. Yet these realiza-
tions, which under normal circumstances would have set off loud

alarms in Angelina's head, launched no panic then. Just the opposite: the news amused her. She found it ironic rather than repulsive
that the person she wanted to spend all her time with lived with one
of them. How curious! How comic! She squeezed the hand still held
and asked him to continue.

He returned her smile. "How about a quote?" She could have
kissed him then and there. "I remember once Dr. Puzo told me—it
was the afternoon I arrived in Naples—that indolence—laziness—is
a hostile foe whose armies surrender to discipline."

He recited the line—or so she believed at the time—as a humorist
would a pun, which helped her overlook its content. "So clever," she
said after he had finished. "Are there more where that came from?"

A spell, a dream-like state, a sustained hallucination: what
should have burned like acid in her ears—the nonsense learned from
a Fascist—instead tickled her with pleasure. A charmed condition,
to be sure, and one that, in some form or another, would survive those
first months and stretch well into the future. In fact, not until Beppe
left alone for Rome did Angelina see the difference in their views as
the impediment it had been from the start. What prior to then had
seemed a minor obstacle when considered next to love now, with
Beppe's departure, sat like a planet between them.

◦◦◦◦◦◦◦

A week, that was all it had taken. Not two weeks or three weeks or a
month or ten, but a week, one short week: the rate at which relationships shifted astonished Tomassino. There were times when it terri-
fied him, when he considered himself fortunate to have remained
unattached. While men and women the world over suffered in the
name of love, he retained independence and, for the most part, emotional control. Yet love fascinated him, too—as it should an aspiring
poet—and he wanted to know as much as possible about the subject.
And he had learned quite a bit, from the arts and from watching others, but like the astronomers who studied the skies, he observed it all
from a distance: he could look but not touch, speculate but never

state for certain. What was it like to sleep on the moon? And what happened to a person's heart when it opened itself up to another?

Angelina had confided in him the previous week, appealed for support, but in the end Tomassino decided that Beppe should come before politics. He still remembered that first kiss, seen from behind a thin curtain, and the tenderness in evidence then convinced him from the start that theirs was a delicate bond. It did seem a risk not to back him, not to want him to honor a deathbed request. So what if it meant that Beppe would have to meet with a few Fascists? Even Tomassino, a former victim of those brutes, would have run the errand if it were he who had been asked. Yes, he still felt indebted to the departed Dr. Puzo, the man who had been so attentive, so tactful, in Tomassino's moment of need: "Mr. Arpino, show our friend here to the bathroom, where he can wash himself and, well, relax."

Without a doubt he had been an odd man, a man with peculiar habits and a more peculiar mind—the stories Beppe told simply confirmed that—but he had also devoted a lifetime to what, mistaken or not, he believed was the betterment of mankind. And on top of those public efforts—the books and speeches, the broadcasts—he had nurtured, housed, fed and clothed, and perhaps even loved Tomassino's soon-to-be brother as a father would an adopted son.

Ah, poor Beppe. Tomassino had come to the door when he arrived with the sad news. "Dr. Puzo," Beppe had said without preface, "is dead." The plainness of the statement and the drained expression on the speaker's face would have turned a hardened criminal, a mass murderer or worse, into a tearful mess. It was all Tomassino could do to offer Beppe a sodden—and unsatisfying—condolence before he retired to the ballroom, where he stayed until, overcome hours later with sudden inspiration, he realized what needed to be done: he would honor Dr. Puzo with a commemorative poem. It took a week then for him to decide upon a title, but now that he had one he was anxious to begin.

The chair centered beneath the center chandelier—were those seashells up there or stars?—Tomassino sat down and opened the slim notebook that contained all the poems he had until then written. The six short pieces, he understood as he perused them, would seem modest, even unambitious, once Dr. Puzo's was finished. Still, Tomassino felt deep affection for the poems, a fondness that most outsiders, at least those not connected with the arts, would have mistaken for self-love. Even the worst lines pleased him, for these testified to the strides Tomassino had made since he started. Whereas he had once likened the sun to a flower—a childish metaphor—he described it in a more recent work as nature's illuminated orb. As for the butterflies and rainbows so prevalent in the first three poems, even the two set in cities, their absence from the three that followed seemed a sure sign of advancement. In other words, the evolution of the poet was evident in each successive verse.

Tomassino flipped past the last poem—a sonnet entitled "Neapolitan Sunset"—and printed, at the top of the first clean sheet, the words that it had taken him a week to find: *Requiem for a Dentist.* But the last several letters sat lower than the rest, which made the title appear to droop, as if tired, at the end, so Tomassino, forever the perfectionist, started afresh on the next sheet. He had better luck the second time, but the line still lacked the evenness he desired. He made a third attempt, the notebook held up before him now like a paper mirror, and believed he would have done the title justice had not a voice startled him from behind. In a house with two dozen rooms and only three tenants, sometimes it was still impossible for Tomassino to be alone.

"I thought I might find you here." Tomassino's father stood at the back of the ballroom, a man dressed for business, a businessman modeled after a tree. "Another poem, I take it?" He advanced across the dance floor, each step the sound of a limb snapped in two.

"Yes," Tomassino answered. "It's a new one. I mean, I just started." He closed the notebook. No one could see it, not a word of it, until the whole piece was finished. An artwork, he believed, much like a fetus, needed to incubate in a protected world. Which meant that Tomassino, a mother to six, had just conceived number seven.

"Well, I won't interrupt." Alfredo Perelli stopped where he was, half the distance from the center. "But if it's not too much trouble, please, do me a favor." He asked Tomassino to check in now and then on Angelina. It was no secret that she had opposed Beppe's trip to Rome. "If there's a problem, I'll be at the office. I have to meet with that Milanese who's interested in our furniture store." Yes, improbable as it seemed, Alfredo Perelli, empire builder, had started to sell off properties.

He then turned around—pivoted, as it were, on a heel—and left Tomassino alone to compose. Or at least to practice his penmanship: several more attempts would be needed before the title as it appeared in the notebook met with the poet's approval.

•••••••••

No question, none whatsoever, that a man could find solace in a paper mill, where the pulp refiner's cadence mimicked the heart's, and massive open vats warmed the air and moistened it and made the space, even in winter, temperate as a womb. A paper mill could also fill a man with awe: to see timber churned into butter, to stand beside steel rollers as tall as a house. And when those first flawless sheets appeared, then satisfaction could be felt and pride. Contemplation was possible, too: Where would that paper be sent? And who would use it? And what would he or she write? Suppose the sheets ended up in a book devoted to the mill that manufactured its pages? A philosopher need look no farther than the place where paper comes from for questions to ponder.

Yet for all the pleasures to be found inside a paper mill—the solace and awe, the satisfaction and so forth—pleasures that Alfredo Perelli, who had owned one such mill for decades, knew well, the time had come for him to put the business up for sale. He wanted to retire, and neither Tomassino nor Beppe was executive material. Better to sell now and deposit the profits than to put a poet or a dentist in control and flirt with ruin. The same applied to the entire Perelli empire: the hotels and restaurants, the electronics plant near Pisa. And while it hurt Alfredo Perelli to dismantle what had taken him a lifetime to build, and he would miss the mill once it was sold, would shed a private tear whenever he smelled sawdust in the same breath as chlorine or heard words like *vellum* and *parchment* spoken in conversation, he also had to think about the future and what would happen after he died to the grandchildren whose arrival he now awaited like a poplar looking forward to spring. Their inheritance needed to be sizable in order to provide them forever with the best, which was more than what a dentist could afford, or an impractical uncle.

Tomassino, the self-proclaimed poet: Alfredo Perelli looked back at him now as he left the ballroom, seated there in the center, hair slicked down to form a helmet. A little decisiveness after that attack in the lane, enough to cause a father to hope, but within weeks the old habits returned: blackouts on the dance floor and breakfast at noon. And now he considered himself a poet. Hours spent in seclusion, rather than at the mill or in the office, just to scribble a few lines about love? The world needed another sonnet like the Mafia needed another Sicilian. Worse than the pointlessness, though, were the prospects for financial reward. As Alfredo Perelli learned from the former business associate whom Beppe was about to meet, "It's more profitable for us publishers to burn such books as fuel than attempt to sell them."

Of course, that information did not dissuade Tomassino, who continued to behave as if love poems mattered, so Alfredo Perelli dropped the subject. He would not let a disappointment control him, at least not now; there was too much to celebrate otherwise: the children who would soon descend upon the house. And if one of them took the name Alfredo, it would make all the accolades received for philanthropic work seem trivial in comparison, so trivial that if ever the local politicians wanted to name a street after the soon-to-be-retired papermaker, he would tell them not to bother. But there was little chance for that in the immediate future, since Alfredo Perelli was not a Fascist. He was not an Anarchist, either. Nor did he support the Catholics or the Monarchists or the Communists or the Liberals. Given the unpredictable nature of politics, the smart businessman never took sides. Oh, one could earn a quick fortune with friends in power, but as soon as their hold weakened—and all holds eventually weaken—the favors would cease and the troubles commence. That said, Alfredo Perelli also knew that sometimes the smart business-man made exceptions, and when he learned that Beppe, despite objections, was determined to travel to Rome, he called upon that publisher friend, a Roman now with political attachments, and scheduled for Beppe a private appointment. The address? Scribbled on a slip of White Linen No. 5. The time? Alfredo Perelli glanced at the clock outside the ballroom. "What a coincidence," he remarked as he set off for work.

∞∞∞∞∞∞∞

The driver pointed to the building. "It's that one," he said, "over there. See the gigantic flag?"

Beppe saw the flag, slack in the distance, and headed in its direction. He climbed out of the car, the report pressed to him like a breastplate, and squeezed between two adjacent cars and the cyclists adjacent to them, all the vehicles for some reason immobile and their owners all irate. Never before had Beppe been subjected to so much verbal abuse. One driver called him a zucchini eater, while another said he had a meatball for a head. Their obsession with food rivaled their love for their horns: the racket these drivers produced made the drills Beppe used on patients seem mellifluous and restful.

The commotion now behind him, Beppe pushed on toward the enormous flag—down the street, through the doors, up the stairs, and along the hall. There were signs posted inside the building to guide people, but he paid no attention to these; Beppe somehow knew exactly where to go. Perhaps Dr. Puzo steered him from above. Or did he simply follow the cigar smoke?

The receptionist had not changed. And her nails still matched the bow tied to her hair, though both now were blue. "Good after-noon," she said before Beppe could introduce himself. "You must be Alfredo Perelli's friend."

"That's right," he answered, "Beppe Arpino."

She told him to take a seat. "It'll be another few moments, I'm afraid. Can I interest you in a drink?"

Beppe declined the offer. "But maybe later," he said in an attempt to be friendly. Next he admired the pictures on the wall, most of which featured the prime minister in one pose or another: the thinker, the pilot, the skier, the speech maker. Beppe knew them all, thanks to Dr. Puzo. He set the report down on one chair and lowered himself into another. It would be a while before he could afford chairs quite as comfortable as these or a receptionist as concerned with her appearance. The office back in Naples was almost bare, not much except dental equipment and a cello, and Beppe's assistant seldom brushed her hair. But deficiencies like these seemed appropriate for a new business, and Beppe, despite Alfredo Perelli's generous offers, was content to finance it himself.

"Sir?" The receptionist again. "Mr. Linati will now see you."

Beppe followed her directions—this time she did not have to write them down—and where the hall took a turn to the left he found, as promised, the open door. And there, behind a desk that gleamed like a concert piano, sat the man who had published Beppe's favorite book. And it was one of Father Vincenzo's favorites, too. A fine white powder like confectioner's . . .

Alfredo Perelli had referred to him as rotund—"And I wouldn't be surprised if he's even bigger now"—but from where Beppe stood at the door the man behind the desk looked merely plump. Yes, the smoke somewhat obscured Beppe's view, and the furniture provided additional cover, but when the man stood up and saluted, all doubts vanished. No matter what Alfredo Perelli had said, Giacomo Linati was not fat.

Beppe returned the salute. When in Rome. . .

"So, you're a friend of Alfredo Perelli." Linati motioned for Beppe to sit opposite him at the desk. "I understand he wants to retire—quite a blow for us publishers." He wore the charcoal suit of a businessman, except for the medal pinned to a pocket: a silver star with a black center suspended from a silver bar. Meanwhile, on the desk, smoke spired from a silver saucer.

"Help yourself," Linati said as he lifted the lid off a box of cigars.

Beppe again tried to be friendly. "Maybe later," he said with a smile, though the box and the smoke and the saucer made him want to frown. Perhaps Linati would find the report that Beppe held offensive. Dr. Puzo did call for a ban on tobacco.

"So, Mr. . . . "

"Arpino," Beppe offered. Names and titles—sometimes even he had to consult a patient's records.

"Yes, Mr. Arpino." Linati unburdened the saucer. "I understand you need some"—the air between them then turned white—"some assistance. Tell me, as a favor to my retiring paper supplier, what can I do to help?"

Beppe had assumed that Alfredo Perelli had mentioned the report. Suppose Linati, publisher of numerous Dr. Puzo titles and no doubt a distant friend, had not heard about the death? Beppe considered where best to start. "Well, sir, I . . . " If only he could have rehearsed. "It's complicated, you see."

"Complicated?" Linati tapped the cigar on the saucer, more for dramatic effect than to remove ash. "Then let's make it simple, shall we?" The role he played now was all too familiar. "Pass me the manuscript you've got there, and I'll take a look."

Like it or not, some people would forever think of Giacomo Linati as no more than a publisher of books. Granted, the business that he founded still churned out texts—thousands per month, now for schools mostly—and Linati did still make the occasional executive decision—he fired an editor just last week—but not since he moved to Rome had he spent much time at the home office. Linati Publishers, he discovered, could thrive without him provided the state renewed its contracts, and that was not a worry, not when the minister for education sometimes dined at Linati's table. Other politicians ate there, too—the ministers for health and finance, as well as several local officials—and once even the prime minister's cousin. As for the prime minister himself, thus far he had not accepted an invitation. But it would happen, Linati believed, sooner or later, just as he knew that with each meal served he drew closer to the dinner at which a book publisher raised on an olive farm would be toasted as the nation's newest ambassador or its most recent cabinet appointee. Soldiers would stand and salute when he entered a room, and mothers would hold up their babies in the hopes that he would kiss them. Reporters would quote him, and newspapers would publish photos: Linati and the prime minister at a Fascist celebration, the same two men in conversation with the Pope. And once that happened no one, not even an old business associate like Alfredo Perelli, would mistake Linati for just a publisher of books, the person to call when a friend needed help with a manuscript.

Linati pushed the saucer aside and set the document down on the desk before him. Based on its thickness and the possessiveness of its author, it was in all likelihood—alas—a novel. Linati took another puff, then waited for the smoke to clear so that he could read the title. Something bleak, he supposed, or something clever. It amazed him, now more than ever, how some people wasted their lives.

◠◠◠◠◠◠

The medal, awarded for service to the Fascist state—he printed selections from the prime minister's speeches and distributed these for free—Linati wore with pride. It marked him as someone special, as in a painting a halo marks a saint. And like a halo, the medal seemed to radiate and shine: a twinkle that could be seen reflected in other people's eyes, which it was now, reflected in the stare of Mr. Arpino—not a novelist at all but a courier of sorts. That lunatic Dr. Puzo followed Linati even from the grave.

The death had not escaped Linati's notice, for he still read a Naples newspaper with his morning cup of coffee. But the event was no cause for celebration. Dr. Puzo's ascent had stalled after those first interviews, and in Linati's mind the man had since taken on a pitiful aspect: too inflexible and unaware, too insistent on perfection. He did have some worthwhile ideas, Dr. Puzo, at least from a Fascist standpoint, but he misunderstood human nature. Most people detested rules, even rules meant to help them, and considered diet and exercise two forms of torture. It took the prime minister, a more sensible man than Dr. Puzo, not to mention more charismatic, to discover the answer: create spectacles that distract the public from the fact that it is being coerced.

"So, Mr. Arpino, you're a friend, I presume, of Dr. Puzo." Linati reached for a fresh cigar. "My condolences, by the way."

The visitor finally blinked. "Oh . . . thank you, sir. I wasn't sure that you knew." He appeared to consider that statement for a moment or perhaps to remember a dead friend. "It all happened so fast."

"And do we know what killed him?" Linati wanted to be sensitive, but he was curious as well. Based on what Dr. Puzo had preached, he should have lived to be a hundred. Come to think of it, he might have written a book by that title—*Living to 100* or something along those lines—which Linati might have published and later might have burned.

"No, sir, the doctors never said what happened. But I was there before he died—in the hospital, that is—and he asked me to deliver this for him." He meant the manuscript still unopened on the desk. "Mr. Perelli thought you might be able to help."

As Linati lit the new cigar—its end now snipped and softened—he considered turning the flame on the papers stacked before him. Why postpone the inevitable?

"Mr. Arpino, I wish I could be of some assistance, to you and to Dr. Puzo, but I'm afraid that my firm only publishes textbooks now, for schools, not books for the general public." He savored the fine tobacco and felt the debt that he owed to Cuba and her people. "I do, however, know of publishers who . . . "

"Sir, you misunderstand." The visitor, polite until now, had begun to wear out his welcome. "It's not a book. It's not supposed to be published. Dr. Puzo wrote it just for one person." He extended a hand across the desk and pointed to words on the manuscript's cover, words that until then had not been noticed. Linati had read the title—*How to Save the Italian People*—and seen Dr. Puzo's name—what a shock that was—but somehow missed the line nestled between them: *A Report for the Prime Minister.*

He scanned the contents: statistics, lots of them, that measured birthrates and deaths, exercise patterns, even water contamination in major cities, plus proposals, dozens it seemed, that described what steps should be taken in the home and in the classroom, on athletic fields and beaches, inside hospitals, factories, theaters—the list went on, but Linati did not. He returned the report to its unopened state and sat for a moment in silence. It was, he had to admit, an impressive document; no wonder Dr. Puzo died after he finished. The report had its flaws, naturally—some people never learned—but its merits, too. In a different form, with a narrower focus and a less alarmist tone, it could be quite effective. Yes, another way to win the prime minister's favor.

"Mr. Arpino, I'm not sure I understand." Linati decided to play dumb. "You don't want a publisher, correct?" The courier nodded. "Yet you came to me, Giacomo Linati, a publisher of books." Time to make another deposit in the silver saucer. "So tell me, please, how am I supposed to help?"

Beppe regretted the confusion. "Sir, let me start over. Right before Dr. Puzo died I promised him that I would deliver this report." Be clear and concise, Beppe reminded himself. "And . . . to be honest, Mr. Linati, I don't know the prime minister or any of the prime minister's friends or anyone, for that matter, who lives in Rome." Beppe would have appreciated some unpolluted air. "So I asked Mr. Perelli, and he mentioned your name." Certain details, such as Beppe's relation to Alfredo Perelli and the latter's use of the word *rotund,* were omitted in the interest of concision. "He said that you're a—and I quote—well-connected man."

The publisher protested. "You flatter me, Mr. Arpino."

"And since you knew Dr. Puzo—*Teeth* is considered a classic—it made sense that I should come here first. I hope it's not an imposition." The speech finished, Beppe felt as spent then as he did after a bout of calisthenics. In fact, he could have used a towel.

Now just to wait and see whether Mr. Linati would offer to help. Given all the pictures on the walls, both in the office and outside, as

well as the silver star pinned to him like a prize, it seemed reasonable to expect that an appointment could be made. If not soon, then
within the week. All Beppe needed was a minute with the man. It did
not even have to be in private. Rather, the transaction could take
place on the street. What mattered most was that Beppe be the one
who handed over the report. Remember the words? "Yes, I promise.
Rest assured, sir, I will."

The air itself now seemed to smolder while Beppe waited for
some response. So much smoke—what a car produced or a truck—
from such a simple appliance. And the smell—as unsubtle as the
perfumes that certain patients doused themselves with in an effort to
mask their breath: horrible odors, excremental. There were times
when Beppe, as close to these people as their lovers—if people who
smelled like that could find lovers—feared he would black out. And
with a hand crammed in an open mouth and in that hand an electric
drill. A lapse like that could ruin a dentist's career.

"Mr. Arpino"—a voice from where the smoke was thickest—"for
Dr. Puzo's sake"—so far, so good—"I'll see what I can do."

∞∞∞∞∞∞

News that the session had, at least in Beppe's opinion, been a success
did not arrive until the letter he wrote that night arrived, a few days
later, at the Perellis' door. Though he had offered to place a call to
Angelina after the meeting was finished, she requested that Beppe wait.

"I'd rather you didn't," she had told him, "not until you're ready
to come home."

And so, alone now in the half-darkened den, beneath a lamp that
she could easily have switched on—its tassel almost touched her
shoulder—Angelina squinted at the unfolded paper. *Dearest* was the
first word, while *Beppe*—another person would have read *Deppe*—
was the last. *I miss you*, he said. *Rome would be better if you were here,
too. But it's not so bad. The room is nice. And I have a nice driver. And
Mr. Linati is nice, too.*

He was not the most eloquent man in the world, nor did he possess
the penmanship one expects of an adult or much historical awareness.

And as far as common sense was concerned, such as what to promise a person and when, he could have used more of that as well.

And Mr. Linati is nice, too. He put the report in a safe for me. Better safe (smile) than sorry.

But in other respects, Beppe had few peers. Next to the bullies and bums, the deceivers and overachievers, who had chased Angelina in the past, he was a wonderful man: decent, honest, affectionate, and kind. Even the faults she found in him could be seen as assets if she so chose to view them. That he let Dr. Puzo twist and, in all senses, contort him also attested to how modest he was, how soft-spoken. Never once had Angelina ever heard him boast. When he first mentioned the cello, for example, on their first date or their second, she assumed that, at best, he dabbled: the sailor who carries a flute. "I'm an amateur," he said, "nowhere near the level of the professionals we've seen." Yet when she did finally persuade him to play for them, in the same room where she sat now alone with the letter, the desire she felt for Beppe quadrupled in size. Just the manner in which he held the instrument, caressed and stroked it, set her ears on fire.

Mr. Linati said that he would help. He said that he was friends with the prime minister's cousin. Can you believe it? I should know more tomorrow. At least I hope to know more. Mr. Linati said . . .

Ever since Beppe left, since he took that report and headed for Rome, Angelina had tried to feel some enthusiasm for the trip. As Tomassino said on one visit to her room, "If it's important to him, it should be important to you." But the words sounded like a formula to her, cold as an equation carved into ice; her brother must have cribbed them from a book. In the real world life was more complicated than that statement allowed. There were hazards out there that some people, for whatever reasons, could not perceive. Was a woman supposed to stand aside and cheer while her mate exposed himself to them? And if not harm in Beppe's case, then certainly embarrassment. All when he could have just slipped that report into an envelope and mailed the envelope to Rome. Would Dr. Puzo ever know the difference?

After another quote from Mr. Linati, the letter ended with praise for Angelina's patience—she did not feel patient—and a reference to the near future: *You're so understanding—you're perfect. I can't wait until I'm home.*

She folded the letter, returned it to its envelope, and placed it, as she would a napkin, flat on her lap. Then her hand reached up, as her mind wandered and her stare fixed itself on a dark corner of the den, and felt the tassel that almost touched her shoulder, its silk threads twisted like the hair on a porcelain doll. What had once seemed too distant for a person to measure—back when he proposed to her and she accepted—now seemed too near. In ten weeks she would be married, after a wait of six months, but suppose the bitterness she now tasted still remained? Bitter thanks to the report, to the promise that never should have been made—or should have been amended to include a postal option or a lesser official—and to Beppe's refusal to bend. Compromise, it seemed, was out of the question. But without compromise, what were their chances, as a couple, as friends, for happiness, for success?

The tassel, the silk threads: as cool in her hand as water, as if the lamp also functioned as a tap. Before Beppe left she would have said that she knew him. Actually, she did say that to friends: "I feel like I've known him forever. He's so open and truthful." Now, though, the comment seemed naive. People were individuals, with their own secret motivations, and no matter how intertwined two lives became there would be unknowns. Her experience with Tomassino, still a riddle after two decades under the same roof, should have told her that. Was he a poet, as professed, or a recluse who hid himself behind a notebook? And what about the interest in love? He asked questions, Tomassino, sometimes ten at a time, but never once had he confessed to a date. Was there someone who met him after hours in the ballroom? A sister could ask, but what was the point? She would never know her brother in more than a superficial sense, just as he or their father or Beppe even would never know the truth about her.

One last touch of the tassel, a trickle in the palm of her hand, before she left the den and its half darkness and went upstairs to the bedroom where she would compose an appropriate response. What she wrote Beppe would be brief, a few sentences at most—it would take a book to describe how she felt and what concerned her—and with luck he would never read them. With luck he would be home before the letter ever made it to Rome.

•••••••••

"Mr. Arpino, for Dr. Puzo's sake, I'll see what I can do."

Those were the publisher's words, as clear to Beppe now, back at the hotel where he awaited further instruction, as when he first heard them earlier in the week. Also fresh in Beppe's mind was the overripe smell of tobacco and the twinkle of that silver star: an award, Beppe supposed, for special achievement, in battle or civilian life, perhaps what Dr. Puzo would have earned had he lived to deliver the report himself, though Dr. Puzo never would have worn a medal, since he frowned on embellishments, as he called them, of all kinds—make-up, perfume, whatever encumbered the body or contaminated the lungs or interfered with the free movement of air across its surface: ventilation, ventilation, ventilation.

Beppe sat at the window—he had repositioned an antique chair—and contemplated, for yet another day, the small piazza and the old stone fountain. Sometimes he listened to music—the tune first heard at the first concert he ever attended—which helped the minutes pass, but more often he preferred silence or what seemed like silence in the center of Rome. Meals he took downstairs, at a restaurant across the street. "You'll like it," the man in the crimson jacket had said. "It's where Mr. Perelli eats when he visits." And though the food there, as at all restaurants, was too salty and rich—Dr. Puzo would have called the chef a public nuisance—Beppe liked the location.

"If someone comes for me or there's a phone call, please, inter-rupt the meal." Such was the request he repeated, before each lunch and dinner, to the man in the crimson jacket. It relieved Beppe's fear that he would miss word from Mr. Linati when word from him arrived. Still, the request led to a few false starts: once when a woman at another table draped herself with a crimson scarf and later when a waiter removed from a table the cloth upon which a patron had spilled red wine. At the hotel Beppe also jumped when he should have remained seated. Footsteps in the hall or a knock on an adjacent door, either was sufficient to make him think, if just for a moment, that the awaited hour had come.

"It could be tomorrow," Mr. Linati had told Beppe when asked for a prediction, "or next week. Who's to say? The prime minister, as you know, he's a very busy man."

Yes, Beppe knew that being a leader was a full-time job. But in addition to the usual activities that occupied statesmen, the pomp and circumstance, the amplified speeches, the prime minister raced cars and rode horses; he owned a violin, remember, and in the winter skied bare-chested. In other words, he had even less time to spare than other politicians, which meant that an insider's help was essential for the citizen, like Beppe, who wanted a minute of the prime minister's time.

"Whatever assistance you can provide, Mr. Linati, is much appreciated. And I'm sure Dr. Puzo appreciates it, too." The words, earnest when Beppe spoke them at the publisher's office, felt the same now at their recollection, with the small piazza there before him and the support of an antique chair. As old, the chair, as the fountain, and carved from wood as opposed to stone, but better preserved than the pedestal and basin outside: not exposed to the elements—rain, sleet, wind, even snow—or to vandals or birds. Or dental patients, either, for whom pain or anticipated pain was often a reason to thrash about. One instructor at the institute recommended leather restraints, even for women and children, which seemed excessive to Beppe, who preferred music, its sedative effects, its pleasant distraction. Perhaps it was time, now, for another spin of the platter.

Beppe rose, as the publisher had risen at the close of their session, when he bid Beppe farewell—"No promises, but as I said before, I'll see what I can do"—and walked around the Oriental carpets, spotless still, past the decorated vase, careful not to disturb it, toward the handsome Victrola, its base reminiscent of the box last seen on Mr. Linati's desk. So close was the resemblance, now that Beppe considered it, that the two could have been fashioned from the same tree. A coincidence, of course. But was it also a coincidence that the cigars housed in one—Beppe stopped in midstride—looked like tobacco-filled cannoli? He stood still, as if posed for a picture. And what about the music—the same here, in a Roman hotel, as at that Neapolitan concert? Even that, however, paled in comparison to Mr. Linati's presence: a friend both to a mentor and to a fiancée's father.

Beppe stared at the Victrola, which he could have reached now if he wanted and put into motion if so desired. For the moment, he preferred quiet—the better to focus, the better to think. Although the influence of Dr. Puzo had burrowed deep in him—the scientific mind had that effect on others—he also came from superstitious people, in particular a mother known for her reliance on charms and occult remedies. When the house collapsed, for example, she blamed it on a curse—a howl that she heard soon afterward confirmed her suspicion—and when Beppe wrote that he had fallen in love with an aristocratic woman, she advised him, in a rare letter, to avoid mirrors and consume more prunes. Thus Beppe, despite the medical education he had received and a skeptical mentor, still had a soft spot for premonitions, and a series of coincidences, such as the one he just noticed—the boxes and so forth—could be interpreted, he knew, as an omen, an indication that in the end all would work itself out. Beneath the chaos and surprise, the indiscriminate attacks and inexplicable deaths, the houses that were there one minute and not the next, an order existed. Dr. Puzo wrote a book that Mr. Linati published and Father Vincenzo later purchased—all before Beppe was born. And now, decades after the first man put pen to paper, their lives intersected again.

From a certain perspective, then, Beppe's presence in Rome, even the position he maintained relative to the Victrola—he could have reached out and lifted its arm—appeared to be part of some elaborate plan. And if there was such a plan, locked in a Vatican cabinet perhaps or filed up in the clouds, detailed in it somewhere would be Beppe's fate: the spiral that started when Dr. Puzo died and accelerated, as if frustrations and complications were fuel, until Beppe was dead, too.

ᴄᴏᴏᴄᴏᴏᴄᴏ

Needless to say, Mr. Linati never contacted Beppe, who waited a week before he returned to the publisher's office.

"I don't have an appointment," he explained to the woman whose favorite color now appeared to be white, "but it's important that I see him."

She wrinkled her receptionist's brow. "I'm afraid Mr. Linati has other appointments. You should have called in advance."

A call? When Beppe had all but abandoned that poor driver? "I can wait," he told her. "The truth is, I have all day."

The receptionist advised him to take a seat. "It could be a while," she said. "I'll let Mr. Linati know you're here."

Beppe appreciated her help as well as her predicament. Dentists, more than most people, knew the difficulties that receptionists faced. Seldom did patients arrive on time, and some never showed at all. So no sooner was a schedule made, with its careful increments, its personalized entries, than the schedule became obsolete. And tempers flared then, thanks to the wait, sometimes an hour or more, and the pain that delivers people to dentists in the first place. Just in the few months since Beppe opened his practice there had been incidents out front. As the assistant he hired remarked after one such confrontation—she doubled as the receptionist—"Thank heaven we use sharp tools."

No need to fear Beppe, though, at least not yet. No outbursts would be heard from him, no profanities or threats. He would take a seat and remain seated, as unobtrusive as a nun, until Mr. Linati invited him in, which could be an hour from now or several hours, after lunch perhaps or late afternoon. Whatever the wait, Beppe was happier to do it here than at the hotel. Yes, Mr. Perelli had provided him with a splendid room—the view, the vase, the Victrola—for which Beppe was grateful, but the more time he spent there, the more isolated he felt. No one, not since he arrived, had set foot in the piazza, nor had a single bird taken a dip in the fountain. And the silence that at first impressed

him—a miracle in Rome—now, after a week at the hotel, sounded
unnatural to ears accustomed from the start to other people's noise: a
brother's snores, a mother's kitchen percussion, the expectorations of
the widower next door. What relief the Victrola offered also diminished
as Beppe's desire for the cello left behind increased. Not since Father
Vincenzo died had a similar separation occurred. Even while Beppe
studied for important exams, studies interrupted by exercise sessions
and strolls, even then he and the cello remained acquainted. He would
pick up the instrument and wrap himself around it—before bed or
whenever he needed a boost—and in that position produce music:
whole notes and shorter notes, melodies and chords, the vibrations
created not unlike those set off by Angelina's womanly touch.

Desire: a topic best not dwelt upon, not if one could help it. But
who possessed such self-control? Not Beppe, not now. Even when it
hurt him, when desire made him ache inside, he could not stop it. To
the contrary, the more intense the sensation, the more stubborn it
seemed. So powerful was the desire Beppe felt sometimes that he came
to fear the arrival of certain memories or the mention of a certain name.

It was lust, he knew, lewd and animalistic, but also the deepest
affection. One stirred the other, and the other stirred the first. What
started with her teeth, at the banquet when she opened wide, now
encompassed all her features: the lips that framed those teeth, the
face that framed those lips, the curls that framed that face, the neck
that supported them all. And her hands: delicate as little birds, as
soft to the touch as feathers.

Desire, lust . . . love. No other woman inspired fantasies in
Beppe. The picture that Dr. Puzo showed him with the bare breasts
and such? It could have been a balance sheet for all the stimulation
it provided. Likewise, Mr. Linati's receptionist, her nails painted to
match her bow, her lips painted, her cheeks as well—no doubt a
woman desirable to some—awoke in Beppe about as much lust as a
clown would, or a bear dressed in pajamas. When she retreated
down the hall to the publisher's office, to announce Beppe's presence, her ample backside incited no lurid speculation, and when she

returned a minute later, the considerable bounce of her bosom failed to capture Beppe's attention. It was as if only one buttocks existed, only two breasts, and the rest were flawed imitations not worthy of a person's time.

"Mr. Arpino?" The receptionist touched Beppe's shoulder, her nails like white pistachio shells. "I spoke with Mr. Linati, and he says that it's more difficult than he expected." She smelled, Beppe noted, like cigar smoke mixed, oddly, with flowers. "He says that you'll have to give him more time—another week, he said, at least."

She talked, and Beppe listened, and the words she used he understood. But when Beppe put the words together, their meaning became confused. "I'm sorry," he said as she clicked back to her desk, "but could you repeat that for me, please?"

While the receptionist told him again what the publisher had told her Beppe separated himself from the comfortable chair. "I don't know," he said, now at the desk, too. "Another week, that's a long time. Any chance he was mistaken? I mean, maybe Mr. Linati thinks I'm someone else."

The receptionist tidied the few papers on her desk. "No, he remembered as soon as I mentioned your name."

At least Beppe had made an impression. "Well, if it's not too much trouble, I'd still like to see him—when he has a minute, that is." She had helped Beppe in the past, and he hoped that trend would continue.

"I'm afraid it won't be possible. You see, Mr. Linati's been named . . . " She made a quick adjustment to the bow in her hair. "Really, I shouldn't say anything until it comes out in the newspapers."

⚬⚬⚬⚬⚬⚬⚬

He arrived on a train to cheers in a black shirt and a borrowed coat. The March on Rome, as the event became known, was not without its ironies: a revolution in which not one shot was fired. It could have been a bloodbath, with Italians dead on either side, because their politics differed, not their skin color or their features, but instead it possessed all the violence of a recital. And that alone was cause for celebration, reason enough to mark each anniversary with festivities, with speeches. With time, however, and further achievements—marshes were turned into farmland and railroad personnel required to follow schedules—the date outlined in red on all calendars became, for most Fascists and quite a few Catholics, more important than Christmas. Parades that once featured five hundred soldiers now had thousands, starched uniforms as far as binoculars could see, and the speeches, though never brief, now lasted until the orators grew hoarse. Similarly, the preparation for these spectacles, each more elaborate than the last, became more and more a collaborative effort between Fascist officials and public servants and civilians recruited for their expertise: poets to pen slogans, composers to set those slogans to music, artists to paint them on banners, and dancers to keep the soldiers in step. One such civilian pressed into service, as the newspapers would soon announce, was Giacomo Linati.

"It's an honor," he had told the reporter who answered the phone when he called the paper, "and such an important occasion; the responsibilities are great. But as I assured the prime minister, the Italian people can trust me to do whatever it takes, even if the effort kills me."

That Linati never spoke with the prime minister—the news arrived in the mail—did not, in his opinion, make the statement untrue, for he would have said as much in person. Nor was it false, he believed, to claim that he could be trusted to overextend himself. A calisthenics routine for fifty schoolchildren dressed as soldiers? Linati would make it a hundred or ten times that amount, from little infants to late adolescents, and arm them all with rifles. It would be a spectacle to remember, on par with a total eclipse or, as Linati once witnessed, a fire at a brothel. Years from now even the most jaded observers would recall it with affection. "You should have been there," they would reminisce, "when the prime minister shed a tear."

Either tears, Linati vowed, or a smile. If he could just break that stern expression, then he would know that the exhibition had been a success and another appointment would follow: an ambassadorship, to Cuba perhaps, or a seat in the cabinet, a position more in line with

Linati's interests and one with some permanence. Not that he was about to complain. No, few events compared in importance to the March on Rome; entire books were devoted to it. And Linati understood—he published those books—that it was an honor to participate in its commemoration. People from all over would attend the ceremonies or listen to the official broadcast. Even in a small town such as the one Linati left at nineteen, convinced still that talented writers deserved to be published—a notion that now made him chuckle—the local Fascists would place a radio in the central piazza and turn up its volume. An Italian would have to be deaf and bedridden or on vacation overseas to avoid the festivities: anthems and speeches, as well as parades or their description, but also, for the first time ever, a performance in which a thousand schoolchildren demonstrated, in unison and uniforms that matched, the latest exercise patterns. For fifteen minutes the nation's attention would be focused on these acrobatics and, it followed, the man who planned them. And to think that Linati, anxious to rid Dr. Puzo's report of its author's madness and win the prime minister's favor, almost deleted the calisthenics routine. Impossible, he had thought, for neither Italians nor schoolchildren could be trusted to follow orders. Besides, he had never attempted a push-up or a deep knee bend, much less instructed others on their execution. Modern science obliterated the need for such exertions, especially if all one wanted was to lose a few kilos. Why jump around like an imbecile, like the victim of some prank, when a simple injection could achieve the same results? But no sooner had Linati posed that question and readied himself for the deletion than he remembered that the prime minister, an outdoorsman and father, loved both exercise and children, and the two combined would certainly appeal to him, maybe even force the desired tear or the never-before-seen-in-public smile. The uniforms, added later, an inspired contribution from the prime minister's office, would help Linati's cause, as would the occasion itself: their leader's favorite holiday, now less than a month away.

"Still there?" Linati asked from behind the desk and the attendant smoke. It was time for him to leave—the doctor expected him, as usual, at five—but between the desk and the staircase an impediment existed.

"Still," the receptionist answered, her voice lowered now to a whisper, the concern on her face, despite all the smoke, as palpable as her makeup. "Should I call the police?"

Linati waved off the question—"He's harmless; we've no need for police"—and in the process opened a window in the haze, which reminded him for the first time in hours that there were pictures framed on the opposite wall: the prime minister here, the prime minister there. He added more ash to the silver saucer, topped it off, made a final deposit, then put an end to the discussion. "I'll talk to him as I leave."

Whether appeased now or not, the receptionist made her exit. Granted, their visitor had become a nuisance—seven hours he had remained there, seated just meters from her desk, oblivious to the excuses she offered and the advice that he return next week—but at the same time Linati needed to be careful not to offend him. He feared repercussions. Suppose someone in power discovered Linati's sources or Alfredo Perelli became upset. Better to proceed with caution than risk embarrassment or a price hike. Sooner or later, the publisher believed, their visitor would lose interest in Dr. Puzo's disposed-of report. Rome was filled with distractions, some impossible to resist. Linati himself had followed the crowds to the Colosseum when he first arrived and at the Sistine Chapel developed a sore neck. The painter must have been a masochist, he decided afterward, or immune to pain, perhaps like that Mr. Arpino who still waited outside.

"Seven hours and he hasn't moved," the receptionist had reported. "I'd think he was dead if I didn't see him blink. Those chairs are comfortable, but . . . "

Linati selected a few cigars to last him until he reached home, then collected the materials he would need that evening: the official exercise manual for the Italian armed forces, printed on Linati's presses, and a Swiss periodical, once purchased from a man in an overcoat, devoted to coeducational fitness. One or the other, he hoped, or both would provide inspiration for the calisthenics routine and clues as to how a person executes the more obscure movements named in Dr. Puzo's report: the deep knee bend was obvious, but what about the crunch or the windmill or the chest press or the buttocks squeeze? As he headed out the door, the materials tucked under an arm, Linati wondered what Dr. Puzo had in mind when he recommended that children perform these maneuvers.

"Mr. Arpino!" The publisher pretended as if had encountered a friend. "Believe it or not, I was just thinking about you." He put an arm, the free one, around the visitor's shoulder and steered him toward the stairs. "I'm off to another appointment now—it's been a chaotic day—but walk with me for a minute, please, and tell me about your adventures in Rome."

"Adventures?" Beppe repeated the word, he realized when Mr. Linati then defined it, like someone who had never before heard it.

"Yes, where you've been, what you've seen—you know, adventures."

After seven hours in the same position, Beppe's head, much like the rest of him, was numb. How fortunate, then, that Mr. Linati offered the support he did: an arm and shoulder, a concise definition.

"Of course," Beppe said, "adventures." He reviewed the previous week, leaving the pace and destination to Mr. Linati—just ahead the staircase awaited their descent—but no adventures came to mind. The farthest Beppe had wandered from the hotel since he last visited Mr. Linati was across the street to the restaurant. "No adventures, I'm afraid, none that I can remember."

At the stairs Mr. Linati released Beppe but continued the conversation. "Not even the Vatican?" he asked, the last word pitched above the rest. "I find that hard to believe."

Beppe joined him on the stairs. "Mr. Linati," he said, less interested in attractions missed than in promises made, "about Dr. Puzo's report. Your receptionist told me . . . "

"Do you realize, Mr. Arpino"—Beppe let the publisher interrupt him—"that in all the years I've known that woman only once"—a turn to the left and then more stairs—"has the bow in her hair not matched her fingernails. And that was after her mother died." One step followed another, each step lower than the one before. "It's probably time I gave her a raise."

Beppe agreed that she warranted it. "But sir, about the report. Your receptionist mentioned certain difficulties." At last the stairs ended, and the main entrance came into view. "Is there anything I can do?"

From a pocket, not the pocket with the medal but another pocket, Mr. Linati pulled a fat cigar. "As a matter of fact," he said, "there is something you can do." He handed Beppe the printed matter that had been tucked under his arm. "Hold these for me, please. This will just take a second."

While Mr. Linati clipped and otherwise prepared the cigar for combustion, Beppe tried again to inquire about the report. "I'm concerned," he confessed, perhaps too abruptly. "What I mean is . . . "

"Listen, Mr. Arpino." A match appeared from a third pocket. "I don't know what influence Dr. Puzo had on you, but trust me when I say"—the match met the publisher's shoe and produced a flame—"that tobacco's not the demon he made it out to be. This cigar"—he torched one end, inhaled from the other—"it's just a rolled-up vegetable, like spinach that's been dried. And since when is a taste for spinach reason for concern?"

A person with less patience than Beppe or someone more interested in Mr. Linati's health would have protested then, stomped a foot or shouted an objection, not nodded when the publisher finished and repeated, in a voice as calm as an undertaker's, words that earlier had been interrupted.

"What I mean, sir, is the report. With all due respect, another week is too long. Isn't there any way we could make it sooner?"

For the second time in ten minutes, Mr. Linati put an arm around Beppe's shoulder and guided him, now out the main entrance into the

street. "I'm trying my best," he said, "but remember that there's a lot
of competition for the prime minister's time." He mentioned the
March on Rome, slated for commemoration in a few weeks. "Even
minor details, I understand, down to what the radio announcers will
wear—not to mention what they say, their scripts—require the prime
minister's approval."

As Beppe listened to Mr. Linati, whose arm still held him in an
embrace and whose feet set a moderate pace, he was reminded of Dr.
Puzo, who had also remarked on the prime minister's attention to
detail. "A perfectionist," Dr. Puzo had called him, "which is just
what we Italians need after all these blunderers and elected buf-
foons." No more shortcuts, he declared, no more excuses. "And no
compromises, either."

As similar, Dr. Puzo's admiration for the man, to Mr. Linati's
obvious affection as the low opinion that Beppe's fiancée held was
different.

"Now do me a favor, Mr. Arpino, and see a little of Rome." The
publisher disconnected himself and discontinued their stroll. "Visit
St. Peter's," he said. "It's an impressive dome." Mr. Linati then took
a final puff and bid farewell, which left Beppe stranded on that unfamiliar street with, as he realized once the smoke had dissipated and
the time had come to retrace their steps, those forgotten papers: an
exercise manual, Beppe discovered, for the Italian armed forces and
a Swiss periodical, complete with pictures, devoted to coeducational
fitness.

•••••••

For her, tea. For him, coffee into which had been mixed a little cocoa.
The waiter placed their cups on the table and received their thanks,
then left them to resume their conversation.

"Where was I?" Angelina asked but the next second remembered. It would take more than a waiter's brief appearance at their
table to make her lose her place. "Oh, the calisthenics routine." It
would take an explosion in the street that fronted the café or a blast

from Mount Vesuvius, its plume a fixture in the distance, but even then the competition for her attention would be fierce. "It's all so peculiar." She considered her tea for a moment, the steam that rose from its surface. "And so frustrating, too."

Her brother, meanwhile, stirred the coffee mixture with a spoon, either to blend its flavors better or to lower its temperature. On the table, within reach, was the notebook he carried with him now at all times, and on the notebook rested a pen. "Yes," he said as he removed the spoon and tasted from it, "I'll admit, it is peculiar, but . . . "

"I know, I know." No reason for another lecture, not when she could predict its content. "You think I should be more supportive, more patient with him." Whatever interest the tea once held for her had passed, so she focused instead on Tomassino: still unblemished and slender, hair still held in place with pomade. "It's difficult, though. Do you understand?"

He nodded, then put the cup to his lips, sipped, and returned the cup to the table. "I imagine it's very difficult, being so far apart."

As happened whenever the matter had come up before, her brother missed the point. "It's not just the distance, Tomassino, the inconvenience, the fact that I'm here and Beppe's there. And it's not just that I miss him, which I do, quite a lot. It's more complicated than that." Her stare returned to her tea. "It's much more complicated." Then it went back to her brother. "So complicated that it makes me confused." And scared, she could have added but decided to leave out.

Across the room the waiter attended to another table.

"But you love him, right?" Sooner or later that word was bound to be heard. Were all poets, she wondered, as fond of it as her brother? "And he loves you?"

"Yes, of course." Tomassino had asked her that at least a hundred times. "I'm not talking about love, though. A person can love someone and still be confused."

He appeared to consider that for a moment and, for some reason, the design of the spoon, which he turned first one way and then the other, this way and that, as if it were somehow unique. When finally he set it down, he reached for the pen, jotted a line in the ubiquitous notebook, then explained the interruption. "An idea," he said, "that couldn't wait. Now, about that last comment . . . "

Her desire to continue the discussion, however, had abated. At some point words became inadequate. She could talk and talk, for a week, for a month, but until Tomassino traded places with her and experienced her life from the start he would never understand. An overabundance of words could even do harm, as Beppe's letters proved. For though he respected her wishes and did not phone—she had needed to set some parameters—he wrote often, and each letter created in her a disturbance. Words that once were filled with special meaning now seemed hollow, even cliché, while references to the future, to the event just around the corner, after which she would be known as Angelina Arpino, made her ever more anxious. And then there were those passages devoted to Dr. Puzo's report and that Fascist publisher, Giacomo Linati, which dampened what little enthusiasm she had been able to muster for the trip.

"You know, Tomassino, maybe it's time we changed the subject. Let's talk about you for a minute." She clasped her cup, still warm despite the steam's disappearance, and lifted it to her mouth. "How's the new poem coming? Almost finished with it?"

While the details remained a secret, even what title it bore and its subject, Tomassino had made reference in recent weeks to an ambitious project. On one occasion he described the piece as a departure for him. "No cherubs," he said, "at least none that I can foresee." On another occasion he mentioned its form. "After much deliberation, I've decided upon couplets." But otherwise he kept "Requiem for a Dentist" to himself, for both practical as well as artistic reasons—not just because, as a new artwork, it needed to be protected from intrusions, from contamination, until its completion or abandonment, whichever came first, but also because, as happens when artists push their limits, some people would find it offensive. In particular, the poem was sure to upset Angelina, for it celebrated the man she held responsible for her current predicament.

"A request that never should have been made," she said whenever the topic arose, which it did now quite often. "Deathbed or no, I still think it was unfair for him to put Beppe on the spot like that." Dr. Puzo's desire for fame, she contended, even posthumous fame, overshadowed whatever concern he had for Beppe's dental career. The answers, therefore, that Tomassino provided to the questions she posed in the café demanded equal parts care and evasion.

"The poem? It's coming along, though it will still be a while before I'm finished." Not one to force the artistic process, Tomassino worked at a pace that allowed him time to think and rethink all decisions: each word's placement, its shape, its sound, the various connotations, the overall effect. Such deliberateness, he was convinced, would make him a better poet than those who felt the need to compose a sonnet whenever their muses so much as sneezed. If it took months for a seed to mature into a flower, the written equivalent deserved at least that much time. And there was even less reason to hurry now: better if Beppe returned before a poem dedicated to Dr. Puzo became public.

The cup emptied and the spoon licked clean, Tomassino ordered another coffee with cocoa in it when the waiter passed their table.

"And another tea," the sister with whom he would soon not share the same surname added, despite the fact that all but a sip remained from her first cup. Tea versus coffee, one mouthful rather than several: appropriate somehow that their last names should also differ. Less alike, brother and sister, than most enemies. She taller and sturdier than he, with curls as opposed to ointment. Her preference in music instrumental pieces, not opera, which he favored, just as he did literature over histories, authors over pamphleteers. Yet Tomassino knew that without her he would be incomplete. Even to consider such an absence made him thankful that there was no coffee at the moment to spill. In that respect what he felt could be termed love—familial love, to be exact, which should never be confused with self-love, unrequited love, or love's other varieties, each with its own pleasures and perils but none more celebrated or more elusive and unpredictable than the romantic sort, the love Tomassino's sister shared with the man who saved Tomassino's life.

"I'm sure Beppe will be back soon," he said with a suddenness that surprised even the waiter about to set down their drinks. "I'm sure he's trying his best. But until he does come back"—again Tomassino dirtied a clean spoon—"you should stop worrying so much." Round and round it went, much like the conversation. "Think about something pleasant instead."

∞∞∞∞∞∞∞

Sometimes their father hired a car for weekend excursions: an hour or two on a dirt road, the landscape blurred impressionistic, the bumps a test for her brassiere. Most often they left after breakfast and returned in time for dinner, but now and then their father reserved for them rooms at an inn, and they stayed overnight. He preferred forested areas and orchards, while she liked open spaces best, unobstructed views and afternoon breezes. As for Tomassino, he claimed that all nature had the potential to inspire an artist; deserts and marshes, he said, were as valuable to the poet as waterfalls and snowcapped peaks. Nevertheless, he did have fair skin, so no matter what their destination or the weather expected he carried with him at all times when they traveled an umbrella. Had Angelina shared that habit or foreseen a particular thunderstorm, perhaps Beppe never would have proposed.

It was early spring, the first warm spell since autumn and their first excursion since then as well. The town was small and perched on a hill, a rustic place, primitive almost, with a quaint hotel, a modest chapel, olive trees in one direction, unplanted fields in the other. Lunch arrived on simple plates, some with chips in them, some with cracks, and the wine that accompanied the meal came from bottles wrapped in baskets that looked as if children had woven them, or arthritics. But the food could not have been more delicious, the wine's earthiness a more perfect complement to the meal.

After lunch Tomassino retired for a nap—under normal circumstances he did not rise until noon—while their father explored the area. "You're welcome to join me," he said before leaving. "You never know what we'll find." But Angelina had no desire to examine trees or make conversation with local farmers. And neither, thank heaven, did Beppe, who had been invited on the weekend excursion when it was learned that he had never left Naples since he arrived there.

"Let's take our own walk," Angelina suggested when the last plate disappeared from the table. Although it was not unusual for her to be alone with Beppe—a date almost every weekend—their solitude here, two hours from home, felt different somehow. In retrospect, she would describe it as filled with suspense. "I feel the need to move around."

Not surprisingly, Beppe seconded the idea. A meal, he once told her, was not complete without a stroll afterward. Such were the quirks that endeared him to her, the peculiar little habits that separated him from the pack. An individual, Beppe, even from afar—consider those oversized clothes—but more and more so the closer to him a person came. "A walk would be wonderful," he told her. "But first, I'd like to floss."

She waited for him outside, near where their driver polished the car—some surfaces, dulled with dust, now reflective as mirrors—and watched as an old man led a mule with a child on it past the driver and the car and her. Then Beppe returned, flossed and eager, and soon their stroll had taken them down the hill upon which the town rested and up another hill, then down that hill and onto a third. The path presented no difficulties, no decisions that needed to be made: no forks, no dead ends. Their arms touched intermittently, as did their hands. When she slipped on loose pebbles, he prevented her fall. And in the excitement then, the sudden breathlessness, the embarrassment and relief—disaster averted—a tender kiss took place. Later another occurred under a tree.

"What is it?" she asked, their heads still bent and shaded, when he paused after that second kiss and appeared to listen, as if in the distance someone called their names. No sounds, though, that Angelina could hear other than those of their own manufacture: air as it entered and issued from nostrils and saliva as it moistened lips. Perhaps he paused, then, not to listen but to think. Yes, perhaps that was when he decided that before their walk had finished he would ask for her hand.

Not quite. As Beppe experienced it, the pause was more delirious than decisive, more concerned with reverie than intent. If not for the recent meal and the ample ventilation, as well as the protective shade, he probably would have fainted then, collapsed in her arms like an accordion with a punctured bellows. The kindnesses that she bestowed on him—these kisses just the most recent example— would have overwhelmed even a man raised in a castle, someone accustomed to excess. Her affection showed no limits or diminution. Rather, with each week that passed, each concert attended, each visit to their café, each kiss, it seemed to increase. No wonder that Beppe, a butcher's son who once pulled a doll from the rubbish, found himself unable to function when faced now with attention from such a beautiful and sophisticated woman. What, he asked himself as the delirium subsided, had he done to deserve her devotion? And how would he ever recover if she decided it had been misplaced?

●●●●●●●●

When the rain came it found them unprotected. First the clouds appeared, the blue turned to slate in an instant as if painted with a celestial brush, then the thunderclaps, loud and explosive, like kettledrums filled with kerosene hit with mallets lit like torches. The temperature's fall caused miniature bumps to appear on their arms, and on his neck Beppe could feel the skin constrict and the hairs there become pins. No shelter except for a few trees between where he stood next to her and the town two hills distant, which would have been closer now had their kisses been briefer or their walk not slowed to a saunter.

Drops started to pat the path behind them. One hit Beppe on the nose. In minutes their clothes would be soaked, their hair slick as Tomassino's, their shoes covered with mud. It had been irresponsible, Beppe knew, to have overlooked the weather. Not that a little rain bothered him. No, he rather liked how rain felt. But a suitor, as Stefano and Marcello had told him, was expected to return a woman to her father in the same condition as when he picked her up. "In other words," Stefano had cautioned, "always cover your tracks."

Another reason for concern was that most women, in Beppe's experience, disliked rain, even feared it. At home he learned about the shepherd fried like a frittata—the same storm claimed several sheep—and others whose deaths were not as swift. "She suffered for months," Beppe's mother once said about the childhood friend who never recovered from chills that started after her exposure to rain. "I can still hear her teeth chatter."

Beppe noted a similar panic in Maria Teresa's voice the time he arrived at Father Vincenzo's soaked to the skin. "Are you crazy?" she asked, then attacked him with towels. Yet that same afternoon Beppe first held the cello, which in turn made the rain seem like a blessing. Still, he now had another person's well-being to consider, a woman whose curls would soon lose their bounce.

"I hope you don't mind a little rain," he called out as the patter became more insistent, more like a snare drum now, now more like ten. The storm would soon be overhead. But rather than make a dash for the nearest tree, she turned to face him.

"Mind?" Never before had there been a reason for her to shout at him. "But I like the rain. And that smell"—she breathed in a manner that would have met with Dr. Puzo's approval—"it's better than perfume."

Beppe also liked the fresh scent that accompanied bad weather, so he kissed her one more time. He kissed her despite the drops that hit them now at will and the potential for chills or electrocution. He kissed her and continued to kiss past the point at which he otherwise would have stopped. And while desire was in part responsible—the cushion that her lips provided, the nearness to her teeth—what sustained the kiss was love.

"Yes," she said when he asked her, "of course I will, Beppe, of course."

oooooooo

An old man, a mule, and a child were the first to hear the news. The storm had passed over, its departure as sudden as its approach, and left behind a sheen, as when a driver polishes a car, and more silence than before. Clothes once wet soon lost their heaviness, if not their dampness, while shoes became difficult to lift, the path now a brown adhesive that affixed itself to their feet.

"Good afternoon," Beppe said when the threesome came upon them. "A beautiful day, isn't it?" Only the mule responded. "Well, would you believe that Angelina and I, we're going to be married?"

Uncharacteristic behavior, to be sure, but still rather subdued. Another suitor would have clasped the old man's hand and embraced the mule, danced a circle around them and performed a back flip. Not Beppe, however, who from the start—that is, if one overlooked the remarks he made at the banquet about her dress and Titian—had proven himself to be different from the rest. Just as he invited her to that first concert while her father and brother looked on, without chocolates to help him, he proposed to her on a sodden footpath and offered no diamond incentive. Even the manner in which he asked set him apart: "I want to be your husband, Angelina, if you'll let me."

The words, whispered into the silence that followed the storm, the silence that followed the kiss that lasted almost as long as the storm, affected her as would a dose of liqueur: a warmth as she swallowed, as the words soaked into her, which spread then to her limbs, her knees and her toes, her elbows, wrists, and palms, wherever her bloodstream traveled no matter how far removed from her heart. She loved Beppe and trusted him and knew in an instant her response: no indecision, nor even the briefest hesitation. If the old man with the mule had arrived sooner and identified himself as a priest, she would have married Beppe then and there. Instead, she returned to the hotel not as a bride but a fiancée and slept in her own bed. Or attempted to sleep. After the drive, the walk, the thunderstorm and kisses, and all that followed Beppe's proposal and their announcement at dinner—the toasts, the quotes from poets—a little rest seemed overdue. But the moment her head met her pillow she found herself wide awake. On a hillside, to be specific: the fresh-scented rain almost as close as her fresh-scented pillow. It would be hours before she drifted into sleep, expectant and fulfilled, convinced anew that Beppe was the one for her. No doubts, none, and no foreseeable obstacles. Her father could not have been happier—he must have made a dozen toasts, most to their future children—while Beppe predicted that back in Cortenza the news also would be well received. As for political differences, with no newspapers to prompt her, no Fascist passersby, the subject never entered Angelina's mind. It was as if, for the weekend at least, the Blackshirts had never marched on Rome, and their ghastly legacy—electoral intimidation, beaten and left-for-dead opponents, coerced oaths from teachers, censorship, inane decrees, a self-appointed leader—not existed. Preferable, without a doubt, but even if politics had intruded upon the weekend—an IL DUCE stenciled on the town's water tank—it would not have altered Angelina's decision, because Beppe was no Fascist. He just happened to live with one. And whatever he said about discipline and the masses or the prime minister's so-called talents came not from personal beliefs or the desire to wear black and administer castor oil to defenseless pedestrians but from respect for an eccentric mentor. More an amusement to her, such remarks, than a cause for concern.

But now, with a calisthenics routine in the works, her naïveté seemed the real joke. For either Beppe shared Dr. Puzo's opinion of authoritarian rule, even with Dr. Puzo dead, or he lacked conviction, lacked a backbone: a man as pliable as heated wax. Too innocent and trustful, too unsuspicious. Yet those same qualities also had their appeal. No wonder she was confused. And worried, too.

"Think about something pleasant instead," Tomassino had said. But when she tried—their weekend excursion—it still led her back to the present. She was still seated opposite her brother in a Neapolitan café, their cups still between them, while Beppe remained in Rome, the report still undelivered, locked still in a publisher's safe.

∞∞∞∞∞∞

He had not even asked for compensation. Instead, he described the work, on the street late that afternoon, as an honor and a welcome distraction. "And I think Dr. Puzo would have wanted me to help."

But the project was not without its costs, as Linati discovered when he received the invoice for their calisthenics props. Despite a volunteer expert, now on the line from Alfredo Perelli's hotel, the publisher still would have to spend a small fortune: uniforms in all shapes and sizes and countless wooden clubs, plus a thousand sheepskin medicine balls.

"A thousand?" Linati puffed into the receiver. "And we really need them?"

Medicine balls, the expert informed him, were crucial to Dr. Puzo's workouts, so Linati initialed the invoice and handed it back to the receptionist who had placed the call for him, then he made a note to raise the prices on textbooks. It all evened out in the end.

"We can store the props at a warehouse I have here in Rome," he continued, careful to speak louder than the static, "which isn't far from where the performance—the calisthenics, I mean—will take place."

The children would come from Fascist youth groups—Rome alone had hundreds—and Linati would lead them. And though the wooden clubs he used would be hollow and the medicine ball filled with straw, the movements he performed, the exercises themselves, these would be the same. A buttocks squeeze? No problem. And a deep knee bend? Give him another week. Between the lessons from Mr. Arpino and the supplemental injections—new compounds, unknown even to most chemists—Linati soon would be as fit and nimble as an escape artist or a double-jointed thief.

"Now, about the routine, without rifles"—incompatible with calisthenics, the expert notified him in a previous conversation—"I'm concerned it won't be militant enough. Is there anything we can do with those clubs, anything combative?"

Linati had made sketches, with arrows and circles, whorls, pointillistic lines, which he studied before bed and when atop the commode, but it would be weeks before he memorized all the patterns in Mr. Arpino's repertoire for wooden clubs—complex movements and, for the children, simple ones as well—and months before he had the confidence to invent such patterns himself. Thus once more he turned to Dr. Puzo's courier for assistance. No fool, Mr. Arpino, not as first suspected, when Linati mistook him for a writer, but nevertheless somewhat slow. Indeed, he still wanted to deliver that long-gone report.

"Combative?" A pause that sounded like sand as it moves in a tin can. "I'll see what I can come up with. Which reminds me, sir, any news from the prime minister's office?" Every day he asked, some days two or three times, but as yet there was no appointment.

"Believe me, Mr. Arpino, you'd be the first to know. Now, I have some other business to attend . . . "

Perhaps tomorrow, Beppe told himself in an effort to remain hopeful. But with the celebrations closer now, the chances that the man responsible for them would have a minute to spare were slim at best, as Mr. Linati had pointed out more times than Beppe cared to remember. And while it saddened him to think that even with help from a well-connected Fascist he might fail, Beppe took comfort in knowing that at least he was able to assist with the calisthenics routine, which would have pleased Dr. Puzo, whose inspiration would be credited, Mr. Linati promised, in all the booklets printed to mark the occasion.

"So I'll see you at six as usual? And afterward we can visit the warehouse I mentioned. Until then, Mr. Arpino . . . "

A click, then the line went dead. Beppe waited a moment— strange to hear the publisher's voice and not smell cigar smoke— before he set down the receiver and thanked the woman behind the front desk and the man in the crimson jacket who first notified him of the call.

"That's what I'm here for, Dr. Arpino. I'm at your disposal."

Beppe crossed the lobby toward the stairs. As he neared them, though, he remembered Mr. Linati's latest concern about the calisthenics routine and returned to the front desk. "Excuse me," he said to the man in the crimson jacket, the man put there to help him, "I don't mean to pry, sir, but were you ever in the armed forces?"

It was as if the question had been anticipated, as if people who stayed in expensive hotels asked such questions all the time. "Nine months in the trenches, then ten at the door of a military hotel."

"The trenches?" Another fortunate coincidence, like the materials that led to Beppe's involvement with the calisthenics routine: two publications, both related, believe it or not, to fitness. "As in hand-to-hand combat?"

Again he showed not even moderate surprise. "Yes, sometimes we used our hands—or sticks, stones, whatever we could find. In fact, I once killed a man with a tweezers." The woman behind the front desk excused herself to visit the rest room. "But remember, Dr. Arpino, we also had our munitions: rifles and pistols, mortars, mines. I found that these were much more effective."

With the front desk vacant, Beppe helped himself to a pen and paper. Then, when the woman returned to her post, he and the man—no, the veteran—in the crimson jacket retired to the small piazza below Beppe's window, perhaps the only place in Rome where combative poses would not attract unwanted attention.

A businessman can never rest, even when he wants to retire.

Alfredo Perelli examined the phrase with a lens attached to a handle. He checked to see if the ink veined into the paper and looked for uneven absorption: areas darker than the rest or still white. Next, he tore a corner from the paper and inspected the result. He smelled the paper, tasted it, crumpled it into a ball. And then he set the ball on fire and afterward scrutinized the remains. Satisfied at last, he replaced the lens in its case, returned the case to its drawer, stood up, switched off the desk lamp, and closed the office door behind him.

"Good-bye, Mr. Perelli," Umberto, the accountant, called out; then Carlo, the foreman; Romeo, who ran the pulp refiner; Elio, the best bleach man in the business; Mario, in charge of drying; Giovanni, who sharpened the blades on the cutter; and others, some whose names escaped him, some whose voices were drowned out by the machinery.

Perelli wished them all a pleasant afternoon, then took a breath and stepped outside, where it was quieter, yes, but not nearly as fragrant or filled with good cheer. He paused then beside the paper mill and planned the route that he would take to the appointment he had hoped would be canceled. If he rushed, he could make a detour to Via Cavallina, which would offer some consolation. At least then he would be able to see a beautiful statue or two and a few ornate street lamps before what promised to be a wasted hour. The decision made, he set off in that direction at a pace somewhere between brisk and hurried.

A businessman can never rest, even when he wants to retire.

The phrase came back to Perelli as he maneuvered around several slow pedestrians. It just flowed from the pen when he started to test that paper. A word would have sufficed, even a scribble. But a sentence complete with punctuation? Even on an incline Perelli kept himself erect. Well, the sentiment must have needed to be released. As Beppe once mentioned over dinner, it was healthier for people to vent pent-up emotion than to hold it in. A lesson from the infamous Dr. Puzo but useful nonetheless—a plateau, then one more street before Via Cavallina—maybe even true. Because Perelli did feel a reprieve after he wrote those eleven words. It was like old times: the lens heavier than the hand, the paper not quite delicious, the smoke listless and sad, the workers all smiles. And then he stepped outside.

"Father?"

"Tomassino?"

The streets in Naples numbered in the thousands, and the Perelli home was nowhere near Via Cavallina. It took a moment, therefore, for father and son to recover from the surprise.

The elder Perelli looked around in all directions. "Is your sister here, too?"

A notebook in one hand and a picture frame in the other—the picture, however, concealed—Tomassino responded after a pause that would have taxed even a cadaver's patience. "No, I think she went to a café."

Alfredo Perelli should have known as much. Her mother had also loved cafés. "And you, Tomassino? Where are you headed?"

"Oh, just doing some research"—he held up the notebook but not the frame—"you know, for one of my poems."

Research? Since when did poets do more than smell roses and toss pebbles into the sea? The hidden picture could help explain the deception, but Alfredo Perelli did not have time then to pursue the matter. Or walk down Via Cavallina. He kissed Tomassino on the cheek. "I have to run to an appointment, son. I'll see you at dinner."

A businessman can never rest, even when he wants to retire.

So much for the statues and street lamps, the small consolation. While Tomassino shuffled past these pleasures on some secret mission, perhaps to find a photo retoucher or a pawn shop, Alfredo Perelli rushed off in the opposite direction for a conference room in which he would have to discuss a transaction that would never take place. But the smart businessman, he reminded himself as he accelerated past a stalled car, listens to all offers, even those that offend him. The driver made an unkind remark about Perelli's mother. Not that these people, the conference room inhabitants, would be rude or expect him to sell below market value. No, it was their intentions that concerned him, and their persistence: despite what he told them at the first meeting, they asked him back for another. But no matter how lucrative the new offer, he would never sell the mill to people with no love for paper. Such action would just ensure its demise: the vats emptied, the workers displaced, the rollers soon frozen with rust, the pulp refiner silent as a heart stored in an icebox.

From somewhere a scream. Perelli looked but could not stop. The scene? A lane, identical to all the others, down which one child chased another and each clutched a balloon.

What should have been a blissful time for him—the trust fund started, a son-in-law almost snared, and grandchildren soon in the making—instead was filled with stress: Tomassino's increasingly peculiar behavior, Angelina's paranoia, Beppe's misadventures in Rome, and now these people who refused to lose interest in the paper mill. No wonder he needed to write out phrases now in order to find relief. But the relief did not last.

"I'm afraid I don't have time," Perelli said to a peddler who invited him to smell her flowers.

A businessman can never rest, even when he wants to retire.

••••••••

The problem was a simple one, Tomassino realized after he solved it. Until then, however, it seemed insurmountable. Never before had he faced such difficulties as a poet. For a few desperate minutes he went so far as to consider a new profession; even papermaking had its appeal. But just as he was about to tell his father not to sell the business, he remembered something he had heard Beppe once mention: Dr. Puzo, before he died, had established a personal archive. And here, Tomassino suspected, he would find the kind of information needed to complete "Requiem for a Dentist." But the solution was not without its own complications: Tomassino would have to risk his life.

A visit to the Naples Institute for Dental Arts and a conversation with its headmaster, during which Tomassino let drop Beppe's name —a recent graduate, a star pupil—and made reference to Dr. Puzo's funeral, provided him with access to the archive. Unfortunately, though, a place at the school had not been found yet to house the materials.

"We're still recovering from the shock," the headmaster said. "It's like we've all lost a father." But if Tomassino wanted, the headmaster would arrange for a viewing. "How about tomorrow afternoon? I can send a secretary over with the key. Do you know how to get there?"

Yes, Tomassino assured the dental school administrator, he knew where Dr. Puzo had lived: a neighborhood safe only for Fascists and people with constipation. Since the attack in the lane Tomassino had avoided the area, even when walking with others.

"But the Blackshirts are nicer now," Tomassino's friend Alonzo recently insisted. "It says so in the papers." Well, Alonzo had never been assaulted with a spoon. Somehow or other, though, Tomassino would find the courage to visit Dr. Puzo's house. Like soldiering or mountaineering, poetry had its perils, and the professional learned to handle them with grace.

"Father?"

"Tomassino?"

The fears proved to be misplaced. Rather than young Fascists ready to chase him down a lane, a possibility that he had prepared for—the picture featured the prime minister in military attire—Tomassino almost bumped into his father, inquisitive as ever.

"And you, Tomassino? Where are you headed?"

A truthful answer would have compromised the poem, while a falsehood seemed too deceptive. Tomassino again chose evasion. Angelina had ended her interrogation at the café after a question or two, and so did their father. As the latter rushed off to an appointment, Tomassino neared Dr. Puzo's door—not the door he entered the last time, when Beppe carried him from the lane, but the front door now, past the crude statuette that matched the portrait behind the headmaster's desk.

A woman let him in, then left him alone. Her only comment before she departed: "Be careful, sir. I know a fire hazard when I see one."

The clutter, the abundance . . . Tomassino could have used a chair. But while all the papers, books, envelopes, and pocket-sized pads in the room threatened to overwhelm him, he also found the sprawl inspirational: to stand knee deep in Dr. Puzo's past made him feel closer to the man and awed. After all, Tomassino had written a mere six poems, a few hundred words at most, not enough to fill even one notebook.

Someone, either Beppe before he left or the headmaster on the weekends or a dental student pushed into service, had separated the material into piles, as Tomassino discovered after the dizziness passed: one pile for correspondence, another for contracts and the like, one for faded newspapers, one for the pocket-sized pads, a pile for thick journals, and several for books, most with L. PUZO printed on their spines but a few stamped with the name often seen in headlines. Tomassino placed the picture that he carried near these last piles, then started in on the first.

Upon some envelopes Dr. Puzo had doodled—studies, it appeared, for a urinal wall—but the drawings revealed little about their maker other than that he had never mastered perspective. Inside the envelopes, however, revelations abounded: as valuable to a poet interested in understanding Dr. Puzo, these letters, as a candle would be to a spelunker. For while Beppe had mentioned Dr. Puzo often and quoted from Dr. Puzo's books, he never discussed the man's private life. Had there ever been a Mrs. Puzo? Tomassino did not know. And the question would still be unanswered even after all the letters were read. Nevertheless, Tomassino did learn that Dr. Puzo had participated in several romantic affairs. In one letter, for example, a woman named Cecilia wrote that she wanted to have children with him, while in another, a Caterina, much to Tomassino's alarm, made playful reference to her bruises. But the most disturbing news of all came in a letter signed by a man.

Tomassino did not realize at first that it was Dr. Puzo writing—the letter penned but never posted—nor did he connect the addressee's name with anyone he knew. And since the letter related to business matters—a fire, lost assets—and not love, he started to skim. But in doing so, the gist of it occurred to him, then the implications, at which point a trembling started in the hand that held the letter, which made the words illegible, so Tomassino set the letter down and read it that way, his attention focused on each word so as to avoid misinterpretation—yet another instance of a poet's skills having their practical applications—but such care was unnecessary, because there was nothing ambiguous about the message conveyed in the letter, nothing to confuse even a beginning reader. In its simplicity, though, its directness, the letter achieved an elegance that perhaps only a student of literature could appreciate. But that was not the reason Tomassino took the letter home with him and left the others behind. No, he wanted it for Beppe, who was under the impression that the publisher now entrusted with Dr. Puzo's report had been its author's friend.

"It's all so peculiar," Angelina had said in reference to the calisthenics routine. And while Tomassino had agreed with her—he found any exercise abnormal—he had not shared her worries. And still he trusted that Beppe could take care of himself. Tomassino's lean attackers had fled the instant Beppe appeared on the scene; a fat publisher should pose no problem. Yet despite the fact that the letter would confirm his sister's suspicions, Tomassino knew better than to share it with her. Better if it remained a secret between him and Beppe. Better to spare her further distress.

∞∞∞∞∞∞

After dinner, as usual, at the restaurant near the hotel, where the man in the crimson jacket, the veteran, knew to find him if someone called—it had happened once thus far—Beppe would cross the street, busy no matter what the hour, climb the hotel stairs, and sit himself above the small piazza in which, just a few days earlier, he had learned how to kill a person bare-handed: an elbow to the throat, a heel to the head, a thumb in the spinal column. He would then pick up a pen, a sheet of paper, and write, as he did every night, to Angelina. He would describe for her new developments, if there were developments to describe—oftentimes there were none—and reiterate the fact that he missed and loved her. The letter would end with a promise to return soon, and after Beppe sealed it in an envelope, he would brush and floss, undress and slip into bed, then lie awake for several hours. The dreaded insomnia, alas, followed him wherever he went. Even at the Perelli Grand, where the rooms were quiet as chapels and the mattresses expertly stuffed, Beppe slept no better than he did in Cortenza, a lumpen mass beneath him and an asthmatic nearby.

Paolo was the snorer, of course; their mother and sister slept quietly. As for their father, Beppe could not recall whether he made noise or not. Apart from that final walk, when Beppe escorted him to the mules that would take him to the train, and a few assorted details—shoes black except at the cracks where the brown showed through, hands poised over a dismantled chicken—little remained in Beppe's head about the man he once called Papa. Rosselli often had told stories about him—"Your father was one of the best"—but these he seldom finished: a customer would walk into the shop or the subject would turn to New York. "Filled with murderous thieves," the butcher would say. "What was I thinking?"

Just as unhelpful was Beppe's mother, who rarely mentioned her husband after he died except to lament. The superstitions were to blame, Beppe knew, and the pain: a lost spouse . . . unthinkable. And now added to that pain was a son's absence. Beppe had promised to return after he finished school, but when the time came he decided to find a Neapolitan office. Cortenza was no place for someone like Angelina. It lacked a concert hall, a decent café, and since Beppe's departure it had become a Fascist outpost. First the mayor was replaced by a Roman appointee, then the town's two unarmed policemen appeared on the streets with clubs. Margherita described these changes and others in her infrequent correspondence—infrequent, yes, but predictably so. She alone kept Beppe in touch. Their mother, as he learned, was not much of a letter writer. Nor was Paolo, now a butcher's apprentice, or Rosselli, now Paolo's boss. Maria Teresa also was slow to return Beppe's notes, and when she finally did write it was just a line or two of thanks. Not surprising, then, that Beppe sometimes wondered whether all those he invited would attend the wedding. Would Dino travel the distance if he never even wrote? Miss Donati? The deposed mayor? Of the many people Beppe knew when he lived in Cortenza, perhaps only the three Arpinos would make the trip north. Such were the disappointments for which he needed to be prepared. Still, no matter who attended or how far their commute, Beppe was certain that the event would please him. The altar could be wobbly and the priest visibly drunk, Beppe's suit could be threadbare and Angelina in sequins, but he would still be there with her, and she would still, once it all was over, be his wife.

But first, before the wedding, before any of the guests arrived, before the dinner and the letter and the insomnia that would follow, Beppe needed to cross the street and wait to be seated in the restaurant where then he would await dinner, wait as he now waited for a pause on the road before him and a minute of the prime minister's time. It seemed as if life itself of late had been reduced to waiting. No doubt Dr. Puzo would have disapproved. A minute wasted, as he often said, is lost forever.

●●●●●●●●

The table was much too large, even for three people. In fact, if elbow room were compromised, it could have seated thirty. More preferable were the tables found at cafés, around which three could sit without feeling like strangers.

"I must say, Tomassino, it was quite a surprise running into you on the street today."

Perhaps that explained Angelina's desire then to return to the café where she had spent all afternoon.

"Yes, I was surprised, too."

It was her first time back, her first time there alone. With hundreds to choose from, avoiding one was as easy as steering clear of a certain dental office had been until now.

"And your research? Did you find whatever it was you were looking for?"

They called it Our Café, though the name painted on the window referred to the concert hall across the street. All afternoon she watched singers come and go—she recognized a few—and harpists, clarinetists, even the violinist who played at her favorite banquet.

"As a matter of fact, Father, I found more than I expected. But all the while I kept thinking about your appointment. I'm anxious to know how it went."

And then there were the Fascists who spoiled her view and the children forced to wear Fascist uniforms. Was it possible that in recent weeks their numbers had doubled?

"Well, for once, Tomassino, I'd rather not discuss business at the dinner table. Let's just say it could have gone better."

The idea was to indoctrinate them early, before their minds were fully formed. Radio shows, sporting events, field trips and summer camps, parades, essay contests . . . all tools of the Fascist's trade. And now another, one that involved medicine balls and wooden clubs.

"Did it have something to do with the paper mill?"

What she pictured was a circus with sinister overtones, a thousand helpless clowns, and Beppe polishing the ringmaster's boots.

"I said I'd rather not discuss it, Tomassino, at least not at the table. But I am interested in that research you're conducting for your poems."

Meanwhile, the dental instruments collected dust, and patients went elsewhere. She walked past the office, and yes, it looked abandoned. A note tacked to the door provided the names of the only two classmates Beppe ever mentioned or ever introduced to her: one, she remembered, carried a cane, while the other wore a coat draped like a cape; more like her former suitors, those two, than dental professionals.

"My research? I wouldn't want to bore you two with the details."

He had wanted to wait until the practice was established before they married. And though she was ready on that sodden footpath where he proposed, she agreed. She even helped find an office that he could afford and asked her friends to schedule appointments. She also went herself once for a cleaning and was embarrassed to face her father when she returned home: a more intimate experience, even with the assistant standing there handing him tools, she could not imagine.

"Well, we'll never know whether it's boring or not until we hear it. Isn't that right, Angelina?"

And the cello collecting dust, too. An old Guadagnini, according to Beppe, given to him by the housekeeper of the priest who taught him how to play, an instrument he later carried all the way from Cortenza strapped to his back. And when he performed on it, as he did sometimes for her—a close second to the cleaning in terms of her arousal—it still seemed attached. He melded with it, enveloped it; at times she needed to look away.

"Angelina?"

But as inseparable as Beppe and the cello appeared to be on such occasions and dependent upon one another—for sustenance, for life—he ignored it now and instead put all his energies into planning calisthenics routines and delivering reports.

"Angelina? Can you hear me?"

"Oh, I'm sorry, Father. It's been a long day."

⊶⊶⊶⊶⊷

She coaxed him off the table and into a chair, the servant who assisted sent then to fetch a bottle from the liquor cabinet.

"And three glasses!" Tomassino called out, the tremble back after a three-hour absence.

It had started quite unexpectedly: one minute they were having a conversation—not exactly candid but nonetheless polite—and the next a napkin hit the floor and shoes were upon the table, the reasons unclear to all except the man who wanted to enjoy dinner for a change. Was it too much to ask, Alfredo Perelli asked himself, that for one meal they put aside their worries and make pleasant conversation, maybe even smile once or twice?

Angelina reacted first, moving the bread basket just in time and the soup tureen less than a second before their father would have stepped in it. But until then, until she saved the soup and perhaps an ankle, her attention had been elsewhere: the usual preoccupations. So obsessed with her own thoughts was she that the content of the conversation at the table now escaped her. Was it wood pulp and chlorine vats? Tomassino with more questions about love? Or was it her own self-absorption that drove their father to undertake that desperate act?

The table was long enough—if necessary, it could fit thirty—for him to build up some momentum before he leapt for the chandelier: a stunt that had cheered them as children. Granted, the ceiling in that house had been lower, which eliminated the need for the table, and the fixture itself had resembled a trapeze—its shape what first inspired him—but based on the calculations Alfredo Perelli made between the moment he threw down his napkin and the instant the soup moved, he knew that the chandelier was within reach. What concerned him was the ceiling that held it in place and the absence of prominent handholds. If he had known earlier that at dinner he would attempt such a feat, he would have hired someone to install special cables and attach a crosspiece. With prescience, though, he also would have canceled that appointment. But it was too late for revisions now, now that he was airborne.

Like a bird, the poet tried, a falcon. No, more like an ostrich: tall and erect and meant for the earth. Or Icarus, who launched himself but later fell. Yet their father soared to the crystals and bulbs above the main entrée—Tomassino too stricken to scream—and remained there, one arm hooked around the taut chain, one shoe due for repairs—a worn spot on its sole—the sound then like a massive wind chime after a blast or a classroom filled with toy pianos. But as the swaying slowed and the tinkling became occasional and the smile faded from the acrobat's face a silence filled the room.

The servant returned with the bottle requested and the three glasses, each of which he then filled with the auburn liqueur.

"Here, Father, have something to drink." Angelina knelt beside him and presented the medication. "It will make you feel better."

She then tended to Tomassino, all shakes and shivers, as if the Blackshirts were back with their castor oil.

"You're spilling, Tomassino. Maybe you should have a seat, too."

And since the servant had filled all the glasses, Angelina helped herself to the third. Then she pulled her chair closer to Tomassino and their father so as to form a small circle. In other words, she tried to make the space more like that at a café.

"Is the drink helping, Father? Is it having any effect?"

It tasted to her, someone more accustomed to tea, like what an overzealous baker would put inside a pastry. Tomassino, on the other hand, if asked, would have likened it to nectar, while their father could discern no taste at all.

"I don't know what came over me," he said at last, the board-like back now bent. But in truth, he did know. It was written on the walls: sell the mill or lose it. If only he had stopped when he saw those two with their balloons. "It's been years since I've done something like that." He sipped more of the flavorless liquid. "But you probably don't even remember."

Tomassino remembered. And now that the trembles had subsided, now that his drink no longer dribbled, he could appreciate the intent. He could even name its source: love, the familial sort. Still, their father, who had seen Tomassino at work in the ballroom count- less times, should have known that, for a poet at least, chandeliers were inspirational and best admired from a distance.

"When all else failed, I'd use that to cheer you up." Alfredo Perelli considered how best to phrase the next sentence. "It seems like weeks since we've had a nice evening together."

Despite the care, however, he knew when she lowered her head that Angelina resented the statement. But he was mistaken: the bow was in contrition, and it accompanied her decision then to remedy the situation. Likewise, she had no idea at the time that the chandelier performance was due more to an encounter in a conference room than to her preoccupations. As for Tomassino, all he knew was that the sooner he mailed that letter, the sooner Beppe would return. And Beppe, who had rescued one Perelli from a Blackshirt attack and dis- covered the crack that threatened another Perelli's smile and provid- ed a third with hope for new heirs, was needed in Naples now more than ever before.

•••••••••

A promise had been made—on a deathbed, no less—and Beppe had tried to keep it, but even he could see now the pointlessness of stay- ing in Rome. Better for all concerned if he went home and waited a few months, until the various celebrations, both political and matri- monial, were over, then returned to make a second attempt. With luck, the prime minister would have more free time then. If a fifteen- minute calisthenics routine required hours and hours of preparation, surely weeks were needed for a long-winded speech.

Rather than admit defeat, Beppe preferred to think of the mis- sion as a partial success. He had made a friend in Mr. Linati, once plump and now almost thin—perhaps those cigars were dietetic— and helped him plan an exercise demonstration that would be per- formed at the prime minister's feet. And while Mr. Linati had invited Beppe to participate in the historic event—a thousand schoolchil- dren, a thousand combatants—the fact was that Beppe was needed elsewhere now. There were music lovers with problem teeth. There was the cello itself—abandoned. And finally, most importantly, there was Angelina, who had never wanted him to leave in the first place. Well, the wait would soon be over. All he had to do was wish Mr. Linati luck and retrieve Dr. Puzo's report.

"I'm sorry that you won't be here, Mr. Arpino." The desk, the smoke—only the sketches spread out now between them were different. "It's going to be quite a show."

Yes, Beppe had attended the first rehearsals and knew from those that it would be impressive. Miss Donati back in Cortenza would have killed for such well-disciplined students. "I'll listen on the radio, Mr. Linati. It won't be the same, but . . . "

"When I say it's going to be quite a show, I mean it's going to surprise even calisthenics experts like yourself." The cigar fed the silver saucer. "Can I trust you to keep a secret?"

Beppe nodded, a sincere, trustworthy nod, and received what he interpreted as the same in return.

"Does the word *pyrotechnics* mean anything to you?"

It did not, though Mr. Linati rectified that situation by explaining to Beppe two of the surprises he had in mind: sparklers on the ends of clubs and, for the finale, the final flourish, a publisher launched from a cannon.

"It's in keeping with the theme," he added, the medal pinned to him twinkling as always. "Believe me, the prime minister will love it."

Beppe did believe Mr. Linati, who had dined with the prime minister's cousin, but he worried that too many liberties were being taken. First the uniforms, which offered poor ventilation at best, then movements borrowed from the trenches—Beppe accepted the blame for these—and now smoke from sparklers pouring into children's lungs: all modifications that Dr. Puzo would have frowned upon.

"But don't despair." Mr. Linati had stood up while Beppe drifted. "I'm sure the radio announcers will do their best." The salute came next. "Your help, Mr. Arpino—you've been indispensable."

Beppe accepted the thanks with a smile. "And I've appreciated your help, too." He waited for the report to be offered. "I'm sure Dr.

Puzo also appreciates it." The pictures on the wall were all familiar. "So, I suppose I'll be going now." The receptionist's bow, he remembered, was purple, while her nails were dark blue. "If it's not too much trouble, Mr. Linati, do you think you could open your safe?"

So close, so very close, that it hurt when Mr. Arpino stumbled. But it was inevitable, and Linati had been foolish to think otherwise. An obsession like that would not vanish overnight. And too bad, because Mr. Arpino, it turned out, had been rather helpful, and Linati would have liked to reward him somehow. Instead, he would have to lie.

"I'm embarrassed to say it, but with all this excitement it seems I've forgotten the combination." Linati tried his best to look flummoxed; he even sprinkled himself with ash.

Mr. Arpino, however, bested him in that department: an expression so perplexed that one would have thought Linati had jumbled the words or left out certain letters. "So, Dr. Puzo's report . . . "

The publisher could not stand to see the poor man suffer. Also, Mr. Arpino had recently studied hand-to-hand combat. "It happens all the time," Linati explained, nonchalant now. "Give me a few weeks, and then I'll have it." He led the way to the door. "Already I know there's a four in the combination somewhere."

There was no four, of course, because there was no safe, at least not in Linati's Roman office—all transactions were handled in Naples—while the report, not unlike a book past its prime, had been cremated, the work of a Cuban cigar.

Linati started him down the hall with a delicate shove. "Remember to keep our little secret to yourself." Another salute, one for the road, just as he had practiced at home, like reaching up for the top shelf with both heels nailed to the floor. "Farewell, Mr. Arpino. And be careful now. Don't hurt yourself on the stairs."

Beppe followed the publisher's advice and concentrated on making an injury-free exit, which proved therapeutic. The puzzlement that turned to panic when he realized that the report was inaccessible soon softened—on or about the second flight—into mere concern that Mr. Linati's memory would fail. And later, once Beppe reached the street, he was able to see that the lapse also had a benefit: what better protection for Dr. Puzo's report than a safe that no one, not even its owner, could open?

The driver was waiting at the car. Beppe would miss him as well. And he would miss the receptionist, whom he had failed to thank for all her help, both recently and in the past: without her directions to Dr. Puzo's house Beppe would be leading a different life.

"Back to the hotel?"

"One last time," Beppe said, the car now in motion, headed toward the Perelli Grand, "and then I'll have you take me to the station."

"But you'll miss all the commotion if you leave now." He meant the celebrations, Beppe understood: the parades, speeches, the surprise pyrotechnics.

He watched the driver watch the road. "Don't worry," Beppe said. "I'm sure there will be a commotion in Naples, too."

●●●●●●●●

How the vase came to be broken he could not recall. The most plausible scenario involved an accidental bump, but there was also a chance that he had pushed it off its pedestal on purpose. Either way, hotel property had been demolished—an artifact, a museum piece—and Beppe held himself responsible. He refused to blame Tomassino, even though it was a letter Tomassino sent that prompted the destructive behavior. Nor did he blame Mr. Linati, despite the fact that he otherwise now viewed the man with suspicion. But while Beppe held himself responsible, he did not make an immediate confession. Instead, he collected the more conspicuous shards and wrapped them in a blanket, which he then placed beneath the bed. It was an unusual reaction to what in all likelihood had been an accident, but the letter was even more unusual.

No doubt in Beppe's mind that it was Dr. Puzo writing. He recognized the voice, emphatic as ever, and the penmanship from their workout schedules, which Dr. Puzo drafted daily. Thus he read the letter as a prank, a joke intended for a friend. It was inexplicable otherwise. But then he recalled that Dr. Puzo had possessed no sense of humor and had hated to waste time: the letter would have taken at least ten minutes to write. In addition, Dr. Puzo had never mentioned friends. Yet even if there had been secret acquaintances, friends that Beppe knew nothing about, none would have smoked. And it was at this point roughly that Beppe lost track of his whereabouts in the hotel room and either bumped or pushed, he could not remember which, the vase from its pedestal.

"What? No valise?"

"A change in plans," Beppe explained to the driver as he rejoined him in the car. "Back to Linati Publishers, if you don't mind."

The driver made no objection, though he did express concern once the car was on its way. "You seem a little agitated, sir. Is everything okay?"

"Some unfinished business," Beppe said and left the matter at that. Meanwhile, outside the window, the flag slowly increased in size until it was, once again, gigantic, flapping arrhythmically.

The receptionist set aside her purple polish. "I'm sorry, Mr. Arpino, but he's not in at the moment."

"Are you sure he's not there?" Beppe thought he could smell cigar smoke coming from down the hall.

"Positive," she said. "You're welcome to look for yourself."

Beppe trusted her more than he did his own assistant at home. "Well, do you expect him back soon?"

"With Mr. Linati, one never knows." She blew on her nails to dry them. "I don't recommend waiting, though, if that's what you're thinking."

The last time he had waited it took seven hours for Mr. Linati to appear, so Beppe appreciated her recommendation.

"Is it something that I might be able to help you with?"

Beppe wanted to spare her the unpleasantries. "Oh, just some papers that are locked in Mr. Linati's safe."

"Mr. Linati's safe?" She looked at him as if he had spoken in falsetto. "You mean the one in Naples?"

"No," Beppe said, surprised at her expression, "the one here"— he pointed down the hall—"in Mr. Linati's office."

A look of comprehension came over her face, then amusement. "That's no safe," she chuckled, "it's a cigar box. Who in the world would put a safe right on top of their desk?"

Soon it became clear to Beppe that Mr. Linati had deceived him. And soon after that, within a minute or two at most, Beppe and the driver were off to the publisher's warehouse.

"You sure everything's okay, sir? I'd be happy to stop at a pharmacist's if you're not feeling well."

As before, Beppe deflected the question. "Thanks, but we're almost there." To answer it would have required an admission on his part that everything was not okay, which in turn could prompt a panic, and at the moment Beppe could not afford that. He needed to remain calm, levelheaded, sane, even if, as the driver's comments suggested, he appeared the opposite to others. Remember what happened to the vase.

"That's it over there, next to where that truck is parked." For the first time Beppe noticed the chimney, ominous after the revelations in Dr. Puzo's letter. The driver positioned the car behind the truck, but before he had finished the task Beppe was in the warehouse.

"Mr. Arpino!" The deceiver saluted, serious for that moment, then all smiles. "I thought by now you'd be halfway home." He waved Beppe over to a crate equal in size to the car parked outside. "It just arrived," he said, patting the crate like a pet elephant. "Remember our little secret?" In a whisper, he explained: "The cannon, it's in here."

Beppe reminded himself to remain calm. At the same time he wondered what had happened to the ever-present cigar. "Mr. Linati, I don't know what you did with that report, but I need it back now."

If the publisher was surprised, he did not show it. "I'm disappointed, Mr. Arpino, and surprised. After all we've been through together, you're accusing me of lies."

"I'm not accusing you of anything," Beppe answered, even though what the publisher said did not constitute a question. "I just want Dr. Puzo's report"—the warehouse had turned abnormally hot —"wherever you've put it."

Mr. Linati walked over to several smaller crates—the clubs and other calisthenics supplies were kept in a separate area—and Beppe followed. "Well, I don't have it."

"But if you don't have the report, who does?" Beppe found it more difficult now to remain calm.

"No one, I'm afraid." From a crate Mr. Linati pulled a sparkler, the absence of the cigar suddenly explained. "It's ceased to exist." He then used the sparkler's uncoated end as a crude dental pick. In almost any other situation Beppe would have advised against this practice.

"You mean you burned it? You burned Dr. Puzo's report?" Beppe felt as if he were trapped in a closet. "But it was written for the prime minister. It wasn't yours to burn."

The sparkler transformed itself into a pointer. "Mr. Arpino, I did you a favor by burning that report." With each stressed syllable, the sparkler connected with Beppe's chest. "I know the prime minister. He's a close, personal friend—a confidant, if you will—and had he gotten his hands on that report, believe me, he would have done far worse things to it, things that make cremation seem pleasant." He tossed the pointer aside. "The way I look at it, I did what any responsible Fascist would have done in the same situation. Now, if you'll excuse me, I have a cannon to unpack."

As happened earlier at the hotel, Beppe lost track of his whereabouts. Fortunately, the car was not far away.

∞∞∞∞∞∞

Dear Beppe,

I hope all is going well for you in Rome. You're probably busy preparing for the calisthenics event, so I'll try to keep this brief. It may be hard for me, though, given that I haven't written much lately (sorry about that). What I mean is that without a little background, you may find some of what I'm about to say surprising. It's not surprising to me, though, since I've given it a lot of thought.

Let me start at the beginning. When I first met you at that banquet, I thought you were just like all the other men my father used to invite to those functions (aside from the fact that you'd rescued my brother). It wasn't until you looked at my teeth that I really started to like you. I'd even say it was at that moment that I started to fall in love with you, though I don't think I knew it at the time. What I did know was that I wanted to see more of you. And you must have felt the same way, because before long we were going to concerts together, sitting in our café (I went there the other day, by the way), taking strolls, kissing. As much as I dislike the word, I'd have to describe that time as magical. And I did feel like I was under a spell. It didn't matter where we were or what was going on around us, all you had to do was look at me and I was entranced.

I notice as I read over what I've already written that toward the end I'm talking about my feelings as if they're no longer there. Sorry if it seems that way. The truth is that I haven't fallen out of love with you, Beppe. I don't think that's possible. I do, however, think that your going away has changed things somehow. Things seem more complicated now and more confusing. One minute I'm convinced that we're perfect for each other, and the next minute all I can think about are our differences. Really, we don't have a lot in common. And I can't say that I understand you very well yet, either. I still don't understand why you're still in Rome, despite all the letters you've sent. And though there's a chance I may never understand, I must admit that the thought depresses me right now. Distresses me, too. I haven't been myself lately, and I think it's because I'm so preoccupied. The other night my father practically killed himself as a result (more about him in a bit), and I realized then that I needed to do something about the situation. It might sound drastic, but I think it's the only way. What I want to do, Beppe, is put off our wedding until things have settled down. It could take a few months, or it could take longer. Whatever it takes, though, I know you'll understand.

Now, about my father, it seems that some people are trying to make him sell the paper mill, people he doesn't trust to run it properly. I don't know the details, but he did mention that they have political

*connections. And since you're now friendly with that publisher who was
once friendly with my father, I thought you could mention it to him.
My father isn't the type to ask for help, but unless someone intervenes,
he'll almost certainly lose the mill (and you wonder why I say that
what this country needs is a good assassin).*

*Well, it's getting late, so I think I'll stop here. I hope we see you
soon, Beppe. And good luck with your calisthenics.*

Love, Angelina

●●●●●●●●

He read the letter carefully, even paused once or twice to review
points, yet oddly, despite the news, Beppe's whereabouts never went
astray. Never did the fact that he stood in a hotel room filled with rare
objects escape him. Rather, after the previous day's events, which
ended with him not on a train but back in bed, the letter seemed to
calm him in much the same way that music settles dental patients.
Since he arrived, in fact, it was the most at ease that he had felt. Still,
he could not overlook the peculiarity of his reaction. Angelina had
canceled their wedding; surely that should have upset him. Yet he
was spared the dizziness and other disturbances that hit when he
learned that the report had been burned. Granted, it was a one-of-a-
kind document without which he would never be able to honor a
deathbed request, but even with those distinctions it remained paper,
whereas Angelina was flesh, a person, the someone he loved more
than dentistry itself. And now he stood to lose her. The calm was
indeed peculiar.

Beppe stepped over to the window, the view so familiar now that
he could have painted it while blindfolded had he possessed a
painter's skills, not to mention the brushes and whatnot, perhaps also
a smock: the small piazza, the old stone fountain upon which the man
in the crimson jacket had demonstrated certain maneuvers. Beppe
would call for him later. In the meantime, he wanted to ventilate himself as Dr. Puzo recommended and, while he still had time, savor the
odd peacefulness that swept over him once he finished the letter.

It was the contrast that made the sensation so palpable now and such a relief. Just an hour earlier he had been filled with desperation, unable to do more than berate himself: he had walked into a trap and not realized it until after the trap had snapped shut. Even to call what he felt desperation—he breathed in the Puzo manner—seemed inadequate; it was closer to suicidal. Not only had he failed Dr. Puzo, he had helped Dr. Puzo's enemy achieve yet another victory. Beppe could not have done worse for the man who had treated him like a son. But in addition to the Roman failures—best to hold each breath for five seconds—there was the humiliation he would face when he returned home. Angelina had tried to keep him there, warned him in advance, and still he defied her. No wonder he climbed back into bed rather than aboard a train. Yet when all seemed lost and humiliation certain, her letter came to the rescue.

It was an elegant solution, and it unfolded as he read her sentences. Of course, under normal circumstances it never would have occurred to him; it would have been unfathomable at best. But now, with the report somewhere in the atmosphere and their engagement on the line and her father in need of a savior, it seemed like a reasonable plan. Yes, there were dangers involved, but these existed everywhere, whether a person knew it or not. One could be giving a speech or icing a cake or running an errand at home, even headed to the lavatory in a hotel, and suffer a fatal attack. To pretend otherwise was foolish. Besides, if Beppe wanted to keep Angelina, uncomplicate things for her, the time had come for him to be bolder than ever before, daring even. As Dr. Puzo had forewarned, women did inspire recklessness in men.

The ventilations completed, Beppe left the window and walked past the pedestal upon which the vase once rested, past the Victrola now silent, past the squat platform that appeared to have been built for no other reason than to support valises, to the velvet rope that hung from the ceiling, which Dr. Puzo would have severed but Beppe instead pulled and which the man in the crimson jacket answered with a haste that made it seem as if he had been poised outside the door.

"Thank you for helping me up the stairs yesterday," Beppe offered as an introduction, "and for slipping that letter under my door."

"All in a day's work, sir." So was killing someone with a tweezers, Beppe reflected. "Is there anything else I can do?" Yet nowhere in the man were past violences now apparent, which comforted Beppe to a certain extent.

"As a matter of fact, I would like to ask some more questions, if you have a few minutes to spare."

He did have a few spare minutes. But it occurred to Beppe then, as he and the man he wanted to interview took their seats, that perhaps it would have been wise before he pulled on that rope to have moved the bare pedestal from its conspicuous location. Well, the time had come for recklessness to prevail.

"Do you remember," Beppe started, pen and paper in hand, "that when I first asked about the armed forces you mentioned . . . "

"The military hotel?"

"No, I believe you called them munitions. I wonder if you could tell me more about those now."

∞∞∞∞∞∞

A servant answered the telephone. Which servant, though, it was impossible to tell. Their voices, like their appearances, were almost identical, and whatever subtle differences did exist the static on the line erased.

"Is Angelina there?" Beppe asked, alone at the front desk after the woman who watched over it excused herself to visit the rest room. Likewise, the crimson jacket was at a courteous distance. "I'm calling from Rome."

"She's out at the moment, sir. Shall I take a message?"

While Beppe was prepared for her absence—all possibilities had been taken into account—the disappointment was nonetheless there, as if he had fallen into a hole. She asked him not to call, and he respected her wishes, but never had the desire to hear her voice disappeared. Or the desire to kiss her: as soft as a velvet cushion; no, softer than that and moist, more like a moss perhaps, but cleaner and sweeter . . .

"Sir? Have we lost the connection?"

Beppe would try her father. "What about Alfredo Perelli? Is he home?"

Alfredo Perelli was not there, either. Given recent developments, he probably never left the paper mill. Such a loss would cut him down for sure. It would strip the leaves off Alfredo Perelli's branches. It would turn the paper baron into pulp.

"Tomassino perhaps?"

"It will take a moment, sir."

The message Beppe wanted to leave was brief but also the most important of his life, so he appreciated knowing that a poet, someone trained to memorize and recite verse, would be conveying it for him. At the same time, though, Beppe remembered that Tomassino's poems, at least the few made public, could leave a person confused. Nature's illuminated orb? Butterflies that talked and painted rainbows? Best if the call were limited to essential details.

"Tomassino? It's me, Beppe." Last names, he assumed, could be omitted, but not all pleasantries. "How are you? How's Angelina?"

Over the phone Tomassino's voice was both the same and distorted. "Beppe? And you're here in Naples?"

"Soon, Tomassino, maybe as soon as tomorrow night." It depended more on the train schedules than Beppe's plans. A national holiday was not the best time for travel.

"So you received the letter, I take it." Tomassino meant a letter different from the one in Beppe's pocket. He meant a letter written by one man and mailed by another.

"I did receive it. And thank you. It's made quite a difference." The rest room now was vacant. "I need you to do something else for me, though, if it's not too much trouble." Beppe related the information: the time to switch on the radio and whom to sit before it. "Can you remember all that?"

"Certainly," Tomassino assured him, "but you haven't said what we're going to hear."

Beppe wanted that to be a surprise. "It will be obvious," he explained, "believe me, and well worth everyone's time."

The call then came to a close, with Beppe's love sent to all the Perellis and one last question from Tomassino: "By the way, Beppe, do you know if Dr. Puzo had a favorite poem?"

Although he did not understand Tomassino's recent obsession with Dr. Puzo—a visit to the archives and now an interest in what Dr. Puzo read—Beppe wanted to help the poet who had promised to help him. No titles, however, came to mind, so Beppe requested more time. "Let me sleep on it," he said. And he did sleep on it. At least he pondered the question while around him Rome slept. But it was not the usual insomnia that kept Beppe awake. The munitions were to blame. To be specific, he spent the night and next morning assembling an explosive device: First he scraped a valise's worth of sparklers clean and combined the powder with shards from a broken vase. The resulting mixture was packed with care inside a medicine ball, which, as a final step, Beppe sutured shut. In some respects, then, the work he performed over those hours—scraping, mixing, filling, stitching—was not unlike that required of a dentist on a typical day at the office.

⚬⚬⚬⚬⚬⚬⚬

The uniform fit, the skies were clear, and in the distance he could hear what sounded like a celebration.

Beppe left the hotel at noon, medicine ball in tow but minus the car and driver. He would walk there and let the volume and collective momentum lead him even if these steered him past the warehouse from which he had helped himself to whatever he needed. With a thousand outfits just like it on the streets—khaki shirt and trousers and stiff black boots, the belt intended for a holster—and a thousand medicine balls, he was as inconspicuous now as a priest out for a stroll around the Vatican and its environs. No one would ever suspect that he was an assassin, especially if he smiled. Certainly the hotel staff had no idea.

"Good luck with your performance," the man in the crimson jacket, a murderer himself, said when Beppe departed, a sentiment echoed by the woman behind the front desk.

A smile no doubt helped, a cheerful disposition, but it would have been hard to appear otherwise on such a beautiful day, a holiday, when festiveness filled the air. Indeed, the sound Beppe followed was boisterous to say the least: part marching band, part chant, part cheer, part overenthusiastic speaker. And the excitement, frenetic at noon, would continue to build for the next hour until, as a climax, the prime minister exploded: an appropriate end for Mr. Linati's friend, the man a fiancée and her father would have preferred dead. Well, thanks to Beppe, soon their wishes would come true.

He walked on, around corners and across crowded intersections, toward the platforms that had been erected and the chairs upon which politicians and their supporters sat. Some streets Beppe remembered from visits to the publisher's office, but the people on these streets—adults and children, obese and thin, more people now than ever before—were all, without exception, unfamiliar to him. The masses, Dr. Puzo had called them: faceless, nameless . . . and Beppe was one, too. It could have been a pumpkin that he carried for all the attention he received. Yet he had the power to kill these people; he held it in both arms.

"Either toss the ball or roll it, Mr. Arpino, but don't nurse it like an infant."

Fear not, Dr. Puzo; Beppe knew now to toss when the time came, when the other medicine balls soared into the air, just as he knew to spark the fuse first with the match hidden in a shirt pocket. Past hesitations, past indecision—nowhere in the present was there a place for these.

Ahead, above Beppe's fellow pedestrians, banners came into view, and police officers atop horses. The pace slowed here, the crowd thickened. The banners, meanwhile, white cloth with red letters, fluttered freely. A number sported slogans—BELIEVE, OBEY, FIGHT and the like—though most featured the prime minister's nickname as a kind of advertisement. Beppe held the ball even more securely as he neared the horses, parked at intervals up and down the street, and was careful where he stepped. Heaven forbid he should slip on one of their deposits and detonate the wrong person. Even to harm the animals would be disastrous. The prime minister alone deserved to be exploded. If not killed, then at least decommissioned: a severed limb might be sufficient, a severe concussion.

On the street before him, the parade route lined with civilians and mounted police, women marched past in columns—Beppe could see them if he stood on tiptoe—with babies in their arms and aprons to their ankles, a platoon of young mothers. An amplified voice—it seemed to come from overhead—praised these women for their fertility, their service to the Fascist state—"Maternity is to a woman what war is to a man"—and the onlookers applauded. Of course, Beppe could not clap just then. But even without the medicine ball, cradled as the marchers held their babies, he would have refrained.

"You'll have to excuse me if I don't join in," Angelina once remarked over tea at their café. "I have a problem with Fascists."

And now, two years later, Beppe did, too. But he was not like most of the prime minister's foes. For starters, he never would have described himself as political in the least. Authoritarian rule? The imprisonment of freethinkers? Widespread censorship? While important to some, these were second in Beppe's mind. Just as he had chosen a career in dentistry over one as a musician because a priest behaved bizarrely at the mention of teeth, he carried explosives now for obscure reasons: a threatened paper mill, a burned report, a fiancée's change of heart. Nevertheless, he understood that the blast would benefit others—the Italian people, for example. He understood it—a recent turnaround for Beppe, very recent—but desperation, really, was what compelled him to act.

More mothers, column after column, and behind them, in the distance—Beppe raised himself even higher on tiptoe—what appeared to be several hundred soldiers, perhaps a thousand, all in khaki and black. Soon Beppe would push forward, between onlookers and horses, and fall in line with these militant twins: some smaller than him, some taller, and one a publisher of books. He would become invisible then, just another exerciser, and later, when it mattered most, use their presence to disappear. The hotel room would follow, the train station next, and finally, in a matter of hours, the Perellis' home in Naples, where dear Angelina, beautiful and impressed, would come running to the door with her arms outstretched.

●●●●●●●●

A fine white powder like confectioner's . . .

Suppose, for a moment, that he had noticed it earlier or never noticed it at all. Either way he might have survived the day and history taken a different course: no Ethiopia invasion, no partnership with Berlin, no anti-Semitic policies, no air raids or Allied attacks. Other men—and at least one woman—had made attempts on the prime minister's life, but none succeeded. Their friends betrayed them; their bullets strayed. The latest failure could be blamed on poor concentration.

From the time Beppe left the hotel until just seconds before the calisthenics routine began he kept the medicine ball pressed to him and both hands pressed to it. But once he set the ball on the pavement and assumed the first combative pose—feet apart and fists raised, like a boxer about to spar—the residue revealed itself on the stolen outfit. That is, the sutures had leaked. Yet Beppe remained unaware. Between the thousand anxious boxers, all posed alike, all dressed alike, a vast piazza's worth, and the publisher before them, also posed, albeit next to a cannon, a little residue did not draw attention to itself. Besides, not far from Beppe, on a platform filled with decorated men, sat the prime minister himself: the square head, like a block, like an anvil, the humorless expression, the lap meant for explosives.

First the thrusts and punches, the kicks and deep knee bends—all in unison, as in some barracks revue—then the movements, borrowed from the battlefield, that featured wooden clubs—topped with sparklers, remember, and distributed lit. All these Beppe performed without incident. He mimicked those around him, even their mistakes, and maintained the serious but festive expression he felt appropriate for the occasion. And as much as he could under the circumstances, he readied himself for the events ahead. He pictured the throw he would make when the time came, the perfect arc, and identified potential escape routes. It was not until after the sparklers burned themselves down that he faltered.

Like the thousand schoolchildren and the publisher before them, Beppe set aside the wooden clubs and lifted the medicine ball. He pressed it overhead—a shoulder exercise performed with Dr. Puzo innumerable times—once, twice . . . but soon the particles were upon him: a mist, a wispy shower. He blinked, and a second medicine ball appeared above him, a second circle. Yes, two holes dusted with a fine white powder. He was fourteen the next instant, still slouched and timid. He still had not handled a butcher knife nor experienced lust. Nor had he ever met a dentist. The tooth extractor was the closest he had come, and their encounter had been brief. Music was what mattered most to him, the cello and Father Vincenzo. In all Cortenza —all the world—there was nowhere he would rather be than here with the priest and the Guadagnini, even now, when one hovered over him uncharacteristically and the other stood silent in a corner.

The two circles then resolved into one: a medicine ball dusted with powder. The illusion over—a few seconds at most, a few lost repetitions—Beppe resumed the calisthenics. He pressed the ball again like those around him and hopped with it, as if over land mines—Mr. Linati's touch—when the time came to hop. As for the residue, the fine white powder that had affected Beppe's vision, he quickly deduced its source: sheepskin requires a tighter stitch than do human gums. At least that explained the powder's presence on the medicine ball. But what about the powder in Father Vincenzo's nose?

No more hops now while the publisher mounts the cannon. A drum roll, please, while he climbs inside.

The question, of course, would remain unanswered; Beppe understood that even as he posed it. All deaths left such questions: priest, dentist, butcher. Who knew what killed Father Vincenzo? And what explained Dr. Puzo's collapse? Or the murder in New York?

A woman approaches the cannon with a taper in her hands. The bow in her hair, by the way, matches her fingernails.

And no doubt Beppe's own death, he was certain, when it came, sooner or later, whatever the cause—he still had no idea—would puzzle others, even those closest to him, though perhaps most confused would be the people, provided they did not expire first, who had wanted him to become a professional musician: Miss Donati and the mayor and . . .

Beppe reached for the match hidden in a shirt pocket, the shirt covered with explosive powder, the same powder that covered the medicine ball, and removed it. He then lifted a boot off the pavement and, balanced there like a dancer, introduced the match to it. One skidded across the other. Sparks appeared, then a flame.

The flame starts the fuse; the woman retreats. Seconds later another woman, her hair minus a bow, her nails unpainted, jumps when from her radio there comes an explosion. "What happened?" she asks, but neither the brother sitting beside her on the flowered sofa, notebook in hand, nor the father in the nearby chair, its upholstery also in bloom, offers an answer. It is the radio announcer who, amid cheers that sound more like screams, soon identifies the blast as a publisher shot from a cannon.

ACKNOWLEDGMENTS

I would like to thank, first and foremost, Lynne Sharon Schwartz for her advice, enthusiasm, and continuing support. Thanks also to Carl Phillips and the Washington University Writing Program for their support. Robert Rebein deserves credit, too, for pointing me in the right direction. Others who helped along the way include Stephen Amidon, Anis Ahmed, T.M. McNally, Dr. Hillard Scott, and Dan Black and Kathy Chao.

Special thanks to my agent, Henry Dunow, and to Chuck Kim, John Webber, and all at Welcome Rain.

And of course, thank you, Tami.